THE
Garden Angel

MINDY FRIDDLE

THE

Garden Angel

St. Martin's Press

New York

AUG 2 5 2004

www.stmartins.com

Portions of this novel have appeared in slightly different form in the Charleston *Post & Courier* and *Night Rally* magazine.

Excerpts from the poems of Emily Dickinson reprinted by permission of the publishers and the Trustees of Amherst College. *The Poems of Emily Dickinson*, Ralph W. Franklin, ed., Cambridge, Massachusetts: The Belknap Press of Harvard University Press, copyright © 1951, 1955, 1979 by the President and Fellows of Harvard College.

Library of Congress Cataloging-in-Publication Data

Friddle, Mindy.
    The garden angel / Mindy Friddle.—1st ed.
        p.   cm.
    ISBN 0-312-32674-2
    EAN 978-0312-32674-6
    1. Women—Southern States—Fiction.   2. College teachers' spouses—
Fiction.   3. Obituaries—Authorship—Fiction.   4. Female friendship—
Fiction.   5. Southern States—Fiction.   6. Home ownership—Fiction.
7. Agoraphobia—Fiction.   I. Title.

PS3606.R49G37   2004
813'.6—dc22

                                                            2004040544

10   9   8   7   6   5   4   3

To my parents, Ron Friddle and Kay Vinson Friddle,
for their love, support, and encouragement

Acknowledgments

I am deeply grateful to the following:

My agent, Judith Weber, for her extraordinary support, wisdom, and insightful comments about early drafts of this novel; everyone at Sobel Weber; my editor, Diane Reverand, for her guidance and superb editing, and all the staff at St. Martin's Press. I thank the Emrys Foundation for years of generous support and encouragement. The South Carolina Arts Commission and the Charleston *Post & Courier*'s Fiction Project opened doors. The Warren Wilson MFA Program for Writers and its invaluable community of writers pointed me in the right direction. The Tuesday Night Feathered Crotch Writing Group provided a plethora of creative jolts. Bread Loaf brought about enormous opportunities and lifelong friends, and the Ragdale Foundation offered time and space. I would also like to thank Ernst & Young for offering flexible work policies that allow a writer time and opportunity to write.

I thank my readers, all of whom offered direction and intelligent commentary: Richard Russo, Julianna Baggott, Ron Rash, Sarah Gilbert Fox, Gil Allen, Kevin McIlvoy, Heather Magruder, Kendall Friddle Neason, Katie Friddle, and Randy Crew. Debra Spark deserves special thanks for her close, discerning reading of an early draft.

The support of friends and family members, too numerous to name here, remains invaluable. I wish to thank my stepsons, Chris and Patrick, and my daughter, Saga, for her sense of humor and patience. I am profoundly grateful to my husband, Mike Cubelo, for his love and sensitivity, constant encouragement, and his faith in me.

A Prison gets to be a friend.
—EMILY DICKINSON, "POEM 652"

THE
Garden Angel

One

THE VIEW FROM THE attic bathroom always broke my heart a little, for it told the story of my family's own fall: our lost property and standing, our dwindling. The land, as far as I could see, had once belonged to us, to the Harris family. Gran said this had once been fields and meadows surrounding her family's house. *Estate* back then, she said, when our house was the hub of Sans Souci. But now Sans Souci was a city-swallowed town. The shopping malls and 7-Elevens, billboards and neon signs, reached for us. The city of Palmetto lapped at the shore of our home.

In the distance, I could make out Sans Souci Mill, where it lay sprawled, monstrous and deserted, some kind of thick brush sprouting from its red brick chimneys. My great-grandfather had established the mill in the last century, had built the neighborhood there on mill hill, had financed the pharmacy and soda shop, the jeweler, the motel, the shoe store—most of downtown. A lot of the storefronts were boarded up now, as if they'd been waiting out a hurricane for thirty years. The houses that remained were mostly rentals; we'd heard some outfit up North owned them. And scattered among them were smaller houses, decaying or already gone: stone steps stopping abruptly, eerily, above a grassy lot; the brick remnants of a chimney strewn about a weedy yard like children's blocks in a playroom.

But on our street, the houses were still standing and faintly grand—gussied up with fish-scale roofs, cupolas, and spires—although our kinfolk and neighbors had long abandoned them. New groups had taken residency: there was the home for retarded men across the way, and the Pinkerton and Colleton homes had been divided into apartments, which seemed to attract Palmetto University students, harried single mothers, and older, grim-faced people who had turned a corner in their lives, who cooked on the hot plates in their rooms and attended twelve-step programs at night.

Our house sat at the end of Gerard Avenue: coquettish and tattered, on tippy toes, it seemed, from the encroaching world. In the backyard, our family cemetery guarded its weed-choked dead beside a two-lane highway that should have been four. There had been talk from the highway people, but there wasn't much they could do about moving a graveyard, and so our cemetery remained, a fort that withstood the city's attacks. The headstones were broken or toppled or unrecognizable; one hundred–year-old marble lambs looked like small terriers. And some of the graves were marked by nothing more than gray, worn-down rocks that poked up in a semicircle like neglected, decaying teeth. Only Gran's grave was new, still unsodded after six months.

Home will keep you rooted through the black clouds of living! she'd told us. *You might dawdle out there in the world for a while, but you'll need a dwelling to protect you.*

I believed her.

The minute they ventured out in the world seeking love, seeking more, the women in my family found nothing but trouble. Now my sister Ginnie was going to college, taking classes over in Palmetto. *Escaping* is how she put it. My sister said *I* was the crazy one, rattling around the three-story dilapidated mansion our great-grandfather had built before he died of syphilis, wondering how I was going to pay the light bill.

But I knew better.

I'd found Ginnie's pregnancy test that morning.

What happened was, I'd set my mind on a morning bath. I'd donned my mother's white eyelet lace gown from the cedar closet downstairs, the gown Gran had hand-embroidered special for her honeymoon. It was dingy now, the color of coffee-stained teeth, and it puckered around my chest and strained a little around my hips. But it floated elegantly about my ankles as I walked up the stairs to the attic bathroom.

I drew my bath and scattered dried rose petals in the water. I stepped into the tub, pinned up my hair, dipped into the bowl of mayonnaise that had been mixed with fennel and rosemary and soaked secretly in the refrigerator for two days. I patted it on my forehead, my cheeks, across the bridge of my nose. I reclined.

That's when I saw the glossy pregnancy-test box sticking out of the old copper wastebasket.

I made it across the floor in two big wet steps. The little color-coded stick was pink. *You're going to have a baby!* gushed the back of the package. I stood for a while, naked, dripping, with the shock of it.

Then I heard her.

The slam of the front door, the heavy thunk of books, and a tinkle of keys hitting the dining room table. I got back into the tub. I slathered on more of the mix, smoothed it on my ears, down my neck.

I heard the grating of the kitchen's swinging door as it scraped the paint from the doorjamb. I listened as Ginnie walked through the bedrooms on the second floor, calling for me. It was easy to track her, even three stories up. The house, like a faithful servant whispering secrets, relayed her sounds to me.

I felt for the cucumber slices and placed them on my face. When the third step up to the attic screeched, I submerged. Water filled my ears. The cucumber slices eddied and drifted. After a minute, I sensed the light shifting and her shadow falling over me.

"What in the hell? Cutter, what are you doing? It *is* you, isn't it? Behind all that stuff?" She was standing over me now.

"I'm celebrating," I said, squinting up at her. "Can't you tell?"

"This is celebrating?" She paused, a little out of breath from racing up all those stairs. "I just want to say that I'm sorry—I'm really sorry—about not showing up last night." This was a practiced answer, without the remorse I required. The day before had been my twenty-fifth birthday, and no one had remembered, not even Ginnie, my own sister, my Irish twin, eleven months younger than I. "So, did you do anything special?" I shook my head. "C'mon. Didn't anyone remember your birthday?"

"Oh, yeah," I said. "There's a happy birthday postcard from the dentist with a coupon for free mint floss."

She sighed.

I had the satisfaction of seeing her mouth tighten to a line. Since Gran had died, we were both in limbo. Also, drifting apart. Ginnie kept telling me that we would have to sell the house. But packing up and selling three generations of our family's leavings felt like betrayal. I still couldn't bear going into Gran's bedroom. The fine, fragrant talc dusting on the dresser, the brush webbed in silver hair, the fifty-year collection of black handbags stuffed in the top of the closet—it was all too much, too much.

"Your face looks like a salad, you know that?" She dragged over a stool from the corner, sat down beside the tub. " 'It's certain that fine women eat a crazy salad with their meat.' " Her voice was patient, like a teacher's.

"Who said that? Julia Child?"

"*Yeats.* William Butler Yeats."

I made a face, felt the cucumbers shift a little. Ginnie reached out and touched my arm with her fingers, left a track in the glob of white on my arm. Her fingernails were bitten, the flesh raw, bleeding a little around her thumb.

"What gave you the idea for this?" she asked.

Gran's old beauty books. But I would never admit that to her.

"*Cosmo.* Last month's."

I had discovered the recipe in a book in the basement just last week, had devoured its advice and warnings about beauty, and instructions for potpourri, herbal masks, and beauty soaks. The stern Victorian words, capitalized and underscored: *The Young Lady is advised to retire to the Privacy of her own toiletry with only the company of her Maid to assist in the Beauty Episode.* When I had leafed through the yellowed, musty pages, a pressed pansy, as brittle and brown as a moth's wing, had zigzagged to the floor in a papery flurry.

"I brought beer," she said. "It's downstairs in the fridge."

"Why?"

"For you. To really celebrate."

"I don't drink beer."

She walked over to an alcove window, stood with her back to me. I wondered if she would even tell me. I glanced over at the wastebasket in the corner where the pregnancy-test box was crammed out of sight. I pulled the mildewed shower curtain between us.

She cleared her throat. "I'm going away this weekend."

"Well," I said, "that's not news."

I spread more of the mix on my shoulders, across my collarbones.

"I mean I'm not just staying away over at Susan's or Penny's— I'm going away. I'm going away—with Him."

Him. Capitalized, as if He were in red like the print in Gran's Bible. The starring parts, where Jesus spoke.

"Your teacher?" I peeked out from the shower curtain and she turned to face me. She nodded, walked over, and sat down on the stool again. Her face was soft now, damp from the steam of my bath and the heat of her news. Her eyebrows were as white as cornsilk, her eyelashes clear. My sister had a certain pale, bright beauty, while I was an almost blonde, a shadowy hybrid. Ginnie was willowy and golden, I was shorter and freckled. I imagined our in utero tug-of-war. How she had seized all those pale, paternal Scandinavian genes, pulled at those chromosomes until they stretched like taffy.

"We're going to a conference today—all day with a stopover in a log cabin tonight in the mountains." She tried to keep her face blank.

"And you're going as his"—I searched for the term, then held it with tongs—"student assistant?"

"Well . . . yes."

"Doesn't he have a family? I mean, how can you forget that?"

"Believe me, I don't forget Wife."

"What if she finds out about this?"

"Wife doesn't go out. Anywhere. Daniel does everything for her. She's like an invalid or something. But there's nothing wrong with her. Wife is just real sensitive or something." She shrugged her shoulders.

I sunk back in the water. I looked down at my knees poking out of the gooey, white water like identical pink islands.

"Cutter, this is important, so listen. If anyone calls me this weekend, I don't care who they are or what they want, tell them I'm at the library."

Ah. So that explained our chat. An alibi. "I'm not going to lie," I said. "It's Wife, isn't it?" It was the first time I used the nickname, and I felt its power to distance, to make fun, even as I felt ashamed for using it. "She knows."

"No, she doesn't. But there's been . . . some gossip."

"I'm shocked."

"Don't, Cutter. Sarcasm is derived from the Greek for 'tearing of the flesh.' Did you know that? It means 'to wound.' "

I rinsed off and wrapped myself in a towel. When I finished she was sitting on the stool again, looking down.

"If Gran weren't dead, this would kill her," I said, shaking my head. "Kill her."

"Who cares about the past? I'm talking about the here and now. And the future. I'm talking about reality." I detected the slightest wobble in her voice. If I thought she'd listen to me, I would have reminded her that our family's motto could be "Love goeth before the fall."

"I have to pack now. He's coming to pick me up." My sister

wrapped her arms around herself, her gaze softened. I knew she was gone from me, then. Love had snatched her away.

It's hard to say even now, two years later, what came first—Ginnie's passion for Daniel Byers or her love for literature. They'd seemed to arrive together. For months, since she'd announced that she was changing majors from business to English, Ginnie had doted on him. She'd taken to delivering rambling lines of poetry and then reciting what Daniel Byers said about that poetry. It was too much for me.

"Look," I'd asked one day, interrupting her midsonnet, "have you got something going with your teacher or what?"

"No," she said, looking shocked and a little peevish. "But we're together."

I'd never met Daniel Byers, but I knew some things about him. I'd heard about his prodigious memory. The previous fall when the lead and the understudy for the university's showing of *Hamlet* had got salmonella poisoning from the chicken salad sandwiches served at the opening night cast party, Daniel Byers had volunteered to step in with only an hour's notice, and he never forgot a line. He'd performed flawlessly, Ginnie said, and she kept repeating that. *Flawlessly,* she'd whispered, shaking her head.

Also, he was a cyclist. One of those serious ones, Ginnie told me, with a tear-shaped helmet, fingerless gloves, and tight, shiny shorts. And he believes in making what he teaches come to life, she said. If you took his class, you would not be bored. He was known to stand on his desk and recite lines of poetry or prose when he saw his students stifle yawns or prop their heads on their books, usually in the middle of something like *The Waste Land* or *Walden*.

I could hear Ginnie in her bedroom drying her hair now, getting dressed. I went downstairs to water the fern out on the porch. A red Toyota pulled in our drive, and I knew it was Daniel Byers. He got out of the car when he saw me on the porch. He had a limp, a catch in his pace like an extra beat in a song, a little flourish in a dance step, so practiced and smoothed over, I knew he'd had that limp all his life. And I thought, Oh good Lord, another thing Ginnie didn't tell me. She's taken up with a cripple! And then he drew closer and smiled, and for a minute—a sweet, forbidden flash of time—I knew what it was like to be wanted, to be the single, sharp focus of another's attention. That was before he squinted at me, confused. I was used to it. From a distance, my sister and I looked similar enough to give people a start. People would call me Ginnie, then pause, take in the darker hair, the freckles, and apologize for the mix-up. I'd come to think of myself as Ginnie on a bad day.

"You must be Cutter." He knew my name and that surprised me. But I refused to be flattered.

"That's me."

He came over to the porch steps. He had on khakis and a denim shirt. Dark hair receding around his temples and a little too long in the back. The ordinary facade did not fool me. There was something pent up, an energy humming below the surface that my sister had tapped into. You could see it in the way he rocked on his heels as he stood on the walkway. He was nervous. He knew that I knew about him and Ginnie. When he smiled, the sliver of space between his front teeth showed a narrow slice of tongue, gave him a puckish grin. I stared for a minute at his outstretched hand until I realized he meant for me to take it. Shaking his hand made me feel stodgy and formal, like a chaperone.

"Your sister told me about you."

"What did she say?"

"Just that you are . . . industrious."

He meant my two jobs. I said nothing. The way he talked was clipped, abrupt. Chopping off the ends of words. Around here, we did not do that. Around here, we let our words linger a little in our mouths like mints.

"I guess she said she wanted me to get back in school."

He nodded. "She mentioned that, yes."

"Well, somebody has to pay the light bill and buy groceries."

He put his hands in his pockets, glanced up at the windows. He took a few steps back. The *For Sale* sign leaned against the porch.

"Had any offers on the house?"

"Nope. None." I waved to Father Bob across the street. He reached into the mailbox and divided the mail into two piles and handed it over to the men trailing behind him. Daniel turned to see who I was waving to. "It's a group home. Father Bob's Home for Men, we call it. They're retarded—"

"Mentally disabled?"

"Yeah." I looked at him sharply. He wasn't my teacher.

"Unfortunately, I guess a home like that might scare off buyers."

"But they're good neighbors. I know them all over there. If Pinky doesn't take his medicine, he thinks his hands will fly off, and Richard wanders away sometimes. Stan has Down's syndrome, he's real easy, and he's affectionate. Alfred's my favorite. I'm trying to have him hired on down at the newspaper where I work. I get a kick out of him."

Silence. Daniel was looking at his watch.

"So, how much land do you have here?"

"Three acres or so. Of course, part of that is the dead garden."

"Dead garden?" He met my eyes. I tried not to smirk.

"The family cemetery. That's what we've always called it." There. See? We're as crazy as hell.

"The family cemetery?" Goddamn him, he was amused.

"Actually, it makes a nice buffer zone. Keeps the city away back there."

"It's not used anymore, is it?"

"My grandmother was just buried there," I said. "If you stand right over there behind the house, you can see her grave. It's got a new stone." I expected him to look uncomfortable, to look away, but he met my eyes.

"Are you trying to spook me, Cutter?"

"Spook you? Nah."

The screen door banged, and I didn't have to look at Ginnie to know she was furious.

"You didn't tell me Daniel was here." A hissing whisper from behind my right shoulder.

"We were just talking till you got ready," I said. "I can't help it if you're up there primping all day. When will you be back?"

"I'll call you tomorrow."

"I'd be honored."

Daniel cleared his throat, and Ginnie's eyes locked on to him. He was standing at the bottom of the steps, staring up at her. It was like I wasn't even there. Like I had been vaporized from my own front porch. I wondered if Daniel Byers was different. Not just a brief stop for Ginnie after all. Not like all the others. And there'd been lots of others. In high school there'd been a parade of lanky runners, a couple of strapping football stars with cropped hair and powerful necks, a German soccer player. Later, a biker named Slick showed up for a while, with a do-rag and raging, tattooed biceps. Then there was the doctor she'd met in the ER where she'd taken Slick after he'd wrecked his Harley. Next was Glen, a social worker from across the street at Father Bob's. Smitten, all of them. Mauled and bruised and besotted by Ginnie, who was amused at their fixation, then irritated, and, eventually, bored.

The sharp, clean smell of shampoo and bath soap drifted over to me as Ginnie stepped down. She carried a haphazard stack of books and files, an overnight bag slung across her shoulder. She must have grabbed everything at once when she looked out and saw Daniel's car. When she took a step down, three giant textbooks tumbled across the porch steps, their covers spreading open indignantly, white pages revealed like petticoats.

The O of her mouth broadened into a smile while Daniel scrambled to gather them. By then I had stepped back behind the screen door.

"I wasn't sure how much reading time I'd have," she told him. "I brought everything."

"Did you squeeze in a toothbrush?" he asked.

Laughter. "Of course."

"Well, that's what matters. Books and a toothbrush—that's all you need in life."

Daniel took Ginnie's bag and tossed it in the trunk. Inside the car, the shadowy silhouettes of their heads merged for a minute, before they drove off, Ginnie not even looking back.

I went inside and got the six-pack that Ginnie had left me. I wasn't one to drink. But on this Saturday morning I sat on the porch in the old mildewed, peeling wicker rocker sipping beer, and pretty soon I'd drunk three of them pretty fast. I stood up and wiped my hands on my sweatshirt. The place looked too good for a Saturday.

That was dangerous.

Mrs. Worthington would very likely come by with prospective buyers, flinging her "excellent first home," "a real fixer-upper," "stunning potential" phrases around like confetti. I needed buyers to see more than benign neglect; I wanted them scared away by a mean dilapidation.

A week ago, when Mrs. Worthington had brought an older man to "have a quick little walk-through," I could tell the clutter in the house and the patchy lawn had gotten to her. A few days later she had sent a pamphlet filled with tips for home sellers. "Make some cookies or cinnamon buns and let the aroma waft through the house," it said. "Keep your lawn lush and trimmed and your yard well maintained. Keep closets organized and keep all personal items out of view." Now I found the pamphlet useful. It was a blueprint for sabotage.

Barry, my older brother, was stationed at a marine base four hours away. He was pushing for the house to be sold, dreaming about the candy-red Corvette he was going to buy with his share of the proceeds. Ginnie preferred living in the clean emptiness of the carpeted condos of her college friends to spending the night with me in her own home. But the day was coming when she would need me, when our home would be a sanctuary again.

I put the *For Sale* sign in a plastic leaf bag and set it out back with the garbage.

I walked around the backyard. Bed linens, a bra, two dish towels, and a tablecloth hung out on the clothesline, snapped in the wind impatiently. I buried my face in a sheet. Well, I would leave the laundry out; it added a certain atmosphere of neglect, as did the lily pad pond overtaken by ivy, the roses choked with weeds. A few hydrangea blossoms hung brown and dry on the shrubs, rattling sadly in the breeze. It was well hidden, the splendor of what had been, and that was fine with me. I could still remember Gran's garden out back the way it used to be—goldfish in the pond; hydrangea blooms heavy and blue, the color of the sky; sunflowers bent down upon themselves.

When Mrs. Worthington figured out that I wasn't going to allow this house—Gran's house—to be sold, she would try to talk to my brother about it. Barry was hard to get a hold of, but Mrs. Worthington would do it eventually. Thank goodness Ginnie was too caught up in her love life to worry about the house. But I needed to sock away money. I needed to find a way to buy out Ginnie and Barry's shares. And with my two jobs, maybe I could find a bank that would let me take out a mortgage. Maybe.

I sighed. The remnants of last summer's kitchen garden—yellow squash, runner beans, cucumbers, tomatoes—were withered, left wild. I got out the hose, watered, and found myself standing where my grandfather had turned mad one day more than half a century earlier at a company picnic he had hosted. As Gran had explained it, his madness wasn't a gradual kind of edging away from reality, it was a sudden release—like a beam breaking. One day he was ringing horseshoes right here, the next day he was shattering every pane of glass he saw. No one's house on Gerard Avenue had been spared. The police finally found him in Sans Souci First Baptist Church scribbling in the Bibles, scratching out the name Jezebel, then writing in my grandmother's name above so that they read ". . . the woman *Myrtle Ann*, which calleth herself a prophetess, does teach and seduce my servants to commit fornication . . ." He ended up in the State Hospital, where he died years later. "I have no idea, no inkling of what brought that on," Gran would tell us all our lives, her voice still full of surprise and sadness. "It was like the man I knew was there one moment, kissing me on the forehead, smiling and holding your mama, and waving to the workers out there, and the next moment his soul just disappeared."

When my grandmother found herself raising a daughter alone, she said she began to realize that as far as husbands, the Harris women couldn't pick 'em and shouldn't pick 'em. Hadn't her own mother nursed her father through the late stages of syphilis? Held the camphor-soaked cloth to his temple as he foamed at the mouth like a stallion run too hard?

Gran warned my mother to wait for a strong, sensible specimen, one that luck looked fondly upon.

My mother picked one U.S. Navy Lieutenant Gerald Johanson, shipped out to Nam, serving two tours before being lost in foreign waters, presumed dead at twenty-three. My mother picked one that left her with two babies and a toddler, a man that left us half orphaned before she, running out for a pound of sugar, a box of Ivory Snow detergent, and a pound of snap beans three years later, finished the job when her car collided with an eighteen-wheeler.

Inside, I got myself another beer, my fourth. I was light-headed and giddy. It was a new experience. *I like it*, I thought, then realized I'd said it out loud. I walked through the house trying to see it through the eyes of a stranger. I tried to forget all the years of my life that lay curled up like cats in the sunny corners, on the stairs, memories that winked and purred as I passed. My parents were married here, at the base of the stairs. I'd studied the portrait showing ivy-draped banisters, my father in his uniform gripping my mother's waist as she clutched white roses. There, in front of the fireplace mantel, Ginnie and I had posed in tutus and tiaras for our dance portraits. And in the parlor, behind the heavy French windows, Gran had huddled weekly with her ever-shrinking group of women friends, murmuring recipes, Bible verses, and gossip over iced tea.

I started to scramble eggs then changed my mind and made egg salad. It would really stink up the place. I made a mental note to buy broccoli later today: I could use its stench, too. While the eggs boiled, I sat down on the couch and reached for the hair necklace I was working on. At the Ripley's Believe It or Not Museum at Myrtle Beach, I had seen an exhibition about the Victorian custom of weaving jewelry from the hair of dead relatives. I didn't have a dead loved one's hair, so I just had six inches cut off my own hair and started crocheting. It wasn't easy. A hair necklace is hard to make when the hair is slick and unwieldy, so I settled on making a hair doily. Ginnie refused to be around when I worked on it. That gave me an idea. I would leave my hair doily out for Mrs. Worthington.

I started knitting but I couldn't concentrate. What a bad day already! I pictured driving Ginnie to the abortion clinic in Palmetto, that anonymous metal building behind a high wooden fence, a constant knot of protestors in front. I'd read *TV Guide* and *Reader's Digest* in the waiting room. Or hold her hand back in an examining room.

Or sign up as her Lamaze coach.

Oh God.

I heard a car drive by slowly, turn around, and drive by again. I froze, listened hard. The whizzing traffic on the highway out back made a steady roar like the ocean, but this was a car right out front. I darted over to the door and peeked through the sheer curtains. Mrs. Worthington's silver Mercedes was nowhere in sight. Instead,

I could see a woman hunched over, motionless, in a brown Honda Civic parked at the curb.

A potential buyer, maybe. Or another Realtor. Nothing good, that was for sure.

Two

ELIZABETH STOOD IN HER driveway holding her car keys, the cold metal warming in her hands. After a while, she fished around in her purse and pulled out the map and unfolded it on the hood of the car. Gerard Avenue was in Sans Souci, just two miles up the road—2.3 miles actually, if the map scale was correct, and she was sure it was, she had done the calculations herself with a ruler. It was simple, really. She would turn out of her neighborhood, take a right on the highway. But the problem was the left there on Main before Gerard. Taking a left on what was probably a busy road. Maybe there wasn't a turn signal or even a turning lane. She felt her stomach tighten. Well, she would just make a right there; she would take four rights and circle round the block and come up to Gerard Avenue the other way.

Elizabeth slid in the driver's seat and started the car. She dabbed at the sweat on her upper lip with a tissue, glanced at herself in the rearview mirror. Her face was pale. *A delicate ivory bisque,* is what the Avon lady had told her when she had approached Elizabeth last week and tried to sell her bronze gel. People were always accosting her in the yard, where she lacked cover, where she could not extricate herself from their stares or questions.

Elizabeth fastened her seatbelt, put the car in reverse, and slowly backed out of the driveway.

Your husband is involved, the caller had said that morning. That was ridiculous! Laughable! And yet, here she was checking up on him. *Forget it,* she told herself. But she couldn't. That whispered, reluctant voice hovered like a hornet in her brain.

Look. You don't know me. I'm . . . I was a student—and I want to talk to you.

Elizabeth closed her eyes now, remembering how the leaky, stuffed-up voice had nervously sputtered on.

I don't know how to say this exactly, except just to—there's this student. She's your husband's student and it's no secret—

The speaker had cleared his throat, a thick, wet sound. Waiting for her to respond. But she'd said nothing, made no noise.

The fact is, your husband and this girl are involved. Her name is Virginia Johanson. She goes by Ginnie. She lives over on Gerard, 102 Gerard in Sans Souci. Listen, I'm sorry. I figured you would want to know.

"Who is this?" Her own voice sharp with fear, and then the click, the dial tone. She set the phone on its cradle, gently, politely, as if it were a teacup.

When the caller had said the name Ginnie, something had clicked.

All those references, "I've got Ginnie working on the research," "Ginnie's tracking down that volume on Byron," flickered. It was like learning a new word and then suddenly noticing how everyone seemed to be using it.

She'd dressed hurriedly, discarding blouses and dresses, slipping them on, peeling them off. It had to be something nice. Something . . . normal. A skirt with cabbage roses. A white blouse.

Elizabeth proceeded slowly down her street until she came to the sign that announced *Ye are departing Olde English Acres.* She pulled off to the side, turned off the engine, and sat there staring. The sign was plastic, fake weathered oak with a seam. It was hollow with a lightbulb inside. She looked down at the map beside her on the seat.

This will get easier, she thought. Once I'm on the road, it will get easier.

She took a right onto the highway. There were cramps in her hands. She made herself loosen her grip a little on the steering wheel, flex her fingers. She was going forty-eight miles per hour in the right lane. Then she came to the intersection on Main, and there was traffic congestion in the right lane. It would be faster to turn left, wouldn't it? There was a left turning lane. She pulled into the left lane, her blinker clicking, a car in front, its taillights pulsing, and then a car in back, too, and there she was wedged in between. I have got to get out of here, she thought. I will just get out and leave the car here, leave the door open, leave the keys. And then the little green arrow appeared and her car sputtered loyally across the intersection.

She rolled down the window, turned on the air. Sweat rolled down her sides, her back, like tears. One more right turn, just up two streets on the right and . . . there it was! Gerard! She turned and drove slowly, passing the house, 102 Gerard, passing it and circling back, and passing it again and then parking.

What had she planned to do once she arrived? She didn't really know, had hoped her fears would somehow be allayed once she reached the address. She squinted as she looked out, saw the sun glance off the hood of her car, a row of silver mailboxes, the flat glint of windows.

> There's a certain Slant of Light—
> Winter Afternoons—
> That oppresses.

Oh, God. That Emily Dickinson poetry—all those lines just made matters worse. She squeezed her eyes shut, willing herself to

shrug it off, this anxiety. The slanted light sliced through her and
for what? For nothing. All this way, all this worry and Daniel obviously wasn't here. His car wasn't. He really was at that conference!

Elizabeth ran a hand through her long, dark hair, her fingers
stopped by the tangled thickness. Her hair was too long; it seemed
separate from the rest of her, the way it clumped and tangled like
an overzealous vine. With two fingers, she traced the angry red
semicircle branded across her forehead, the result of resting against
the steering wheel for how long now? Twenty minutes? Her foot
was asleep. She sat up cautiously, made herself take another quick
look around. It was an old street, with grand houses, towering oaks,
a grass median thick with rosebushes—all unpruned and weed
choked. Porches crowded with rusty lawn chairs and pots of pansies or gobs of ivy, a broken stroller. She did not like this disrepair,
this giving into the natural rot of things. But, Daniel. Well, Daniel
would love it. He, who had acquiesced to living in a new house
(for her!) that even now still smelled of new paint and carpet.
Daniel always enjoyed a good-natured wrestle with entropy.

Elizabeth studied 102 Gerard, stared at the wraparound porch,
the large windows, the peeling paint. There were three little square
attic windows at the top, the middle one stained glass. Some of the
gingerbread trim was rotting or missing, which gave the house
raggedy, dingy edges. And the side of the house was a mess where
someone had attempted to mount a patch of vinyl siding.

Before she was an English major, Elizabeth had been premed,
immersed in chemistry and biology. And sometimes her thoughts
were stained with the worst of both worlds: dark lyricism and
mean facts of science. Looking at 102 Gerard, Elizabeth couldn't
help thinking, *reducers.* You couldn't fight them. Reducers had a
job to do: decompose waste and remains. As far as the fungi and
bacteria and termites were concerned, wooden planks and porches
and shutters were delicious.

Dilapidation's processes
Are organized decays.

She felt a shiver pass through her then, a coldness in her finger-tips. Frozen with fear . . . and for what? A rumor? An ugly anony-mous phone call? A lie? Daniel was softhearted, had just yesterday gathered up a spider from the bathtub, held it in the folds of a Kleenex, whispered, *Just a minute, old fella,* and freed it on the back porch. Being alone in her house all day made her suspicious. At least it was a good sign, wasn't it, doing something active about her fears? It would make them proud, those doctors who tossed off her diagnosis as casually as lint from a lapel—free-floating anxiety— words that left her feeling betrayed and puzzled, because they weren't the right words, they held no pain, only made her think of things filmy and fluttering: butterflies, autumn leaves, chiffon.

That morning, just hours ago, Daniel, his old soft leather suitcase and black bookbag at the door, waiting like pets before a romp, had laced his fingers through her hair, kissed her on the forehead while she'd crouched over her desk, pretending to concentrate. It was a lie, of course, the concentration, the props: files and books and typed notes scattered about, index cards bundled and stacked like corded wood. But it made both of them feel better: she couldn't go to the conference with him, couldn't go anywhere with this disser-tation hanging over her head. She was close to completion.

"So you'll be all right . . . just until tomorrow night?" He squeezed her shoulder. She was busy looking busy, sorting index cards, not even glancing up at him, just nodding. A car trip, an overnight stay, two days away from home? She couldn't.

"I'll be fine." Was it guilt that made him hover over her, mur-muring about helping with her research? She thought of his eyes on her—dark and green and a little perilous, too, like moss-covered rock. No. Not guilt. Urging her on from the sidelines—that was nothing new. He was her coach.

Once, though, the roles had been reversed: she'd been his coach, demanding his concentration. *The Krebs cycle involves ten major reactions,* she'd make him repeat. When they were sophomores at the University of Virginia, she'd been sent in like a SWAT team by their biology professor; she was charged with saving his scholarship by helping him pass biology. Oh, and she was so serious. So firm with him. How could someone who memorized all 434 lines of *The Waste Land* not remember the first step of the amino acid cycle? By the end of the semester, when he squeaked by with a C— then persuaded her to take American Lit with him, how could she resist? He loved her. Her! Pale as a pearl, bluish veins like wires in her thin white arms. The bent can on the shelf, that's what she was, and he picked her anyway, devoured her, left bite marks on her neck and raw, red rashes on her face and breasts from his unshaven burrowings. When she'd heard him quote lines of poetry in class, or even lines onstage, the words seemed pampered and plumped, glistening, until, for some reason, she'd blush, stare down at her textbook or hands, not daring to look up or even follow along. *Close your eyes, close your eyes,* he'd whisper to her at night and she would and she never knew if he'd kiss her or recite a line of Shakespeare or Auden or Yeats. How could she not follow him, a man like that? How could she not jump off the sturdy bridge of scientific facts—leave isotopes and mitochondria, synclines and anticlines behind—and plunge into a sweet rich pudding of words? Days or weeks after cramming for a Shakespeare exam, the lines, the words would come to her, swooping down like a birds of prey, nipping her at night. But she could never recite as he did. Not like him, no. *Close your eyes,* he'd say. *Let go.* And he'd kiss her, untangle her braid and fan her hair out across her shoulders, through his fingers.

She won the English department's highest award her senior year for her Dickinson paper—for exploring botany and garden imagery in the poems of Emily Dickinson. And he was so proud! They were a couple, then, intended to marry soon after their college graduation, their grad school plans—their life together— mapped out like a vacation.

But that was twelve years ago. A dozen. It made her think of rows of white eggs: smooth, identical, fragile, nestled in hollows of Styrofoam, one egg for each year they'd been together. Where were the fellowships she'd been ripe for? Where was the travel to Tuscany and London they'd set their sights on? Where were the babies? Their own green-eyed, dark-haired sons?

She should start up her car and go home. Nothing was to be accomplished by coming here, sitting in her car at the curb. Someone had played a joke on her, to see if she would come out, leave her house. She knew the students, the faculty, too; they probably talked about her. Maybe now someone was hiding and watching her, laughing at her.

She pictured walking up the porch, the front door being thrown open by the guy who made the call—*I'm really sorry but you have to admit it's kinda funny. They said I was the only one who could sound serious enough about it. What a bunch of jokers, huh? No hard feelings?* Then she would see her, this Ginnie, sitting on the couch with her boyfriend. That would explain things, wouldn't it?

Except it was crazy. Crazy.

But what if she's not here now? Ginnie. What if she's at the conference with him?

Elizabeth pressed her eyelids with her fingertips until she saw colors, whorls of blue and black. She didn't know anymore. She didn't know what Daniel would do.

Crumbling is not an instant's Act.

Elizabeth got out of her car and walked right through the grass median, around those sad rosebushes. She made her way up the front walkway of the house. She couldn't believe she was actually doing this, but she pictured herself sitting at home, unable to eat, sleep, read—not knowing.

What if there were cars around back, hidden? She paused at the porch, pushed her hand through her hair. What if one of them was a red Toyota? She walked past the concrete planters full of scrubby weeds. She stepped slowly up onto the porch, felt the hem of her chintz skirt graze the wood. She looked though the heavy, beveled glass.

One of the shutters lay propped against a porch railing, the hinges broken. The crescent moon cutout on it reminded Elizabeth of cold, white things, of ice, of marble. She never was one to gaze at the moon, at space, at stars. *It makes you think of possibilities,* Daniel had said once when they stood together, looking up into the black of night. But she never thought so. All those hard stars reminded her of being small. She was living and they blinked cheerfully, she would die and still they would blink, and the moon would rise all the same.

She backed up and stumbled over a dirt-caked Reebok tennis shoe, laceless, wide and gaping like a toothless mouth. A broken umbrella lay inside out, halfway down the porch. It all looked so carelessly intimate, like someone's messy closet. She turned around, headed back to her car.

Then the door opened behind her. A girl stood there, her eyebrows raised, her head tilted, her brown eyes too dark for her pale, freckled face. Her blonde hair was halfway out of a ponytailed little nub at the top of her head. Her sweatshirt was inside out. She was here. This Ginnie. She was here, not at a conference after all. Elizabeth backed up. "I'm looking for—sorry, wrong address." She started back down the steps.

But the girl was saying something. "Look, the house can't be seen today, okay?"

Elizabeth was off the porch steps now, on the walkway. Under her feet, the gray cement had cracks like lightning. Like bare trees in winter.

> *As if my life were shaven,*
> *And fitted to a frame.*

Elizabeth stopped, her back to the girl. She swayed, unsteady, sweat prickling under her arms.

"Are you all right?"

Elizabeth looked down. An ant on the cement crawled and disappeared through one of the cracks. Underneath the sidewalk were ant beds and tiny, tiny crawly things and worms and moles and layers of soil and fossils. Dirt, layered like cake, spiking and sinking, swirling. And here she was between the buried and the cold expanse of the sky.

"Maybe you need to come in." The voice was softer now with concern.

Elizabeth found herself in the arms of the girl, a stranger, and realized she had started to faint. The girl had a strange scent, herbal and earthy. Oregano? Fennel? She helped Elizabeth up the steps, the two of them making scuffling noises across the wooden porch. And then she was inside, behind the heavy double doors with their yellowed pleated curtains. A terrible stench nauseated Elizabeth. As the girl guided her to the couch, Elizabeth's foot hit three beer bottles on the floor. They teetered and fell like bowling pins. She sat on the heavy, dusty tapestry of the couch and caught sight of the coffee table, at the horrible-looking tangle of hair and knitting needles there, as if a small animal had been butchered.

Three

WHEN SHE FINALLY GOT out of her car and came up to the porch, I was ready for her. But then, I forgot what I said after all that beer. My tongue felt thick and unwieldy, a small toad. *I'm not showing the house.* Something like that. Maybe I was rude. She had a string of pearls around her neck, beads of perspiration on her upper lip. I could picture her pressing a calling card in my palm with a white, slightly damp gloved hand. She headed back down the porch steps. She swayed, then crouched on the sidewalk. It was horrible, standing there and watching that. So I brought her in.

When she sat down in the living room, she hugged her thin, flat arms around herself like a child. I left her there, on the couch, its tattered, lumpy cushions smothering her in a musty, bosomy embrace.

"It's all right." I headed to the kitchen. I would give her a beer and make myself a cup of coffee.

But as I measured out the coffee, I turned to find her standing in the kitchen doorway. "I have to go," she mumbled. "I'm sorry."

"*I'm* sorry about the mess," I lied.

"Oh, I can tell your house was beautiful—could be beautiful."

"You can?" That scared me.

"Well"—her eyes scanned the high ceiling, the windowsills—"but it would be so much work, fixing it up."

"Then you're not interested?"

"Interested?" she whispered.

"In buying."

"I'm sorry . . . buying?"

"Isn't that why you're here? I figured you were waiting on the real estate lady."

"Oh no. No. I'm not—I mean, that's not why I'm here at all."

"Well, that's about the best news I've had all day." I raised my coffee cup in a toast.

"I was just . . . lost." I handed her the beer, but she refused it. Her hand fluttered to her mouth, and she looked distracted, in pain. She squatted on the floor, right there in the doorway, just kind of folded herself up in a heap.

"I'm feeling . . . a little light-headed."

"Would you like to lie down?" I asked. "Could I call somebody for you?" She shook her head. "Listen," I said. "You should come in the living room and sit down." She seemed to shrink like paper curling in a fire: she drew in her arms, hugged her knees, hid her face. Then she stood, caught herself on the door frame, and headed down the hall. Before I put down the bottle of beer, she was back.

"There's a strange man in your living room." She was wide-eyed. "There's a big—very big—man looking under your sofa cushions."

"That's Alfred. He lives across the street in a group home." I handed her the beer again, then led her to the living room. She had a brittle, small-stepped walk.

"Alfred, put down the cushion. Okay?"

"Hello," he said softly, then closed his eyes, and groped for crumbs and lint.

"You can stop now," I told him. "Please don't clean today."

His back was quivering with effort. His white shirt looked big as a sail, the dark of his skin showing through in circles, muted brown. There were Cheetos and pennies and two dusty Certs in a neat pile on the floor.

I touched his arm. I would have to have a long talk with Alfred soon, tell him how I needed to keep the house messy in case the real estate lady popped in. I lay my hand on his back. "I left some Pepsi in the fridge for you. In the bottles, the way you like."

Alfred nodded to himself and headed for the kitchen. Then I looked at the woman. She tucked her hair behind each ear, swallowed hard, looked at the floor.

"Does he always just . . . come in like that?" she whispered. "I mean, do you hire him or—?"

"Well, yes, he always comes in like that, and no, I don't hire him. He likes to—hang around. He's good company. Father Bob couldn't manage things over there without him."

"Oh."

I smiled a little, thinking about how I'd gotten to be buddies with Alfred. It was something else that Ginnie and I now fought about.

Just last month, we'd come down to the kitchen only to discover all the dishes had been washed and laid out on the counter. Sometimes we found our food—even the cereal boxes—covered with plastic wrap. It was like discovering glistening spiderwebs spun overnight and strung out across your yard, knowing something had worked awfully hard while you slept. One day Ginnie pulled out the cheese slices in the refrigerator and waved them in my face.

"He's been sucking cheese again, Cutter! Look at this. Look!"

I shrugged. Putting cheese slices in a zip-lock bag and sucking the air out of one corner was Alfred's way of vacuum packing.

"Alfred really enjoys cleaning," I said now. "But I don't want a clean house. Especially with Realtors and buyers popping in." She looked confused. Of course she looked confused. "You see, I don't want the house to sell, that's why it's a mess. I mean, my brother is the main one who is trying to sell it, and my sister just goes along—I know it looks pretty bad, which is kind of good—at least for me." The beer made me chatty, made my words tumble out faster than I could catch them.

"So you're keeping the house in disguise."

"Exactly!"

" 'One need not be a Chamber to be Haunted,' " she said in a low, stilted voice. " 'One need not be a House. The Brain has Corridors surpassing Material Place.' "

I shrugged. "Yeah. That sounds about right."

Alfred came back with the Pepsi and sat in the wing-back chair. He swigged his drink, making wet, popping sounds. Between sips, his eyes darted around the living room, fixing on the drapes or the mantel or the overhead light.

"Dude," he said, and looked at me. I smiled.

"I miss Glen, too," I told him. Alfred was grinning now, his teeth shining out from his dark face. "Glen was the social worker who came on the weekends there," I explained, "at Father Bob's. They called him Dude. The three of us spent a lot of time in here drinking Pepsi, playing Hearts."

"I miss him bad," Alfred said.

"Glen's in California now, studying to be a chiropractor," I said.

Alfred moved to the floor, his large, powerful legs out in front, feet knocking. He looked at her. She was silent and tense. She glanced at her watch.

"Stay," I said. "Just until you finish your beer."

Alfred took a last swig of his drink and walked to the kitchen, his head held to the side as usual, as if he were listening very hard to something far away. I heard him start in on the breakfast dishes. I shouted for him to stop, that I wanted it messy today.

"Half the time, he doesn't pay attention to me."

Her eyes, still round with worry, were focused on me. She lifted the bottle and took a sip, and it looked so strange, such an unlikely thing for her to do—drink out of a bottle—that it reminded me I hadn't offered her a glass. When I brought one from the kitchen, she waved it away.

"No, no. This is fine. It's very—collegiate. I like it."

I watched her take in the pile of spiral notebooks on the coffee table, the fat English literature textbook on top of the family Bible.

"So. Are you a student?" she finally asked.

"Me? No way. I'm no student. I work."

She looked at the books in front of her.

"Oh, that stuff isn't mine. That's my sister's."

"Your sister?"

"Yeah. She's one of those professional students, you know? I think she's changed her major, like, three times."

"I see." She stood up and walked over by the fireplace mantel, where old photographs of my family sat displayed, some propped on others, some knocked down, none of them in order, as random as memories. She picked up Gran's wedding picture, a photograph I had studied for most of my life. The picture was taken in the back of our house underneath the rose trellis, my grandmother's face blurry, my grandfather squint-eyed and barely smiling. How many times had I stared, looking for a trace of the madness that would later claim him? He was like a battery before it went bad, before the acid corroded, before the crusty poison oozed. She picked up another picture, this one of my father in uniform, too young, his skin tight and pink and healthy, his hair short, marine style. She gazed at my mother's high school senior picture with her off-the-shoulder black velvet, her blonde shoulder-length hair flipped, teased.

"I was named after my father," I volunteered. "I mean, I ignored my given name and took my father's name. I'm Cutter, by the way. Cutter Johanson."

"And what was your given name?"

"Catherine." She put the picture down, looked at me, nodding slowly, waiting for an explanation. "My father was killed in Vietnam. Years later, his best friend visits, just out of the blue. He was in Nam with my dad. They enlisted together out of high school. So, this guy—his name was Henry Junket—he shows up and says it's part of his therapy to visit us, that he needs closure in his life. Apparently, he'd been bonkers for a while. He sat right here in the living room and told me how my father was a born warrior. That's the word he used, *warrior*. Only, my father hadn't planned to fly, he said. He'd wanted to be on the water. He wanted to be a sailor and that's how he got his nickname. Even in high school he was Cutter—you know, like the boat. But he died over there. His plane crashed in a bay. They made him fly, but in the end the water claimed him."

"And you decided to take the name?"

"Right then, at nine years old, I did. I ordered everyone to call me Cutter, and if they didn't, if they slipped and called me Catherine, I ignored them, or I cried. And it worked."

"Your mother—"

"She's dead, too. And so is my grandmother. There's no one left but me and my sister and my brother." She turned her back to me, looking at the pictures, then moved to the sofa. I noticed she'd started having that pressed, nervous look again, her eyes darting to the door.

"By the way, I don't know your name."

"I'm Elizabeth Byers."

Wife!

"I owe you an explanation," she said, looking down.

"No," I said, my throat tight, my voice too loud. "No, you don't."

Wife! Wife! Wife! Like a siren.

"You were kind to invite me in. I've not been feeling well and . . . I'm embarrassed, I really am. As I mentioned, I was lost. I was just . . . taking a break, because I've been so busy and cooped up. And so I decided this morning to explore Sans Souci and somehow I got turned around and then I saw your house and it seemed the most . . . authoritative one on the street so I thought I'd stop and ask how to get back on Palmetto Highway. I'm terrible with directions."

Wife doesn't go out. Anywhere. She's like an invalid or something. I swallowed the last inch of my coffee. It was bitter and cold.

"So you must have just moved around here, then," I managed.

"Let's see . . . I guess it's been two, going on three years. But I've been busy, as I said, and I'm ashamed to say I'm just now getting out, exploring. You see, I've been working on my dissertation. On Emily Dickinson. I think I'm close to finishing, I really do, but she hasn't been kind to me, I'm afraid."

"I thought . . . isn't she dead?"

A polite smile then, gone so fast I thought I had imagined it. "What I meant is, I seem to feel such a connection with her work sometimes . . . and then—" She lost it. She tried to control herself, I could tell, sucking in her breaths, discreetly swiping at her eyes with a finger. "I started exploring the garden imagery in her work—poems and letters, you know—and then—after—I just couldn't finish."

Alfred came in from the kitchen, wiping his damp hands on a towel, looking at me sheepishly. I motioned for him to be quiet, to sit beside me.

"The poetry—just never leaves. I mean, all the gardening information I've read. I know what varieties of sweet peas grew on her fence, for goodness's sake. And then I started a garden myself just as an experiment, and it got better for a while, I started really making some progress, I made some great notes, I felt such—empathy. But now that doesn't even—I started moving everything inside. My plants, my seeds. I froze up. I couldn't go to my garden outside—I mean, I can't go anywhere. Not to the library. Not to get groceries."

She was the private type. This would kill her. She would hate herself later for opening up to me. I thought of Ginnie then, listening to something like "A Feminist Reading of *Bleak House*," pretending to be interested, sitting right next to Elizabeth's husband, their thighs touching, their pinkies entwined.

Elizabeth stood up. "Can I ask you a question?"

No. "Yes."

"What is that?" She pointed to the coffee table.

"Oh." I hoped she couldn't hear the relief in my voice. "That's this hair necklace I'm working on. Well—it started out a necklace." I had to admit it looked sloppy and uneven, a jumble of needles and hair. "Now I think it's going to be a doily."

"The hair is—"

"It's my hair, don't worry. It's not from some dead person. You're familiar with the custom?"

"I've read about it." Her face was guarded. I couldn't tell if she was repulsed or genuinely interested.

"What is your sister's name?"

"Virginia."

"Ginnie?"

"Yes. Ginnie. She was named after my great-aunt Virginia Louise. I was originally named after my other great-aunt, Catherine—"

"Are they involved, Cutter?"

"Involved?"

"Your sister. My husband. Please don't make me say it."

I looked at the pattern on the rug. I had seen that threadbare Oriental rug a million times, had walked on it, slept on it, stood on it; I'd spent a whole summer when I was ten analyzing the design after reading a Nancy Drew book about a secret treasure map woven into a Turkish rug. But now I cocked my head, following a swirl, the way it entwined with the border like roots from a plant. Maybe I should play dumb, like I didn't know a thing. I could even lie, make her feel better. I didn't look up.

"It's just a rumor, isn't it?" Her voice was a whisper and I looked up then and saw how her hands started to move again from her mouth to her chest to her mouth. I hadn't thought her face could look any paler, but it was now.

"I don't keep up with rumors—or Ginnie. Like I said, I'm not a student. I don't get over to Palmetto much. And the university? Never. My sister—she's not here much anymore, anyway. She just pops in once in a while. So I don't even know the rumors, much less the facts." The beer buzz was fading. My head was starting to pound.

She closed her eyes, took a breath. After a minute, she stood, smoothed her skirt, thanked me for the beer, and left.

"Wait, let me help you to your car." I followed her across the street where she was parked. The keys in her hand were shaking so badly, she could hardly unlock the door to her car.

And then it wouldn't start.

"Sounds like your battery is dead," I said. I opened the door. A map covered the passenger seat, a jumble of yellow Hi-Liters and pencils nested in the middle of it.

"But how can it be worn out already? I barely drive this car—"

"That's the problem. It can be fixed. Don't worry. I'm always having car problems. I'm used to it." But she kept trying the ignition over and over until even the sickly engine grunts stopped.

I sent Alfred to get Father Bob and the jumper cables.

"Do you think I'm crazy?" she asked me, whispering, as I drove her home. We were in her car. Father Bob and Alfred followed, so they could drive me back. I wasn't entirely sober, but I was in better shape to drive than she was.

"No," I said, but I don't think she was listening. She was just gazing out the window and grasping the door handle, white-knuckled. "I'm lost," she said. "I don't know where I am." She rolled the window down and her hair blew around. It seemed to betray her that way, lifting and whipping happily.

She lived in a new development called Olde English Acres. A name like that was supposed to set up a theme; it was supposed to make you forget the tract housing and the chain-link fences glimmering in the sun. Make you think of thatched roofs, Tudor cottages, and deep green forests.

When we pulled into her drive, she ran to her front door. The door wasn't locked and she disappeared inside. I turned off the engine. She'd left her purse in the car. It was leather, worn soft and a little dirty with use. The snap was broken and I could see a lipstick in there and a comb with missing teeth. I carried it up to the porch. Father Bob and Alfred pulled up then—you couldn't miss the clacking of the compressor in Father Bob's Dodge Dart. They got out of the car.

"Is everything okay, Cutter?" Father Bob whispered as he and Alfred joined me on the porch. His face was seamed, sagging kindly. The frail hunch of his shoulders was hidden under a flannel shirt flecked with paint. He smelled of turpentine.

"Oh, sorry," I said. "We got you on your day off, didn't we?" On Saturdays, a social worker relieved him for the day so he could turn to his projects: he'd tended banana trees in his greenhouse last winter. They'd withered and blackened and then filled the yard with a noxious, swampy odor. He'd spent the spring building soil beds for an earthworm farm. We found those worms on the sidewalk for weeks, dried and curled, entangled in lumps, like ramen noodles. Now, he'd turned to painting sunset scenes on dried gourds.

"Oh, I'm glad to help."

"The battery is fine now, I think."

"No, I mean the lady. She's ill, isn't she?"

I shrugged. Father Bob had an antenna for fragility, and it was quivering.

I knocked. "Your purse," I said, when Elizabeth opened the door. The three of us stood there, a knot of concern. Her eyes widened.

Father Bob said, "You're all right, dear? Is there someone you could call?"

"Oh no. No, I'm fine." She reddened. "Why don't you all come in?"

All the blinds were closed in the living room, the lights off. It was a small, dark burrow. The sofa was covered in books and journals and papers, their pages branded with taupe coffee rings. Clear plastic trays and soil-filled egg cartons and a few limp, yellowed seedlings were spread on a coffee table in the middle of the room.

"Thank you all again for helping me." She clutched the purse to her chest awkwardly, then began to clear stacks of paper off the sofa. "Please have a seat, if you can find a place. I wasn't—you know—prepared for company."

Father Bob leaned over her seedlings. "You simply must come to our greenhouse. You must come and see our orchids."

"They give them names," I said.

"My flower's named Ladybug," Alfred said. "It has freckles."

"Would you like something to drink?" she said. The crisp civility was meant to mask her awkwardness, but it didn't. Her discomfort and fear lingered there in the air among us. "I can make some iced tea." She darted to the kitchen and rummaged in the refrigerator.

"Please don't worry about it," I said as I followed her. She stood there gazing into the refrigerator. It looked mostly empty except for a box of baking soda, some pickles, a jar of mayonnaise.

"It's just . . . I'm not really prepared for guests."

"That's okay. We have to get back."

She held up a bag of gray slimy mushrooms and a bottle of Worcestershire. "I went to the store the other day, and I meant . . . I thought I got beef Stroganoff ingredients. But there's no meat on . . . What was I thinking?" She looked at me, puzzled, as if I could answer her. "I ran out of time. They changed the aisles around. I hate that."

"Yeah, I hate those big stores, too. I stick to the local places, the farmers' market and vegetable stands."

"Would you like me to pick up something for you?" Father Bob said from behind me.

"Oh no." She seemed to snap out of a trance. "No. I didn't mean I needed—"

"You will come and visit us soon?" He smiled at her. "Promise?"

She nodded hesitantly.

As Father Bob and Alfred stepped out on the porch, she gripped my elbow. "What kind of priest is he?" she whispered.

"Mail order, I think."

"What?"

"We've called him Father Bob as long as I can remember. I think he believes it."

"So you've known him—?"

"All my life. He married Ella Hollis late in life, and when Ella died, Father Bob inherited the Hollis house, and also Ella's brother Pinky, who lived in a home for retarded men way down in Charleston. Father Bob brought Pinky to live with him, to keep him company. That was the start of Father Bob's Home."

"Oh."

"It's a nice place to visit. You'll see." As a little girl, I'd spent my summers sitting on Father Bob's screen porch helping him or one of the men put together jigsaw puzzles, the cardboard pieces plumped and soggy from humidity. We never did complete one. The Mona Lisa remained one-eyed, Van Gogh's sunflowers blighted, the roiling seascapes wrecked with jagged holes.

"Look, why don't I leave my number with you? And, well, if you feel uncomfortable about calling me at home with Ginnie there"— she winced—"call me at the newspaper or at the Pancake Palace. That's where I work. In case you need groceries or something."

I scrawled down my name and the phone numbers. She took the slip of paper between her hands and held it there, flattened and hidden, as if she were praying. I got in the backseat of Father Bob's car. We waved to Elizabeth as she stood in the doorway. She did not step out onto the porch and did not wave back. She squinted out at us as she closed the door, until the house swallowed her up. I sighed. I knew the signs. With Gran, life had been like a rail she rode on, with fewer and fewer stops, until she never stepped out of our house at all. The beauty parlor on Tuesdays, the farmers' market on Fridays, church on Wednesdays and Sundays, gardening and sitting on the porch summer evenings—one by one she stopped them, until all that was left was her path from the kitchen to the bedroom to the attic bathroom. Homebound.

Four

NIGHT. ELIZABETH WAS IN bed, her back to her husband, the covers pulled up to her ears. She listened to his pen's quick bursts of scratching as he wrote comments, pressing down so hard the bed quivered. She turned slowly and glimpsed the red-inked scrawl of his handwriting across the page of a student paper. *Are you saying Miss Havisham symbolizes the withering of capitalism?* She closed her eyes again. Once in a while, she felt him glance at her as she lay beside him, pretending to sleep, the faint trembling of her eyelids betraying her. She yawned.

"Are you awake?"

She nodded. The writing stopped. Her grogginess was wearing off now, but the sedatives still lay on her, heavy and warm like a lover. When Daniel had arrived home earlier that afternoon, she'd been in bed. In bed all day.

He reached out, squeezed her shoulder. "Can I get you anything? Hot tea?" She could feel his stare on her face, her closed eyes. "An IV?" She did not smile. She kicked off the covers and lay flat on her back, staring up, listening to the ceiling fan's whirring, its faint breeze rattling the dying fern's leaves on her dresser.

There was so much they didn't talk about, the things they did say to each other jumped out, had a special resonance. And sometimes their sentences even rhymed, spare like poetry:

Have a good day, honey
Do you need grocery money?

I'm starving something smells great
I've already eaten but I fixed you a plate.

The scratching sounds of his pen began again.

After a while, Elizabeth sat up, hung her feet off the side of the bed, wiggled her toes like a little girl. It was a very high bed, old and rickety. A wedding present they'd given themselves right after they'd married. She'd seen it in a window at an antiques store; the four carved posters and an elaborate walnut headboard reminded her of an altar. A solemn, solid presence that they'd managed to squeeze into apartments and finally here, their first house, although it always meant taking doors off hinges and hiring men to maneuver it through narrow hallways.

Without looking back, she walked out into the hall, bumping the walls with her shoulders. She made her way to the kitchen.

"Elizabeth?" He called to her from the bedroom.

She opened the refrigerator, blinked from the light. He had been to the store. The refrigerator was full: luncheon meat, a roast, eggs, lettuce, milk. Well, good. She wouldn't have to go shopping tomorrow. She opened a can of ginger ale and gulped down half of it. Cottonmouth. She had forgotten how the pills did that. She put the can back in the refrigerator, sloshing it. The carbonated bubbles fizzed fiercely, secretly.

When the phone rang, she jumped, and picked it up before it could ring twice.

"You sound sleepy. Don't tell me I woke you up at nine-thirty?"

"No, Mother. I'm just tired."

"Did you get that brochure on Bermuda? It's a great package, the three-night-four-day little minicruise at that price. I immediately thought of you and Daniel."

"Mom, you don't have to sell me." Her mother, for thirty years a housewife, had packed up and moved to Miami from the Chicago suburbs two years before, when Elizabeth's father had died. She was a travel agent now, her obsession with her new career desperate and sudden, like a religious conversion. She was lonely without her husband, and Elizabeth knew loneliness made people do strange things. She was actually the kind of mother who stayed up late sewing a felt costume for a second-grade Halloween party, or mailing a supply of brownies when Elizabeth was in college. Elizabeth tried to think of those things now, when she lost patience with her mother, dodged her insistent questions.

"Well, did you look at it? Talk about it? Did you even get the thing?"

"Yes. I got it and looked through it. We can't consider a trip right now."

"Is it money?"

"No. It's not money." If only it were, Elizabeth thought. If only it were a vexing normal worry like being broke that stopped them from vacationing. Elizabeth's inheritance from her father was still mostly untouched, socked away in savings for emergencies. Hospitalization for long stretches of time wasn't cheap. Even for the insured.

Her mother sighed. "How is Daniel?"

"Fine. Daniel is . . . fine." What could she say to her mother, who, along with letters and recipes for blueberry buckle, sent her articles from *Good Housekeeping* and *Redbook* about How to Keep Your Marriage Alive? How to Scratch His Seven-Year Itch?

Her mother loved Daniel. At twenty, when Elizabeth had told her parents about dropping chemistry and biology for literature, they'd been relieved. Her mother had patted her hand across the dinner table, her father put down his knife and fork, pushed aside his plate to look at her and nod. The two of them peering at her, cheerful with relief.

At sixteen, she'd had two weeks of electric shock treatments, which left azure bruises on her forehead, like watercolor prints of hydrangeas. That had scared them a little.

You just need a little extra help sometimes, her mother had explained when Elizabeth was twelve and could only get through her piano recital after she took a little lavender pill that numbed her, escorted her worries out of the building, let her mind drift away, somewhere up and to the left, on the beam above the stage with the strip lights and the dusty red velvet curtains.

"Well, you two can always come to Florida and visit me for a little getaway, you know." Elizabeth felt herself tense from the implied worry in her mother's voice. And then her mother changed subjects, began to tell about a small cold that Elizabeth's niece had caught. A hacking cough in a two-month-old that had them all scared to death. Elizabeth thought of her sister Marley with her husband and four children, straggling in late at Christmas while she and Daniel sat on her mother's couch watching them arrive, the whole noisy, sweet, marsupial bunch of them.

"What have you been up to?" Her mother's question was too probing to be offhand. It meant, Are you venturing out in the world? Are you pregnant? Her mother was like a night nurse, coming in to check the vital signs.

"Gardening a little, finishing up my dissertation. The usual."

"Oh, honey."

In the corner of the living room, her black Underwood typewriter sat neglected, the piece of paper in it curled. It had been days since she had typed. Tonight she must, she *must*. She would start doing more reading. She would finish the notes she had begun last month. Even the pretense of work would make her feel brave.

Elizabeth sat rigidly on the sofa, as if she were an obedient guest in her own cluttered, small house. The metal springs grated, but the crushed velvet, worn nubby and thin, comforted her. It was a shabby sofa, left over from graduate school, one they had found on the curb. She had meant to replace it soon after they moved in, but then she had meant to replace all of the furniture—the makeshift metal bookcases, the sagging tweed reading chair, the dust-filled pleated floor lamp. She needed to buy new furniture and put up wallpaper; she needed to paint and plan color schemes and make curtains and arrange cut flowers in crystal vases.

She glanced at the yellow legal pad fanned out beside her. Daniel's presentation. *Metaphoric cannibalism . . . mimetic view of literary form . . . historical context of the alienation of the labor force.* She closed her eyes. It was like a foreign language now.

She sat at the table and typed *I Years Had Been from Home, Poem LXXIX.* Her typewriter was loud, not sleek and secretive like a computer. She actually liked the squeaking and slapping sounds of each letter, her words as measured and powerful as a judge's sentence.

She heard the bed creak in their room, Daniel's footsteps in the hall.

"Who was on the phone?"

She looked up and the sight of him leaning in the doorway, his hair sticking up on one side, his sleepy, puzzled look, made her ache for him. She felt the anger inside her shift, breaking up like ice, the fear of losing him like a welder's torch, blasting away at her.

"Mother. Pushing a trip to Bermuda. I told her we didn't have time." Elizabeth thought of him naked, his body covering a lean blonde moving slowly beneath him in a motel's wide bed. She shut her eyes and, when she opened them again, saw that he had moved closer to her, stood behind the sofa.

"I didn't mean to interrupt you," he said.

She shook her head. "You're not."

He made his way around the sofa then in the slightly irregular gait that she barely noticed anymore, even though it was one of the first things about him she had loved. A tic of vulnerability. A relic of pain left over from a birth defect. An atrophied leg, a too-small foot, a sentence of abnormality that he had overcome. She watched him, and in those three steps he took, remembered the way her own stride would change when they held hands and walked together, his limp a rhythm she would give into.

"So, how are the plans for your conference coming?" She thought she saw him flinch a little. Was it that surprising, her asking?

"It's coming along. Just wrapping things up at this point."

"It's—when?—next month?"

"Next week. You know, I talked to Carter Price this weekend. I just happened to run into him. He's back from a year in London. But he's agreed to come, maybe even present although it's a little late in the game for that."

"Carter . . . who?"

"Carter was two years ahead of us, remember? He helped me land the assistantship with Gardener."

The vague image of a ruddy-faced, short man shimmered for a minute, disappeared. "Oh, I remember now."

"Gorney is out of his mind. He can't believe it. I mean, we're pulling in some big fish for this conference."

He stood up and stretched, his arms and fingers spread. His raised shirt revealed a band of flesh, dark knots of curls. They blinked at each other awkwardly. The fact that her husband could be considering leaving her even at this moment floated up to Elizabeth cruelly. But they had been happy once. And twelve years together. She had so much to tell him now, so many promises to make. Except it would sound like begging. It would be begging. He leaned over her, murmured "Good night" in her hair. An award. He was glad to see she was working.

After he went back to bed, Elizabeth could not concentrate. She just sat for a while, an hour maybe. Or ten minutes. Lately, time had done nothing for her but plod slowly and drag its slippered feet, padding around her house like a fat lady in pajamas.

She read the top sheet from her haphazard stack of notes.

Dubbed the Moth of Amherst, Emily Dickinson almost exclusively wore white, and was known as a kindly but eccentric loner who rarely left her house and garden. Indeed, her garden became the poet's escape into creativity, a rich source of allegory and metaphor that inserted itself repeatedly in her poetry.

She crumpled it up and flung it across the room. This wasn't what she meant at all. A kindly but eccentric loner? It was the pity that got to her, the amused tittering of all those critics, in all those books and articles that seemed to creep in and poison her own notes. *Her poet's soul demanded a solitary life,* they wrote, or, *She displayed remarkable discipline in sequestering herself, for she was devoted to her art above all else.* As if she chose to live that way, as if she enjoyed it.

"You're not writing some psychological treatise," Daniel had warned her. "Stick to garden imagery in her works and letters, remember?" He had said it tenderly and had stroked her hair.

Their first year of graduate school, it was she who had tried to do too much, never missing a deadline. Daniel had laughed when he'd found out she used index cards to memorize lines of poetry and scenes. *King Lear* had taken 184 cards, all color-coded by act and scene. He'd flipped through them, smiling at her, shaking his head, kissing her. She had a way of bringing out the gentleness in him. He loved dragging her into life, pulling her along with him into his rounds of parties, through strings of friends and colleagues, meeting more people than she could remember. Singing out his lines in the shower, the *Forsooth my Lord!* and *Prithee my Lady!*

Elizabeth thought of all the times lately he had gently nudged her to stay on track, to finish papers, to give teaching another try. He carried her failures cheerfully. He ignored them and explained. He rationalized. He hoped for the best. And she disappointed him again and again.

For someone who'd grown up in a household where book learning was discouraged—who managed to land a full college scholarship
despite his mother's genuine puzzlement about why he wanted more
school when his uncles were ready to hand over the family business to
him—understanding her failed scholarly life took extraordinary
patience. Elizabeth knew that. There were no obstacles to her success,
Daniel had seen to that. She had a home, a quiet place to read and
research, a job waiting on her. And him. She had him. At the end of
the day, there was someone who wanted to listen, to help chart her
progress, even if she didn't have much progress to report.

As much as she loved Daniel, would do almost anything for him,
she would never go back there, to teaching. No matter how much
he begged or talked about getting back on the horse when you fell
off, she just couldn't do that. One time had been enough—too
much. She could still see all those faces now, looking up at her
expectantly, every one like a firecracker that popped out at her:
You're in charge! You're in charge!

That day two years ago when she'd found herself behind a
lectern staring at four rows of empty desks, she knew she had made
a mistake, a terrible mistake.

Jumping a little at the sound of the bell, she had watched them
file in: twenty-two freshmen, backpacks slung gracefully over their
shoulders, flip-flops and tennis shoes scuffing, T-shirts with beer
slogans. She remembered looking out and seeing a room of
beauty—of youth; a group of people who saw their lives stretching
on before them like smooth, satin ribbons that would never fray or
tangle, that would never end. The carefree, clean-slate newness had
filled the room. She watched them whisper together, the girls with
their belted, snug jeans and too-tight shirts, their hair straight and
limp, still damp from rushed showers, the boys in tank tops and
baggy shorts. They were waiting for her, suddenly, quieting down
and watching her every move, studying her face. They were
expecting her to smile, to joke, to welcome them with a loud, clear
voice as Daniel did.

And then the slant of light, like a laser.

She knew that she needed to begin passing out papers, to announce *This is English Composition 102* in a clear, firm voice. To close the door and turn to them.

They were waiting for her to begin, waiting for her to take charge. But she said nothing, did nothing, only felt her heart race, tasted the curdling sourness of nausea. She almost retched, right there at the lectern. Right there, in front of them. Some of them glanced uneasily at one another, waiting for her to start.

She had turned and left then, running down the hall, her high heels echoing like shots. Whole seas of faces turned to stare as she passed classrooms. A janitor shouted that the floor was wet.

Two of the girls found her in the faculty rest room, leaning to look up at her from under the stall, asking over and over if she was all right. "Please fetch my husband, Dr. Daniel Byers, in 501," she whispered stiffly in a small voice, like a lost child reciting her name and address. For the three minutes it took them to bring Daniel back, she kept herself busy thinking about the word *fetch*. Why had she chosen that word? It was one of those words hardly used anymore, like *muss,* or *swum.* Fetch, fetch, fetch. She said it over and over until it sounded strange and lost meaning. With all the strength she had left, she stood beside the leaky industrial commode, trying to avoid thoughts about what had just happened, pondering instead etymology and a strange, archaic word. *From Old English, feccean, fetch also means ghost, a doppelgänger.* And then, finally, finally. The familiar scuffed loafers under the stall, his voice, his coaxing, his strength.

"Take me home, Daniel, I want to go home now."

Had she said it or just thought it? It didn't matter. He knew.

In the bedroom, Elizabeth saw that Daniel was asleep, his papers stacked on the bedside table. He was wearing sweatpants and a T-shirt. When had he started wearing all those clothes to bed? She slipped beside him, pulling the blanket up, covering them both. She lay a hand on his chest, let it rest there under his shirt, her fingers spread. He stirred then, turned on his side, crumpled up his pillow, moved to the edge of the bed.

In college, they had slept crammed in his single bed, every night together on the hard, narrow mattress a luxury. Now they had this large, too-soft bed, creaking and listing like a ship with their slightest movements, so wide they could sleep all night without touching.

She began to rub Daniel's back lightly now, her hand moving in slow circles. His back was hard and muscular from cycling, miles every week. But where? Where did he ride? Elizabeth pictured him riding down suburban streets, stymied by cul-de-sacs, sprayed by the fine mist of sprinklers in the Pleasant Valley golf course, past ornery drivers on Palmetto Highway. He was not one to meander, to venture without a destination. No, he would plan his routes. She closed her eyes. He was like a falcon floating away in a widening gyre, and she was the falconer, in the center, gloved and peering upward, waiting for his return.

The bike riding wasn't recent. He had bicycled for years, had started after they lost the baby. The week after she'd come home from the hospital, he'd brought the bicycle parts home in a box, assembled it himself in their tiny apartment. He'd even rebuilt the left pedal, altered it for his leg. They'd only had one car then, and he explained how he could ride the bicycle to the university, and leave the car for her so she wouldn't feel stranded.

It had been in her twenty-second week, the miscarriage, just after they'd timidly begun to furnish their tiny campus apartment with a rocking chair, a Winnie-the-Pooh lamp, a small white dresser. One Sunday morning she awoke to find herself drenched with blood. She felt it before she saw it: the dried, chocolate color that stained the sheet, the scarlet red, still-moist circle underneath her, the smudge of her own blood on his leg. When they stood, when Daniel called the hospital, she saw they were both covered in her blood. By the time she was wheeled into the hospital trauma room on a gurney, she knew it was over, could feel the warm, thick mass begin to pass from her. She'd heard the nurses say it was a boy. *The fetus is a male, approximately twenty-two weeks.* He'd had fingerprints, and a heartbeat, his lungs soft and jellyish, like a halved grape.

Sometimes when she took the pills, she dreamed of the blood: whorls like fingerprints, thick, rich dollops like berry cobbler, thin rivers of it, splattered and smeared and pooled. What a wicked comfort it brought. For the grief had brought her a secret, delicious excuse for staying inside, staying apart, staying away from the world. She knew that now. All those months before—years, she realized, years—she'd found herself dreading to leave their apartment, she'd fought the fear.

Grief greeted her like a friend. She took to it. She began to feel more and more detached from things, like old wallpaper buckled and loose, the seams not meeting. For weeks, she'd had visitors: her sister, her mother, Daniel's mother. Telling her she was healthy and young, telling her she needed to get out, to go shopping, to go on a vacation. Everyone's words wormed their way in her fuzzy cloud, eating little holes, biting her. She got good at not listening. The radius of her life was shrinking.

Elizabeth ran a hand across the firmness of her husband's shoulder.

"What is it? What's wrong?" He fumbled for his glasses on the bedside table. She realized she had begun to rub his back harder, too hard, like a shove.

"Nothing. There's nothing wrong."

She embraced him, her head on his chest. She could not meet his eyes. Not yet.

"Daniel?" His hand was in her hair now.

"I'm here." His voice was thick with sleep.

She moved her hand over his chest, down his arms. She shivered a little as she drew closer to him. When he ran his hands down her back, she sat up, slipped off her T-shirt, rolled down her panties. She saw he was bleary-eyed and a little confused. What hurt her, when she finally met his eyes, was his polite compliance. The distance in his eyes, the same expression she'd seen when he'd painted the deck in the backyard or read over a stack of freshmen papers.

His mouth moved over her, touching down haphazardly on the mounds and lengths of her. It had been so long since they'd made love—months? seasons?—and Elizabeth felt herself warm and loosen. *Oh, this,* her body answered. *I remember this.* Still, when he moved above her, inside her, she felt herself shrink away from him, as if she were watching from a distance. When he shuddered and let out a low moan, his face was buried in her neck, and she could not see the pleasure move across his face, could not take credit for it.

The noises of him trying to move quietly in the morning awoke her, the soft thud of the top, sticky sock drawer, the gentle clanging of sliding hangers. Elizabeth watched him rifle through the closet, looking for a shirt. She turned on her side, reached for her pillow.

He selected a beige button-down, frayed around the collar, a faint ink stain on the pocket. He'd already showered, standing there in underwear and a T-shirt, his hair damply tussled. She watched him hold three dark socks in the light of the window, searching for navy blue or black. He was tall, she had always loved that about him, how he stood over people, bent his head down to listen.

"I love you," she whispered, her voice catching a little. She should pick up the dry cleaning, do the laundry today.

His wedding band caught the morning sunlight, twinkled

cheerfully. He leaned over her, his shirt pocket inches from her face. The faded ink stain—three little circles—looked like Mickey Mouse.

"I love *you*."

"Your shirt," she said, pointing.

He looked at the stain, took off his shirt, grabbed another from the closet. She got out of bed and went to the kitchen, where she drank a glass of water at the sink, watching him move to the den to gather his things for the day: a folder, a dog-eared anthology from the shelf, a stack of graded papers, a spotted banana. He glanced at his watch. He was running late.

"I'll be coming home later tonight, after six. I'll call you at lunchtime."

Coming home later. She walked over to the window and watched him put everything in the backseat. But he forgot something. He jogged up the drive, burst through the door, grabbed his bike helmet from the top of the closet. "I'm going to try to ride at lunch."

"I've got an idea," Elizabeth whispered. It stopped him. He stood, his hand on the knob of the front door. He shifted a little, slowly leaning, a tall pine caught in a sudden blast of wind. She hadn't noticed how long his hair had gotten in back—creeping over his collar.

She found herself saying it: a reception here to start the conference, very informal, and small, very small. Her heart was pounding at the thought of it. Hors d'oeuvres, heavy hors d'oeuvres. Maybe even a light dinner, just to kick things off. He looked down before he met her eyes. Surprise and puzzlement did a funny little dance across his features, then nothing, then calm.

"Elizabeth, are you sure you want to—"

"I'm sure."

"It's only days away. Are you up to—?"

"Yes."

He nodded. "Okay."

She realized that she expected him to say no, that he appreciated her courage, her thoughtfulness, but no, an opening dinner was already taken care of. Instead, he said yes. With a faint, surprised, sad look he had said yes and left carrying his bike helmet under his arm like a knight with a headpiece.

Five

MOST DAYS I HAD to be at the Pancake Palace at 6 A.M.
sharp. On Monday I took a little longer getting there. I tiptoed
around the house—careful not to wake Ginnie—and made small
messes. She knew I was gone a lot of mornings—she would pass
that on to Mrs. Worthington. I left my bed unmade, dribbled an
invisible trail of honey for the ants to find around the back door,
scattered sofa cushions, rumpled rugs, dropped dollops of corn-
flakes and milk in the sink and on the floor to harden, heaped
damp, musty towels on the bathroom floor. Ginnie waited until the
last minute to get out of bed and get ready for class. She would
never have time to clean up.

I closed the front door softly behind me and stood on the porch.
It was chilly and overcast, barely dawn, but the sun was sliding up.
I felt its brightness more than I saw it—and its faithful, ordinary
rising made all those high school facts I'd memorized about fission
and fiery, atomic explosions seem mythic, silly. I walked out to the
driveway, reverently laid a hand on the hood of my Fiat Spider
convertible. It was a ritual, this laying on of hands, a response to the
car's 50 percent failure rate . . . or 50 percent success rate, if you
were an optimist. And I tried to be. I needed it to start now,
because it was too late to walk to the Pancake Palace. I moved my

hand from the hood to the leaky ragtop with the split back window, applying a gentle pressure.

The car had been a gift from Glen, my one close call with love. Glen was a student at the university, and he worked weekends at the group home. The first time I saw him, he was leading the men from Father Bob's for a walk, pointing out the maples, the oaks, the dogwoods, while the men clutched small branches in their fists. The next time I saw him, he was sitting on the porch with Ginnie.

They were on the porch swing, swaying a little, Ginnie holding a box in her lap. I could tell from the faded ribbon and dusty red plastic rose that it was a box of chocolates from Randy's Candies downtown, a store that had been holding a going-out-of-business sale for three years. The candy box looked so fusty and stodgy, so un-Ginnie I almost burst out laughing. But Glen's face, his earnest, eager, *desperate* face, stopped me.

"You're sweet," Ginnie told him.

Nights, Glen and I would play cards at the kitchen table, waiting until Ginnie arrived, or later, waiting until she didn't. He taught me five stud poker with a deck of cards, soft and dirty with use. One night he offered to align my back, and he stood behind me, put an arm across my chest and cupped my chin. My back pressed into his chest and my bare feet lifted off the kitchen floor. There was a small pop just as he'd promised. He asked if I felt better and I lied and told him much better, but I was in pain because I was on fire. I could still feel his arms around me, the bristle of his unshaven chin, the cool grip of his hand on my face.

And then came the night when he didn't show, and Father Bob told me he'd quit working there and was moving to California. Gran had been dead for close to three months, and all I could think about was how for years I had held out for her, had turned down, turned away from any male who looked friendly, but I decided I wouldn't any longer. I found Glen in his apartment, a room over the Shell station with greasy dust on the windows, boxes of books, crates of records, a microwave on the floor, the cot squeezed in as an afterthought.

"Don't go," I said.

I paced around on the gritty hardwood floor, my shoes making dramatic scratchy noises, while Glen packed his clothes. I knew he was not a man to foil a Harris woman. He was kind, unassuming, and Father Bob liked him. He had a dimple in his chin, curly blond hair that was already thinning. He was my friend.

When he finally met my eyes, sitting there on his cot, patting a spot next to him, I joined him. He hadn't washed the sheets for weeks. "You don't want to sleep here, Cutter. I'm talking the Shroud of Turin." I told him to stay in Sans Souci. I told him I loved him. I told him a lot of things that night, but nothing helped. Because Glen couldn't bring himself to finish what we both wanted. I thought it was me. I kept feeling guilty; I was a virgin and it was a burden of ignorance. His face lunging above me, trying, then closing up and weeping, made me love him more, and I told him that. "I can't," he said. "I look at you and I think of her. Ginnie. I see Ginnie."

The next morning, I found his Fiat convertible parked in the front yard, a note scrawled on the back of a Mr. Monkey's Transmission Service bill tucked under the windshield wiper.

Cutter,
You deserve better. Keep the car.
Love,
Glen

And I did. I kept the car.

The parking lot at the Pancake Palace was nearly full. If I was lucky, I'd make twenty-five bucks. That seemed an awful long way from all that money I needed to save Gran's house. I felt my spirits sag.

Inside, a small crowd was milling around the gumball machines and the newspaper rack, waiting to be seated. Mr. Demitriopolis was too busy ringing up bills at the cash register to see me slink in and throw my purse under a sink in the waitress station. While I tied my apron, I took a look at the damage. My six-top was seated with suits, two tables sat looking at menus, one table with coffee just sat looking around.

"You're late." Jolene, the head waitress, came up behind me carrying two pots of coffee, her stiffly sprayed hair already wilting. She swiped at her forehead with the back of her free hand, filled two pitchers of ice water, and started three new pots of coffee. She pushed a crumpled wad of tickets into my hand. "We're eighty-six hash browns, but if they raise hell, tell 'em they can get a double order of grits free. Three-four wants two sunrise specials, three-five wants more time. Other than that you're on your own. I suggest you kiss ass at your six-top, those suits look like bankers."

I picked up a menu. I noticed a hair had been laminated in it, a curly, suspicious-looking body hair, right over the number-three scrambled egg special. I felt my throat tighten up. I realized how things could build up, hollow you out with hopelessness. My plan of saving money, of saving my house, seemed far-fetched and impossible. My life was too small to be this complicated.

"Jolene?"

"What?"

"I don't think I can take this place today. My sister—you know, Ginnie? In college? I just found out my sister is pregnant and I'm about to lose my house. My life is going to hell, Jolene."

"I ain't takin' the two-top off your hands, so don't give me no sob story, Miss."

"I'm not. It's the truth."

Jolene took a discreet look around and squatted down. I knelt down, too, watched as she lit a cigarette.

"Do me a favor, will ya? Double-check and make sure Mr. D is still at the front?"

"He is," I said, standing, then squatting again. Jolene sucked the cigarette, inhaling deeply. Her earrings were clear plastic balls with a tiny, dried starfish in each, souvenirs from her latest trip to Myrtle Beach. The leg of one starfish had broken off and was rattling around when Jolene fiercely tapped out her cigarette on the floor and put it back in her apron pocket. She stood and loaded herself up with coffeepots and water pitchers.

"Cutter?"

"What?" I stood up with a groan. She gestured to the dining room with a little roll of her head, and I looked out at the disgruntled faces at my tables, people looking around, holding up coffee cups.

"You are in the *weeds,* hon. That's your problem right now. And you can do something about that."

"I'm looking at three stiffs, Jolene. What's the use?"

But she didn't hear me as she dodged chairs and tables down the crowded aisle. I watched her scurry into the double doors of the kitchen, like a fiddler crab zigzagging to a hole. The kitchen clatter sneaked out as she backed into the swinging doors, the noise rising and fading with their swishing. Jolene was a career waitress; she had the system down pat. Her secret was never to let her mind spill beyond the boundaries of her work. She didn't care if a couple were man and mistress, sister and brother, father and daughter—she never speculated, she never wondered, and she had warned me to stop looking so hard at the customers, "staring a damn hole in them. You're here to serve 'em, not figure them out."

I walked over to my section, sizing up table 3–5. Two silver-haired ladies half hidden behind menus. Mr. D, the owner, liked the waitresses to say, "Hear ye, hear ye, welcome to the portals of Pancake Palace!" But this morning I didn't have it in me. I stood at the table, tipped my head to the side, and found myself looking into the placid, hard, powdered pink face of Mrs. Lucianne Kincaid, Sans Souci's own Queen of the Dead.

"Oh, hello, Mrs. Kincaid. Why, I had no idea you were here at my table."

"Hello, dear." She flashed a coral-lipsticked smile that quivered over large yellowed teeth. "I requested your table."

"I guess you heard about poor Mr. McGill?" I asked, pouring her ice water. "They found him stretched out on his La-Z-Boy recliner. Doc says it's stroke."

"Linoleum, dear."

"Linoleum?"

"Yes. The oil man was coming by to fill the furnace and found him lying flat out on the kitchen linoleum. Coffee everywhere, powdered doughnuts scattered, and him with hardly a stitch on. Just up and died. Of course, stretched out on his recliner, that sounds a might more peaceful. That's why the rumor."

"Ahh."

"Even the preacher doesn't know yet, so keep it under your hat right now. I'll call you with the details this afternoon."

"Sounds good."

She winked at me, smirked before she sipped her coffee. We needed each other, Mrs. Kincaid and I. She was my inside source for details of local deaths, and that helped me in my obituary write-ups at the newspaper. She honored me with her behind-the-scenes knowledge because she'd been Gran's friend. Of course, I wouldn't want to be on her bad side. As Queen of the Dead, Mrs. Kincaid was in a powerful position. A lot of times, she was the first person called by families when someone died—even before preachers and funeral home directors, for it was Mrs. Kincaid who spread the good word, or leaked the bad, about the recently departed. In fact, she had gotten the position chairwoman of the Sans Souci Baptist Church Grieving Committee through a coup d'état of sorts, deposing Mrs. Violet Diddley, who'd failed to share the details of a double drowning in an aboveground pool.

Mrs. Kincaid looked at the woman across from her now, a shy, dowdy little gray woman. "We're celebrating," Mrs. Kincaid told me, tipping her head toward the woman. "Rose here has been appointed chair of the Sans Souci Baptist Membership Committee."

"Congratulations. Membership, huh? I suppose that's a lot of work." Rose opened her mouth to speak, but Mrs. Kincaid interrupted her.

"Oh, you have no idea." Mrs. Kincaid closed her eyes and shook her head. "You just have no idea. There's so much witnessing to be done, what with all these new people from all over the country moving in, who weren't raised right. Who have never even attempted to have a friendly conversation with Jesus, much less been saved by him. We have our work cut out for us." Both of them were shaking their heads. Finally Mrs. Kincaid looked up at me again. "We'll have more coffee, dear, and toast."

As I filled their coffee cups, Mrs. Kincaid pulled out a list of names from her purse. Her voice lowered. "Don't worry, we're going to *get* her," I heard, and left them to their Baptist hit list.

When I got back to the waitress station, Jolene was shaking her head.

"I don't see how you talk to those old biddies. It gives me the creeps the way they always talk about who kicked off."

"I need the info."

"Hey, you got closing duty in the kitchen?"

"Yeah."

"How about saving me the bacon and some biscuits. Wrap 'em up the way you did last time."

"Okay," I said. The food was for her two kids and her husband, Mack. I knew things had been rough for them since Mack had been laid off. Jolene was losing patience. She was starting to have daily Mack-the-Fool stories.

"You know what that fool done now?"

"What?"

"Well, I told him to go to the welfare office yesterday. I don't like taking handouts, but might as well see what we got coming to us, you know? So he drove all the way to Social Services in Palmetto and sat there for three hours in their waiting room and then the lady that finally talks to him tells him he should go to their satellite office in Sans Souci."

"Oh yeah. The local office down there on Main and Broad. Did he have to wait there, too?"

"No, because he didn't go. He ended up at the satellite dish store down there on Main. That's what he thought they meant, he said. He walks in the place and asks around, and of course, they didn't know nothing about welfare checks, but plenty about satellites. Now we got one of those god-awful satellite dishes in our backyard. Rent to own, he says. Eight hundred channels."

"Oh, Jolene. That's awful."

"Yeah. You think you got problems."

I looked over at the door. Mrs. Kincaid was leaving. She waved, and I waved back. I elbowed Jolene. "Wave, Jolene. Just try to look friendly." She scowled.

"You know," she said, "that whole group of old-timers grew up together. Christ, they graduated from Sans Souci High when it wasn't but three rooms, and now they act like they're planning some big senior prom or something, except it's funerals."

"Well, planning funerals and proms are a lot alike, when you think about it," I said. "Everyone gets invited eventually. And everyone gets a last dance."

She looked at me, puzzled.

"With the Grim Reaper," I said, making a slicing motion on my neck.

"You ain't right, girl," she said, laughing. "You are one weird, weird girl."

At the end of the breakfast shift, I tried to spot-wash my uniform in the bathroom. I was sticky with syrup and damp with perspiration, but I was thirty bucks richer. The businessmen had come through after all and left me a twenty. My afternoon shift at the newspaper started at noon and I had less than an hour to go home, eat lunch, and change clothes. I untied my wrinkled, slightly damp apron. My uniform was stained with orange juice and coffee splashes. They only gave me one uniform. If I didn't wash off all the gook from my shift, I ended up having to put it through two wash cycles. I tried to wipe the stains off the front, but the water beaded. Plastic, I thought, I'm wearing plastic. It was hard to believe anyone liked the look of a polyester mock dirndl but Jolene swore it turned men on. "Polyester," she said "is the poor man's silk."

For a while, I'd actually gone to the newspaper office straight from waitressing, still in my Pancake Palace outfit. After all, I was just an obituary clerk sitting behind a desk talking to undertakers. But I'd started dressing up ever since Curt Sams, my boss at the newspaper, had started to call me in his office for long talks. I'd grown to take an odd delight in rushing home to don heels and hose, slip on the smartly cut wool-blend suits with peplum and ruffles that I'd found in my mother's cedar closet. *Now you're a Career Girl!* said a manual from 1960 that I'd happened upon under a hatbox. It was clear from the black-and-white photographs of lean, beautiful models bending over typewriters or pouring coffee for men or taking dictation with coy glances from behind notepads that dressing like a career girl was just a way to get a man's attention. And that wasn't me. Still, the college intern at the paper had been impressed and told me I'd had the best vintage wardrobe she'd ever seen. Where in the world do you find all that stuff? she asked. My mother's closet, I said. She asked me if that was a shop in Charleston, wondered why she'd never heard of it.

Now I thought of the navy skirt and blazer I'd laid out the night before at the end of my bed, the string of freshwater pearls draped there on the bedpost. They were my very best clothes, reserved for funerals and job interviews. I took my ponytail out, combed my hair with my fingers. It smelled of smoke and syrup and stale coffee.

Just then, the rest room door burst open.

"Well, well. We was wondering where you ran off to."

"I already did my closing duty, Jolene. All those lemons are sliced for tea—"

"You got a phone call up front."

"Oh."

"Hurry up. She's been waiting a long time while I been hunting you down."

I walked over to the cashier's station and picked up the phone. I knew it was Ginnie, all worked up about waking up to the messes I'd left behind.

"Cutter, it's Elizabeth Byers."

"Oh." I tried to cover my surprise. "Hi. How are you? Is anything wrong?"

"I remembered what you said. About, you know . . . about helping me with a trip to the grocery store." Her voice trailed off. "Something like that . . ."

I thought about how the old A&P used to deliver. That's what she needed, really. Good old home delivery. Gran used to call Mr. Miller, the manager at A&P, and place our order every Friday. Mr. Miller would bring it himself, or send one of his boys on a bike. The cardboard box they brought to our kitchen was packed elegantly, with tender economy: a head of lettuce and a loaf of Merita bread on top of a netted sack of oranges, a bag of Dixie sugar, a pound of butter, the pork chops and bacon still cool in waxy wrap. This was before the A&P closed down, and the new, huge Lo-Bi opened. "I didn't even know there were twelve different kinds of cornmeal," Gran said when I took her to the grand opening and we walked down the aisles. "Strawberries aren't in season now. And watermelon? In December? Why, who are they trying to fool?"

"Do you know of a place nearby that would carry . . . specialty items?" Elizabeth asked.

I didn't. Between the deep freeze in our basement and my weekly trips to the farmers' market, I had no need for grocery stores. "I don't cook much," I said. "Especially not fancy stuff."

"The gourmet food is on the other side of town. I'm searching for shiitake mushrooms—do you know where I could find those?" I pictured Elizabeth in that tiny boxy house with all those books and papers, nothing but sour cream in the refrigerator, fluttering hands, her wilted seedlings. I wondered if she'd confronted her husband about Ginnie. Why didn't Daniel Byers help his own wife with shopping?

There was a long pause. Jolene glared at me from the waitress station, pointed to a dirty coffeepot.

"I have no right to bother you," Elizabeth said. "It sounds busy there."

"No . . . it's really not—"

"When I think how silly this sounds—"

She hung up.

Oh, Jeez. Somehow I'd insulted her. And I didn't have her number. I would have to look it up. I remembered how shaken she'd been on our porch, how she had collapsed on the sidewalk, and I knew my thoughts would snag and eddy around that vision of her all day. I decided to call her back from the newspaper.

I walked out to the parking lot, got in my car. I turned the key in the ignition. Nothing. In my hurry, I'd forgotten the laying-on-of-hands ritual. "C'mon, girl," I whispered. I looked up at the cloud-less sky. My Fiat almost always started on sunny, dry days, 70 to 78 degrees, low humidity, like it was solar powered or something.

I tried the ignition again. Nothing, I beat my hands on the steer-ing wheel, and in a wheedling tone told the car how beautiful it was, how proud I was of it, how I knew it could start if it just tried. Jolene came out of the restaurant and walked toward me. She had teased and resprayed her hair. She had put on red lipstick. She tapped on the glass. Her long nails made little clicking sounds. I rolled down the window.

"Your car not starting again?"

I shrugged, turned the key again. Nothing. I looked at my watch. I would try again in exactly thirty seconds.

"Look," she said. "I'm on my way to pick up the kids. I'll drop you off where you need to go."

"Nah. I can walk if I have to."

Jolene lit a cigarette and shook her head. She perched on the hood and looked up at the sky. "Is it your battery?"

"No," I said. "It's not my battery."

"What did you say that thing is?"

"A Fiat."

"A who?"

"It's an acronym, Jolene. It stands for Fix It Again Tomorrow." But Jolene didn't laugh.

"Well, damn," she said. "The car's uglier than a bowling shoe. Why don't you get rid of the thing?"

I sighed.

"I'm going to try one more time," I said. I did, and it started, the engine purred smoothly, innocently, and I sped off, leaving Jolene shaking her head.

When I got home, Ginnie was semireclined on the sofa, papers stacked beside her, a book propped upon her knee, a pile of boiled peanuts nestled in a newspaper on her lap.

"Since when do you eat peanuts?" I asked.

"I dunno. I just . . . felt like having something salty." Cravings. *Ginnie is pregnant.* The thought jolted me. It had been the same when Gran died. Sometimes I would come in the house half expecting to find her making corn bread in the kitchen, and I would remember suddenly—*Why, Gran is dead.*

Ginnie put a handful of the wet peanuts on a page from yesterdays' *San Souci Citizen* and handed it to me. "I don't have time," I said. But I collapsed in the gooseneck rocker across from her anyway. I opened a soggy, warm shell with my thumb, exposed the two pink, soft nuts inside, fetal in their curled plumpness.

"How was your weekend?" I asked.

"Frustratingly romantic." She looked up at the ceiling, distracted. It was Ginnie's closed look, a warning not to probe. "How about you? How was your weekend?" she said after a minute. "Did anyone come by to look at the house?"

I searched her face. "Why?"

"Why? Because we're trying to sell our house, Cutter."

"Oh."

"House. Realtor. Buyers. Money. Remember?"

"Well, there was one."

"Yeah?" She sat up straight. "What did he say?"

"She." Wife, I thought. Wife came by. But I couldn't say it. As hard as I tried, I couldn't. "This woman was—I think she was lost."

"Oh, please. Don't get my hopes up. It's getting discouraging. Another weekend without a single prospect."

"What are you doing home now?" I asked her, changing the subject. "Don't you have classes?" It was hard to tell when she'd be home. There was no rhythm to her comings and goings anymore, no pattern that I could tell.

"I had classes this morning. I'm cramming for a test." She looked over at me. More and more my sister had taken to wearing glasses, instead of the contacts she swore by.

"I almost had to walk home from the Pancake Palace again. The car was being stubborn. I think it's getting worse about not starting. Maybe I should sell it. For scrap."

"No! Sell it? Did I ever tell you that it was your car that brought Daniel and me together?"

"My *car*?"

Now, despite all her pensive lip biting, my sister seemed suddenly on the edge of a smile.

"It was like magic."

"Magic."

"Yes."

An early unexpected frost had set in and she was already late to class, she explained, so she had jumped in my car. She didn't have time to put the top up. It wasn't until she got on the freeway that she remembered the defrost in the car didn't work, and there she was with the top down, her ears and hands red and hurting, the windows hopelessly fogged. I could just see her swiping at the windshield with a shredded, lipstick-kissed Kleenex.

"When I pulled inside the university gate on the traffic circle, there was this crunch, which turned out to be Daniel's bicycle wheel. I looked into the rearview mirror, and I saw this man rolling on the grass median by the yield sign and I screamed."

She got out of the car, watched Daniel stand up. She saw how his hair was rumpled, as if some giant hand had reached down and given him a cheerful little tousle on the head. His tie was crooked, his sweater hung off one shoulder. There was a faint grass stain on one knee of his gray corduroys. The effect was of a disheveled little boy who had just fallen out of his tree house. And then, Daniel got himself back in order. He started at the top: smoothing his hair, tugging at his shirt, brushing off his pants, tying his shoe.

"And then he mumbled something about not properly meeting. He could tell I was upset, and we both knew it was my fault, running him off the curb like that. He leaned over to shake my hand. Calm me down. I told him to pop the bike in the back. He said no. He would manage, his office was in sight. And of course, I thought his limp was . . . my fault." My sister stood there watching his flawed stride, as he gently guided the bicycle upright on one wheel, as if it, too, were injured.

The next semester, already half in love with him, she registered for his Victorian lit class.

"Did you get these peanuts from Mr. Gordon?" I said, watching her hazy half smile disappear.

"I don't know. Just some little old man on the corner of Church and Marion with a big black pot of boiled peanuts."

"That was Mr. Gordon. I saw him last week out there. Remember how he used to come by and bring a box of leftover vegetables and a bag of peanuts to us when we were little? Gran would give him a jar of fig preserves."

"Nope."

"You don't remember?" How could she forget a man like Mr. Gordon? The small, round watermelons he peddled had always reminded me of eggs, as if he were an alien foisting off pods.

A crashing sound came from the back of the house. "What was that?"

Ginnie looked at me calmly. "Relax. The monsters are in the kitchen. If you want anything to eat, you better grab it now."

"What do you mean, monsters?"

Ginnie smiled. "You didn't see the TransAm out back?"

I could hear him now, my brother, his laughter coming from the kitchen. Barry's laugh hadn't changed much from the time we were little. It was the same burst of staccato punches.

Gran had sent Barry away to boarding school after he got his fellow Boy Scouts smashed on Jack Daniel's, then had them vomit in their beanies, which they left in a smelly, damp heap on the mayor's front porch. He was twelve, and it hadn't been the worst thing he had done in Sans Souci, but it had been the last. "He needs good, solid men to lead him," I remember Gran explaining to us, "he needs something that I can't give him." That was the first time I looked at Gran and thought, Gran is old. "But I'll raise my girls right," she said to us then, "that's what I'll do."

I found Barry and two of his friends clustered around the refrigerator, devouring cheese sandwiches. My brother and his fellow marines. They were sunburned, their hair cropped short, their T-shirts and jeans tight, their arms knotty and hard, ready to spring.

"Whoa. Cutter. Lookin' good, babe. Love that cute little waitress costume."

"It's not a costume. It's a uniform."

"Ohhh. A uniform." Snickering. "Stick around. We'll put on our dress blues. They're uniforms."

"No thanks."

"Especially Steve here." A tall guy guzzling a Schlitz looked at Barry and laughed. He had a chipped front tooth and thin lips. "Yeah, stick around while he takes off his uniform. He hasn't got any for a while, have you, Steve? This bastard is horny."

"Barry," I said. "Why don't you try to call sometime and let us know before you swoop in here like this. I mean, are you planning on replacing all that food?"

"Hey, look. We were on the way to the beach, and thought we'd stop by for a little visit. Which reminds me—"

I knew what he was going to say and I steeled myself.

"—when is this goddamn house going to sell, anyway? Where is the *For Sale* sign, for God's sake? I got my eye on a new car." He stood there, looking into the distance, his hands making sweeping motions, the vision overtaking him. If we were in a musical, this would be the part when he would break out in song, his two friends behind him singing backup. "A Corvette, cherry red, convertible—"

"Sounds like a pussy-eatin' dream," chipped-tooth said.

"Oh man, I'm going to be getting so much leg, I'm going to be begging you guys to take 'em off my hands."

"Yeah, right," the other one said. "You been talking that game a long time. You ain't never going to get you a car, and you ain't never going to have too much pussy." I saw Barry's face redden, and I knew enough to leave. I kicked the stopper out from the swinging door, let it close behind me.

"Cutter," my brother bellowed, following me. I felt the house shrink around me a little, draw nearer like a shy child watching, appalled at the anger. "What's the name of that woman selling this house? I lost her card."

I looked down at him from the top of the stairs. "I don't know."

"What the hell you mean, you don't know? She should be bringing people in here every day. And if she's not, I'm gonna make sure she will."

I went to my room, closed the door, but still I could hear his rumblings.

"Don't try to pull no sneaky shit, Cutter. We're going to sell this fucking house. She's just like Gran," he yelled to Ginnie, "just like her. She'd rot here, if she could."

I peeled off my polyester, slipped into my skirt and blouse, then tiptoed down the stairs, skipping over the third, tenth, and thirteenth steps, the ones that squeaked, so quiet that Barry wouldn't hear me leave.

I tiptoed past Ginnie, but she looked up and saw me and made a motion to come closer.

"He's just scared about the house not selling," she whispered. "That's why he erupted like that."

"Ginnie, pimples and volcanoes erupt. Nature's scourges erupt."

"To tell you the truth, I think he owes money, gambling. I feel sorry for him."

"Well, I don't. Gran's house shouldn't be on the block for his gambling debts."

Her mouth puckered, skeptical, as she looked over at me. "I know what you're going to say. Don't even start."

"Just listen. I can buy out your shares in this house, both of you, but I need some more time."

"That's not going to work, Cutter. Even if I agreed, you don't have that kind of money, and we don't have time—years—for you to scrape it up from the Pancake Palace."

"Ginnie, I won't sell."

"Listen to me. The house will be sold. Even without your permission. But I don't want to go to court and get an order to make you. That wastes everybody's time and money."

"Why are you in such an all-fire hurry?" I studied her profile, the button nose and smooth forehead. The delicate way her upper lip was thin, her bottom lip full, just like our grandmother's had been, just like the portrait of Gran as a debutante sitting right there on the courting sofa, right where Ginnie sprawled now. A pang of grief moved through me. I missed Gran so much.

"Look," I said. "I've been meaning to ask you. Can you meet me in the dead garden after work? We need to do the plantings for Gran."

"Today? I've got all this stuff to do—"

"Ginnie, it's spring already. There's nothing on her grave but a big hump of red dirt." I squeezed my eyes shut for a minute, sniffled wetly. "Besides, I've already got the plants together."

"Jesus, pull yourself together. I told you I'd help, didn't I?"

"Weeks and weeks ago."

"Oh, all right." She sighed.

"Five sharp," I said. "We'll have enough daylight left to make a good start."

She seemed to snap out of a daze, then looked up at me sharply.

"By the way, try not to leave this place such a wreck from now on, all right?"

She said something else, but I couldn't hear her. The barking laughter from the kitchen drowned out her whispers.

"I'm going now," I mouthed silently.

But I didn't fool Barry. He came around back just as I started the car. He was bare-chested, and held a wadded-up T-shirt in one hand.

"Cutter, wait." He was running now, trying to slip the T-shirt over his head at the same time. I pretended not to hear him. I turned my head, began to back out of the driveway.

"Hold up." He ran alongside the passenger side and opened the door. I put on the brakes.

"We're going on a little ride, me and you."

"No thanks. I have to go to work."

"Yeah, yeah. Spare me. This will only take a few minutes. The guys are about to go to the store for another beer run, so now's my chance to sneak out. I'm buying a present. I'm trying to keep it a secret."

I sighed. "Fine." Although it wasn't.

"A present?" I asked as he got in.

"Yeah. For my buddy back there. He's a week short. And once they leave the Corps, you never see them again. Swear to God." He shook his head. I sensed the house issue crouching between us, large and silent, a voracious, invisible beast.

"Where to?" I asked.

"Straight up Gerard here, then Main. I'll tell you where to turn."

He tapped two fingers on the dashboard. "How's she running?"

"A little temperamental, but nothing I can't handle."

We passed Sans Souci High School, up on a hill, looking tired and defeated. It was a red brick building with wide white cement steps that were cracked and sprouting grass. In its glory, sustained by the money of the mill—Harris money—it was once home to the best high school football team and marching band in the state, one of the finest-equipped science labs. That was before my day, even before my mother's. Now air conditioner units sagged out of the windows, gray and unsightly, like warts. The tennis court was a makeshift parking lot. The same velvet purple curtains hung in the auditorium—musty and moth-eaten, faded to lavender—despite years of bake sales and car washes to raise the funds to replace them. Four years at Sans Souci High was a rite of passage, an initiation, for just about everyone in our town. Except for Barry. I stole a glance over at my brother, who hung an elbow outside the window. A raised silvery scar snaked down his neck and disappeared into his shirt. Tumbling from the top of an oak tree had done that—broken his collarbone, snapped his arm like the branches he'd fallen through. He was ten then, young enough to cry and cling to Gran as she crouched over him, holding his head to her talc-scented chest, her apron still damp from morning dishes, reciting the Lord's Prayer over and over until the ambulance came. He'd always been a blustery kid, a boy who broke things. His footsteps thundered up and down the stairs, down the hall. The porch door banged like shots behind him, the chairs he sat in screeched like fingernails on blackboards, the silverware and dishes he touched clattered and cracked. As he got older, Gran took to her bed with headaches. The boarding school she sent him to had been a military school for boys. It was another sore subject, another thing my brother and I couldn't talk about.

We passed Sans Souci Baptist and a Little Cricket convenience store.

"Hang a left here, okay?"

I turned onto a narrow, rutted road that curved and thinned until the asphalt gave way to gravel.

"I thought you said you were going to get a gift. Where are we going?"

"Affirmative. And you can stop here."

There was a trailer in the clearing. A single-wide, with a broken slide in the front yard, an inflatable pool gone slack and mossy, a truck-tire flower bed.

"My man's waiting in there. It's set up, he'll hand it to you. You give him this." He handed me a crisp bill. Benjamin Franklin looked out sternly, too regal for this transaction.

"You've got to be kidding. I might get caught. I could end up in jail."

"You and half the town. Toy McCoy comes here all the time. You know him, right? The sheriff's son."

"Oh, that Toy McCoy," I said flatly.

"And preachers' boys, too, I can't even begin to name them." He rubbed his face with one hand. "It's just I got more at stake, I'm in the service. They'd let you go, a pretty little thing."

"Don't they drug-test you?"

"Like I told you, it's a gift. It's not for me."

The curtains parted in one of the small windows. "Who lives there?" I asked.

"Parker James. You know him?"

"I know *of* him." He was Jolene's little brother. He came into the Pancake Palace sometimes, and he always requested her table. Mostly I knew him from tenth grade homeroom, where he sat in the back with his head on his desk, the kind of kid who always forgot his picture money and lost his textbooks, who grunted during roll call and slept through announcements.

I got out of the car.

"Hey, if he gives you a hard time, just yell."

"Yeah, thanks a lot."

By the time I crossed the scruffy, sun-baked lawn and reached the front steps, the door opened.

"Come on in."

It was him, all right—Parker. The same narrow, brown eyes as Jolene, the same sinewy, freckled arms. I squinted until my eyes adjusted to the dimness of the trailer. He pointed a finger at me. "Don't I know you?"

"I work with Jolene. At the Pancake Palace."

"Yeah? I always welcome new clients."

"I'm not," I said loudly. Then quieter. "It's for my brother."

"I'm just pulling your leg. I seen Barry out there in the car."

"Oh."

It was small and dank, the room, just as I expected.

"Haven't seen Barry in a coon's age."

"He's in the marines," I said. "He hardly comes home."

"So I hear."

I handed him the money.

"Shit, I hope I got change." He said something in Spanish and a woman came out of the kitchen with a bundled-up Kmart bag. She was small, swallowed up in a REM T-shirt that must have been Parker's. A dark, thick braid hung between her shoulder blades. She did not meet my eyes or say a word. She handed the bag to

Parker and then knelt down and picked up a wadded-up gum wrapper by the sofa. Parker took out a roll of cash and counted bills out in my hand. He clicked out coins from a change belt like an ice cream man.

"You give back . . . coins?"

"It's good business practice. I don't give a penny less than people owe. I'm what you call one of them entrepreneurs."

"Really?"

"Yeah. I'm getting out of this supply business. I'm looking to market an idea I thought up. It's really going to take off."

He waited a beat. "What idea is that?" I asked.

"The breakfast hot dog."

"The breakfast . . . hot dog?"

"The breakfast hot dog. Think about it. People rush around in the mornings, kids are off to school, people driving around all crazy trying to eat biscuits and gravy. With a breakfast hot dog, you got one hand freed up. And you got your various varieties—scrambled egg hot dog, pancake and syrup hot dog, grits hot dog, hashbrowns hot dog—all in the convenience of a classic American favorite—the hot dog." He grinned. "I've been working on my spiel."

"I can tell."

"The whole idea came to me one day a couple of weeks ago." He nodded at the woman. "See, me and her are having a kid."

The woman blushed a little.

"Congratulations."

"And I ain't smoked or drank a drop since she told me. That's what has me so fired up. That poison kept me in a fog since sixth grade. Now, I don't touch the stuff. I just think about the breakfast hot dog. I tell you, it's like the whole world just opened up." He threw back his head and spread his arms wide. "Hooowee!"

The woman's hooded, black opal eyes glittered. She was holding a dishcloth. She began to wipe off the two plastic placemats at the table. Despite its shabbiness, the room was neat, the top of every surface shiny.

"Thing is, it's going to take cash—capital—to start this thing." Parker spoke louder now, and faster. I glanced out the window. I wondered if Barry would come to the door. "I already wrote me up a business plan. I'll need investors. See, all I need is ten men— or women, 'scuse me—that's good for ten grand each."

"Well, you're barking up the wrong tree. I don't have anything to invest."

"I already cased out a place. One of them old empty Harris manufacturing buildings down by the rail line. Realtor says it will go for a song. But I got to get some machines in there that will stuff the weenies."

"Stuff the weenies?" In a Harris building? I felt sick.

"Yeah, I didn't explain that? See, you gotta have these special machines that will take the scrambled eggs or grits or whatnot and cram them in the weenie skins."

"Yes, but do you think anyone would—I mean, it doesn't sound too appetizing." My hand covered my mouth.

"Ever eaten Tator Tots? Spam? Devil Dogs? Cheez Wiz? That's some weird-ass food when you think about it, but people love it. See, that's part of my plan. Get people to like breakfast hot dogs by having free samples at the malls. People will try anything on a toothpick."

The horn honked outside. Delivered!

"That's Barry. He's so rude. Good luck with your, uh, project. I'll see you around sometime."

"Oh." He looked crestfallen. "Well, maybe you could ask him about being an investor?"

"Okay, but my brother's money situation isn't much better than mine."

"Tell him it's a ground-floor opportunity," he yelled, as I sprinted across the yard.

"I honked because I wanted to let him know I was watching," Barry said as I slid in the driver's seat.

"Oh, please," I snorted. "He's harmless."

"I knew that."

"Although he did talk a lot about stuffing weenies."

"You're shittin' me."

"Yeah."

I handed him the dime bag and his change.

He folded the bills back into my hand. "Keep it. For your trouble."

"But that's a lot of cash."

He shrugged. I could not figure out his moods, his back-and-forths, his swings from rage to concern. "If you had to hear about stuffing weenies, you deserve it."

"Jeez. Thanks."

At Gran's funeral Barry had worn his dress blues. He'd been the only young pallbearer—all the rest were over sixty—and it was as if he carried her coffin alone, his arms trembling with the effort, his mouth worked into a frown, a roll of flesh squeezing over his collar, his white gloves smudged.

He'd brought a woman to the funeral, someone he'd met at a club off base. She was skinny with a gob of curly, beige hair and she clung to him, her small tanned hand hooked in his arm for hours.

"You think she'll let Barry take a piss alone?" Ginnie had asked me bitterly from the corner of our living room. "I guess she'll need to hold his dick."

"Ginnie," I hissed. Our house was filled with Gran's friends. They balanced plates and cups of coffee on their knees, shook their heads at us, murmured *poor dears, poor dears.* Later, I went down to the basement for a jar of blueberry preserves, and I saw Barry and his girlfriend on a cot in the corner. She straddled him as he lay beneath her, her head thrown back, her narrow hips moving slowly. There was a rose tattoo at the base of her humped-up spine. He was her big man, she moaned, her big man, oh yes, oh yes. I tiptoed back up the stairs before they could see me. But I'd seen Barry's face, turned to the side, his expression far off and flushed and miserable, as if he'd been weeping.

When we pulled back in our driveway, Barry got out and thumped the hood with a fist. I jumped.

"Hey, thanks."

"Hey, you're welcome."

"He'll appreciate this gift, let me tell you." He began walking back, raised an arm, and gave me a sad, stiff wave without turning around.

I started working the dead beat the same week I began waitressing. The dead beat—that's what I called writing up obituaries for the *Sans Souci Citizen*—a struggling, anemic daily that should have been a fat weekly. The politics of death wasn't easy. Disgruntled relatives and undertakers tried to get the *Citizen* to print family pictures or entire family trees, to list surviving pets, or bully me into running elaborate life histories of the deceased that practically needed footnotes. If it weren't for Curt Sams and our talks, well . . . with a little surprise, I admitted to myself then that if it weren't for Curt, I'd quit. We were breathing life into the Sans Souci paper, he told me, rescuing it. I'm not sure I believed him yet, but I liked listening to him. I liked hearing about his plans to save the paper and our town.

Gradually, as the town of Sans Souci had succumbed to the city of Palmetto, everyone in Sans Souci started getting *The Palmetto News*. So, the *Sans Souci Citizen* started relying more and more on social snippets, on elaborate wedding descriptions (*the bride wore a delicate candlelight cathedral-length gown, with princess sleeves, beaded with seed pearls . . .*) and on long, detailed obituaries and death notices. Focusing on community news was a strategy devised by Curt, who'd come in as the new managing editor the summer before. He had a theory about how to increase circulation: "Geezers. We are tapping into the community factor here. The double-knits in Sans Souci have money."

I guess that's why he hired me. That and my friendship with Mrs. Kincaid, Queen of the Dead. When I mentioned her in the job interview, his eyes lit up. Deaths were to be glorified, detailed, even more than the weddings—those were my orders when he hired me. And I had the sources for all the insider stuff. "The obits are the first thing they look at, Cutter," he said. "What neighbor died? What Sunday school pal? Only we're going to offer them a lot more than *The Palmetto News*. We're going to offer them details." I considered it a kind of dubious honor—being the first real obituary clerk the *Citizen* ever had—and although the money wasn't great, the hours were good and I didn't have to wear polyester.

Four obits were already on my desk, ready to be written. Four. The first person had been a member of the Sans Souci Mission for Wayward Women—that meant a huge write-up. And there was one of those "in memory" anniversary pieces sent in by a family. We'd been running more of them lately. Curt said they paid well. This one had a photograph of a florid-faced, grumpy-looking man and a poem printed out on pink stationery with a rose in the corner:

> *It's been a year you big lug*
> *We really miss giving you a hug*
> *But you're not in the ground*
> *You are up there chasing pretty angels around*
> *Driving a brand new Ford*
> *Telling jokes to the Lord*
> *Fishing like crazy*
> *Just being lazy*
> *Tell Jesus we said hi*
> —*Love from Jimmy, Momma, Buzz, Marney and Joe, Jr.*

I put my purse away, sat down at my desk. Might as well get comfortable. This was going to be a long afternoon. I leafed through the phone book, under the B section. There was only one listing for Byers. I wrote the number down.

I looked up to see Curt walk into the newsroom with a plate of takeout barbecue. He motioned me to follow him with a slight nod of his head. I stood and tugged at my skirt. Why hadn't I ironed it last night? I wandered over to his office. He had a large window that looked out onto the newsroom, tinted so he could see out but you couldn't see in. He said it encouraged productivity from the staff.

I knocked softly on his door. He was cradling the phone on his shoulder and squeezing barbecue sauce on his sandwich. He licked a finger and motioned for me to have a seat. Yes, he would have a photographer there. No problem. The story could run on Sunday.

"That's all I need," he told me when he hung up. "More barbecue."

"The fire station?"

"Yep. Their annual barbecue is this Saturday. I was thinking it was next weekend. I'm gonna send Fred."

"But you shouldn't miss it. The fire station barbecue is the best. Better than that stuff you call barbecue that you're eating right now. The firemen's five-alarm plate is vinegar based, the best."

His starched white shirt was like a blank canvas just waiting for a dramatic dollop of ketchup or red smudge of sauce. Curt was the only man I'd ever known who wore cuff links in the daytime. His pants were creased, his collars as crisp as paper. His mouth he kept in a tense line, like a kid up to bat, and his small, deep-set eyes bored into you. His yellow hair was too short, the curls there tamed, clipped back, all of it to show how serious he was about things.

"How's obits?" he asked. "People dying to get in there?"

"I guess you could say that."

"That was some fine work you did yesterday with the former Sunday school teacher, what's her name—"

"Alice Swan."

"Yes. That old photo of her with the governor all those years ago. How in the world did you know we even had that clipping, from what? Fifty years ago?"

"I have my sources."

"And what is the Queen of the Dead up to lately?"

"I spoke to her this morning. She's going to call me this afternoon with some info."

"That's a talent you have, communicating with her."

"It's not hard. You just gotta know the code."

"The code?"

"Yeah. Like when she says 'bless her heart' right after a name, then you just substitute 'that damn fool.' 'Bless her heart' means she's got some dirt on somebody. Like last week when she called and said Martha Gilchrist had succumbed to pneumonia, bless her heart. And then she told me Mrs. Gilchrist had this secret marriage years ago and the guy went to prison for robbery, and here she was married to a deacon and no one—well, *almost* no one—in Sans Souci was the wiser. She said it was our duty to print that Martha Gilchrist was survived by her first husband of Central Correctional Institute, Cell Number Eleven, Columbia, South Carolina."

"Oh God." He laughed, then crumpled up the Styrofoam lunch plate and crammed it in his overflowing trash can.

Curt's mother owned the paper, so naturally he was secretly called Mama's Boy—M.B. for short. He grew up in Green Mountain Estates, a country club neighborhood that, while technically in our town limits, held itself apart from Sans Souci, like an aloof relative at a family gathering. He'd gone to private school north of Palmetto where they wore jackets and ties, while the rest of us at the *Citizen* had graduated from Sans Souci High School.

His mother breezed in and out of the newsroom in her tennis dress or navy suits, which embarrassed him and amused the staff.

But she bankrolled the place, and everybody knew it. I'd heard all about the day last year she'd bought this place, how she'd had more windows put in, had more fluorescent lights installed, had all the desk cubicles hauled away, and left everyone confused and blinking.

And then Curt came aboard. He was young to be a managing editor, even for a daily the size of the *Citizen,* and he was full of contradictions. Sometimes I thought he just didn't want to be figured out. He'd graduated with honors from Emory but hated school. He'd told me that my not going to college proved I was smart. He came from money, but eschewed the world out there and seemed happy to settle down in Sans Souci.

He had a wide forehead, and a sharp but regal profile, like faces of men on the backs of coins. The truth was, Curt reminded me a little of my father. I thought of the black-and-white photographs on the mantel in my living room. My father newly enlisted, shorn and eager, then home between tours in Nam, his arm around my mother or holding babies, his expression burdened, secretly overwhelmed, and a little worried.

I looked now at the collection of framed yellowed issues of the *Citizen* displayed on Curt's office wall, headline letters as big as my hand screaming about world wars, new presidents, plant shutdowns. It was all there—Sans Souci's glory days in the bright heat of commerce, when the mill machines roared and hummed so loudly you could hear them from Gran's house, when everyone's days were pierced and punctuated by the mill whistle. And the decline, it was there, too; the Depression and slow-downs that descended like a sickness.

I cleared my throat. "I wanted to talk to you about . . . well, I have this friend. He's a neighbor actually. And I think he could do a better job of cleaning up around this office than that night crew you have coming in." He followed my gaze to his trash can. "He lives across the street from me at Father Bob's. His name is Alfred. But he's really sweet and he's dependable and once he sets his mind to something, like cleaning, there's no stopping him."

He nodded. "Well, bring him in the next day or two and we'll give him a try."

"Just like that? No application or—"

"Cutter, I trust your judgment. Believe me, yours is the only judgment I trust around here anymore." He looked out at the newsroom from the one-way window on his wall, then smiled at me sheepishly.

I knew that was Curt's way of telling me he was having problems with the staff, that they still didn't like him. His mother made things worse. Her shrill orders to wipe out the filthy microwave in the snack room echoed for days.

"Why don't you call a meeting?" I said all of a sudden. "Call a staff meeting and just, you know, talk to them out there. But talk to them the way you talk to me."

"What will I tell them?"

"Tell them some good news, not just rules. And tell them the truth. Tell them how you love Sans Souci, and the newspaper, and that we all need to pull together to make it work. To save the paper. Maybe they still don't understand that. And joke with them, like you do with me. Relax and let them see you relaxed. Let them like you."

He sighed. "I'll think about it."

I stood up, my hands sweaty and stiff, and realized I'd been clutching my skirt, had left two fistfuls of wrinkles. "Well, back to the dead beat for me."

"Don't tell me—you're buried with work."

"Ha ha."

"We're just a couple of working stiffs."

"Yes! That's what I mean," I said. "About joking. Let them see your funny side, too."

He nodded and looked as if he were going to say something. I saw him glimpse at my legs, his gaze traveling from the modest side slit of my skirt down to my mother's worn leather t-straps, where my cramped toes throbbed a little. His glance quickly took in the length of me, seemed to flicker there on my legs, like a sun ray bouncing off chrome. My stomach fluttered. Then the phone rang, startling both of us. When he answered it, I left. I walked across the newsroom to my desk, felt his stare from behind his office window, and I didn't mind at all.

It wasn't like I was a management guru or anything. I was just an obit clerk, a girl from Sans Souci. But he'd listened. And didn't he say he trusted me? That I was the only one he trusted anymore? And the way he looked at me . . . Pride whirred in me, a band seemed to tighten across my chest. I knew I had to stuff my feelings back down deep inside or they might pop out all at once, sticky and soft, like canned biscuits.

"Let's get this over with," Ginnie said when I got home. She was sitting on the porch in jeans and an old flannel shirt. I changed into overalls and went to the back porch, where I'd hoarded seed packets all winter. I crammed them in my pockets. Together, we dragged bags of soil and compost from the shed out back and loaded them into a wheelbarrow and rolled it down to the cemetery. Ginnie closed the iron gate with a lonely clang behind me. The evening shadows were already lengthening and had begun to swallow light that, even on the brightest summer days, filtered in softly between the oaks. We walked to a row of three stones: our grandmother and grandfather and, between them, our mother. There were crocuses and daffodils and snowdrops blooming on my mother's grave. Gran had always carefully tended it. After Sunday dinners, when we were little, Gran would put on her wide-brimmed gardening hat and gloves and take along her basket of garden tools and bring us down here. She would plant lavender petunias and purple bearded irises. She would deadhead the spent daylilies and pull up weeds on my mother's grave and on my great-grandmother Beulah's grave back in the corner. She barely touched my grandfather's grave, scratched in some monkey grass and ivy and told us even that was too good for him.

I began spreading soil over the red clay hump on Gran's grave. "First we have to amend the soil," I said. "Then we plant." I took out the little cluster of sweet alyssum I'd stuck in the wheelbarrow and a handful of larkspur seeds. I turned to find Ginnie plunked down on the cement bench behind me.

"What's wrong?"

"I just don't feel like digging in the dirt right now."

"Well, I'll just add some compost here and we'll be done."

"Jesus, what is that smell?" She stood, held her nose, and looked accusingly at me.

"It's mushroom compost," I said, as I poured the dark thick globs out of the plastic bag.

"It *stinks.*" She jumped up and stumbled over to the far side of the cemetery, past the snaggled gravestones half swallowed by roots and vines. She dropped to her knees and retched under a newly green weeping willow that seemed to arch protectively over her. I walked over and kneeled beside her.

"I'm pregnant."

I nodded.

"You're not surprised?"

"I found your pregnancy test last weekend. You left it in the trash can in the attic bathroom."

"And you didn't ask me about it?"

"You didn't tell me about it."

She retched again, coughing and sputtering, while I watched helplessly. I fished a rubber band out of my pocket, pulled back her hair from her face and knotted it in a ponytail.

"I'm okay now."

"You're sure?"

She nodded, sat back on her heels. "Last weekend, when I was together with Daniel at that conference? He kept calling her. Wife. Like every hour. He doesn't leave her long, ever. He's afraid of what she might do. The way she controls him! He'll never be free of a woman like that."

And it was then, in the sour stench of Ginnie's sickness, that I remembered I hadn't called Elizabeth back that afternoon.

"He berates himself, Cutter. It breaks my heart. You see, anybody's failure seems to insult Daniel, to hurt him personally. That's how I got in to see him in his office the first time . . . I told him I was failing postmodernism." Ginnie took the corner of her flannel shirt and wiped her mouth, dabbed at her soft, pale face. "Last semester, Daniel had the chance to teach in London, but he turned it down because she wouldn't go. He even got her a job teaching once at Palmetto, and she blew it the first day. She blows everything. But him."

"That's mean," I said. "Someone like that probably needs help. It sounds like she has no control at all."

Ginnie closed her eyes for a minute, wiped her mouth with the back of her hand. "The only thing that gets me through this is how I bring him back to me, to happiness. Every time he pulls away, I go in after him, I bring him back. Wife would drown him in her weakness if she could. But I'll always dive in after him and bring him back. I love him."

"Is that why you want to have this baby? To bring him back to you?"

"I can't believe you said that. I didn't mean to get pregnant, Cutter."

"Well, I just mean . . . from the way you describe—"

"It was an accident, okay? Do I have to go over the mechanics with you?"

"No." My face burned with anger.

"Not only did you not tell me you'd snooped around and found my pregnancy test—"

"I didn't snoop! It was sticking out of the trash can."

"—but you made me come down here and dig fucking holes in the dirt with you when you knew how shitty I've been feeling?"

We stood then and she waved me away.

"Just forget it," I said. "Let's just go home." I began packing up the wheelbarrow. Ginnie walked over and got the hand trowel and began to hack away at the vines entwining the iron gate.

"What are you doing?" I said, alarmed. "Stop it."

"All these creepy stalks and vines are smothering things," she said. "It's strangling, this stuff is taking over everything. Look around you, for Chrissake."

She slashed the tendrils and stems snaking their way between rusty tines of the gate and low-hanging tree limbs, covering the tombstones themselves. I grabbed her wrist. "Listen to me," I said. "You're going to kill them. Stop. These vines will be blooming by summer don't you remember? It's just the bones of the garden you're looking at right now." I thought of the trumpet vine and honeysuckle that would green and flower; the jasmine that would sweeten the air, its perfume drifting in the windows of our home.

Ginnie released the trowel which fell to her feet. She leaned limply against the gate. I exhaled slowly, as if she'd just dropped a gun. There were faint half-moons of sweat under her arms and her damp bangs hung over her eyes. "The hell with this."

"Go rest awhile," I said. "I'll fix us dinner when I get back up to the house."

As she turned to leave and made her way up the path to our house, Ginnie leaned into the slope of the hill, clutched her waist, and I saw that my sister looked sick and too slight to carry a child, too frail even to carry herself.

Six

"IF I WERE YOU, I'd sprinkle me some Pine-Sol in that chipmunk den there."

Elizabeth looked up at her neighbor, then followed her hard stare to a small hole in the ground by the azaleas. Elizabeth knew Patsy was testing her, waiting to see when she would be a normal neighbor, do normal things. Like killing chipmunks.

"Or just pour some bleach down the hole," Patsy added. Elizabeth watched Patsy lean with an exaggerated groan on the chain-link fence that divided their yards. Patsy was pregnant.

Elizabeth looked back down at the little patch of soft earth where months earlier she had planted tulip bulbs. She kneeled down, took off her gardening gloves, and inspected the soil for any sign of green fingers reaching skyward. It would have been nice to have the tulips blooming in time for the party. She'd thought for sure she'd find enough of them to cut and bring inside. But there was no sign of them. What had she done wrong? In the fall, she had mixed the soil with fertilizer and bonemeal, and gently placed one hundred dollars' worth of bulbs, white nubs pointing skyward, in a hole exactly six inches deep. It was supposed to have been a beginning for them, a little warm dirt womb where they could start to grow. But she couldn't get the idea of burial out of her mind. They had seemed so tender, so defenseless as she covered them with the thick black soil.

"They will eat them bulbs, you know. Every one. Chipmunks, I mean. They are the biggest pests."

Out of the corner of her eye, she saw Patsy look across her back-yard, taking in the four bird feeders, all of them rocking and sway-ing with quarreling birds. Patsy shook her head.

"Lord. They do make a mess, don't they? I want you to look at all that bird doody on your deck. I bet your car's covered, too."

"We don't mind," Elizabeth said. She meant the answer to come out archly. Instead it was quiet. She watched the early-morning sun filter out from the trees still glistening from frost, and imagined the way her perennial beds would be thick and wild with beauty in just a few months. And her zinnias and sunflowers and trumpet vine would cover the fence and keep Patsy out.

The messy look. That is just how Patsy described it last summer. After Elizabeth dug up the boxwoods and hollies with their geo-metric precision, their obedient square ugliness, she planted daisies, black-eyed Susans, coneflowers, and phlox. She planted zinnias and cosmos that she had grown from seed. The border had exploded in color and texture. The plants had flowered wild and strong and generous. Every morning, Elizabeth had fingered the velvety petals.

But Patsy had called her and complained. By then Elizabeth had learned not to be caught outside at five o'clock when all the neigh-bors, wilted and ornery, returned from work. As usual, Patsy's voice had that curious mixture of cheerfulness and irritation. Elizabeth recognized her immediately. "I'll get to the point," Patsy had said. "What's with the messy look, hon?"

Why couldn't she have a neighbor like Cutter? Cutter would never accuse Elizabeth of the messy look. She would never try to kill chipmunks or complain about bird doody. She was knitting a hair doily, for goodness's sake.

Suddenly, the clouds hid the sun and Elizabeth, frowning, looked up to search the sky. A minute ago, the morning held the promise of a clear spring day, with just the mixture of sharp coolness and warm sunshine that coaxed the winter-weary from their homes. But now everything was gray, shadowy. It was as if the sun were betraying her, as if it were reminding her how the day could turn dark so suddenly.

> *The blonde assassin passes on—*
> *The sun proceeds unmoved.*

Not one flower blooming to bring inside. Not a camellia or a lily of the valley or a daffodil or a tulip. She would have to go in search of flowers. She would have to buy them, from . . . where?

Now Patsy's voice seemed to be speeding up, getting higher, shrill and hard. A cartoon voice. She was counting the days until the baby was born so she could put it in day care and go back to work; she hated staying home all day and wondered how Elizabeth could stand it.

"By the way, Daniel mentioned you were real busy finishing up your work—your, uh—"

"Dissertation."

"Yeah. So I'd be glad to pick up some things from the store for you. Seems like I always have to run to Winn-Dixie every day anyway. Just give me a call anytime and tell me what you need."

Is that what Patsy was doing? Keeping an eye on her? At Daniel's behest?

Elizabeth felt her heart speed up. It was beating against her chest now, a red, soft, fluttering bird, trapped in her rib cage. Her panic was in full throttle. She inhaled cold air, sucked it in until it burned. The fence, her Honda Civic sitting not twenty feet away, Patsy's wide, white face, all twisted together, all melted and rippled like a surrealistic painting.

"That's very nice of you, Patsy, but I don't think—"

Elizabeth crouched on the ground again, stared at Patsy's

immaculate white Keds through the fence. There was razor stubble around her ankles. Probably she was too big to reach down and shave her legs. She had a sudden picture of a naked Patsy, reaching over her balloon-white belly, taking halfhearted swipes at her ankles with her Daisy razor.

"Hey, I got a joke for you, okay?"

Elizabeth ignored her, grasped two handfuls of grass. Patsy was staring at her.

"Know what's better than roses on a piano?"

Elizabeth shook her head. She prayed the laws of gravity would stop suddenly, just for one instant. The end of the world was just the break she needed to recollect her senses.

"Tulips on an organ. Get it? *Two lips.*" Patsy giggled. "Hey, I think I hear your phone ringing."

Elizabeth stood, then dashed across her yard, but she was too late. By the time she got to the porch, she heard the answering machine cut on: Daniel's cheerful answer, then Daniel's cheerful message. He was checking to see if she needed anything. He would call later.

She sat down, pressed her hand against the cool flagstones of her own pseudo-porch, a porch too small even for one rocking chair, for one wicker love seat. Once she'd been sure she would like living here. But now she hated it. Everything was false, small, and reduced: the boxy, ranch-style houses, the tiny yards and porches. All of it phony, silly, like a cheap movie set.

Elizabeth was wet with perspiration, felt it drip down her sides, between her breasts. She walked inside and headed for the kitchen. She drank a glass of water, almost gagging on the metallic, tepid no-taste of it. There would be no pills today, she'd promised herself. She needed energy and clear thoughts. She had to plan.

She glanced at the box of recipes and cookbooks on the counter that she'd dragged out in a flurry of terrified optimism after Daniel had left that morning. Somehow, she would find the courage to go to the store, to start cooking today. She picked up a stack of recipe cards. A newspaper clipping, yellowed and stain splattered, stuck to the back of a recipe for Roquefort-stuffed grapes. She unfolded the article, and looked into her own face, a picture of herself smiling, holding up something, a tray of fruit. And there was Daniel behind her, holding up a book. The headline said FOOD FOR THOUGHT: A REVIVAL OF THE SALON ON CAMPUS MAKES FOR HEARTY DISCUSSIONS AND DELICIOUS MEALS! And underneath the photo: *Graduate students Elizabeth and Daniel Byers at one of their recent gatherings.*

"It started with a few neighbors and my wife's cooking," Daniel Byers, a graduate student in the English Department, said. "We all began talking about our different fields and about our graduate studies but we always found common ground—whether we were studying English, philosophy, engineering, medicine . . . whatever."

Now the Saturday night think tank has gotten popular, and the Byers have gotten calls from students and professors on campus who want to know how to become a part of what Byers has termed "a salon, in the true sense of the word." Byers said he was surprised by how the weekly gathering grew, but thinks living on campus helped since "we're all too poor for real entertainment, and all our lives revolve around books right now."

But he also points out that many of those who attend are hungry for more than knowledge. "My wife's cooking is out of this world."

Mrs. Byers, a graduate student studying American literature, says she tries to offer their guests international cuisine, or foods that complement the topics to be discussed. "One night the discussion centered on Nietzsche, Wittgenstein, Hegel—so we had German food: bratwurst, schnitzel with German beer and wine. Real heavy food—but then it was a heavy discussion."

The Byers generally welcome about 15 to 20 people at a time because "that's how many our modest minuscule apartment will hold," Byers said, adding, "and I hope the fire marshal won't read this." But the couple has had no problem squeezing in those who want to come.

"This is what academia is really about," said a smiling Dr. Joel Karikoff, chairman of the Philosophy Department as he settled on the floor one recent Saturday with a bowl of coq au vin. The French cuisine was being ladled up, the French wine chilling— the topic? The mind-body problem as defined by the French philosopher René Descartes. "Let's define body first," Karikoff began. A chorus of voices rose to answer him, and the discussion began.

Elizabeth folded the clipping, slid it into a cookbook. What did women do when they lost the love of their husbands? Call up their best friends? Their mothers-in-law? Elizabeth thought about calling Daniel's mother, Davida, and telling her everything and asking for her help. But calling a man's mother to help referee . . . that was so desperate.

And Davida would just shrug her shoulders anyway, shake her head, the way she had when, years ago, Elizabeth and Daniel had sat at Davida's kitchen table, told her they were getting married and going to graduate school. *Is she pregnant?* This said as if Elizabeth weren't there, weren't sitting between them staring at the bowl of dusty plastic fruit in the middle of the table, the grapes gray and slick like tumors. *No, Ma. No, she's not.* Davida for a minute looking like a bird of prey, cocking her head, staring at Elizabeth, comparing her to the other girls, so different with red lips, loud laughs, curves. And here was Elizabeth, her braid hanging down her thin neck like a rope, Daniel's hand moving from her bare knee to her thin wrist.

"What kind of life is that? Teaching, reading books?" Davida asked them. "What about being doctors like you planned?"

"Ma, you can call me doctor. I'll have a doctorate. Both of us will."

She shook her head, sighed. No doubt Davida, who had raised her son alone since he was seven, would be the first to say that he was a mystery to her. She had seen to it that his uncles had trained him to take over Rossi's Garage so the boy would have a future, so he wouldn't end up like his father. A failed librarian. And what does he do but go off to be a teacher, a book reader himself!

It was something Daniel joked about. *Stock from a failed librarian. How's that for a gene pool?* His father was the town librarian when he met Davida at the dry cleaner's where she worked, taking his order of four white shirts to be pressed, medium starch, every Friday. And Davida, as voluptuous and sultry as George Byers was reed thin and pale, developed a sudden urge to get her first library card and check out books, mostly heavy coffee table travel books with lots of photographs. She invited him to dinner. He reluctantly agreed. She cooked meals for him—heavy cream and pasta dishes, spicy roasted meats—that must have made his bachelor dinners of soup or Chinese take-out seem niggardly, almost unbearable. They married quickly after Davida found out she was having Daniel. Elizabeth could only imagine how a quiet, shy man like that would be overwhelmed by Davida's brothers, three burly mesomorphs, who clapped hands on his back hard enough to take his breath. All three of them were mechanics, owned Rossi's Garage, and when Daniel was two, when it was clear a librarian's salary couldn't support a family, they persuaded his father to give up the library job, to help manage their garage. He wasn't a mechanic. White hands, narrow shoulders, tall and gaunt—how could he be? But he could keep the books, mind the payroll, he could manage the place. He didn't, of course; he didn't manage, not well.

Sometimes after school Daniel would walk to the garage, sit quietly in his father's office and drink his bottle of Coke and eat his Nibs crackers, and watch his father do nothing more than read. Pensive and withdrawn, his father kept his office door closed, unwrapped the salami sandwich Davida had lovingly packed, and dove into Joyce or Faulkner or Emerson.

After my father left, Daniel would say *After my father left, my uncle Tommy put a hole in the office wall with his fist. After my father left, my mother stopped cooking, started drinking, and there was always the glass in the sink the next morning.* When he left, Daniel's father took what cash the garage had taken in that week. There was no embezzlement, certainly no calculating siphoning of money. He simply took $822 and left that night in his Chevy, headed to Florida or Canada, they guessed. Where criminals go.

After that, Davida got a job as a secretary in a tire factory, where she cried her lunch hours away in the ladies' room. She came home, eyes swollen and red, smelling faintly of rubber as she poured red wine from a screw-top bottle into a cut-glass decanter and then a juice glass. Daniel retreated to his room and read books or magazines that he had sneaked home under his shirt or in his bookbag or that he'd bought on the sly at the corner convenience store. *Oh, come on. No Playboys?* Elizabeth had teased him when he told her. *You were sneaking books?* At first Superman comics, *Mad* magazines, then the Hardy Boys, then books his teachers pressed on him: *Huckleberry Finn, The Catcher in the Rye, The Great Gatsby.* But he knew enough about his family to keep his reading a secret. After all, the one time his uncle Joe caught him on the back stoop of the house behind the clothesline with his Superman comic, he grabbed it and spit on it. "This . . . it's what your goddamn father did. A loser, Danny. A loser. You got better things to do. Real things."

After my father left, my uncles took over like the National Guard called in after a flood. Most Saturdays one of them came to visit and repair things for him and his mother in their run-down apartment—tightening leaky faucets, caulking the bathroom, cleaning the storm windows. They would cuff Daniel, their large meaty hands like paws. *You're the man of the house now,* they'd say. By the time he was thirteen, Daniel was working in the garage, turning over the limp, soiled dollar bills to his mother. Afternoons, after school, the poetry he'd read at school echoed in his head, whinnied like a wild horse as he padded brakes, rotated tires. It was then he taught himself to memorize words. He played the role of Mercutio in *Romeo and Juliet* his senior year in high school, explaining away the rehearsals to his uncles as a senior project, reviewing the lines in his head as he tightened lug nuts, scrubbed the rinds of grime under his fingernails. It was not the spotlights, the anonymous, delicious attention of the audience, the strip lights, the adrenaline on stage that he liked, it was the language, being transported, leaving his life behind. By day he staved off disrepair, he got things running, he made them go, but evenings he earned the privilege of hearing and saying those words, the lines that carried him off to other lives; it was a luxury he earned. And it was the way he came to understand how a man like his father would leave him and his mother for something more.

How could a man love something like words so much, the idea of words? Elizabeth had wondered, and found herself dropping everything—the chemistry, the biology, the premed—to find out for herself.

In the bedroom, Elizabeth stripped off her damp shirt and jeans and found a sundress in the back of the closet. She slipped on sandals and grabbed her purse. She slammed the front door closed, locked it, got in her car, took out the city map from under the seat, just in case. Just in case she took a wrong turn, she would be prepared. She took a deep breath, and backed the car out of the driveway. First to Belk's for a new clutch purse to match her shoes. Finding a little cream-colored purse wasn't important, and that was why she had to do it: to prove she could do trivial things, could act impulsively, like normal people. The mall was five miles on the right. The mall was easy to find. She chanted those words—*easy to find, easy to find*. She pressed on the gas, and she was gone.

She knew she was in trouble when she walked through the automatic double doors and found herself in Housewares. Everything in Beds and Linens looked like part of a period set. There were odd-sized little beds in pretend bedrooms that were supposed to look lived-in—with a pair of glasses on a bedside table, a coffee cup with a cinnamon stick, a Dickens novel. But when Elizabeth pressed down on one of the beds, there was no mattress at all, only plywood. "We order the beds made especially for the sets," the saleslady whispered from behind her. *The sets.*

On the second floor, in Cosmetics, the salesgirls were concentrating—their arched brows raised, their red lips pursed, their cotton balls stained pink—dabbing thick creams, spritzing perfume, to cover, to disguise. Elizabeth looked down at the little scrap of paper in her hand—*BUY A PURSE TO MATCH YOUR SHOES,* it said and she did, bought the first beige purse she saw, but then she got turned around and forgot where she came in. On the way to the escalator she thought about how everyone around her perched on the horny, hard back of reality like birds on a rhinoceros—superfluous, silly, flapping things. "But linen—I just wear it wrinkled," she heard in Career Separates. In Juniors, no one talked, they smacked gum and closed their eyes while they folded sweaters and moved to the music blaring from speakers.

Elizabeth was running! She stopped when she realized it, stood and met the gaze of two mannequins who stared down at her scornfully, glass eyes, nipples like bullets. For some reason, the mannequins were dressed like pirates. It was a look this season: rakish eye patch, billowy white blouse, thigh-high boots, with a stuffed parrot on the shoulder, a saber at the side. People walked around her as she stared back at the pirate mannequins. People were so accepting that way. It wasn't sane being sane, that's what she thought. You dress like a pirate, and worry about a wrinkled jacket.

She looked at the floor: she concentrated on the precisely cut squares. The marble was mottled and pink like canned meat and that made her think of dead things. Over in the shoe department, people were mulling over the shoes as if they were works of art in a museum, twisting their heads this way and that, like puzzled dogs hearing a far-off, high-pitched sound. "The finest leather," she heard a salesman say—trying to sell a dead thing's skin. Elizabeth held her hands over her ears and imagined the shoe salesman coming near. People were going to stare at her. In a minute she would be lying on the floor screaming and they would be fighting over her—"Call security!" one would shout, then "For God's sake, no—an ambulance!" Elizabeth opened her eyes, dropped her arms by her side. She stretched a tightly curled foot, ballerina style, on the floor. The marble looked cool, hard, surprisingly clean, recently waxed. It invited her down, but she declined.

Back at home, Elizabeth got out the phone numbers Cutter had given her. Cutter told her to call anytime. And she meant it, Elizabeth knew she did. She was probably waiting for Elizabeth's call. She dialed the number for the Pancake Palace. While she waited for Cutter to come to the phone, Elizabeth listened to the hoarse orders, the clatter and chatter in the background that reminded her that she was not part of that world, the world of work, where people did things and had schedules and got paid.

"Hello?"

Elizabeth almost lost her nerve, came close to hanging up.

"Cutter, it's Elizabeth Byers." Elizabeth felt her face grow hot with embarrassment as she explained about needing groceries, a trip to the store for food and flowers. When she heard how strained Cutter sounded, awkward but polite—very polite—she'd wished she hadn't called her at all. She'd put this girl in a terrible position, going on about how hard it was to find good mushrooms, asking for her help. After Elizabeth hung up—too abruptly, she thinks, but she simply did not have enough energy to sound casual—she looked down at the carefully organized grocery list she'd written out.

She proceeded to Plan B.

The story was that Elizabeth had to wait for the cable-television repairman and she couldn't very well leave the house even for thirty minutes because as soon as she'd dart out to the store, then he'd come and she'd miss him and have to wait another week before he'd reschedule. Something like that. She forgot exactly what she'd said. But it had come out all bubbly and run-together and it must have made sense. Patsy had nodded, seemed eager to help out. Missing the cable-TV repairman was serious business. Patsy took the list and the money that Elizabeth handed her and told her she'd be back within the hour.

By then, Elizabeth would have everything in the kitchen ready to go, the flour and sugar premeasured, the butter melted, the rice cooked. She was going to try out some old recipes again—salmon quiche, maybe a little shrimp mousse.

She'd surprise Daniel. Shock him.

While she waited for Patsy, Elizabeth washed three loads of laundry, vacuumed and cleaned all the windows with vinegar and ammonia. She made up the bed, and did something she'd never tried before, one of those hints from the "How to Keep Your Marriage Crackling!" articles her mother sent her. She sprayed perfume between the sheets. Then she lay on them and closed her eyes.

Would he make love to Ginnie in his office? No. No, Ginnie had her own big house, she would have friends with apartments. But still. Was it his office where it first happened? He was used to the crushes, the flirtations, surely he was. He had held them off for years, their infatuations, their eagerness; he had risen above the cloud of their tugging. But with Ginnie . . . Elizabeth pictured Cutter's face. She would look like her, wouldn't she, this Ginnie? Was Daniel wordless, almost sad, touching Ginnie's face lightly as if he were daubing a wound?

After a dozen years of marriage, she and Daniel had discovered their own shortcut to satisfaction. There was a gentle efficiency to their pleasure. First, his tongue flicking on her left nipple; then his hand moving in small, slow circles across her stomach and thighs, between her legs. They could finish the whole act, they could both come, in under ten minutes. No awkwardness, no pain, no disap-

pointment. There was something to say about the comfort of cho-
reographed love, wasn't there?

Were they crazy like animals, her husband and Ginnie, fumbling
and rushed? Fucking. Like in the movies. With a white surge of
energy. Sloppy. Aching. No tenderness, surely not.

Elizabeth stood up, smoothed the covers, went to the kitchen to
wait. The water was boiling, the lemon butter simmered. She
peered through her kitchen window and saw Patsy pull in her
driveway. At the door, Elizabeth thought the bag that Patsy
handed to her was too light, and the puzzlement must have shown
on her face. "They didn't have some of that stuff on your list,"
Patsy explained, "so I just got the next best thing I could find.
Oh, and they had this great two-for-one deal on Dorritos so I got
you some. You know they're always great for parties." Elizabeth
looked at her blankly. "Didn't you say you were having some
kinda get-together?"

In her kitchen, Elizabeth looked in the grocery bag and found
two cans of asparagus, a box of frozen fish sticks, three heads of
iceberg lettuce, and two bags of Dorritos. She moaned, covered her
face with a hand. Her list had said *salmon filets, or the freshest fish you
can find*. And where was the Boston bib lettuce and rosemary? The
fresh stalks of asparagus?

She would have to go herself. She remembered the department
store that morning, the mannequins, the crowds, the mean business
of it all. She looked at her watch. She didn't have much time if she
expected to have everything ready when Daniel came home.

The important thing when grocery shopping was to stick to the
items on the list. Just pick them up, put them in the cart, and go.
No distractions. Just breeze through, be efficient. She made herself
walk casually; that is what people who knew what they were doing
did. They sauntered wearily and leaned on their carts and stared at
food under hooded, bored eyes.

She walked through Produce first, past a mound of strawberries, a wizened, lone kiwi, piles of green and yellow apples. And a pineapple—always good for a centerpiece—but, no, this one was overripe, the bottom soft with decay.

She strolled past an elderly couple, their doddering gray heads bent together, contemplating the grapefruit. She forced a grim smile. *So far, so good. I'm fine, this is normal, everything's just great, yup.*

She picked up a bell pepper, smelled it. She squeezed it slightly, felt the hollowness inside. The eggplants were overripe and spongy but she selected three anyway. She passed up the plums; their tight rosy skins hinting at the yellow flesh underneath were somehow disconcerting. She wheeled around a frowning, jowly woman in bedroom shoes picking out sweet potatoes.

And then, heading down the cereal aisle, she felt fear brush by her. She made a mental note: aisle two—cereal, flour, sugar . . . She picked up her speed, the grocery cart wheels going *fa-lak, fa-lak*.

The crosshairs were searching her out now, she could feel them, the fear like a bullet, hard and hidden, ready to enter her and explode. *Slow down your breathing, count to ten.* Just get enough to make the quiche, maybe tomato bisque. She pictured his face then, his surprise and pleasure just hours from now, coming home and finding she'd made his favorites and . . . But in aisle three the tomato sauce wasn't there. Why, that was the silliest thing—not to have the tomato sauce with the canned tomatoes. She turned to a stockboy who was squatting, stamping stickers on cans of green beans.

"Excuse me? The tomato sauce is . . ."

Panic screwed her down in a fierce, casual grind, like a foot on a cigarette butt. Her stomach tightened. She exhaled slowly. "The tomato sauce?" she repeated.

"Ma'am?"

The stockboy stared. She looked away. She could see the refrigerated cases at the end of the aisle, the meats gleaming pink against the cellophane. The bones and limbs and skin were clean, neatly arranged in trays, compactly pressing against the plastic. Cross-sections of horror. Little captured deaths. *Stop it.*

"Aisle six, ma'am." The floor was dirty, the white tiles had gray swirly designs, and they were shiny, but dirty. And cold. So cold when you sat on them. She hid her face under the tent of her hair as she slowly slid to the floor. The stockboy ignored her, looked away as she sat by her cart. Thank God.

When she looked up, he was gone, and the older couple she had seen in Produce were making their way up the aisle toward her, close enough so that she could hear them discussing ketchup brands. The coast was clear—go! Go! She stood up and pushed her cart to the front of the store. She found herself in line at the express lane behind the sweet potato lady. Elizabeth saw the cashier was hands-on-hip exasperated: out of quarters! She yelled into the silver microphone beside the cash register—*Manager, register two!* The cashier shook her head, looked at her nails. This might take a while, she said. Elizabeth looked around. People thumbing through magazines, studying labels. My God, the luxury they had! Bored. While she gripped her grocery cart with white knuckles, and silently recited multiplication tables just to stay sane.

The potato lady's housedress was loose, sleeveless, and little hairy rolls of skin pooched out from her underarms, soft and fleshy and fuzzy, like a seal's whiskers. She was buying sweet potatoes and Pampers. Six boxes of Pampers.

Six times six is thirty-six. Behind her, a couple argued, because he had added a dozen eggs, orange juice, and bacon when the woman wasn't looking. Elizabeth closed her eyes and concentrated on their bickering. "Breakfast? You're counting on breakfast? That's insulting. How could you just assume I would stay over?"

The cashier sighed. "I swear he is so slow. All I need is one roll of quarters."

Elizabeth walked out, left her cart. They might be staring, or calling out, but she left it, her cart with the eggplants, the rice, the tomatoes. She walked through the automatic doors, with their sucking sound, the street air whooshing in on her, lifting her hair.

At home, Elizabeth studied her calendar. No matter what, she was trapped, she was contained; the days pressed down on her like a wire cage. She was suffocating thinking of him, of Daniel. Thinking of him with her, Ginnie, his naked ass pumping into her. And now she was planning this perfect party as if she could go through with it, as if everything could be like it was before. She had to make everything all right; she wouldn't let it end like this. She wouldn't lose Daniel.

Lose him.

The room was spinning now, and she was hot, she was sweating. She was so ensnared in here, in this house.

She opened all the windows and raised the blinds. She knocked out screens, took deep breaths. If she could just clear her head and breathe, she could figure out what to do. She could stop feeling trapped. She took off her earrings, threw her wedding band and watched it roll with a ping behind the refrigerator. She took off her clothes and walked through the house naked, her head back, her fingers spread.

In the bathroom, she studied herself in the mirror. Her hair lay stringy and limp on her shoulders. It was not young and silky anymore, it was neglected. Damaged, like the old part of her. If she could only change . . . right now. If she could only show him she could change. The pills, she really needed to take a pill. She could sleep this off. But no. She promised herself.

She looked for scissors, a knife, anything, and she found Daniel's old shaving kit behind the Clorox in the linen closet. The scissors were small, but sharp. As she was finishing up, she heard him come in. He was home. Finally, he was home. Where had he been? Riding again for miles. Or maybe basketball, that team he was on. She heard him running down the hall, into their bedroom.

"Elizabeth?"

His footsteps closer now. He knocked on the bathroom door.

"Elizabeth, for God's sake, open up. What the hell is going on? I tried calling earlier. Every light in the house is on, the screens are lying on the lawn—"

"What was the score?"

"I thought somebody had broken in. Sam and Patsy Rogers are standing out in the driveway, ready to call the police."

"What was the score?"

"The score?"

"Basketball tonight. The score."

Silence. "It's a pickup game, Elizabeth. It's not competitive. We don't keep score." And then, quieter, "I brought Chinese. Shrimp fried rice and egg rolls. Elizabeth? Come out."

She looked down at her feet. Her hair lay on the bathroom linoleum: S's and C's. She peered in the mirror, at her newly shorn head. She was different, but not changed. She was not her new self at all. Not yet.

Seven

THE BLACK-AND-WHITE GRAININESS OF the photograph in the real estate magazine made my house look beautiful, silvery and forlorn. I sat down at the nearest table, holding a hand over my mouth as I felt all the free Pancake Palace coffee I'd bolted down threaten to come back up. I forced myself to read the description.

> TURN-OF-THE-CENTURY BEAUTY! You've got to see this beauty to believe it. Five bedrooms, oak floors, high ceilings, wraparound porch, large kitchen, brass bathroom fixtures, claw-foot tub, stained glass, four fireplaces. An outbuilding and guesthouse in back perfect for mother-in-law suite or studio. Located in quaint Sans Souci on several acres. Great for residence or business. How about apartments?! Mr. Businessman, bring a great offer. Daddy, bring your hammer and saw. This one won't be on the market long! Call Priscilla Worthington.

Someone had left the magazine that morning at one of my tables. I'd picked it up as I bussed the table. *The New Sans Souci!* the front cover said, and I skimmed the words inside, my heart racing: *marketable . . . on the brink of taking off . . . an art gallery.*

I waved it furiously in front of Jolene. "Can you believe this?"

She looked up from the table she was wiping.

"Yeah, I took a gander at it when I came in."

"Did you see my house? Do you believe what they say here about how everything's changing and prices are going to skyrocket—"

"Honey, I'll believe anything now that I found out they're opening a new Wal-Mart. Things are changing. Yes, they are."

"You heard about that, too?"

"Yep, they gonna build it across from the old icehouse. Mack told me."

"Mack knows about it?"

"Yeah, Mack. You know what that fool done now?"

"What?"

"He's got it in his head to invest in this new thing that's gonna be big. It's—well—I might as well tell you if you promise not to breathe a word. They don't want someone to steal the idea."

"What idea?"

"The breakfast hot dog. My brother came over the other night and him and Mack were up half the night making plans, they were so excited about it. They want to make breakfast hot dogs and sell them wholesale. Have you ever heard of such a thing?"

"As a matter of fact, yes."

"I must be the only person doesn't know squat about this stuff. Even you heard of it. They want me to talk to Mr. D about it." We both looked over at the cash register where Mr. Demitriopolis stood ringing up orders. "Seeing as how he's the owner of a breakfast place, he could start a drive-through window with breakfast hot dogs to go."

"Is Mack putting up any cash for this?"

"That's the other thing they talked to me about. They want me to get some cash out of our house. A second mortgage. Said we'd make a lot of money back in a couple of years once the breakfast hot dog takes off."

"Well, it's none of my business, but I think it sounds like a risky venture. I don't think it's a good idea to—"

"You're right. It is none of your business."

"Sorry."

"Never mind." She stood up straight and stretched, then squeezed out the dishcloth into a bucket of filthy, gray water. "I know that magazine with the picture of your house has got you all torn up."

"Well, I can't help but worry when—"

"Don't worry, no one in their right mind is even going to think about buying that falling-down claptrap of an eyesore."

"You're just saying that to make me feel better."

I braved Jolene's scowling to slip out early from my breakfast shift. I decided on a quick mess-making trip in case Mrs. Worthington had plans for showing the house. I drove with the top down on my car although the spring day was still chilly and the cool air left the tips of my ears stinging. I zigzagged impatiently between trucks and cars; I didn't slow down until I neared home, leaving behind the freeway with its hissing din of traffic, its slick, black asphalt running through Sans Souci like a black snake through a garden.

I pulled into Mr. Heller's old filling station with the rusty bed-springs sitting out front, the honeysuckle vines scaling a bedpost. The station bell rang, and he lumbered out from the garage in his slow, big-bellied way. He wore his usual uniform, dark blue like a cop's, with *Buddy Heller* stitched in red above one pocket, an orange dipstick rag hanging from another. He carried a tire gauge and a wet squeegee.

"Fill 'er up?"

It was a joke between us. I'd never not filled up.

"How are you today, Mr. Heller?"

"Never been better." His face was hidden beneath his cap. It was hard to tell if I'd insulted him; he might think I was asking about his health. Since his heart attack last winter, he'd been sensitive about greetings. "I'm healthy as a goddamn racehorse and I ain't about to keel over," he'd told Mrs. Kincaid after she'd inquired about how he was feeling. *Just got himself all riled up,* she said, *all riled up, right up in my face. That kind will drop dead right in the middle of an oil change one day. You mark my words.*

"How about popping your hood for me?"

"I just did. Remember, it opens the other way. Up here, near the windshield wipers."

"I tell you, these foreign makes don't make a lick of sense." He shook his head. "Did Misty call you?"

"No. Why, what's wrong?"

"She's in the office. Go have yourself a Coca-Cola and say hey."

"Oh, she is? She's back in town?"

He nodded grimly. "Just got in this morning. Said she was going to call you."

Inside, I found Misty sitting on the counter swigging Orange Crush, a brown ledger in her lap. She was Mr. Heller's daughter, his only child, a girl I'd grown up with.

"You're all dressed up," I said, eyeing her tweed, her silk, her thin gold chains.

"This old thing? I have to wear suits every day now. I'm used to it." She ran her hands through her short, curly hair. "And how do you like this new do?"

For years, Misty's red hair—the color of dried blood—had stuck out stiffly in a triangular mass like a shrub. In sixth grade, her long feet, baggy jeans, wide, awkward stride, and sparkly purple lipstick were clownish. That was before she'd grown into herself, before the scholarship and business school.

"I like."

"Thanks. Aunt Darla did it this morning."

"You mean you passed up the froufrou salons of Atlanta to get your hair done in Sans Souci?"

"Can't touch Aunt Darla. She's the best."

I went to get myself a Coke from the refrigerator in back, but found myself standing by the freezer.

"Hey, mind if I have an orange push-up?"

"Help yourself."

"Or . . . hmmm . . . maybe a Nutty Buddy? I can't decide. Oh God, it's agonizing, Misty. Help me lick the ice cream problem."

She did not look up from her ledger. "You're funny. Take one of each. Just like old times."

Having Misty as a childhood friend meant free ice cream after school and all the Lance crackers and Moon Pies you could eat. But it was having no mothers to raise us that drew us together. *Momma run off, period,* Misty explained over and over in the same toneless way in kindergarten, and you could hear Buddy Heller's furious grief parroted in that grim sentence.

"You still working at the Pancake Palace?"

"Ha. Well, I'm not wearing this uniform for kicks, friend. And how's tricks with you?"

"I sit for my CPA exam next week. I'm a little nervous."

"When are you moving back?"

"Here? God, never. Toss me an ice cream sandwich?" She caught it, unwrapped it and licked the foil, holding the wrapper gingerly with her long, pale pink nails.

"You don't play your violin anymore?"

"No, not much." She wiggled her fingers. "Noticed them, huh? They're fake. At least I can have manicures now." At fifteen, Misty had been the star of the school district's string orchestra. She'd never been without her small black violin case, had carried it to pep rallies and driver's ed classes, cradling it in her lap or setting it between her ankles, like a pet. She must never, ever lose her violin, she'd told me, and she couldn't take a chance on having it stolen. Her father couldn't replace it. She was already keeping his books by then, after school. On slow days, she played her violin in the hot, cramped office—something jaunty like "Turkey in the Straw" to amuse her father, who told customers with a thumb over his shoulder, a sideways grin, *That's my daughter in there making that music. She's a fiddler.* But it was Misty's talent for numbers that took her away from her music and from us, from our town. It was that gift that helped her land the full scholarship to Georgia State, that took her to another kind of life altogether.

"Don't you miss it? Your music?"

"Nah, I got other things." She wiggled the finger of her left hand. "Notice something else?" She pointed to her ring finger. "Look—I'm engaged!"

"You? When? Who?"

"His name is Richard Thompson and he lives in Atlanta. We work together."

"Oh, well . . . that's great news."

"Don't look so shocked. I guess everyone thought I'd end up an old maid." She giggled, thrust her hand out so I could examine the ring. "It's a marquis cut," she said. "I thought it looked the most sophisticated."

"Wow. It's really nice."

She watched me carefully. Her gray eyes looked enormous, rimmed with a dark waxy line, a shimmer of powdered gold on the browbones. In eighth grade, Misty and I had learned to put on makeup by giving each other makeovers. I knew the arch of those brows and had powdered those cheekbones and mascaraed the auburn lashes. "I want you and Ginnie to be my bridesmaids. You will be my maid of honor, right?"

"Only if I don't have to wear chiffon. And no bows on my butt."

Mr. Heller came in then, took one look at me and said, "Well, from the look on your face, I guess you heard."

"You're getting yourself a son-in-law."

"Did she tell you about the scheme she's got, trying to get me to move down there, too?"

Misty sighed. She closed her eyes for a minute. "Oh, boy. Here we go. Richard and I think it would be a good idea if Daddy came to live with us, is all. At least for a while."

I saw right away what was happening, that they were arguing with each other through me, so I took great pains to avoid eye contact with either of them, instead examined my second ice cream, unwrapping it slowly.

"With his health—I mean, he doesn't need to be alone all day in this ramshackle place."

"It's worked for me thirty years, little girl. When I die, you can have it and do with it what you will. Until then—"

"Honestly, Daddy, these books are a mess. What if you get audited?"

"I'll tell the government to kiss my ass. It's tied up behind the store."

"Daddy, please." Misty's face was splotched in anger. "Haven't you noticed this is the only full-service gas station left around here?"

"That's the point," he said. "This town needs me."

"They're not good businesses anymore. Cutter, tell him."

I shrugged. "I don't know much about business."

"I'll tell you what's not good for me," he countered. "Atlanta. It was ruint when Sherman burnt it, and it's not any better now. There's nothing to see but shopping malls and office buildings and highways. Cars going every which a way on twelve lanes. You're liable to get killed just getting from one place to another."

"Cutter, he came down for one day—"

"I spent hours in traffic." I could feel their glares, knew each was waiting to catch my eye, which made me even more determined not to look up. "Miles and miles of traffic cones and blinking signs, and finally at the end of it all, one construction feller standing there scratching himself. No kind of work going on nowhere that I could see."

I cleared my throat. "Is it my imagination, or are these Nutty Buddy ice creams getting smaller? There's like three nut pieces on here. There used to be scads of peanuts on top, remember?"

"That's because you're bigger now, you goof," Misty said. "Everything looks a lot smaller when you're grown up."

"Except for problems," I said. "They get bigger."

"They probably make them in China now," Mr. Heller said. "Everything comes from there now, and that's why everything has shrunk up so awful."

A pickup truck pulled in by the pump out front. The station bell rang morosely.

"I better get going," I said. "I need to get my car out of the way."

"Why would anyone want to leave Sans Souci?" Mr. Heller asked. "Cutter, tell her we got good reason to stay." He winked at me in his rare, gruff, kind way.

Misty was shaking her head, looking hard again at the ledger in her lap.

I squinted at the trash can across the room, tossed in my balled-up wrapper. "It's true. We have everything we need right here."

I drove down Main Street, where the world narrowed and seemed more important, past buildings with their wide glassed storefronts, their glass bricks gleaming, past the old Star movie theater and Klein's Drugstore. By the time I turned onto my street, I felt the beauty of the day, the shimmering magic of the spring working through me, gurgling around me like a stream around a rock, dissolving, nudging away my worry. It wouldn't work, selling the house from under me. Surely no one would want a house like mine.

When I turned onto Gerard, I drove under the trees, arched protectively, their limbs meeting, clasping above me. There were no strange cars, no signs of Realtors anywhere. I parked at the curb in front of my house, a warning to Mrs. Worthington to stay away. For a while I did nothing. Just sat in the seat and looked around, watched the budding trees wave a little in the breeze. The wind whistled down our street, through our windows, across our weathered porches, and over our glass transoms and did us no harm. I saw that the rocking chairs and the swing on my front porch shuddered a little. I could feel the presence of my ancestral shades there, and I found this comforting.

After all, the porch on our house had figured prominently in my life, a kind of thrust stage that had snagged destiny when my parents met and fell in love there. Gran had told us the story, always with a mixture of regret and detachment, of that August day in 1964. My mother, eighteen year olds and set to begin Miss Sylvia's Business School for Ladies in Palmetto the following Monday, sat out on the porch shelling peas. Gran was in the kitchen rolling dough for biscuits, glancing up just in time to see the commotion. Billy King from two houses up was chasing another boy, both of them landing in the shrubbery in our yard, right in front of the porch. *And there they came busting through my red tips,* Gran said, *crushing my geraniums, rolling around on the ground something awful—those two boys wrestling—well, you couldn't tell if they were fighting or just playing, they carried on so.* Billy King had just graduated high school with my mother, then enlisted in the army. He was going to Vietnam. He'd met my father in basic training and invited him to visit for ten days of home-cooked meals before they shipped out.

Everyone knew Billy King had always loved your mother from the time they were children, Gran said. That's why he had come over to our yard, to impress my mother with his new hand-to-hand-combat skills. While Gran watched from the screen door, my mother stood and leaned over the railing, looking at my father and Billy, with their shorn hair, their sweating, flushed faces, the two of them tumbling like puppies. *Then your daddy, well, he caught sight of Caroline. He stood up, his mouth dropping open, his eyes big, standing there swaying and staring. Drunk! A Yankee! And they have to go fall in love. Your mother was a Harris woman through and through to pick one like that.*

It was true. The end of my parents' tragic lives crouched before them, even then. But what a story. To fall in love like that. And here I was able to stand where my mother did on the porch, and imagine my father staring at her.

Tonight I would have to clear the air, I would have to talk with Ginnie about that real estate ad. And Barry? For a while Ginnie had let Barry and me fight about selling the house, rolling her eyes when I yelled at him over the phone. She hadn't cared about the house, whether it sold, whether I could buy it, but something had changed. I wondered if selling the house was part of her plan. The money and moving out went along with the baby and Daniel Byers.

A few cars lazily made their way to the end of the street. Two doors down, old Miss Jamison was inspecting her pansies. She stopped and waved to me, pointing to her forsythia bush, a yellow explosion. I smiled and waved back.

As I headed up the front sidewalk, whistling, swinging my purse, I looked across the street at Father Bob's.

Alfred and Father Bob stood over a hole in the ground. Father Bob was leaning on a shovel, a long, black vestment flapping wildly around him. I saw Alfred gently placing something in the hole and Father Bob reaching up to place a hand on Alfred's shoulder.

"What happened?" I asked, walking over.

"It was just one of those things, I'm afraid," Father Bob said. "A hit-and-run." His eyes were red and his hair was stiff and gray and stuck out from his temples in little clumps. "Spot just darted out and a car hit him. It didn't look too bad at first—I mean, he wasn't mangled—" He sobbed. "Oh, I can't do this, I can't *bear* it. But I must be strong for Alfred. There's a lesson to impart in this, I know."

"Where are the others?" I asked.

"Inside."

Three faces pressed at the screen door. I waved and a desperate chorus of moans and whines rose. "It's okay," I yelled out. "Everything will be all right." It seemed the right thing to say. I did not meet Father Bob's eyes. I looked down at Spot. He was a big cat, white with a large gray spot on his side, a gray-ringed tail. He lay on his side, as if curled in sleep.

"I'm so sorry, Alfred," I said. His tears had left two slick trails that shined on the brown of his skin.

"Spot—he's in heaven."

I saw Father Bob's head nod, his eyes close.

"He's gonna wait for me up there. Spot is gonna sit in a big window in heaven and look down and see me."

"Yes," Father Bob said.

"Jesus is gonna pet him."

"Oh, Alfred," Father Bob said. "That's a lovely thought." He blinked hard, cleared his throat and looked at me. He took a minute to get himself together, his face moving, crumpling, then settling into a pinched sadness. "Alfred and I have discussed how death is a part of life, and how funerals and mourning are ways of dealing with death. Let us join hands and begin."

I thought about trying to excuse myself—I had my second job to get to, after all—but when I looked at their solemn, bent heads, I knew I couldn't leave. I closed my eyes. I waited. Then I peeked and saw Father Bob frantically flipping through his Bible. I thought maybe he was out of practice. I searched my own limited memory of Baptist services and Sunday school, realized all I remembered of churchgoing was a kind of conglomeration of verses and vague threats, a white noise of theological terms caught in passing.

"Isn't there some kind of Book of Mourning?" I asked.

"You're thinking of the *Book of Mormon,* dear."

"Oh." A few years back the Mormon missionaries had descended on our street, their lanky, ungainly legs poking out from their bicycles. They'd asked to talk with us, left pamphlets and books, refused our offers of iced tea. They'd reminded me of locusts that swarm suddenly, rising together frenzied and thick in a cloud before disappearing.

"I'm looking through the index now. I thought for sure there would be some mention of animals."

"Try *beasts,*" I whispered, and he nodded fiercely. I looked at Spot, still casually curled up. You could see the top of his little pointed teeth sticking out from his thin pink lips. His eyes looked pinched shut in that lidless way cats have.

"'*Beasts*—see *sacrifice.*' Oh my stars! That's not—" Father Bob looked up at us, his robe snapping in the breeze like laundry on a clothesline. "Perhaps you two should give me a minute to peruse this." Alfred stood staring hard into the hole.

I kneeled, threw down a sprinkling of dirt, and grabbed another handful. "Bye, Spot," I said. "See you in heaven."

But Spot opened his eyes.

Then Spot jumped out of the hole and ran, leaving a little dusting of kicked-up soil on our feet.

I looked up to see Father Bob's mouth open in surprise, his eyes busy scanning the shrubbery across the street where Spot had disappeared. Alfred smiled slowly. His hands were held flat and tight in prayer and I watched as they loosened like petals.

"Spot—is a ghost," Alfred said finally. Then, more loudly, "A ghost."

"No, no, Alfred," Father Bob said. He still looked surprised, his eyes darting around the street. "I think Spot was just hurt a little and . . ." He looked at me for some help.

"Spot was knocked out," I said. "I think Spot was sleeping—but now he's okay. He was never—"

"A miracle! A miracle!" Alfred jumped up and down. Pinky opened the screen door, the two others behind him, grinning and gaping.

"Spot's been re-erected," Alfred yelled to them. "A miracle from the Lord!"

"Well, maybe it was a miracle," Father Bob said. "Maybe Spot was resurrected . . . Yes—why should we be cynical, Cutter? Maybe that's what happened."

"I guess we could use some miracles on this street," I said. "I could, anyway."

Father Bob stopped watching the men and turned to me, his smile gone. "Ahhh. The house. I noticed the *For Sale* sign disappeared. The work of vandals?"

"Apparently."

"Unfortunate."

"Very." I smirked.

Alfred was on the porch now, with Pinky and Jerry and Larry. All four of them turned to look at the street.

"Remind Alfred that the job we talked about at the newspaper starts tomorrow," I said.

"Wonderful, Cutter." He beamed at me. "You're good to him."

"It's not a big deal," I said, blushing a little. "I knew Alfred would like it. Tomorrow is my day off at the Pancake Palace, so I'll take him a little early to the paper and introduce him around and stuff."

"I'll tell him. And, Cutter?"

"Yes?"

"There's something I forgot to ask you."

"What is it?"

"I don't know! I forgot." He clutched his head with both hands, began walking in a tight circle. "What was it? What was it?"

"It'll come to you."

"It's important. I can feel it. If I can just—Oh! I remember now." He clapped his hands in front of him in glee. "The lady! The sick lady. When are you bringing her to visit us?"

"I don't think we really planned—"

"Oh yes. Yes. She said she would come and see us. Remember? To see the greenhouse. No doubt she'll need one of us to pick her up, she obviously can't drive."

It was my turn to clutch my head. "Father Bob, I think she was just being polite, okay? And I don't know if she's sick. Not that sick, anyway."

"Why, she certainly is. Terribly ill."

"Look, it's complicated. More complicated than—"

"You will bring her, Cutter, won't you? Today or tomorrow would be marvelous."

I sighed. As usual, Father Bob's stubborn buoyancy ran roughshod over me. "I'll see what I can do."

He nodded, smiling.

"By the way," I asked, "have you seen the real estate agent poking around lately?" Not that I was calling in any favors, asking Father Bob to keep a look out. He would never intrude in our family like that, never take sides. Still, I knew he'd rather I stayed.

"Why, no, I haven't."

"Just thought I'd ask." I turned to leave.

"There was just the one car today, Cutter."

"One car?"

"Yes, a little one. I believe it's still behind the house."

When I opened the front door, I stood in the foyer for a minute wondering if I should leave. Feeling like an intruder in my own house was new to me, and I didn't like it.

The dining room table had been set for two. Gran's fine china anchored a white linen tablecloth branded with a grid of yellowed fold marks. A gravy boat tackled a humped-up wrinkle. On either end of the table, two white candles flickered. In the middle, a large crystal vase held a small clump of daffodils; their bright papery heads peered over the glass like curious children.

I smelled burning bread, and I walked toward the kitchen. I could hear them talking in there, my sister and her lover. I recognized Ginnie's sadness right away, her words whispery ribbons around Daniel's rumblings.

But for how long?

Until I can get her some help.

They stopped talking immediately when I came through the door. It was like pushing the mute button on the television controls. "Sorry," I said.

Ginnie turned and looked out the kitchen window. She had her arms wrapped around her waist in a sad self-hug. Daniel was standing against the kitchen counter, his hand rubbing her back in slow circles. I couldn't help thinking of Elizabeth then. Just days ago she'd stood near where he was standing, awkward, embarrassed. In fact, much like he was now. I noticed the stiff way he dropped his hand from Ginnie's back and drew himself up, the brittle way a man moves in a tuxedo, the way he had looked that day he'd picked up Ginnie, standing there adjusting his sunglasses, his legs planted wide and sturdy, like a ladder. The rigid way he stood just made him seen more formal, more important.

Ginnie's eyebrows shimmered golden over the red-flushed bands around her eyes. She'd been crying. "No, don't sweat it. Really."

"I smell something burning," I said.

She grabbed a dish towel and took out a pan of smoking biscuits from the oven, slid all of them into the sink and turned on the disposal. She darted back to the oven and pulled out a large dish of something bubbling and crackling. There was a jangling crash as it clattered in the sink.

"I burned myself," she said quietly, her face grim, half hidden by her hair.

Daniel grabbed her arm and held it under running water. The beginnings of a long welt rose on Ginnie, from wrist to forearm. *Ice*, he whispered to me. I handed him an ice cube.

"I feel like you're putting us on this abbreviated schedule or something." Ginnie's whisper hiccupped with a sob. "I don't like being cut off from you so much. Daniel, it scares me." She was looking at his face, her eyes searching.

"Is that better?" he asked, rubbing the ice on her.

"I need a Band-Aid," she said.

Daniel turned off the water and clutched her hand, pressed it to his mouth fiercely, closed his eyes. It happened so fast, that quick burst of passion, like a flashbulb that left me a little dazed.

When Ginnie went upstairs for a Band-Aid, I headed out of the kitchen, but Daniel stopped me.

"I'm going to fix that deadlock." He made a motion with his head to the back door in the kitchen. "I couldn't help but notice that it doesn't close all the way."

"Don't worry about it." I bristled a little.

He opened the door, walked out onto the little back stoop. He stepped over the crumpled, mildewy kitchen rug that lay on the top step, ignored the dried-out mop that hung on the railing.

"It's not safe, this lock."

"We're safe here," I said.

He took off his jacket and draped it on the railing beside the mop, loosened his collar, rolled his sleeves up. There was a kind of needless masculinity under his shirt.

"A screwdriver might help." Despite his looking worried and determined, there was something friendly about him. He squinted up at me. "Do you have a toolbox?"

"A butter knife and duct tape." But I got out the old half-bushel basket of haphazard tools from the pantry and crouched down beside him.

"Wow." He plundered through the basket. "Haven't seen one of these before." He held up a rickety wooden yardstick, folded into hinged sections. On the back were advertisements for headache powders and shoe polish.

"You like doing this kind of handyman stuff?" I asked.

"No. But I grew up working with my hands." He closed his eyes for a minute as he fiddled with the latch, as if he were tuning an instrument. "I can fix anything, but it's the cerebral life I'm fond of."

"I heard you . . . juggle." He looked over at me, turning the doorknob. "That's working with your hands, isn't it?"

Ginnie had told me how he'd come in the classroom one day juggling four tennis balls, talking about rhythm, about sonnets and balance. But I meant it as a challenge.

"Yes, well, that's in my bag of tricks."

He stood and tried the lock, but it still didn't work.

"Here," I said a little petulantly. "I'll hold the lock." There was something familiar about the clean scent drifting off his damp hair, and I realized it was Ginnie's shampoo.

"What about you, Cutter? What is it you like to do? Somehow I think serving pancakes and writing about funerals is not your life's ambition."

"There's nothing wrong with good honest work. And it is hard work living the life you want, especially if people keep interfering, trying to take it from you."

He was studying the lock. My shadow fell over his face.

"But what about your next life?" he said after a minute. "If you knew you had a second life, what then?"

"Well, then I would be a pilot."

"Ah, now we're getting somewhere. Have you ever been on an airplane?"

"Once, when I was thirteen." It had been eighth grade. I'd been selected to go with a group of teachers and students to Washington, D.C., since I'd gotten the top score on my school's history exam. I remembered flying through clouds, disappointed as the solid spun cotton faded into blurs and wisps, then into ordinary fog. But when I looked down between the clouds, I saw the Blue Ridge Mountains rumpled below us like a kicked-up rug.

"Our father flew in planes," I began, "and he was—"

"What are y'all doing?" Ginnie stood in the kitchen, her eyes red, her hair tangled, a haphazard snarl of bandage and tape on her arm. She plunked down on one of the kitchen chairs, willowy and limp. I stood abruptly, dropping the door handle, but Daniel caught it with a practiced gesture.

"You're okay?" he asked.

"I'm fine. No big deal." She started fanning herself with the newspaper. "It's hot in here."

Daniel tossed the screwdriver in the basket, flipped the latch several times. "Well, it's not perfect, but at least you can lock the door now." I followed his glance to the clock above the stove. It was one of those Green Stamp prizes from years ago, a little faceless, bonneted milkmaid whose outstretched milk buckets served as hands on the clock. "I've got to go," I said.

I excused myself, but looked down from the top of the stairs to see them hug so tightly that Ginnie let out a little gurgle. He planted three fierce kisses on the top of her head. Their parting looked like an airport hug, travelers clinging to each other.

I changed clothes, then went into Gran's room and opened her jewelry box. I couldn't find my favorite pearl choker, a gift from Gran's mother. I looked in all the drawers, even in the cedar chest. I searched through her old suits, and all those hats: pillboxes, straw wide-brims, rigid, elegant ones. I sat on my heels in the middle of Gran's closet. I must have left it in my purse.

I passed Ginnie's room on the way downstairs. A froth of pale green covers and lace-bordered sheets were rolled back, a small rumpled wave. One of the pillows lay on the floor, and there was a knot of Ginnie's clothes in the corner. The room was stuffy and close, briny heat still lingering.

They had spent the morning there.

I heard her in the bathroom, the faucet screaming on and off, on and off. She was taking a whore's bath, something she'd done since we were in high school. She'd come in through the bedroom window at dawn, rumpled and half drunk. She'd head to the bathroom, yeasty and smoky, red-eyed and sullen, not bothering to close the door, letting her clothes drop softly on the cold tile around her feet. She'd take a small linen hand towel from the closet and a bar of Ivory soap and she'd wash her face, between her legs, under her arms.

It wasn't unlike Gran's own sponge baths, a habit she had begun when the daily trek up the narrow stairs to the bathtub became too much for her. She'd fill the bowl and pitcher in her bedroom with warm water and daub herself with scented cloths and lavender talcum powder, finally hobbling down the hall to the kitchen in her damp robe, one step at a time, to make us breakfast.

I knocked on the bathroom door.

"Have you seen a pearl choker around here?" I asked.

"No."

"Are you sure? It's the one I wore last—"

"I'm sure."

She opened the door and brushed past me. I followed her down-stairs to the dining room. She blew out the candles on the table, and the sharp, acrid smoke tickled my nose. She sat down and pushed her hand through her bangs, stared at the daffodils.

"You didn't tell him, did you?" I sat down at the opposite end of the table.

"No."

"Why not?"

"He's so distracted right now." She buried her face in her hands for a minute, then looked across the table at me. "We're not alone much. And in class, or in a crowd, there's this kind of barrier between us. Not a wall, because we can see each other, but we have to pretend we don't. It's more like a curtain descending, dividing us."

We would manage, I told her. She didn't even need to tell him. We would live in this house, the baby, too, and I would work and we would do fine, all of us. Why, there were baby clothes in the attic. Our old baby clothes and maybe Barry's, too, I had just stum-bled across them last week, I knew exactly where they were. Tiny bonnets and pale pink blankets. A spindle crib and wicker bassinet.

"Oh, please. Baby clothes, Cutter? From the attic?"

"What's wrong with that?"

"Those things are so old they should be burned. You're so . . . God, look at yourself. The stuff you wear. Like, that dress you've got on looks about a hundred years old."

I looked down at the navy linen with the Peter Pan collar, the three little tarnished buttons. "It's from Mom's room."

"Half the time you reek of Eau de Mothballs. I'm just telling you that for your own good."

"You're trying to change the subject."

"Well, not that it's any of your business, but I've decided to wait until next weekend to tell him. We'll have some days together then. The conference he's planning will be finished, and Wife will be committed to some—"

"Committed?"

"Cutter, she's disturbed. She needs help. Serious medical help. Which she refuses to get." She rubbed a wet finger around the top of the crystal goblet in front of her until it made strange deep ocean noises, whale sounds. "Apparently she's had some kind of breakdown."

"What happened?"

"Well, she practically shaved her head, for one thing. And she decided that they should have this party—she and Daniel—before the conference. No students allowed, of course."

"Do you think she knows about you?" I looked down, flicked imaginary crumbs off a plate.

"No. It's just that she's drowning in this—sickness. And she's trying to drag Daniel down with her." She looked across at me, her eyes gone flat. "Just like Gran, in a way. The three of us rattling around in this old barn like seeds in a dried gourd. Twenty years of mourning and grieving."

"That's not true. We have a home because of her," I said quietly.

Ginnie did not look at me. She'd spent her life hating my ideas, dodging me when I followed. Not that I wanted to shadow my sister. By the time I was in sixth grade, there were days Gran took me to the side, whispered how I should stay close to Ginnie. And I knew what she meant. Gran must have sensed something was wrong, must have found the tubes of melon and bubble-gum lip gloss, compacts with little mirrors and beige face powder hard as clay, pink razors, panty hose—all those taboo items we weren't allowed—stockpiled in Ginnie's room. She'd gotten so fast, so smooth, I'd hardly noticed when my sister swiped things. When I finally confronted her at the dime store, she bribed me with Tootsie Rolls and a *True Confessions* magazine. One day we walked home together from school and cut through the woods. She took me to an old stump near a clearing, and we sat on it. In front of us was a view of one of the newly constructed neighborhoods. There were humps of red clay around us—leftover dirt bulldozed into piles—and heaps of lumber. I looked out onto the blacktop between the lines of houses. There was a row of identical black mailboxes, scores of them. If I'd had a deer rifle, I could've shot a hole in all of them with one bullet.

"You wanna spy?" Ginnie had asked me.

"Spy on what?"

"Sometimes I come here and I just watch them."

"Who?"

She stared and didn't answer me. A few minutes later a small dark car came down the street and pulled into the driveway of the house nearest us. A man got out and the front door of the house burst open and a redheaded child waddled across the lawn. The woman following him, big with pregnancy, waddled, too. The man kissed them both. The woman took his suit jacket and briefcase and the man began to toss the little boy up and down and swing him around. Then all three of them went in the house.

"When do we start spying?"

"We are spying, stupid."

"But this is boring." I stood up, pulled on my kneesocks, spit out my gum and buried it with a deep grind of my shoe.

I remember the look of desperate adoration on Ginnie's face then, the stunned love as she watched the family, transfixed. It was the same look she had now.

I sighed. "How did you manage to lug up all the fine china from the basement?"

"What do you mean?"

"It was in the basement, wasn't it? With all those boxes of silver-ware?"

"I dunno. I picked a box and got lucky."

"Will you be home tonight?"

"No. I'll probably stay over at Penny's." I thought of the condo where Ginnie stayed. The carpet, pale as loaf bread. There was a chrome and glass coffee table in the living room along with a huge television and an exercise bike. It was spare and empty and square like a walk-in freezer.

I stood and turned, felt the lace edge of the tablecloth snag my belt. Two crystal goblets and a salad plate plunged to the floor. I looked down at the broken glass stems, a Blue Willow plate cracked in half. My sister and I stared at each other from across the room, our grandmother's wedding crystal and china in shards between us.

"Oh no," I said.

"I'll sweep it up, just go on to work."

"No! No, I want to save the pieces. I'll glue it all back tonight."

"Oh, Cutter, don't be ridiculous. Glue it back?"

"Don't throw it away. Don't. I'll fix it. Promise me!"

There were two pink "While U Were Out" notes on my desk. The first from Barry. The receptionist had gone to the trouble of transcribing his words. The "Extremely Urgent" box was checked. *Mrs. W. will be in touch about showing house. Clean up the damn place.* The second message was from Mrs. Kincaid. Betty Rush, former Sans Souci Garden Club president, was dead. Mrs. Kincaid would have more information for me at the Talbot Baker Mortuary this afternoon. "She called right before you got in," Charlie said, from behind his newspaper. "Mrs. Kincaid, that is. Not Betty Rush." He chuckled, lowered the paper to look over at me. "Now that'd be a story."

Charlie had covered crime and politics—he claimed they were one and the same—for twenty chain-smoking, snack-cake–eating years.

"Is that the Palmetto paper you're reading?" I asked rather sternly.

"Hey, I got to get my news from somewhere."

"Well, if anybody should ask, I'm off to gather details for the Rush obit."

"Deathtails, you mean."

"Yes, deathtails."

The Talbot Baker Mortuary was on the outskirts of town. On the way there, I detoured through Olde English Acres and pulled in the Byers' driveway.

After I knocked, Elizabeth opened the door a crack and peered out at me, blinked in the daylight. Her hair was cropped and she looked a little weary, with sleep lines on one side of her face. I tried to hide my alarm.

"Hey," I said. "It's just me."

"Oh. Cutter."

"I didn't mean to bother you. But I promised Father Bob that— I mean, he's convinced that you are eager to visit them. Plus, I wanted to tell you that I'm sorry about not calling you back."

"Oh, well. I didn't expect you to call me back. You sounded very busy." She looked down, but didn't invite me in, did not open the door more than her foot's width. I took in the wedge of chaos from behind her: haphazard stacks of measuring bowls and bags of flour and mess. "I'm getting everything ready. For a party."

"Looks like you're busy. I don't want to hold you up. But, hey, you know what? I just thought of something. I've got an errand to run. Well, actually it's work-related. Obituary stuff. I have to go all the way to Travelers Rest for this one. But there's this place out that way that might be good for you to visit. A little crossroads grocery. You said you were looking for unusual food? They've got it."

"Thank you, but no. I have all I need. We made a trip to the store just this morning." Emphasis on we in a snide little way, like being back in sixth grade.

"I see." I half turned to go. "You'll really like this place, I promise."

"Well, I don't—"

"It's just a little outing. You'll have fun. C'mon."

Her eyes flickered from me to my car parked there in her drive. She stepped out onto the porch. I watched her reluctance soften, dribble away in the sunlight.

"I'll have you back here in an hour."

She nodded slowly. "Okay."

Travelers Rest Grocery was the kind of place you could find homemade apple butter, fishing line, and live crickets on the same shelf. We passed the lone rusty gas pump out front, then clattered across the wooden porch and approached the wide screen door, propped open with an old Dr Pepper crate. The smells of damp wood, cinnamon, and kerosene greeted us. A faint draft stirred from the dusty fans circling lazily above our heads. Elizabeth hung back by the shelves crammed with blackberry jam and local honey.

"You can poke around in there for a while, and I'll go to the mortuary over there across the street," I whispered. "I shouldn't be gone too long."

"But I . . . don't really know this place." She clutched my elbow. "I don't know where things are."

"You've got a list, don't you?"

"Well, yes, I jotted down a few things here." She took a crumpled piece of paper from her purse.

"Believe me, that's all you need."

Silver-haired Mr. McKeen, the owner, made his way from the back where he'd been cleaning the iron stove. He bobbed and weaved through the aisles until he appeared beside us, gnarled and hairy as a moldy potato.

"Well, if it ain't Miss Cutter. I guess you're here for more string for your runner beans."

"Actually, I brought a friend," I said. "She has a list. She needs things." By then, Miss McKeen, his sister, came up the other side of the aisle and the two of them stood there together, hunched and

toothless, grinning at us like two fairy-tale trolls. "This is Elizabeth," I said.

"How doody," Mr. McKeen said.

"This your list, honey?" Miss McKeen whispered, then quickly
slipped Elizabeth's list from her hand.

"Yes, but . . ." Elizabeth sputtered.

Miss McKeen squinched her face up, then plucked a twisted,
taped pair of glasses from her apron pocket. She read the list slowly,
moving her lips. "Let's see here. Cream. Eggs . . . Oh, we got the
prettiest speckled eggs you ever seen from the guinea hens out
back. Fresh from this morning." Her wide blue eyes, magnified by
the glasses, blinked damply at us. She turned and hobbled through
the aisles then, filling a little basket. Elizabeth followed her.

"Cutter, you got to take a look at the collection up here," Mr.
McKeen called over to me. He was standing behind the counter
now and took a wooden box from a shelf. I knew what was coming. I headed for the door, tried to make my excuses. "We got us
some good ones this year."

Mr. McKeen lived for "the contest." Every year, folks for miles
around brought over any vegetable or fruit they'd grown that
looked like a celebrity and entered it into the McKeens' contest.
There was a different panel of judges tapped for the honor of
examining the entries every year. A daylong festival was held and
prizes awarded. The *Sans Souci Citizen* ran a big spread featuring
photographs of the winners. Mr. McKeen rustled around in the
box, held up a sweet potato. "Look here. This one came from the
Spencers just last week. Looks just like that Russian feller. Spot
right there on the forehead and everything." He held up a gourd.
"This one is the best Elvis so far."

Across the street, the Talbot Baker Mortuary was quiet. As I walked
toward the office, someone stepped out of one of the side rooms
and grabbed my elbow. I screamed.

Mrs. Kincaid looked irritated. "Dear, get a hold of yourself."

"I'm sorry—you scared me. And it's so silent. No organ music or weeping or preaching. I guess they're between shows?"

"Viewings, my dear. Yes, they're between viewings."

"Where's Mr. Talbot?"

"No need to worry. I've already talked to him and have all of our information right here." She rattled a sheet of paper. It was the obituary form, filled out in Mrs. Kincaid's spidery scrawl.

"Oh," I said, trying not to sound disappointed. Mr. Talbot was my favorite undertaker, a jolly man with an unbridled laugh.

"He's occupied now in his office. There's a family in there and an . . . unusual situation." She lowered her voice. "Cath-o-lick. They want drinking. And a dinner. Can you imagine? After a funeral?"

I looked over the form.

"I've penciled in some details right there, as you can see."

" 'Famous for her cream cheese potato chip chicken casserole, of which she won many accolades,' " I read.

"Yes, that's right. The casserole with the potato chips and crunchy Chinese noodles on top? She brought it to covered dish at church every Wednesday night for thirty years."

" 'Cultivated the first triple-stitch speckled sweet-faced tiger lily for the Sans Souci Garden Club.' What's that?"

"What's what?"

"A triple-stitch speckled sweet-faced tiger lily?"

"Just put it in, dear. It will do her proud. I promised the family."

"Do you know if there's a photograph her family wants included?"

"Right here." She handed me a black-and-white photo. "It's her engagement picture from years ago, but it's what she would want, I'm sure." The photograph was a close-up of a young Betty Rush looking out rather sullenly, her chin resting on her white-gloved hands, her hair gathered in a snood. "She looks a little put out there, because her father had forbidden her plans for travel. After graduating from Sans Souci High, she got it in her head that she wanted to leave Sans Souci and take off to London and Paris and New York. Well, it was 1930 and back then it just wasn't proper for a young woman to up and leave by herself. I don't think it's any better of an idea these days, by the way. Hence the engagement to Mr. Rush, a fine choice of a husband, sanctioned—some might say handpicked—by her father."

"Poor Mrs. Rush," I said. "I can still see her tackling those rose-bushes in the median of Gerard."

"It was the cancer, you know."

"Really?"

"Yes. In January, they opened her up, took a look, then sewed her right back up. Nothing they could do. But that makes it worse, you know. When they take a look. They don't tell you, but it does. The air gets inside when they open you up and just feeds it. She's already laid out in the East Room over there. Would you like to see her?"

"No, no, that's not necessary. I think I have all the information I need."

"You know, Cutter, you're still a young thing, but as you go through life you'll notice we all either wither or bloat with age. Betty Rush withered."

"Thanks for your help, Mrs. Kincaid. I'm going to—"

"They're burying her in her favorite garden gloves and hat, holding a hand trowel just as she requested. It looks as if she plans to scratch herself out."

I found Elizabeth and the McKeens in the middle of the peach orchard out back of the store. I waded through the tall grass, the grasshoppers fleeing and careening around my steps. They were standing by the beehives. Miss McKeen was explaining all about gathering honey. She was making elaborate sweeping gestures with her hand and wore a white-veiled hat and oversized boots, like a child in dress-up. I walked over to them sheepishly. I was later than I expected and Elizabeth would be miffed. No doubt the McKeens had subjected her to detailed discussions on the collection and marched her around explaining the perils of raising guinea hens and growing peaches.

"Sorry for the delay. We can go now," I said a little breathlessly. The three of them looked at me, startled, as if I'd intruded on a classroom lecture. "I need to get back to the paper."

There was a fine sheen of perspiration on Elizabeth's upper lip. A cluster of beggar's-lice splayed across her skirt. I felt a wave of admiration for her, standing out here in the humidity, a captive audience of one. Mr. McKeen pressed a jar of honey into her hands, and the four of us began a slow procession back to the store. Inside, they packed up Elizabeth's items in brown paper. She cradled a jar of peach butter and a handful of homemade herb soaps, smooth and beige like stones. Mr. McKeen tallied up the prices with a bitten-down nub of a pencil on a scrap of old newspaper.

"The strawberries will be in directly, so y'all come on back in a week or so," Mr. McKeen said.

"Goodness, yes. And peaches will be ready before we know it, too. And scuppernongs! Honey, you come dig yourself up one of them little fig trees out back anytime you want to," Miss McKeen whispered to Elizabeth. "And, like I said, just hang some pie tins on it when the birds start making a nuisance of themselves. They'll swaller figs up faster than you can say boo 'less you scare them off with some shine."

Outside, a butterscotch-colored dog sprawled across one of the benches, panting cheerfully.

"I see Candy has seen fit to come visit us again," Mr. McKeen said, as he scratched the dog's ears. "She's got her a litter somewhere, the way her dinner buckets are dragging the ground."

In the car, I apologized for leaving Elizabeth stranded. "Usually it just takes me a few minutes in cases like that," I said. "I'm sure it was exhausting, listening to those two."

"I wouldn't have thought to go in a place like that. . . ."

"Yeah, it's kind of in the middle of nowhere, isn't it? But it seems the McKeens' place has been there forever."

"Do they live there? I didn't see a house."

"Actually, they live right over the store. Never lived anywhere else. They took over the place from their daddy, who took it over from his, and so on and so on. That place has been there through all the wars."

"You mean before World War One?"

"I mean the Revolutionary War."

"I've never seen handmade herbal soaps like these." She rattled the little brown package in her lap.

"Yep. Like I told you, all you need is a list. They take it from there."

"Do you think we could go back? I mean when the strawberries come in in a couple of weeks?"

"Yeah. No problem. I'm around those parts at least once a week. I guess we could go by next week sometime."

"I'm not even sure I could remember how to get back here myself," she said. "But you seem to know about places. You know where everything is."

I nodded.

We were coming to the highway now and her neighborhood was just a few streets away. Her hands tightened around the packages on her lap as we pulled into her driveway. "Thanks, Cutter. For the . . . outing."

"Don't forget your visit to Father Bob's," I called to her when she got out. "I could pick you up tomorrow. We could go by the farmers' market."

She stood awkwardly, shifted her packages, looked across her front yard. "Yes," she said, after a minute. "I'd like that."

Eight

ELIZABETH OPENED HER EYES before dawn, watched the daylight begin to leak through the bedroom blinds. Outside, the stars would be disappearing, the black sky fading to the color of worn denim, a symphony of birdsong swelling. Daybreak was so . . . optimistic. So up and at 'em. From beside her, Daniel rose and disappeared into the bathroom, the shower surging and splattering like a sudden rainstorm. She got out of bed, tiptoed to the den, found her desk calendar, still on January, and turned it to April. She grabbed a felt-tip marker, drew a black star, and wrote, *Conference Open House HERE!* It was only two days away. She wrote down terse orders (*Clean bathroom! Freeze spinach quiche!*). She began a list of groceries. She heard the shower stop and made her way to the bathroom, knocked gently, then pushed the door open, the steam billowing around her. She blinked until Daniel came into focus, standing in front of the sink, rattling his razor in the water.

"You're up early."

"Actually, I'm planning." She watched him pat shaving cream on his cheeks, his chin, his neck, so there was no smile for her, no kiss, his expressions distorted by the poses and contortions of shaving. The sharp, clean smell of menthol reached for her, prickled her nose. She looked down at the list in her hand, felt it go soft and limp from the steam. *Honey*, she almost said, then stopped, realized she hated that word *honey,* that sexless, ugly, wife word.

"Do we have a final number yet?"

"Final number?" He looked puzzled.

"Yes. For the party. A head count."

He wiped down the mirror with a closed palm, met her eyes, and she watched the razor sliding sideways, a skier in the white lather snow moving over the plains of his cheeks, the hills and valleys of his chin and neck. He took the towel from around his waist, blotted his face, tousled his hair. Something in her stirred. She was suddenly conscious of her oversized Palmetto University T-shirt, the razor stubble on her legs, the clumps of her uncombed hair.

"Elizabeth—"

"Don't."

"I thought we agreed to reconsider this dinner."

"I want to have it. I told you. I can do it."

He rubbed a hand through her hair—short now, so short—and she felt his mouth graze her ear and then he sighed.

"I'll get a count today. I'll let you know this afternoon."

She nodded. She thought of how the night before he'd brought home square, thick Sicilian pizza—her favorite—a bottle of Burgundy, and a video. They'd sat together on the couch watching the movie—grim, Swedish, beautiful—and sipping wine. He'd rubbed the tops of her arms, squeezed her knee rhythmically. Like a heart pumping.

She followed him to the bedroom now, his gentle lope, watched him from the doorway, thought of how she used to secretly observe him from afar in an airport or restaurant lobby or class registration line, while he waited for her. It was a mischievous, daring habit she'd secretly cultivated their first years together. How many times had she lurked behind a post or potted palm, under a stairwell, beyond a store window watching him wait for her? Seeing him half distracted as he paced, scanned faces, gave directions, petted dogs, nodded to strangers. And she, hidden behind a clothes rack or crouched in the back of a bookstore, anticipated the moment of his delight in her.

But now he was all business, sorting his socks.

She saw him glance at the clock on the bedside table, watched him speed up his movements, sliding on clothes. Still, still . . . he did not turn fully to her, did not quiet her request with a kiss. He was careful, handling her as if she would break. She gathered her courage, thrust a question at him.

"Why did you sigh? I don't think I've heard you sigh . . . like that." Her voice was too high, thin. After he left, she would shower and dress, she would get ready for Cutter to pick her up. They were going to the farmers' market today. She would get all she needed there, she would begin cooking the side dishes tonight. The calendar in her head appeared, the grid of hours like a net.

"Sit down for a moment," he whispered. "I want to talk to you." She saw he had three different shades of navy socks in his hand. Mateless. He put them away, turned to her, rested his hands on her shoulders.

"I . . . I don't have time to sit."

"I made an appointment for you on Monday, with Dr. Grayson." The memory of nurses startled her like a flashbulb. Their efficient whispers, their sensible, rubber-soled shoes squeaking on immaculate hallways. "I've been worried."

"Why? I feel fine now. I'm—"

"Pale and sad," he said, cutting her off. "The other night . . ." His eyes were focused on her, glittering, dark green. Did his students ever see him like that, she wondered—humorless, almost stern? No. No, he would ignore the drowsy few pupils in the back rows, those who slumped in apathetic shoulder shrugs to questions. They would not draw his ire or his interest. Enough eyes were on him while he punched verses to life, caressed lines of poetry. She could see the rows of them, their rapt faces opening up to him like a time-enhanced film of tropical flowers bursting wide. And there were those who doted on him. Well, yes. Waiting for him, maybe, as she did once, at the end of a hall, in his office, in the library. She closed her eyes.

"You're stressed. And I don't think you need this Friday get-together to worry about." The pressure of his hands on her shoulders was insistent, and she let herself be seated, the bedsprings sighing softly, her feet dangling from that high bed like a child's.

"No! Daniel, really. I told you I'm perfectly fine." She felt as if she'd been slapped, looked it, too, judging from the bureau mirror that showed her the scarlet splotches high on her cheeks. "I'm fine," she said again. Then wondered about it. Maybe he was right. Maybe she wasn't fine at all.

The fat white mushroom of fear grew inside her.

"I think you should relax for a few days. Rest." He was tender but firm, the way he'd been after they lost the baby, when she'd come home from the hospital, lying in bed for days with her book of poems, leafing through, not even pretending to take notes anymore.

"I've got things under control," she told Daniel now, not quite meeting his eyes, instead noticing the furrow of lines that had deepened on his forehead. "Trust me."

She turned her back to him, began selecting a skirt from her closet. She put on her best blouse, determined that its starched whiteness, its round collar, its tiny perfect pleats would stay impeccable. She held her shoulders back, walked slowly into the kitchen, where Daniel drank a glass of orange juice, waiting for her.

"Do you need to go to the store this morning?"

It would be the easiest thing to do. He would drive them to the store and she would reach for his hand and he would keep it there, driving with one hand. He would swing the grocery cart wide at the end of food aisles, half reading a folded newspaper. He'd join her in the produce section, where she'd watch him gently cradle a peach in his palm, like holding a newborn thing. Daniel was her safe person.

"No, not today."

"I'll come home at lunchtime then and we—"

"No! Don't come home. There's no need. I have enough here at home to keep me busy."

He raised his eyebrows, and she felt a little thrill at the lie. By noon, she and Cutter would be at the market. She began a kind of cheerful busyness, a brave dismissal of him. Assembling ingredients in bowls, perusing her spice rack.

"You're sure? I've got some time around noon—"

"I'm sure."

"Okay, then."

He stood there for a minute, but she did not turn to him for a kiss. Finally, he left, the front door clicking shut.

She went to the bedroom and took off her blouse, examined it, ran her fingers over the pleats, the inside seams. It was wrinkled where she had tucked it in her skirt. She held it close to her face, and smelled herself there, the faint oily smell around the collar, the pungent prickly scent under the arms. She crumpled it, tossed it into the basket of dirty clothes, then emptied out the laundry on the floor and inspected it—balls of socks, damp towels, inside-out T-shirts. She moved to the closet, began to go through Daniel's clothes on hangers, running her hands down lapels, in pockets, frisking them, hating all those shirts and folded khakis for hiding secrets; they revealed nothing more than a crumpled gas receipt and a foil gum wrapper.

The pile of books and papers beside the bed was more promising, and it was there she found a letter still tucked in its crisp buff-colored envelope, addressed to Daniel at the university, her mother's handwriting slanted and cool on the thick paper with the gold-embossed *Mrs. David Cades III* on the top.

I have made some delicate inquiries. I have some contacts in a nearby very reputable Christian agency, one that would guarantee the birth mother's prenatal care, and so on. Please do not be offended, but I would gladly take care of the fee, the $10,000 they ask up front. Please, Daniel, do talk to Elizabeth. I am quite excited about this and have decided I'm through walking on eggshells around you two! Surely adoption is the right choice. (And really, how many times does a couple adopt and then find themselves pregnant. It's practically a cliché!) There are so many desperate young pregnant girls out there. This time next year you will have a child, and I will have a new grandchild! Take a look at the forms I have enclosed. My contact at the agency has assured me that you need only to show you are a stable, loving couple with solid finances, and a birth mother can be found quite easily. . . .

Her own mother. To send this letter to Daniel at the university and not to her, not to their home. And he didn't tell her.

The phone rang, jarring her.

"Elizabeth?"

"Cutter? Is that you?"

"Can you hear me? I was called in to work this morning, at the Pancake Palace. It's really noisy back here in the kitchen."

"Yes, I can hear you." Elizabeth found herself yelling in her own quiet house.

"We're slammed. One of the cooks didn't show. I hate to do this, but can we reschedule?" Cutter asked.

Elizabeth felt disappointment like a blow to the chest. It took the wind out of her, this news.

"You mean"—she didn't want to say it—"later today?"

"How about tomorrow?"

"Oh no! I can't. Not tomorrow. The party is coming up. . . . I mean, I have to . . ." Elizabeth closed her eyes for a minute, swallowed.

"Well, you could always drive over to Father Bob's if you like. I'll meet you later. Or you could call him yourself."

"Cutter, what if I meet you there at the Pancake Palace? I'll drive there and we can go to the market in your car. That would save some time, wouldn't it? If you didn't pick me up?"

"Well, yes. Sure. That would help. I can't promise I'll be through, but—"

"Just tell me how to get there, and I'll be on my way."

At the Pancake Palace, Elizabeth spotted Cutter right away. She was at the cash register ringing up a bill for a group of construction workers. After the line cleared, she looked over at Elizabeth.

"You're here!"

"Yes." Elizabeth looked around for a place to sit.

"Well, it doesn't look good. There's still silverware to roll and lemons to cut and salt and pepper to refill. And I'm stuck here at the register." With her sprinkle of freckles, her crooked half-smile, her tangled yellow thatch of hair, Cutter reminded Elizabeth of a doll played with too much, left ragged and soft in a corner.

"Oh. I see. I'll just . . . wait for you. I don't mind." Elizabeth sat down on a vinyl stool by the gumball machines.

Cutter screwed her eyes up a little, cocked her head to the side as she peered over at Elizabeth. She closed the cash drawer with a little *ka-ching*. "I was thinking. Since you're here and all . . . maybe you could help?"

"Help? With . . . *here*?"

"You could refill the salt shakers."

"Oh, Cutter, I don't . . . I'll just come back when you're—"

"No, really. It's easy. I'll start bringing the empty shakers and you take this"—she lugged a big carton of salt from under the counter with a grunt—"and just fill 'em up. Okay?"

Elizabeth nodded. "Oh, well, okay."

"I really hate to ask you, but we are so buried this morning."

Cutter disappeared into the dining room. After a few minutes of topping off salt shakers, Elizabeth glanced up to see a waitress motioning to her from the back of the restaurant. Elizabeth looked at her blankly, until the woman began wagging her arms fiercely, as if she were trying to flag down a motorist. Elizabeth pointed to herself, and the woman nodded vigorously. *Yeah, you*, she mouthed. Elizabeth felt a slow warm flush move down her face and throat. The woman began hissing and whistling. Where was Cutter? Elizabeth looked across the dining room and spotted her, standing at a large table writing down orders on her little pad. Elizabeth tried to catch Cutter's eye, but instead was snagged by the woman's frantic stare. Elizabeth finally put down the salt carton and tentatively walked to the back.

"Well, thank the Lord. You're the pal, right?"

"I beg your pardon?"

"Cutter's friend? I see you're helping up there, but we need you worse back here. I can't leave the grill, and I got to see to my tables. I thought maybe you could keep an eye on things for a minute."

The woman had moved back behind the grill, where bacon burned, and she began fanning smoke away with a movie magazine, coughing distractedly. "I'm Jolene, by the way," she managed to croak.

Elizabeth shook her head. "I'm sorry, but I'm not—"

"Now what you do is just finish up the eggs and stuff I already started here." The woman began to pour a cup of something yellow and slippery over the large grill. She coughed again from the steam and smoke. Now she was handing Elizabeth an apron and a spatula. She was giving her orders! "Sound like a plan?"

"No, it's—I mean it's not legal, is it, for me to be back here without—"

"Oh, now don't worry about that paperwork stuff. Half the people who work here are off the books. They don't exist in the eyes of Uncle Sam, if you know what I mean. As for pay, well, today I'll personally give you half my tips if you cook just long enough to get us the hell out of this jammed-up morning."

Elizabeth wondered if she should return home. Or find Cutter. This wasn't very calming or sensible. What was she doing here?

"Okay, so like I said, just throw some more bacon on there, add about a dozen eggs scrambled light, two over easy, and four more pancakes. Batter's right over there—"

There was a tattooed barbed-wire chain around the woman's wiry little bicep.

"—the bacon and country ham is back there. Grits right here and I got a little pile of hash browns going back there. . . . Think ya can handle it?"

But before Elizabeth could answer that no, she didn't think she could handle it, that she couldn't, wouldn't handle it at all, that she should just fold napkins or restock Sweet n' Low packets or something reasonable, the woman was heading to a table halfway across the room, drawing out her little pad of paper from her apron and the pencil from behind her ear. Elizabeth began to poke at the link sausages until they bubbled and hissed, like disturbed vipers.

They were in Cutter's car now with the top down, winding through the narrow streets of Sans Souci.

"I can't believe we made it out of there with time to spare. That was incredible. If you hadn't helped, I'd still be there."

"I'm not sure how incredible the food was," Elizabeth muttered. "As a matter of fact, it looked pretty dreadful. I still can't believe you actually served it to people. I can't believe I was cooking like that."

"Are you kidding? Compared to what folks there are used to getting, that was downright gourmet."

They turned onto the highway, the air snatching their words.

"Oh, did I tell you? Later on this afternoon I'm taking Alfred with me to the paper," Cutter shouted. "His first day working there. He's really excited."

"You really look out for them over there at Father Bob's, don't you?" Elizabeth asked. Screamed.

She wasn't accustomed to a convertible, the way it called attention, the way everyone stared at you at red lights. There was no place to hide. You were there, exposed, in the front seat. It was like being onstage. Like being naked, for God's sake. Like being famous. A truck honked behind them on the highway, a hand waved. She'd heard whistles. "Don't pay attention to that. You get used to it in a car like this." Cutter smiled, her blonde hair snapping in the air like whips.

"Somebody has to look out for them. This morning they had a fence put up so the cat can't get out. Can you believe that? Like a fence is going to contain a cat. And Alfred told me they picked up a load of kittens from the animal shelter. That's what he said, a load."

Elizabeth sat up very straight and touched her hair again. She found herself combing her fingers through her hair a lot now, feeling the shortness of it, the unevenness. Funny how cutting her hair made it more important to her. She had to make an effort to feel it now, to remember it with her hands.

When Cutter had appeared at her door yesterday, Elizabeth noticed that her newly shorn hair hadn't shocked her. That meant she knew, had heard about Daniel coming home to find Elizabeth holed up in the bathroom, hacking at her hair. And that made her wary for a minute. Did they all talk about her? Were they going to put her away? When she looked into Cutter's eyes to tell her she was sorry, that she was fine, she just needed to be alone, Elizabeth saw something that beckoned in Cutter's expression: pity, yes, but a stubborn kindness, too, and that demanded a response, didn't it?

Cutter was leaning near her, saying something about her house.

"What?" Elizabeth asked. She looked down at her own hands, at her squared-off, nail-bitten fingers. So far she was holding up okay, she was all right.

"About the house—I'm getting desperate. Mrs. Worthington figured out when I'm not there. I know she's going to start showing the house then." Elizabeth could see herself reflected in Cutter's sunglasses—shrinking, squinting, smallish. "My brother is hounding me. I'll feel a lot better when the house is off the market."

"I'll feel better when I can get this party over with." She saw Cutter study her for a small sharp instant, before she turned to stare back at the road. She had noticed Cutter had looked at her like that several times, tilting her head, sneaking glances when she thought Elizabeth didn't notice.

They turned off the highway, entered the town limits of Sans Souci. They stopped at a red light, and then Cutter was honking the horn, waving at someone coming out of the post office across the street. Elizabeth felt herself stiffen. She didn't feel like talking to any more strangers today. When the light turned green, Cutter swerved in the parking lot, and the man walked over to them, younger than she had thought at first, late twenties, maybe, wearing a yellow tie, a dark suit, a starched, crisp white shirt. Cutter pushed her sunglasses onto her head, looked up at him, beamed.

"I'm taking my friend on a tour of the town," she announced. She and the man both looked at Elizabeth, who managed a tight smile. "Curtis Sams, meet Elizabeth Byers." He offered his hand, and Elizabeth shook it, felt her own hand shrink in its too-warm meatiness. "He's my boss," Cutter explained.

"Join me at Painters for a shake?" he asked.

Elizabeth looked at Cutter, mouthed, *Painters?*

"It's just over there," Cutter whispered, pointing to a little storefront across the parking lot. "The drugstore. But they have the best ice cream around."

"I've got to get back soon," he said, "and take a look at the photos from last night's basketball game that new stringer brought in." He was drawing himself up now, this man, all serious. "But we could just get a cone or something."

"Okay, we'd be honored." Cutter was cheerful and eager, her hands splayed flat on the steering wheel, pinky fingers curled.

Inside the store, he insisted on ordering and paying for three milk shakes, told them to pick a booth and sit down, all the while maintaining he was in a hurry, had deadlines. He liked taking care of things, Elizabeth saw that right away. His smile was pleasant enough, she told herself, politeness sparkling there in the white, straight work of some country club orthodontist. When they all sat down, and he began a courteous conversation with Elizabeth, asking her about where she grew up, how she liked Sans Souci, she began to like him. He was mannered but not too stuffy, civil in the way that gets strangers through awkward moments, and there was something to be said about that. It was a dying art. She began to relax a little. Why, these were her friends. She was having a snack at a little café in town with her own friends, and she was enjoying it. She was not feeling numb, the way she sometimes did when she took pills, when the world around her grew flat and gray and sluggish. At any other time, panic might be hiccupping inside her, the black-and-white tile floor here confusing with its demands of yes and no, night and day, good and bad. The smell of the grilled ham and cheese sandwich that wafted over from the next table might repulse her, remind her of the process of digestion, of absorption, converting matter into energy, as any Biology 101 student knew.

"It's right up here," Cutter yelled. "See up there above the light?"

Elizabeth nodded.

"You never know what stuff the farmers' market will have. Pole beans, tomatoes, okra, potatoes, peanuts. But that's part of the fun."

They pulled into a half-empty parking lot. "There's a trick to opening the car door," Cutter said as Elizabeth struggled with the handle. "The passenger door has never recovered from—some trauma, I don't know what. Here, I'll open it for you."

A layer of duct tape on the seat grabbed Elizabeth's skirt as she got out. She could see the mildewed foam rubber underneath, like a wound. She stood for a minute looking out across the parking lot to the market.

"Usually I just walk from home," Cutter said. "But I knew you'd want to load up on stuff. I figured we'd need the car."

Elizabeth shielded her eyes and squinted, as if she were looking out over the ocean. She saw stalls and tables, a pickup truck loaded with cabbage. She and Cutter walked between two large sheltered areas lined with boxes of fruit and vegetables.

"Oh yeah. Another thing. You're expected to bargain here," Cutter whispered. "Don't get suckered in."

Walking between the stalls, Elizabeth felt the wind tease her skirt. A family dumped out a sack of red potatoes, the clumps of dirt rolling across the table and landing on her sandals. They passed a stall heaped with tomatoes. A toothless woman wearing a Braves baseball cap sat in a rocking chair, holding a kitten, stroking it slowly.

"Here's your tomaters, girls," she said.

"Don't stop," Cutter whispered. "They don't look so good."

"Well . . ." Elizabeth said, slowing down despite herself. There was country music coming from a radio somewhere, tinny, sad voices, drawn-out words. Someone else's sadness. Someone was out of a job, out of love. The woman looked at her. She had the innocent, gummy smile of an infant. Elizabeth stopped. The woman took it as a yes.

"Hold Puss here, while I getcha some." Elizabeth stroked the purring kitten, scraggly, as light and soft as a cotton ball, and then she found herself with a bag of green tomatoes. When she tried to hand the kitten back, he mewed miserably, his tiny curved claws pulling at her sweater. It had been so long since she's held anything so . . . helpless. Her eyes watered. Oh, for goodness's sake. Getting choked up over a kitten. But she hadn't expected the maternal instincts flooding her veins like a drug. The need to cradle something, protect it, just for a minute. Awhile longer.

"Why don't you just borrow him awhile? When you finish shopping, then you bring him back," the woman said, winking at her.

"Oh, well, no. Here, I better give him back now." The kitten would have none of it, clinging and hissing. Finally, the woman reached over and took the kitten back in one firm swipe. "There, now," the woman said, holding it to her chest. "Purring already."

Before they left the market, Elizabeth bought fresh chives and dill, rosemary and oregano, two bags of onions and potatoes, a box of green peppers, a string of dried red peppers, eight crooked neck squash. She purchased a framed collection of butterflies, pressed into yellowed cotton, the glass dusty and cracked with age. And then there were the flowers, the half-torn quart milk cartons with the beginnings of black-eyed Susans, coneflowers, butterfly bush. And a dozen little bags of seeds—hard and small like pills, large fluffy burrs, little soft and striped globes. All kinds, all colors. Seeds.

"You liked that kitten, didn't you?" Cutter yelled as they zipped back down Main Street. "That one back at the market. Why don't you have a pet?"

"I don't know, out of the habit of having one, I guess."

They were heading back into downtown Sans Souci. They turned onto a side street. The Bradford pear trees in front of the town hall were shedding petals, and they blew across the road feathery and white, like snow.

"Cutter?" Elizabeth wanted to go home. She wanted to be home now. "I'm really ready to go home." But Cutter was ignoring her. And speeding. Elizabeth leaned and rifled through the bags of herbs and vegetables at her feet, dug through them and let her fingers run over the knobs and lumps and leaves. She found a potato, closed her eyes and smelled it. The earthy dampness of it calmed her. She held it under her nose, breathed in deeply, like fending off a heart attack with nitroglycerin.

They turned onto Gerard Avenue and pulled into the driveway of an old two-story brick house. Elizabeth glanced at Cutter's house across the street, then looked away quickly. Maybe Ginnie was there, even now. No. No, Cutter wouldn't do that, wouldn't bring her here if Ginnie were anywhere near. Still, she felt the house's presence behind her like a stare.

"They must have finished it this morning."

"Finished what?"

"The fence," Cutter said, pointing to a wooden fence that severed the front yard of the brick house from the sidewalk. "This is Father Bob's. Remember I told you about the fence to keep the cat in?"

"I'd like to go home now, if you don't mind. I'm tired and I don't know where I am and I have a lot to do."

But Cutter did not appear to hear her.

"Cutter, I said I'd like to go home—"

"They told me they went to the animal shelter yesterday after Spot didn't come back. They went to get a new cat, that's what Father Bob said. And, of course, they got an extra one—I mean, Alfred and Father Bob in an animal shelter with all those animals on death row, of course they're gonna get an extra kitten or two—"

"I can see where this is going. I can't handle a pet right now."

"C'mon." Cutter was already out of the car.

Elizabeth shook her head. Why couldn't Cutter understand that being this close to where Ginnie lived was hard? Almost unbearable. "I just want to go home," she yelled. "Can you make my excuses to Father Bob?"

The front door of Father Bob's house opened. Alfred appeared and stood on the front porch, smiling. He waved to them. He was cradling something, its longish arms around his neck, its slight, thin body hanging down on his chest, like a heavy black amulet. He walked over to them. The thing on his chest was making covert, hostile little movements and when Alfred got closer they saw it was a monkey.

"What have you got there, Alfred?" Cutter asked. Elizabeth struggled with the car door until it opened, stepped out. Cutter turned to her, hissed, "I should have never let them go to the animal shelter without me."

They walked past the wooden gate to where Alfred stood, still grinning. Elizabeth reached out and began stroking the stiff, black fur on the monkey's back. It turned its face to her, a little leathery old-man face. It bared its teeth.

"He likes me. He don't like no one else."

"So we see," Cutter said.

Father Bob ambled out from the backyard. He wore overalls over his black shirt, and his clerical collar was limp and translucent from perspiration. He carried a shovel. He swiped at the beaded sweat on his forehead with the back of a hand and fumbled for his glasses in a pocket.

"Cutter." He said her name sheepishly. "I should explain"—he gestured with a half roll of his head—"all this. Oh, hello," he said, seeing Elizabeth, sliding on his glasses. "Elizabeth, isn't it? I'm so glad you could visit." He reached out his hand to her then noticed with a start the rinds of black under his nails, drew it back and smiled instead. "I was glad to be of service the other day with the jumper cables, my dear—" He broke off when he saw the way Cutter stared at Alfred and the monkey.

"Crusty is a monkey," he explained.

"You adopted a monkey named Crusty?"

"Crusty was in one of those horrible zoos at a gas station. Horrible places."

"And?"

"And—" Father Bob cleared his throat. "And he irritated the customers, so he ended up at the animal shelter, where we saw him, and, of course, we—"

"He irritated customers."

"He was practically being tortured." Father Bob looked at Elizabeth now, pleading with his eyes.

"Does this monkey bite?" Cutter asked. "Does he attack?"

"Oh, heavens, no."

"Because the state will be out here in no time to close you down—"

"He doesn't bite or scratch. He's not aggressive that way at all. He—"

No one spoke and Cutter raised her eyebrows then shifted her weight to her other leg, the gravel crunching under her feet. Father Bob shifted his gaze back to Elizabeth.

"He has been abused, we feel certain, you know. But he's not violent at all. He just—he acts out his aggressive tendencies by—" Father Bob paused again and looked around at the two of them, peering over his glasses. His face twisted painfully as he spoke. "He climbs to high places and—defecates in his hand and then throws the offensive matter at round objects."

"Round objects? Like what—balloons, plates?"

"Yes, yes! Or balls or—heads." He chuckled uneasily. "For some reason he despises roundness. It has something to do with his torture, you see. Balls were thrown at him to win prizes. As you can well imagine, taking into consideration the basic Pavlovian concepts of conditioned responses and association, he would, quite naturally—"

"What do you feed a monkey?" Elizabeth interrupted, a silly question, but she had to say something. She felt sorry for Father Bob.

"Well, fruit. We've found he's especially fond of pineapple," he said, looking at her, half smiling, grateful for her question. "And, believe it or not, Purina does make a monkey chow."

"Monkey chow?" Cutter snorted.

"Yes. It comes from Frank's Feed and Seed. Of course, you have to special-order it."

Alfred, knees bent, was swaying, rocking the monkey gently, and it appeared to be asleep. Its eyelids, black and rubbery, reminded Elizabeth of bat wings. "Monkey chow comes in *great* big old bags."

Father Bob had walked behind them and closed the gate. He had a pinched, nervous look. "The men have been working on the pens and the fences in the back," he said hesitantly. "It's a good project. Good for the men."

A shrill warbling rose from the back. The four of them walked to the side yard silently, Father Bob leading the way with a nervous trot, not turning back to look at them even when Cutter groaned. Across the lawn and in the small garden were a sleeping pile of kittens, several scraggly hens and roosters, a dog, and a peacock.

"Oh my God," Cutter said.

Elizabeth watched a pudgy, bald man hammer a plank of wood, his round tongue wiggling in his mouth like a parrot's. The dog was tugging at his shoelaces, but he didn't seem to notice. He waved to them, still holding his hammer. Elizabeth stood beside Alfred, just watching. Those chickens—such nervous, twitchy things.

Elizabeth watched Cutter take Father Bob's arm. She escorted him away from her and Alfred. Still, she could hear parts of their serious, whispered conversation: *regulations, zoning, rules, health department. What about when all the families visit on Sundays? What then?* Alfred was slowly swaying, still staring down at the monkey. "Spot is our first cat," he said, looking up suddenly at her. "He's a miracle cat, but he don't like kittens."

Elizabeth walked over to the kittens. She picked up two of them. She stroked their faces and their whiskers, already coarse and stiff, like fishing line.

"I'll take these kittens," she said. Father Bob and Cutter stopped talking and stared at her. The monkey jumped out of Alfred's arms. It sprinted toward Father Bob and leapt onto his shoulder. The creature peered at Elizabeth with a flat, dark gaze, then drew its lips back in a scowl and applauded. Elizabeth heard herself laughing then. Laughing.

They had one more stop. The last one, Cutter promised. A favor, a gift to Elizabeth for taking the kittens. They drove a street over, parked, and got out, each of them holding a kitten. They walked around to a basement entrance of a weathered little bungalow, and

Elizabeth saw it was a beauty parlor. Inside, there were two large
sinks in the back, a row of old-fashioned hair dryers flanking a
wall, the smell of permanent solution and hair spray crashing down
on her, pummeling her like a wave, sucking away her breath.

"Lord, what you got there, Cutter?" A lady in a pink pantsuit
and puffy red hair stopped sweeping and squinted at them, her
shiny blue eye shadow crinkled.

"Kittens."

"Well, looka here now. I don't need no kittens round here so—"

"Oh, we're not here to give away the kittens, Darla. These kittens belong to my friend here. Elizabeth is new in town and she
needs a trim and I recommended you, of course."

"Oh, well, why didn't you say so?" She pointed to a chair where
Elizabeth was to sit. Cutter held the kittens in another chair and
twirled around while Darla adjusted her hearing aid.

"You want a lollipop like the old days?"

"No." But Cutter smiled.

Darla chuckled, began to comb out Elizabeth's hair. "Used to do
her grandma's hair every Friday at four. Shampoo and set."

"Uh, Darla, I think Elizabeth just wants a touch-up."

Elizabeth nodded. It was easier just to go along.

Darla made a quick fierce face. "Mercy! Who got ahold of your
hair last time? Musta been blind. Or drunk. Bet you went to one
of those mall places over in Palmetto? Well, I'll fix you up good."
She sprayed water on Elizabeth's hair and combed and combed
until Elizabeth began to feel her eyes half close in drowsiness, her
shoulders slump.

"Oh, she used to just tickle me no end, that Myrtle Ann." Darla
glanced at Cutter. "That time your grandma came in here fit to be
tied 'cause she had cut herself on some rusty barbed wire out in her
garden and the doctor's office told her she was gonna have to come
in for a tetanus shot. Well, she told me she cut a tiny hole in her
underdrawers where they could give her a shot, 'cause she wasn't
getting nekkid for no one. I like to died. I said, 'Myrtle Ann, you

ain't got nothing no doctor alive hadn't seen.' But she said, 'Well he's not seeing mine.'" She chuckled, looked at Cutter in the mirror. "She was a might old-fashioned, your grandma, but she was funny." She began snipping at Elizabeth's hair, slowly at first, then faster. "Oh, she was funny."

"I ran into Misty. Her hair looks really good. She said you did it."

"Yes, she came in here the other morning fit to be tied. Her daddy worries her so, being alone at the station so much and him with that bad ticker. I told her Buddy was stubborn and ornery as a mule, always has been, and there was no need to try to change him now. I guess she told you she's engaged?"

"She showed me her ring. She wants me to be maid of honor."

"Her fiancé is coming up in the next day or two."

"Tell them to come eat at the Pancake Palace so I'll get to meet him."

"I sure will."

"If they miss me, tell them to come by the house one night. I'm always there."

"Cutter, honey, how y'all getting along in that big old house?"

"We're not. Getting along, I mean."

"I guess everything will work out when it finally gets sold."

"It's not, Darla. We're—I mean I'm not selling it." The snipping stopped as Darla looked at Cutter.

"Oh, well, I didn't know that. I'm glad to hear you're staying." She started combing out Elizabeth's hair now, blew it dry, then took off the plastic smock so Elizabeth could stand up, take a closer look. She looked elfin, unfettered, her hair a tight shiny cap, her small ears pleated and pale as orchids.

"You know, I don't get your type hair round here too often. Most of the time, the bigger the better. That's the way the ladies want it." She picked up a comb again, touched up Elizabeth's hair. "But I declare, I think this look does right well. It suits you." Cutter was nodding, and Elizabeth ran her hands through her bangs. "It's very chic," Darla said, with satisfaction. "Very chic." But she pronounced it *chick* and Cutter and Elizabeth looked at each other, shared a stifled giggle as they left.

They put the top of the car up before they headed back to the Pancake Palace to pick up Elizabeth's car. Elizabeth held the kittens in her lap, their triangular, startled faces peering up at her. When they mewed, she could see their pink trembling tongues, their tiny teeth.

"What happened to the rest of your family?" she asked Cutter when they were back on the highway.

"You mean who's left?"

"I mean what happened to everyone?"

"Well, I told you about my dad, right?

"Vietnam."

"Right. After two tours. He'd come back and then my mother would be pregnant and then he'd go back and then finally he didn't come back at all. After my father died, my mother moved us in with Gran. And my grandmother died last fall, suddenly. She went to bed one night, didn't wake up. Like she refused to wake up, seems to me, like she decided to just . . ."

"What happened to your mother?"

"Car accident. I was only two when she died, so I don't remember much about her. Just little pieces of things. Like, when she thought we were asleep, my mother would come in and lie down between Ginnie and me. She would smell like cigarette smoke and lilac perfume. I remember that. My grandmother would put us to bed at night while my mother typed and typed because she was trying to finish her degree in secretarial science from Miss Sylvia's Business School for Ladies. Gran said my mother would type half the night, trying to get her words per minute up. And I can remember that—*punch punch click* from the typewriter. I guess that's why she smoked. To stay awake while she did all that typing. Funny, though, my mother had three children, was twenty-three years old, and still hid her cigarettes from Gran." Cutter smiled a little. "Then one day, my mother was dead, killed by a trucker who had driven a produce truck straight up from Miami. The trooper said he fell asleep at the wheel."

"That must have been horrible. For all of you. Your grandmother left to raise three babies. How did she do it?"

"That's what they kept asking her, all those ladies from church. The casserole brigade, we called them. They kept bringing fried chicken and Jell-o salads and casseroles for months. But I remember one of the women came up to Gran and asked her, 'Whatever will you do, Myrtle Ann?' My grandmother said, 'Why, we'll go on. We have to.'"

They pulled into the parking lot of the Pancake Palace, and Elizabeth got into her car. Cutter insisted on following Elizabeth home with the kittens and packages. "That way we'll only have to unload once," she said, and Elizabeth couldn't argue with that logic. She realized she wasn't ready for the afternoon to end anyway. When they got to Elizabeth's house, Cutter dragged the box of vegetables up to the door while Elizabeth struggled with holding two kittens and finding her keys. Inside, Elizabeth put the kittens down and helped Cutter slide in the box of produce and the bags of cat litter and cat food that Father Bob had insisted they take.

"Here, have a stuffed grape." Elizabeth came from the kitchen and held out a plate.

She watched Cutter start to nibble delicately, tenuously, then take bigger bites. "Delicious. I mean, they're nutty but they're juicy, too."

"Help yourself."

Elizabeth watched Cutter finish, then use her finger to sponge up the last of the crumbs on the plate. "These are good."

"You think so? Nothing tastes quite right yet. I mean, the soufflé wasn't fluffy enough, the quiche was runny, the crusts weren't flaky. I'm so out of practice. So far, nothing is good enough for . . . the party."

Elizabeth started unloading the dishwasher. She moved quickly, shoving wooden spoons in the crock on the counter, knives in the block, the pastry cutter in the utensil drawer. She looked down at Cutter, who was on her knees putting up the vegetables in the produce drawer of the refrigerator, and said, "I'm afraid I can't 'go on,' as your grandmother put it."

Cutter looked up at her.

Elizabeth realized how strange she must seem, blurting out something cryptic like that. "By now, I thought we would have a baby, maybe two. But I realized I just couldn't handle a baby until I—now I think I've been selfish. Daniel has been patient."

Cutter still stared, and something passed across her features—what? shame? shock?—before she looked away.

"And I'm not going to pay someone a hundred dollars an hour to tell me to go to my imaginary happy place." Elizabeth closed a drawer hard. Cutter perched on one of the stools at the island. "I'm okay if I just stay in the house and once in a while I'll cook or do a little gardening. If I have the dirt to plunge my hands into, the food creations, and now kittens . . . well, that makes me stronger. I can even handle people now. Honestly, I feel better! I think you've jump-started me. I really do. Daniel and I—well, we go through periods of being shut off from each other, but we have times of perfect contentment. We love each other, and we'll get it together again."

It occurred to her then how she'd had her own affair—with despair, coddled fear like a mistress—but she didn't say it. She leaned back against the counter, relief washing over her face. "Cutter, it's not like me to talk so personally, but I guess I'm telling you this so you don't feel like you have to take on the world for me. You've taken on enough. And there will come a day soon, very soon, when it won't be possible for us to be friends. I understand that, and you should, too. I won't take offense when you don't want to talk to me anymore." Elizabeth smiled again, but Cutter was looking down, very still, and all Elizabeth could see was the part running down the middle of her blonde hair, like a fence dividing a field of hay.

Nine

"Look," I said to Orrin Jones, the pushiest undertaker in town, "you can't list every relative the guy has. You know that. And as far as the Jenkinson obit? We don't print 'survived by a bunch of relatives and friends.' It's not our policy. You have to be specific. But not too specific—no half-nieces, or stepuncles . . . Sir, will you listen to me?"

Charlie scowled at me over his glasses like a fierce figure on a totem pole, all downturned mouth, saggy jowls, and long, fleshy ears.

I hung up the phone and turned to him. "On top of listing every relative this dead guy had, the funeral home wants us to promise not to print his real name in the obit. They want him listed as 'Shortcake' Johnson. They said it was his dying wish."

He grunted. "That's what they all say. Everything's a dying wish."

Charlie looked at Alfred, who was standing at the end of my desk, hands on hips, eyes on the ceiling, then the windows, the heaps and piles of paper on desks and in corners. For Alfred, who loved order, the clutter of the newsroom teetered between overwhelming and irresistible.

"Who's your friend?"

"This is Alfred," I said.

"What is he, deaf or something?"

"He's going to help out around here. I cleared it with Mr. Sams. And, no, he's not deaf."

I put my hand on Alfred's arm. "Come on. I'll show you where the break room is."

We walked down to the basement. The break room, across the hall from the large, rumbling furnace, was small and windowless. The intricate network of pipes that protruded from the ceiling reminded me of submarine scenes in old war movies. You had to scrunch yourself down to walk around in there. Everyone looked hunched and humbled. There was a microwave (with a *Clean up your own mess. Your mama don't live here* sign), a sink, a refrigerator, a drink machine, and a table with a few orange plastic chairs. Half a dozen white dress shirts and a gaggle of loud ties fluttered and jostled from hangers on a ceiling pipe. One of the sports reporters and a copy editor, Marti Miller, who was loud and funny and often rude, sat at the table. Marti should have retired years ago, she looked ancient, but claimed she was needed here too much to quit. Her raspy, deep voice regularly boomed across the newsroom. ("Okay, everyone, pick up your goddamn AP style books. Got 'em? Now turn to page seventy-eight. See the entry on *further* and *farther*? Now read it!") Alfred and I sat down on two of the chairs with our drinks, glad to be ignored.

"They're going to sell, mark my words," Marti said to the reporter. She had nicotine-stained fingers, a droopy, wrinkled face with wide, rubbery lips. She wore pink or orange or beige knit pantsuits with vests and white sandles.

"Who would buy this place?" he said. I remembered his name was Joel. He was a hard worker, put in extra hours all the time. You could see he was hungry to move up and out. He'd come aboard the *Citizen* right after college.

"I have it on good authority that one of those mega media companies is eyeing us. They'll snap us up, just like they're snapping up the Palmetto rag, and fold us inside like egg whites in a cake. Sans Souci will be lucky to have its own half-page section."

"But what about all the news, the coverage—"

"News? Huh, huh. News. This is about advertisements. About revenue. Not news."

"What makes you think the Sams will sell? They don't need the money."

Marti laughed, a bark that ratcheted up to a smoker's wet cough. "Have you ever heard of anybody rich who didn't need more money? They're cheaper than anyone. They're addicted to money. That kind always is. And let me share another little tidbit. This paper hasn't turned a profit for a while now."

"So what are you saying? We're going to be bought out by one of those news companies that nixes any kind of in-depth reporting or special features or long articles?"

"You got it, kid."

"Nothing longer than six inches?"

"That's their rule. Reminds me of my ex-husbands. All of them."

When Alfred and I left, we could still hear Marti's cackling halfway up the stairs.

Back in the newsroom, Charlie waved me over to his desk. "M.B. was looking for you."

"He was?"

"Said it was important."

I found Curt in his office, putting on a tie.

"What took you so long? Have a seat."

I sat down across from his desk. His nameplate said *Curtis Galli-van Price Sams,* a name that sounded like an entire law firm.

"Chocolate milk shake," he said. "Lucky I keep a few extra ties here."

I nodded. It was one of those new rules he had instigated: all male staffers had to wear ties. It had caused a lot of grumbling, especially in the sports department, where the editor, Rooster Russell, was considered dressed up if he showed up in pants instead of shorts. But Rooster had finally given in. Sort of. Actually he kept a black polyester clip-on tie in his desk drawer and he just stuck it on his wrinkled, faux-Izod shirt. I'd heard him mumbling about how he wasn't going to be "out on the goddamn green or the fuckin' football field dressed like a pretty boy—like a damn fruit." I looked out through Curt's one-way window and watched Alfred cleaning desks, shooing people out of the way, then turning chairs over and cleaning springs.

"Is this about Alfred?"

"Alfred?" He looked up at me blankly. "Oh, that's right, your friend." He glanced out into the newsroom. "Looks like he knows what he's doing."

"He has this preternatural talent for seeing order."

Curt stood up, stretched, cracked his knuckles. Out of the one-way window, two reporters scurried between desks, slinging papers to each other over desktops. I was mesmerized, but in a guilty way, as if I were spying.

Curt took off his glasses now and rubbed his eyes, blinked at me, looking vulnerable and a little weary. It occurred to me that I was about to be fired, that I was going to hear a speech about tightening belts and profit and loss and how the paper could no longer afford the luxury of the dead beat.

"I was wondering if you might be interested in a little something new I'm trying. I'm thinking about a small column or sidebar on the editorial page, an 'on this day fifty years ago' kind of thing."

"You mean instead of the dead beat?"

"In addition to your obituary duties. With a little research, you find some historical anniversary dates. And maybe include local people and what they're doing now—like the veterans. You could go and interview them."

He leaned back in his chair, his forehead shining a little from the fluorescent light.

"Check out the veterans' hospital in Palmetto or the Sans Souci nursing home. Or just check with your usual sources in town and follow your nose. I trust you."

He was doing me a favor.

"Okay," I said. "I'll do it."

"It just fits in the plan, doesn't it?" He was excited now, stood up and began to pace. "Push community. Inspire loyalty, sell those ads here, right?"

I nodded, half distracted by Audrey, the lifestyle editor, a heavy-set, red-faced woman who wore her suits too tight, her Windsong perfume too strong. She huffed and puffed by the window with a stack of bridal photos. She paused at her desk looking lost in thought, then began flexing her butt cheeks rhythmically, a secret exercise, or maybe just a nervous habit. I looked away, embarrassed, but Curt hadn't noticed.

"Cutter, we have got to keep them subscribing. We have to keep this town alive. Not let Palmetto gobble us up. We're fighting for our lives, you know, when we're fighting that city. People don't realize . . ."

He turned from me, settled back in his chair, the rich, confident sound of leather crackling. "Of course you'll receive a small raise. We'll talk about that later. Agreed?"

"Okay." I stood up.

"Everything in the morgue is pretty well organized," he said. "The back issues are all there. Your research should be a snap."

I nodded.

"What's wrong?"

"I was just . . . well, have you given any more thought to calling a meeting today?"

He sighed. "To tell you the truth, Cutter, I'm not prepared."

"I've heard some things. There are rumors that you might be selling the paper to some big company that will fold us into the Palmetto rag."

"Where on earth did you hear that?"

"And that the paper isn't making a profit and that you're looking to sell it."

"That's ridiculous. That would be the death of the paper. I'd never consider—"

"Well, then you better tell them."

"And how does one allay their fears when indiscriminate rumors are flying around and they choose to listen to them?"

"Tell them what you just told me. The truth has a better ring to it."

"You think so?"

"I know so. And there's something else. You need to prove you didn't hatch from a pod or beam down from an alien craft and that you're warm-blooded after all and not zipped up in a humanoid suit."

"But how am I going to hide my Day-Glo green skin and these almond eyes?"

"I have a couple of ideas," I said.

"I have a few announcements, folks," Curt said, "if you'll gather around."

He stood on my desk in the center of the newsroom. There was a lot of grumbling and eye rolling and muttering *what now?* But after a minute he got his audience, the staff swelled around him.

"Thanks. I, uh . . . I won't keep you long. I just want to start by saying . . . I'd like for us all to have a dialogue and start meeting weekly. There will be food"—he tapped the Krispy Kreme dough-nut boxes beside him—"and, I hope, your ideas on how we can improve the *Citizen*." He held up his hand. "Some of you may have heard rumors about our paper being on the block, and that's just not true. Now, don't get me wrong, you'll always have compa-nies sniffing around, especially papers like ours with strong reader-ship and solid ad history. But our circulation is up. Ad space is looking good. Still, we have little margin for error. I'm not going to lie to you. We are now in the shadow of a very aggressive big-city paper out there. We have to keep an edge. Better news, more coverage . . ." He looked at me. "But, uh, basically what I mean is you all are doing a great job and we're carving ourselves a niche out here, we're a vital part of the community, hell, we *are* the community. By next week's meeting, I'd like everyone to bring an idea to the table about a way to improve the paper. News, sports, ads, delivery, whatever. The next six months are crucial."

Tell them, I thought. *Tell them.*

"There's one more thing. I—I'd like to announce a change. From now on ties are no longer required in the newsroom." There was an outburst of deep-throated yells and claps. Ties were flung in the air. The sports guys were whistling.

"I would just hasten to add," Curt said, "when out covering events in the community or interviewing, I'd like you to use your judgment and, of course, if the situation calls for . . ." But his voice was drowned out. "Are there any questions?" he added, louder.

"Yeah, you got any custard-filled doughnuts in there?" someone asked.

"I've always loved this street," Curt said when we reached Gerard Avenue. "Which house is yours?" I pointed. He parked at the curb. "Wow. It's a beaut."

My Fiat had balked about starting, so Curt had given Alfred and me a ride home. His navy blue Buick still smelled new. A graduation present, he murmured, as if ashamed, and I knew the car was his mother's choice, not his. When we got out, Alfred walked over to Curt and stood there for a minute. Curt looked at me, a little puzzled. But Alfred extended his arm and shook Curt's hand in three hard shakes, the way Father Bob taught his men to do.

"Good to have you on board, Alfred." We watched him walk across the street. "See you tomorrow," I yelled.

I turned to find Curt sitting on the top step of my front porch.

He smiled, and I watched his thin lips parting, nervous, his teeth glimmering in the dark. He did not smile enough. He shrugged his shoulders. "I guess I won't be needing this for a while," he said, loosening his tie in a zigzagged, casual, masculine gesture that left me a little weak. The porch light shone down hard, like an accusation, and I could see the pale pink of his scalp. He would be thinning soon. He unbuttoned his shirt, pushed back the crisp collar, revealing the white undershirt underneath.

"You can just look at a house like this and picture Sans Souci in its grander days," he said. "The debutante ball, the servants, all that."

Servants. It was hard to believe we'd once had them. Gran had grown up with a cook, a maid, gardeners. I thought of the buzzer in the dining room floor, a nipple of a button hidden under the table. It was there so the hostess could buzz the cook or the maid with her foot while conversing with guests. I had played with that buzzer when I was a little girl until one day it just stopped buzzing, and Gran saw no reason to spend money fixing it.

"When I get a place of my own, it's going to be here, on this street." Curt made a sweeping motion, and I noticed his watch, white-faced and gold, expensive and beautiful.

I should have invited him in then; it was rude not to. But I thought of the bathroom downstairs, the stack of *Life* magazines teetering in the corner, the limp hand towel that was bunched in a dark velvet fold, like a bat; the almond-sized lumps of soap remnants nestled in a heap.

"How do you think the meeting went?" he asked.

"I think it fulfilled your objective."

"The doughnuts and the ties . . . that was a really great idea. Thanks."

I nodded.

"I don't know what I'd do without your wise counsel. Without you."

"It's nothing, really."

He sort of winked at me, and started to say something. But then he blinked, and swatted at a gnat. He stepped down to the sidewalk. His eyebrows arched, and he cleared his throat, but whatever question he wrestled with was swallowed up in a sudden shyness between us. He stood under the oak tree. His deep-set eyes were shadowed in the dappled dimness, and I was thankful for the cover of darkness to hide my own flushed face.

"I think I'll take a quick walk down the block. I'll just leave the car here at the curb, if that's okay," he said. "I have to go back to the paper in a while to check off the pages in layout."

"Of course. You can park it here as long as you need to."

Did he want me to go with him? He hadn't asked me. Perhaps I should volunteer to come along. Wasn't that what he was waiting for? Wouldn't it be presumptuous to invite myself? How did these kinds of things work, anyway?

He ambled away from me, across the yard and down the street, meandering over the humps and cracks on the sidewalks, where tree roots were slowly shrugging off squares of concrete. He turned to wave again, a few houses down. I waved back, then went inside, up the stairs to the attic bathroom and looked out, following his progress through the streets. In the pale light from the street lamps, I could see him walking two streets over, then stop in front of the Gaslight Grill. He stood for a minute in the glare of blinking neon lights before making his way through the mass of pickup trucks surrounding the place. I hadn't been in the Gaslight since I was a little girl, when Ginnie and I would ride our bikes there after school and buy bottles of frosty Coca-Colas, but I knew it was not the kind of place for Curt. I imagined the blur of work boots and uniforms and curious stares that would meet him.

I went down to the basement and selected a jar of okra and tomatoes from the shelf. The jar was cool and dusty in my hands, the top faintly rusty, but I knew it would give a short, sucking gasp when I pried it open. I shivered in the dank dustiness, batted a cobweb. The naked lightbulb swayed a little overhead, its beaded chain rattling, its shifting radius landing on the rows of jars that served as a kind of historical record of our summers. There was the stock-pile of preserves Gran had made from the bounty of figs we'd managed to salvage after the birds' ravenous assaults. Behind that, shelves of apple butter from the autumn our apple tree bore gener-ously; in the front, an abundance of stewed tomatoes and okra from the drought-ridden summer two years before. Despite my having pilfered from it nightly, the basement shelves still had a comforting supply. Between the jars of vegetables and jellies in the basement, our kitchen garden, and weekly trips to the farmers' market, I had all I needed. When I replanted the garden, I could begin stocking my own supply of jars and frozen bags of corn and okra.

In the kitchen, I warmed up the stewed tomatoes. I baked myself a little cake of cornbread. For dessert, I found the last remaining pickled peach in a large jar in the back of the refrigerator. Pulpy and brown, the peach lurked with the cloves and cinnamon at the bottom and looked faintly forbidding, like a creature in an aquar-ium. I stabbed it with a barbecue fork and ate it over the sink.

I went back outside and sat on the porch. After a while, I saw Curt walking up our street, his face flushed and happy under his pale hair.

"Happy hour," he said. " 'Grab a Busch Night.' Pitchers of it. Cheap." He turned and walked over to his car, then pounded the roof of it with a fist. "You know what, Cutter? We've got six months."

"Six months?"

"To put the *Citizen* in the black. Or Mother will sell it."

"Well, that explains the rumors, I guess."

"I wasn't being disingenuous today, okay? Because I'm not going to let it happen. Do you believe me?"

"Yes. But that's a lot of pressure."

"Right now, I need to clear my head," he said. He looked at his watch. "Before I have to sign off the pages."

"Yes," I said. "You do." We both knew the last editor lost his job by overlooking an error that cost the paper ads. A full-page color ad by Miss Huffstedler's School of Dance with a photograph of the town's dancers in their costumes marred by a Presidents' Day illustration on the opposite page. Young George Washington chopping down a cherry tree had been overwaxed in paste-up and migrated down the page, the ax appearing to embed itself in one of the dancers.

Curt turned, began once more to walk down Gerard Avenue.

"Where you headed?" I called. "Don't you need to get back to the paper?"

"Eventually," he said, without looking back.

"Wait. I'll come, too."

We passed a vacant lot, the stone steps from the sidewalk leading up to a grassy hump of dirt where rings of blooming daffodils and crocus marked the borders of a vanished home. We were coming to the end of the neighborhood, entering Main Street.

"You know," he said, "it's funny. This town was made up of dirt farmers who felt damn lucky to find jobs as lint heads, to keep their families fed. And I understand that, you know? I don't have any desire to go out there and conquer the world. I really don't."

"Sometimes," I said, "it's hard enough to hold on to what you have." I looked up at the sky: dark, very dark, with its little hook of moon. "I come from the Harris family," I added, as if that explained everything.

"Cutter, half this town is named Harris."

"I am descended from Henry Haynes Harris," I said. "Founder of the Sans Souci Manufacturing Company. *That* Harris."

"No shit?" He'd stopped walking, stood looking down at me, nodding a little. We were nearing the mill.

"Where are we heading?"

"Over there," he pointed. "To Ninth. I hope you don't mind."

Before I could answer, he took my hand and I stumbled behind him in uneven spurts, like a tin can tied to a car.

"Wait. Slow down. Are you looking for something?"

He didn't answer. After a few minutes, we stopped in front of a little house with cement figurines covering the lawn: giant mushrooms and elves, a two-foot-tall squirrel holding an acorn the size of a melon. A tall, life-sized statue stood near the door. When we drew closer I could tell it was supposed to be Snow White, but her concrete features were coarse and grainy. She had no eyeballs, like that famous bust of Nefertiti, and her toothless smile was twisted, ferocious. The cement apron she held dipped into a bowl filled with blackened wet muck and dead leaves.

"Is there some girl you used to know here?"

"No," he said, sinking to the bottom porch step, "no, nothing like that." I sat down beside him. He reached out and held my head in his hands. "Oh, Cutter. You don't know how much I admire you, the way you take care of things. You dig in. I mean, Jesus, to hold down two jobs so you can save your house. The Harris homestead, just think of it! When I saw you come in the newsroom that time with that Pancake Palace outfit and then dive into those fucking obits . . . Oh, Cutter." He was stroking my face, slowly. "Oh, Cutter—I don't feel—well."

The door of the house opened and an old woman came and stood there in a nightgown, her arm held across the shelf her large breasts made, resting there more for comfort than modesty. She held a cigarette in her other hand, and the smoke snaked up in a stream before it spread out.

"Canna hep you?"

Curt squinted in the porch light. "Is this the home of Jarred P. Hollins?"

"Who wants to know?" she asked.

"I do," he said. "I'm his grandson."

The woman pursed her lips and looked at me. Curtis Sams, the whole Sams family, were supposed to be blue blood. Descended on both sides from *Mayflower* pilgrims, Confederate generals, all kinds of stories that left most people feeling potato-farmer poor.

"He was my mother's father," Curt added, then swallowed hard and swayed slowly on his feet.

"Well, honey, he's done passed. You know that, I imagine."

"Oh, yes. Yes, ma'am."

"But I knew him. He was a good man. He was my daddy's cousin. I grew up right on this street, right up yonder on Third."

"I—I used to stay here, when I was young. Very young. Three or four, I think. I visited them then—my grandparents."

Curt was swaying again, almost wobbling.

"You better get this boy home, honey." She yawned. "He ain't holding his liquor too good. He's liable to be sick all over my steps."

"I'm okay," he said defensively. His knuckles were white where he gripped the handrail. "Can I have a look inside?" he asked. "In the house?"

I gasped. "Curt, we can't just show up here and—"

"Help yourself," the lady said. "We're kin, after all."

"I think I'll wait here," I said. But Curt was already inside, had left me standing out by Snow White.

"Hey, you goin' to a party?" In the doorway a bare-chested man, bald and ponytailed, held a can of Schlitz. "You know where there's any good parties?"

"No," I said. "I certainly don't."

"Well, you look all purty and all, like you been to a party." He grinned. "Wanna cold one?"

"No thanks."

"I'm Roscoe," he said. "And that there's Buddy." He pointed to just inside the door, where a boy of about twelve stared at the television.

From where I stood, I could hear Curt talking with the woman. "'Course they was built like this, you know, without no plumbing," I heard her explain. "The johns were added later. When I was growing up we just had the outhouse. And then you went to the bathhouse once a week. You'd use the company scrip for that, too."

"Scrip?" Curt asked. He stepped back out onto the porch. "Here's your first interview, Cutter. Fifty years ago Eileen started working at the mill."

She chuckled, hacked out a wet, rattling sound. "We was paid with scrip, you know. Wasn't no cash or checks. You just took your scrip the mill give out to you and went to the company store and traded it for food, or a haircut, or clothes—whatever you needed, the company had it all right there. Like game money or something. They was like family providin' for you, I'll say that for 'em. Everything you needed. They built the churches for you and the ball fields and then, of course, they rented you these houses here. Everyone paid twenty-five cents a room a week. My daddy paid a dollar a week rent for our house."

"What about the unions?" Curt asked.

"Oh. Them. They was run out of town on a rail. Super would just make arrangements with the churches—the Baptists and the Methodists—and the mill would make sure they had them some new pews and a new organ, a bigger parking lot. Then come Sunday, preachers would have a sermon about Revelations, about how anybody who talked to one of them union reps would have the mark of the Beast and be stung by devil wasps and be tied and roasted on a spit for eternity. They knew who buttered their bread, those preachers. Old man Harris wouldn't tolerate any of those shenanigans from the union."

Curt's silhouette shifted in the doorway and he looked at me. I knew he was considering telling her I was a Harris. My face flushed.

"I'm leaving," I said. When I reached the sidewalk, I heard the porch door slam and felt someone's hand on my shoulder. I thought of the bare-chested man, his leer, his beery whisper.

"Cutter," Curt said. "Hey. Slow down. Cutter, I've been wanting to do that for a long time, visit that old house. Thanks for coming with me."

"That's okay," I said. "But that man back there . . ."

"I'm sorry. I really am."

We walked in silence for a while, made our way around Sans Souci Mill. Abandoned, it was just something you didn't even see anymore, something you went around.

"So I guess you know now, I'm from lint-head stock," he said.

I shrugged.

"They say you can tell what a man did in the mill by where he lived in the neighborhood. The closer you were to the mill, the lower the position and the smaller the house. My grandfather was a doffer. I don't even know what the hell that is, but it must not have been too high up, judging from his house."

He laughed a little to himself. "It's something my mother was never proud of. She always pretended she was from the city. My father never said anything much about it, and after a while she had us all convinced she had grown up on some avenue in Palmetto. We even stopped visiting here." He looked at me. "But I always loved it. I loved staying with them, my grandparents. By the time I was five, they were both dead."

He pulled me close and kissed me. Our teeth clanked. His tongue darted around my own, slick and warm. His hands moved over my dress, down my back, then up in my hair. And though heat seared through me, lingered across my chest, between my legs, there were goose bumps on my arms. I shivered and he wrapped his arms around me.

He looked at his watch then.

"Oh my God. I'm late. I should have signed off on those pages an hour ago."

"You can take me to the paper, too," I said. "There's a pretty good chance my car will start this time."

When we got to Gerard, I could see Ginnie's room was dimly yellow inside. As we got in Curt's car, all business now, I looked back and I could see Ginnie climbing to the top of the stairs in the house, turning to watch the car pull away, her face silvery in the dimness. The headlights swept over her, her white T-shirt, her slow glide up the stairs. A specter, my sister. A haunt.

In the parking lot of the *Citizen*, Curt turned to me. "Before we go in, I need to say something," he said. There was a formal edge to his voice, and I felt my excitement whither. He crossed his arms, looked straight ahead. "I hope you won't . . . I mean, I think we should be—"

"Discreet. I know, Curt."

He looked so relieved, it hurt. He crumpled behind the wheel, took off his glasses, and rubbed his eyes.

"I know, I understand." I managed a smile, the muscles in my cheeks tight.

"It might undermine what little authority I have, is all. If people thought we were . . . well, it would mean more gossip."

We got out and walked over to my car. I got in and tried to start it. A couple of clicks and then nothing. I looked up at him from the driver's seat.

"I'll keep trying. It's close to starting, I just know it."

"Just go upstairs for a while. Pretend you have—I don't know— an emergency obit or something."

I nodded.

"It usually doesn't take me long to check the pages. And I'll give you a ride back." He put a foot on the hood of my car. "And get this baby towed."

"It doesn't need to be towed. It'll start." He shot me a sideways look. "It will. You'll see."

I went to Curt's office, closing the door behind me. I looked out his window into the newsroom and waited. After a while, I watched him walk across the room, drawing closer, looking over his shoulder, searching for me.

"Oh, you're here."

"No one saw me come in. I promise." He'd put on his tie again, though it wasn't knotted, just hung around his neck like a priest's vestment.

"I guess I need to try my car again."

The voices of two men outside the door made us both stand ramrod straight. Curt leapt to the door, shut it.

Wait until they leave, Curt mouthed.

Okay.

We were standing so close, he almost took a step backward. But he didn't.

"I'll go now," I whispered. He grabbed my wrist and kissed me hard. A faint scent of fixative floated up to me. His bristly evening stubble grazed my cheek, my neck. He turned away and locked the door. He cleared his desk with one swipe of his arm—the pictures, nameplate, pens, Rolodex, stacks of newspapers clattered to the floor.

"I thought you said—I mean, what happened to discreet?"

"My door's locked. We're alone. This is discreet."

And then I lay there, on Curtis Gallivan Price Sams's desk, my bare butt on the calendar At-a-Glance, my head dangling off the end, a button from my blouse pinging across the floor. Curt peeled off his undershirt. His pants fell to the floor, the belt buckle rattling. Both of us were pale as squid. He had a hairless chest, two bright pink nipples, a gold wooly path that led to his groin. I turned on my side, my arm over my breasts; I thought of their unevenness. The amused hand-patting promises from our family's semiretired doctor, *No one is perfectly symmetrical, my dear,* had failed to assure me. I had two tits at war. And the left one was winning by a cup size.

Had I shaved my legs this week? I tried to remember.

"Don't. I want to look at you." He was passionate, nibbling his way down my neck, lingering on my earlobe. He moved aside my arms, began kissing my breasts, worrying my nipples with his tongue. I thought of love scenes in the movies. They all faded out right before this part. Right before things got ridiculous and messy and wet. He was back at my earlobe now, my gold stud earring clinking against his teeth. Maybe it was my move. I couldn't just lie here. I had to reach for something of his, didn't I? I had to stroke or rub or lick him, isn't that what you did?

I watched the newsroom upside down through the one-way glass. It was strange. What in the hell was I doing? And with my boss? Was I completely crazy? Desperate? A slut? Frigid? Easy? On his desk, for God's sake?

But I was lucky to have a man who desired me, who kissed me, who, in fact, was a little desperate for me now. He rose above me then, took my hand and moved it to his stiff penis. I gripped it clumsily; the skin was loose and thin. I tried not to think of the turkey necks Gran used for soup. "Guide me," he whispered. He took out a little square foil pack and opened it with his teeth. He slipped on a beige condom and then rolled beside me on the desk, cloaked and ready. As Curt lunged into me, it was Parker James's face that came to my mind. My stomach tensed, I squeezed my eyes shut. It was Parker's desperate, earnest face wavering there when I shut my eyes. It was the memory of Parker's frantic insistence on finding a way to stuff the weenies that prompted my loss of control.

A snort ripped from me like a wicked fart. Curt looked up. I'd ruined it now. Oh my God, ruined everything. *Get a hold of yourself.* I bit my hand and turned aside, the laughter choking me, my chest convulsing. Oh God, I was dying. *Stuffing the weenies.* I tried picturing all the couples I knew having sex. Now that was a sobering thought. Dammit, everybody was getting laid but me—Daniel and Ginnie, Misty and her faceless fiancé, Jolene and Mack, Barry and his girlfriend. I tried my hardest to think of them naked, roiling and panting, stroking and kissing and . . . But Parker's machines—his rows of phallic, thrusting pistons cramming grits

into pale pink weenie skins, Parker's breakfast-hot-dog manufacturing world—would not leave me and so I . . . guffawed.

Curt's passionate embrace loosened.

"I'm sorry, I'm so, so sorry," I said in a high, quavering voice.

"Hey, it's okay." He fondled my hair. "You're beautiful. I'm with
you, I'm here."

I blinked at him and he wiped away the tears that spilled down
my cheeks. My stomach muscles quivered threateningly. "Cutter, I
didn't know. I didn't know it was your first time." I took a deep
breath. I swallowed another spasm of laughter. He was touched, he
said, his own eyes welling up with tears. He was moved that I was
overcome, undone by passion.

He kissed me tenderly, then lay his head on my belly, moved his
mouth across my hips, plunged his face into the warm wetness of
me. I tried to protest, but only whimpered. I closed my eyes. He
took the breath out of me, the laughter, the fight. I forgot the window, the newsroom, the hard desk pressing into my tailbone,
Parker's breakfast hot dogs, my grandmother's warnings. For a little
while, I forgot it all.

We left separately. I was to head for the parking lot and wait for
him. I didn't bother to open my car door, just jumped in like some
kind of superhero. I took in a deep breath, smelled rain, and
laughed. Convertibles were made for optimists. I turned the key
and it started. Of course it started.

How flat my life had been before tonight. How clogged and
darkened by worries.

"You got it running. I can't believe it." Curt had come out, was
hunkered in the shadows by my passenger door.

"You look like a vampire or something." I laughed. "Lurking
like that in the dark."

Someone came out the back door, the slam echoing across the
parking lot. I could see the embers of cigarettes glowing.

"Well, I'll see you tomorrow," I said quietly. He nodded. "Tomorrow."

Ginnie sat on the floor of the living room between two stacks of books, scribbling furiously on notecards. Her hair, pulled back severely in a ponytail, shone like bleached pine. When Ginnie ignored her appearance, her beauty popped back with a vengeance, multiplied.

"What are you doing home?" I asked.

"Peace and quiet. Penny's having a party, and I've got a paper due. I came home to work on it, but I fell asleep." She looked at me and yawned. "I'm not into parties anymore. I'm so tired." She poured herself a cup of tea from the silver tea service on a tray beside her.

"Why on earth are you using the best silver?"

"Why not? I got it out and shined it up. Seemed too much work to put it back."

She scratched something down on a card, then looked back up at me. "It's really late. What are you doing, working double shifts or something?"

"Why do you assume I'm working?"

"You were out . . . with somebody?"

"Shocked?"

"You had a date?"

"As a matter of fact, yes."

"You're kidding."

"No, I'm *not*."

"Why didn't you tell me before?"

"I'm telling you now. It wasn't planned, really. It was just this evening that things got serious."

She let out a little bark. "Oh my God! The virgin has jumped in the volcano of love!"

"Ginnie. Stop it. It's not a big deal, okay? It's kind of new . . . I mean, not sudden, not like we were strangers, but—"

"What's his name?"

I ignored her question. She studied me for a minute. She closed her books and put up her notecards. "You're really gone on this guy, aren't you?"

"I'm going to bed." I stomped up the stairs by twos.

"Wait a minute," she said, following me. "It's just—well, I don't want you to get hurt. Take it slow, that's my advice. Look, you're new to this, and it takes some experience dealing with . . ." Her sentence trailed off. "I mean, what do you really know about him?"

"Well, he's not married." Even as I said it, I thought of the agreement to be discreet. Our own lie.

In the bathroom, I stood under the shower for a minute before turning on the water, my fingers gingerly probing my body, my own angles and slopes. After my shower, wrapping a towel around my wet hair, I thought of the game Ginnie and I used to play after our girlhood baths. We would wrap the towels around our heads. We thought we looked like nuns. Sister Cutter and Sister Ginnie. We were Baptists, so nuns in a convent seemed as romantic, as forbidden, as princesses in a tower. Rosary beads were like magic beans, genuflecting like some mysterious ritual.

I stood at the sink, wiped away the steam on the mirror, peered at my freckled, pink face, wimpled in a towel. There was a soft knock on the door. Ginnie came in.

"Cutter, I'm happy for you. I want you to know that. It's great that you . . . are in a relationship. Hopefully you won't have to slog through all the muck I did to finally find someone you love."

"Slog through what?"

"The losers. You probably don't even know about all the nights I would sneak out back in high school. Lots of nights you and Gran were both asleep."

I nodded. I knew. "You were always leaving."

"Remember how we'd pretend to run away?"

"No," I said, looking down. "Well, a little."

"We were what? Nine and ten? That was the summer Gran kept going to bed so early. When she stopped paying the lawn man and the fix-it man."

I nodded. We used to wait until Gran was asleep and tiptoe out the back door and then run through the neighborhood, our gauzy gowns floating around our knees, our feet and legs stippled with grass clippings "I just followed you," I said. "I was sure you'd die if I wasn't there."

"I came up here to tell you that you're doing the right thing, finally taking a chance on love. Because if you find it, oh, Cutter, when you find it, you'll know it. There's nothing better on earth."

"I don't know about that," I said. "You seem pretty tormented lately."

"That's because I hardly get to see him. And when I do, it's like I'm extracting venom from him. Her poison. It's not easy right now, but things will get better. I want to wake up every morning of my life beside Daniel. That's what gets me through. Can't you understand that?"

"Why is it we can't talk anymore without one of us blowing up?"

"I don't know," she said quietly. "Come here. I want to show you something."

I followed her into her bedroom. There were empty shopping bags covering the floor, a stack of shoe boxes by the bed. She picked something up and squatted down beside the bed so I couldn't see her.

"What is all this? A shopping spree?"

"Check this out." She stood and pulled up her T-shirt, and tugged two flaps on her bra. Her breasts popped out, *shoop*, just like that, white and round, pink peaks, like two perfectly decorated cakes.

"Thanks for sharing."

"It's a nursing bra."

"It looks like the Frederick's of Hollywood special."

"They have these little flaps so you can just—*voila!*—open and feed the baby. Neat, huh?"

"Yeah," I said. "Neat. So, I guess you've been to the doctor?"

"Yes. And we set up this schedule. I have to start going once a month and then twice a month, and then on ultrasound at sixteen weeks if I want, and then—"

"Did you go alone?"

"As a matter of fact, yes."

"Did you get another credit card? How are we going to pay for this? Clothes and doctors and—"

"I'm not sure yet, if you want to know the truth. I'm still working out the details, you know? But don't worry, it's not your concern."

"Yeah, right."

"Do me a favor?"

"Probably not."

"Let's get something to eat. I'm starving."

"Just like that? 'Here's my nursing bra, let's get a cheeseburger'?" I shrugged and walked downstairs to the kitchen.

"There's not much in there to eat," she yelled. "C'mon. Let's go. I'm buying."

"Well, I guess the Gaslight's open."

"The Gaslight Grill? I haven't been in that place for years. Is it safe?"

"Yeah, it's safe."

"I'm not walking," she said, as I bent down to tie my sneakers.

"But you can practically see it from here. And I have to watch my gas. I try to make a tank last a week. It's not cheap, you know."

"I'll buy you a full tank. Deal?"

Afterward, she insisted on driving. That should have tipped me off.

"But I only had one beer," I said.

"Don't ever, ever make me go to that place again."

"It wasn't so bad," I said.

"It was the worst."

"You run into people you see around town at the Gaslight Grill. You can catch up on things. If you'd bother to talk to people, you'd know. Hey, you just missed our turn!"

"I thought it would be nice to take a midnight moonlight drive."

She turned onto the highway, and I knew then where we were headed.

Old English Acres was dark, a few moon-dappled shadows spilling from the trees onto driveways and sidewalks. The horsey smell of freshly spread mulch greeted us.

"He lives here," she said. "Somewhere."

"Maybe we should stop and put the top up on the car if you're on a covert mission."

"We're taking a drive. There's no law against that." She slowed down. "I'm not sure which house is his."

I had to stop myself from pointing it out.

"There's his car," she said quietly. "Right there." She slowed the car to a crawl, the engine hiccupped.

"Change to first gear before she chokes," I said.

Lights were out at the Byers house, except for a dim golden glow that shone from the side. A reading lamp, maybe?

I looked over at Ginnie. She was crying.

"Why are you doing this to yourself?"

"It's tears of relief. I feel better just being near him. He's left her."

"He's left her?" That was news to me.

"Every way you can leave, except physically."

"Except physically? Ouch."

"Ouch?"

"Yeah, ouch. That's the sound of my brain trying to wrap itself around that concept."

"Cutter, do you mind? Do you fucking mind? This is not a

funny situation. I would have never brought you if I'd known you'd just make jokes."

"It's a deal. Next time, leave me at home."

We turned around on the cul-de-sac and headed for the Byers house again. I began to feel predatory. "You should have told me I'd be doing reconnaissance. I would have worn my camouflage makeup."

"He's there in the house. Asleep, I bet. But I have so much of him."

She stopped the car in front of their house. She looked into the side-view mirror, wiped her smeared mascara with a finger. "I feel better," she said again, sniffing. She searched through her purse and handed something to me. It was a business card. An appointment card, I saw upon closer inspection. Palmetto Women's Services Pregnancy Termination.

"You have an appointment next week?"

"I went there yesterday. Preabortion counseling."

"You should have told me. I would have come with you. I thought you said everything was set up with the doctor. All the prenatal stuff. Why don't you tell me things? Why don't you trust me?"

Silence. A train whistle echoed mournfully in the distance. She took the card from me, tore it into pieces, threw a fistful of Palmetto Women's Services confetti toward the ashtray. "When he leaves her, I want it to be for me. Not just for the baby and me. But today, it came to me. I decided what to do. I canceled the appointment."

"You canceled the appointment?"

"Then I bought the nursing bra, and filled a prescription for vitamins. I called the doctor to set up my prenatal schedule. I was right to wait to tell Daniel about the baby next weekend, after he leaves Wife."

A blue recycling carton on the curb overflowed with milk cartons and newspapers. The flag was up on their mailbox. The two people in there were carrying on with life, I thought, bagging trash and paying bills.

"But I'll do whatever I have to do to get him out of there."

"Ginnie, you sound like you're going to spring him from the Big House. He's not a prisoner, you know. He's got a mind of his own."

"Yes, he is. He is a prisoner. You have no idea what it's like for him." She snuffled. "In there." She stared at the Byers' front door.

Was this love? Lurking in the bushes in the middle of the night, sobbing, claiming to feel better just being in the proximity of a man who was, very possibly at this moment, curled up with his wife? Spouse spooning?

I got out of the car and walked over to the driver's side.

"I'm driving us home."

"I'm not ready yet."

"Well, you can sit out here behind the boxwoods with the recy-clables and the soaker hoses and the leaf bags, but I'm going home."

"Fine," she said a little wearily. She slid over to the passenger seat.

"And I'll go with you to the doctor. You know that. If you're sure about—"

"I am. I'm sure about this baby. There's no need to discuss it, okay? I've made my decision. And I can take care of myself."

The phone ringing by my head woke me up the next morning. When the fog in my head cleared (Curt!), I reached for the phone.

"Miss Johanson?"

"Yes?" My voice was thick and crackly with sleep. I could hear the soft pattering of water down the hall. Ginnie in the shower

"So nice of you to call back promptly yesterday. Such courtesy is so refreshing! A teensy-weensy little problemo has come up, but nothing we can't handle." It didn't take long to recognize Mrs. Worthington—she always sounded like she was talking to a pet poodle. But what she was saying—that took a minute to register. Suddenly her voice dropped in pitch. I sensed danger, grew instantly alert. "The buyer would like to change times. May we discuss coming a little earlier today, perhaps?"

"What?"

"Oh, do forgive me for calling this early. I tried to call the other number—that friend of yours, Penny, I believe? She said you'd be there at your house this morning tidying up. It's just that you mentioned about your sister being there later on, so I wanted to call to find out a good time to bring the interested buyer, you understand. How about three instead of four? Would that be—er—a safe time?"

I flung the covers off, sat up. "Mr. Conrad really is taken with the place, you know," she rattled on like an old buggy over rocky terrain. Filling silent gaps was Mrs. Worthington's business. "And I think converting the house into apartments is a wonderful idea, very trendy, and close enough to the university for students—"

I was dizzy. "Three o'clock will be fine," I managed.

"Excellent. And would you mind letting your brother know the house is being shown? He's left me a dozen messages this week, and I did want to assure him we're getting closer to a sale. I'll let you know how things go. Good-bye now!"

I slid on jeans under my T-shirt, grabbed my tennis shoes, and tiptoed past the bathroom. I padded down the stairs and out the front door.

I drove two streets down, parked on a vacant lot at the corner. Standing on an old stump at the back, I could just make out the front porch and driveway of my house. I waited. Within ten minutes, I saw Ginnie's ride.

Back at home, I called in sick to the Pancake Palace. When Jolene screamed at me to get my sorry butt down there, I hung up. I pulled out the mahogany silverware box from the china cabinet in the dining room. I knew suddenly what I'd find, and what I wouldn't. Twelve silver place settings were there, but the serving spoons, the butter knife, and the sugar spoon were gone. In the china cabinet, all the crystal goblets—my grandmother's gold-rimmed wedding crystal—all of them were gone, twelve identical circles in the dust forlorn reminders. Upstairs in Gran's jewelry box, a pearl choker and my mother's opal pendant necklace were missing.

Ginnie was taking them, secretly pawning them, selling off the estate to pay for doctor's appointments, for nursing bras, for shopping sprees. To pay for her mistake.

Ten

"YOU SAY YOU WANT the lawn tilled up?"

"Yes."

"You want it all tore up?"

"Yes, I do. All of it." The grass was patchy and gray, bald in spots, mangy. Elizabeth wanted a field with a path, she wanted purple coneflowers and cosmos, sunflowers, Queen Anne's lace and daisies. She wanted clumpy bundles and long, bent stalks. Tall, spindly perennials. She would plant all those seeds from the farmers' market. And if she ran out—well, then she and Cutter could go back and get more.

The man was friendly enough, seemed good-natured. Just a bit wary, a little concerned, working hard on that wad of tobacco in his cheek and sizing her up. She could just imagine what he was thinking: *Tear up the lawn to grow those things?* Why, those were weeds, plain old field flowers. The whole point of living some place like Olde English Acres was a nice square green yard. He gazed down the street, taking in the neighborhood lawns, measured and square like quilt pieces. He spit a quick brown stream from the side of his mouth that shot out fast and unexpected, like a snake's tongue.

He walked on out to the curb, and she stayed behind. He mopped his face with a handkerchief. It was nine in the morning, very warm. But then this was the type of man who would sweat in snow, you could tell. A small-time peach farmer who tilled gardens on the side. She had seen his advertisement in the newspaper. *Part-time farmer will till your garden cheap.*

"I remember when this was plain o'l pastureland, part of Burroughs' farm, butted right up to the Harris's land in Sans Souci. Cattle, mostly, but they was into a little of everything—potatoes, corn." He shook his head. "And this neighborhood was part of a field I used to play in as a boy. It ran clear down to Cold Stream, then landed at Puddin' Swamp—well, the stream ain't there anymore, really, now it's that ditch right by the McDonalds."

He had begun walking to his pickup, and Elizabeth strained to hear his last words, then watched as he unloaded the tiller. "My mechanical mule," he said, groaning cheerfully as he lifted it down.

The chunks of lawn parted easily enough, and she followed behind him in her white shorts and shirt and sneakers, stepping high-kneed, gingerly, through the muck. Like one of those gangly white birds that walked around behind cows, scrounging for insects. She began scattering seed. *Broadcasting* seed, her gardening book called it. And here it was already April. Time to get these seeds in the ground.

Patsy peered through her front window. Just wait until she found out that Elizabeth wasn't reseeding a lawn—God, no, she was killing it. She was welcoming the dandelions and goldenrod and daisies and clover that Patsy and the rest of the neighbors assassinated every week with their round, nozzled cans of poison. Elizabeth's yard wasn't going to look like a green shag rug. She was inviting nature back in, she was offering it what little she had: take it, come back, stay awhile. It was beauty she was seeking, beauty that she and Daniel needed.

And then maybe she could love it here.

And next week she would hire the farmer to take up that chain-link fence around the backyard. God, that fence was awful, institutional. She would put up a picket fence, a rock wall, maybe. She would have to dip into their savings, all that mad money, as she had come to think of it, the money for hospitals, for doctors, just in case. It was just another thing they didn't talk about, but she knew, she knew. It was socked away, that money her father had left her. Reminders came in envelopes addressed to her every month, charts and tables and letters about funds and bonds and accounts; thousands of dollars she dared not touch.

"Boy, these lawns," Patsy yelled from over the fence, "sometimes you just gotta start over, huh? Start fresh and replant that grass."

The farmer stopped tilling then, turned off the machine, and glanced at Patsy. He did a double take when he noticed how big she was. She never wore maternity clothes. She told Elizabeth she didn't want to waste the money. Mostly she wore her husband's shirts. Like today. A T-shirt with an American flag across the front, stretched and pulled so tight the red stripes were pink and the words distorted, though you could barely make them out: *Try to burn this sucker.*

Elizabeth called to Patsy, "Oh, it's not grass I'm reseeding."

"Well, that oughta do ya," the man said, loading the tiller back up. Elizabeth looked across her yard. It was rather shocking with the grass gone and the lawn transformed to lumps and rows of red clay. She hadn't pictured such a drastic change. And it would be six weeks before the seeds sprouted. She swallowed.

The farmer cleared his throat. "You sure this is what you wanted?"

"Yes," she said quietly.

She counted out $50, which he crammed into his pocket. She shook his hand then, callused and smooth, like a foot.

"Thank you," Elizabeth said. "Thank you for coming out right when I called."

"I usually make it within the hour, what with how impatient people are. You can't wait around in this business anymore."

"You won't believe how much better I feel already."

He screwed his eyes up, looked at her sideways. "You sick?"

"Suburbia toxicosis. Heard of it?"

He stared at her impassively, lumpy potato face plain, not even chewing now, just staring.

"Chief symptoms include loathing of neighbors, isolation, anxiety, helplessness."

He settled himself in the truck, then hung an elbow and his head out the window as he looked back at her. "Don't believe I ever heard of that," he said.

"Just one more load." Cutter's hair was rain darkened, dripping in pointed clumps, the pink of her skin showing from underneath her drenched blouse. A few minutes ago when Cutter arrived, so had the rain. And as she unloaded—Elizabeth didn't know exactly what was in the boxes Cutter was unloading—the shy pattering had turned to a loud, galloping downpour that pummeled and kicked up a sweet smell of soil. Elizabeth heard the clink of china as Cutter handed her a box and dashed back to put the top up on her car. Elizabeth breathed in the old, dank smell of wet cardboard and moved the box to the living room.

On the porch, Elizabeth watched the tributaries across her front yard organize themselves into small streams that moved with the busy, proud bustle of volunteers as they lifted her seeds, carried them down past the curb, and dumped them into the muddy red puddles that flanked the road. All those puddles with undulate edges, like leaves, full of seeds now, making their way down the street drain to the sewer. She stood there and knew the storm was an omen: tomorrow's party was going to be a disaster—a flooded, ugly, red-clay disaster.

Cutter's splattering footsteps drew closer, her face hidden behind the box she carried. She brushed past Elizabeth and set it down on the living room floor. She was swiping at her eyes, her face wet from rain. Or maybe she had been crying. She swooped up one of Elizabeth's kittens, mewling and trembling at her feet.

"How are these little fellas doing?"

"Good. They're quiet, really. Mainly they stay hidden in the laundry room." She paused, watching Cutter's fidgeting.

"I see you got the yard tilled up."

"Yes . . . wonderful timing with this rain." Elizabeth smiled ruefully. "I'll need to go back to the market next week to get more seed."

"I haven't forgotten that tomorrow's the big night—your party. I know you're probably busy. . . ." Cutter looked around. "Uh, how are things going?"

"I'm . . . things are all right."

Cutter released the kitten with a plunk on the floor. After a minute, she looked up at Elizabeth, who was still standing, leaning on the door. "They're going to sell the house—right out from under me. My brother Barry and Ginnie and that—Mrs. Worthington—are going to sell it. I found out today. You won't believe what I found out." She moved to the boxes, rummaged around and handed Elizabeth a large platter.

"Look at this. My grandmother's wedding china. Ginnie had all this stuff organized—she was planning on selling it. Can you believe it? My grandmother's wedding china and silver and crystal pawned. And behind my back, she made arrangements for Mrs. Worthington to show the house to a man who wants to make apartments out of it. Our house—my family's house—cheap apartments." She choked, struggled for a minute, then looked up. "Jeez. I didn't mean to bring up Ginnie's name again—"

"It's okay." Elizabeth looked down at the platter and caught a glimpse of blue; a river, bent willows, a minute cottage, the blur of a delft world.

"I know that I have no business asking you to do this." Cutter looked through the contents of the box, still not meeting Elizabeth's eyes. "Like I told you on the phone, I was wondering if you could keep some stuff here for me until I figure out what to do with it. I'm going to look into renting a storage space somewhere."

Cutter's hands fluttered over the boxes. "I can't ask Father Bob. He can't keep a secret, and Alfred would end up dusting it all off and bringing it back. Maybe my boss at work, or I could talk to one of the girls at the Pancake Palace about letting me store stuff."

"We can put it under the guest bed."

"Here?"

"Yes, we'll put the boxes in the guest room. We'll drag them back there and shove them under the bed. For as long as you need."

"I may have more."

"Well, bring them on, whatever you can. No one will know, believe me."

Elizabeth knelt down and peered into the nearest box. She held up a sterling serving spoon, dimpled with clusters of imprinted grapes, and a knife, its handle choked with silver vines and shards of slender, shiny blooms.

"Leaving dirty dishes in the sink and balled-up socks in the corners just isn't going to stop this guy from being interested in my house." Cutter cocked her head sideways, sighed, her eyes wide, watery, forlorn.

Elizabeth sat on her heels, looked over at her. "I've got an idea," she said.

They had divided the job into two sections, interior and exterior, and Cutter was still adding some last-minute touches to the inside of the house. She was in the attic now, pausing occasionally to stick her head out a window and wave her yellow, rubber-gloved hands. Elizabeth, who was handling the outside portion of what Cutter dubbed "Operation Sabotage House Inclusively and Totally"—O SHIT for short—found herself coaxing, leading, dragging a dog, a kitten, and a peacock from Father Bob's across the street.

On one side of the porch, Alfred napped in the rocking chair, his eyes closed, his face malt-ball smooth, the monkey huddled in his lap.

Elizabeth led a three-legged dog up the steps, where he hobbled hobbled hobbled then settled with a satisfied groan. She squatted down and scratched the dog behind the ears. He rolled onto his back and offered his belly, cheerfully wiggled three paws and a stump. She glanced up—Alfred was definitely asleep now, his breathing heavy and even, his head lolling down from his thick neck, like a top-heavy sunflower. Elizabeth tiptoed down the stairs and crossed the street for another load of creatures.

There were the chickens. One or two would have been enough, but when she managed to chase two across the street the others followed, as if they were going to miss out on something exciting.

Two roosters squabbled then broke away, then fought again in a tangle of feathers and screeches, the other chickens gathering in a circle, clucking madly like street punks cheering on a brawl. The commotion brought Father Bob running across the street, yelling, "Oh, stop it—now do stop it, please!"

"They do that all day," he told Elizabeth, gasping. "I'm afraid a fatality is bound to ensue, and it will be all my fault."

"I don't think you can teach chickens not to fight."

"Well, don't I know it—and it pains me so! I can't imagine why they are so cross with one another. I thought they would be peaceful creatures. When Alfred and I brought them here from the shelter, I had visions of the men having fresh eggs every morning."

"How many chickens did you get at the animal shelter?"

"Oh—why, twelve. Six hens and six roosters."

She almost laughed, but caught herself. This serious-faced, kindly man in plaid golf pants and a black shirt with his important sliver of clerical collar was looking up at her. The man's cheerful gullibility sucked you in, she thought, engulfed you. "I don't think chickens pair off," she said. "One rooster has to be in charge of a group of hens. That's just the way they are. They're fighting over the hens."

"Oh, my word—why, I never thought of that." She watched his eyebrows knit, thick and woolly as Halloween paste-ons. He frowned. His eyes watered. He turned away. "I guess that makes my city upbringing painfully apparent. Oh dear—I am embarrassed. What a silly thing to do—and the way they must be suffering! Fighting over—over companionship."

"You don't mind if I borrow them for a little while? Just keep them in the yard over here a little bit?"

"Why, certainly not." He looked pleased then, the sunny smile was back, and she realized his facial expressions could be as fickle as March weather. "A change of scenery may be good for them. Why, of course I don't mind, Elizabeth. Help yourself to the bag of cracked corn on the porch, if you want to feed them. But I must warn you—you should tell Cutter that the men and I have discovered the chickens make quite a mess on the porch. For some reason, they have a fondness for roosting there on the railings and their droppings take the paint right off. Right off! We've had to string all manner of nets on the porch—fishing, volleyball, badminton—to no avail. They just love roosting there."

"I don't think that will be a problem." She looked down at his dusty, scuffed-up loafers, his feet turned in like a child's. "And I wanted to tell you that, well, I think your going to the shelter and adopting all these animals no one wanted was very noble."

"Foolish, too, I'm afraid, as Cutter predicted."

"Yes, but kind."

"Why, thank you," he said. "Of course we meant to get just one kitten, but to see those creatures caged, their eyes begging, paws held out between bars swiping at you when you walk by—well, Alfred and I couldn't leave them there, you understand."

"By the way," she asked, "how is the monkey's—condition?"

"Oh, that. Well, he's not showing as much progress as I had hoped. His anger, his fear of round objects, is just a classic generalized phobia. But when I lose patience, I think of that poor creature all those years in a cage at that gas station where people paid to throw rubber balls at him. Just think of it! So we have learned to make certain allowances. At dinnertime, we put him in the back room because every time we got out the paper plates—"

"I don't want to think about it."

"Yes, well. And I don't want to think about how many times I have wiped off and sanitized the kitchen clock after it drew his ire. It's round, you know, so of course—"

"Ugh."

Father Bob smiled, then started across the street again, but paused and walked back over to where she was standing. "And by the way," he whispered, "I know what you two are up to. It's the house, isn't it? Cutter is up to her tricks—thwarting buyers?"

"Yes."

"Well, I must tell you I don't—can't really approve. I mean, it's not quite ethical behavior, is it? But Cutter does so much for us, so much. She loves Alfred. And she deserves some happiness, you know."

"Yes."

"Oh, I wish Cutter could just have a little more faith that things will turn out well in the end. Now Ginnie, she's the lighthearted one. Just a joy, that one. But Cutter takes on the world, doesn't she? Our Cutter just frets and frets."

Elizabeth smiled. It wasn't easy. *Ginnie . . . the lighthearted one.*

Father Bob looked over at Alfred dozing, chuckled, and turned to her and winked. It made things feel worse then, being near happiness. Just when she thought she could join in, her panic swallowed her. She felt herself seal up as if she were in a jar, looking out, trapped in the sour vinegar of her own life.

Panic, taken from the root Pan, from the god Pan, meaning "everything."

Here she was talking to a man as strange and innocent as his mentally disturbed charges. Here she was dragging animals to the house of someone she couldn't help like, someone whose sister was possibly, at this very minute, in the walls of a higher-educational facility just miles from here, seducing her husband. Seduced by

Daniel—never; he might fall out of weakness, but he would never willingly jump. Would he?

She forced herself to stand up straight. She kicked at some grass between slabs of the sidewalk, saw that sweet alyssum was growing there, the seed blown over from someone's yard, probably. She looked at Father Bob. "Do you think things really turn out for the best?"

"Do they what, my dear?" He had already begun to walk away, but turned back to her, cupped his ear.

"Do things really turn out for the best in the end?"

"Of course," he yelled. "Of course. Splendidly, always." He blinked and grinned and slapped away a gnat, all in one move.

After she scattered cracked corn for the chickens all around the porch and front yard, she stood on the little porch off the kitchen eavesdropping. She'd been hovering over the potted herbs, dead and overgrown, that were heaped on the top step. A sprig of rosemary reached through a layer of dead oak leaves, like a hand. She picked a little spike of it, crushed it in her palm, heard Cutter talking on the phone. How could she help overhearing when the kitchen window was open? *Curt, he wants to make it into apartments.* She was speaking with the man they met up with at the ice cream place. Wasn't his name Curt? He was her boss. And Cutter was talking to him intimately. Elizabeth sat on the top step, breathed in the oregano and rosemary that lingered on her fingers. Cutter was in love with him.

She remembered loving like that. That summer she had worked at the college bookstore, missing Daniel so much, aching for him. They had been together that spring, and he had gone to London to study for a month. She was wretched in her loneliness, working at the bookstore just to stay busy. And then, one morning Daniel showed up in a long line of students at her register. When she looked up wearily from her cash drawer, counting out ones and fives, there he was grinning at her three students down the line.

He'd come back a week early, surprised her. She let out a small sound, came from behind the counter to be swept up by him, enfolded in his arms. Looking back, Elizabeth realized that's what she liked best about new love: leaving yourself, leaving your place, even just for a while. The wings it gave you, the flight.

"I'm finished," Cutter said as she emerged from the house, disturbing the chickens that flapped and strutted about on the porch. "And with time to spare." She brushed herself off—her yellowed shirt was wrinkled and smudged, like an artist's smock after a day at the studio. "So, you want to meet the rest of the family?"

"What?"

"Come with me."

They walked in the back, past the caretaker's cottage.

"Stop for a minute," Elizabeth said. She looked through the smudged windows, green with pollen, filthy with dust. "Oh, my."

"Sometimes we called it the cottage. It was a carriage house first, then servants' quarters and then the caretaker's cottage. It's a mess in there. Mice everywhere. Roof leaks."

"It's lovely," Elizabeth said, still peering in at the stone fireplace and the rusty iron bed in the corner.

They walked through a glade of trees in the back, squeezed through two boxwoods left to grow ragged. They came to a foot trail at the bottom of a small hill that brought them to a cemetery beyond a rusting iron gate, massive oaks hunkering like sentinels, two willows weeping profoundly over the graves.

"It's always cooler here," Cutter said, "because of the trees." She opened the gate. It screeched like a prehistoric bird.

"I always called this place the dead garden. It was a joke with Gran and me. We'd walk down and visit the dead garden a lot. On Sundays, Gran would wear her gardening hat and bring her trowel. We would weed and plant bulbs and seeds. Gran's headstone is over there," Cutter said, pointing to the glossy marble that stuck out from the other tombstones like an overdressed guest at a party. *Myrtle Ann Harris Chapel.*

Elizabeth walked by an urn, cracked and filled with dank water. Moss covered everything: it was underfoot, on tree trunks, on the headstones and graves themselves. But it was the broken statue in the corner that drew Elizabeth's attention: a seraphim in despair leaned casually there against the back gate.

"That's Beulah," said Cutter, following her gaze. "Well, *for* Beulah. Beulah was my great-grandmother and the angel was there on her grave till the storm of sixty-eight knocked her over. She's my garden angel."

"Your garden angel?"

"When I was about seven or so, I heard about guardian angels, how everyone's supposed to have one. Only I heard it *garden* angel. And I thought of Beulah's angel in the dead garden. I knew she was my garden angel."

Cutter's hands fluttered over the statue, her touch reverent, light, brushing off leaves, stroking the stone face, like feeling the forehead of a feverish child. Moving closer, Elizabeth saw that Beulah was not in despair after all. She was just waking up, maybe, shaking off an afternoon doze, one arm thrown over her face, a dimple in the elbow of a plump arm, her mighty wings curled around her body like wilted leaves.

"I can't tell you how many times I've thought of her before exams, my driver's test, job interviews, even when Gran died. I close my eyes and picture her and I know things will be all right. At least they seem better."

Elizabeth smiled at the whimsy, at Cutter's grim nod.

There was the sound of a car pulling up to the curb then and Cutter paled, her freckles standing out on her nose. "The buyer. That son of a bitch is here," she whispered. "I was hoping somehow he'd cancel."

They made their way back up the hill, between the boxwoods, in time to see Mrs. Worthington's silver Mercedes, the electric windows *zzzz*ing up before she emerged. Son of a bitch had hopped out of the passenger side pretty fast, Elizabeth thought. Was he that excited about seeing this house he wanted to gut? Mrs. Worthington nodded while he pointed and talked. Elizabeth watched his finger trace alcoves, his hand moving up and down, M's and V's, like directing an orchestra. *The place will need a new roof.*

"You could pose as a neighbor or something," Cutter whispered. "Hang around and listen."

Elizabeth nodded, walked up the side yard to the far end of the porch corner, crouched casually, her face half hidden in her hands. Mrs. Worthington bobbed up the steps in her polyester double-breasted powder blue suit and inserted a breath mint in her slot of a mouth with a smooth and practiced gesture. She reached a hand up to pat her stiff beehive. Like two scoops of ice cream. Hair that was sprayed and sprayed and sprayed. She unlocked the front door. Elizabeth could swear she saw Mrs. Worthington's bosom rise and her chin lift the slightest bit, but even the chickens fluttering and squawking around her ankles as she opened the screen door didn't visibly faze her. Just a little narrowing of the eyes when she looked down.

The man kicked at the chickens, paused, held the screen door open, as he took in Alfred and Crusty, both still sound asleep in the rocker. Madonna and child.

"He live here?" the man asked Elizabeth, who had taken a seat beside Alfred.

"No. He lives across the street." The calmness of her own voice surprised her.

"Hmpf."

She flinched as the screen door banged behind him.

After a while, Cutter came from around the back, tiptoed across the porch and plunked down beside her, hidden behind the rocker.

"You know what they'll find in there?" she asked. "All those loose linoleum tiles in the kitchen and hall—I just peeled them up. And the loose wallpaper, too. I shredded it. I left a box of Tampax lying around, and panties and bras, and some of Gran's old girdles. I think that kind of thing will really humiliate Mrs. Worthington. I flushed the commode that runs and runs and makes that horrible screech unless you jiggle it a certain way. Listen—you can hear it from out here! I dropped a Snickers bar in there! Ummm, let's see—I boiled a dozen eggs and left them all chopped up in the sink so the kitchen smells like something died in there, I cleaned out my hairbrushes and left great balls of hair in all the bathroom sinks—"

"Oh, Cutter. Yuck. I think I've heard enough."

They waited. Two minutes, five minutes, ten minutes.

"They're coming," Cutter whispered. She squatted behind a pile of rotting firewood on the other end of the porch, a baseball cap pulled down over her eyes. Elizabeth tried to look bored as they emerged from the house. There was no clever chitchat coming from Mrs. Worthington, no Realtor-client pleasantries.

Mrs. Worthington shot an icy glance at Elizabeth, who stared straight ahead. From the corner of her eye, Elizabeth caught a flash of furtive movement, saw that Crusty was awake now and peering at Mrs. Worthington.

She was chubby. Her buttocks under that polyester suit and girdle no doubt as white and round and pocked as the moon.

Her hair stiffly set in those pouffed buns.

Mrs. Worthington was nothing but a group of floating circles—even her ankles as plump as peaches.

Crusty's cranky brown eyes took in *round round round*. He jumped down and squatted then, the ammunition rolling with soft, sickly thuds on the porch. Mrs. Worthington stared in disgust, her mouth open (unfortunate—another circle). Crusty climbed up a railing, lobbed, and missed. The second time, harder this time, with the fury of failure, and it was bull's-eye.

Mrs. Worthington screamed, clawed at her head.

There was shit in her hair. Mrs. Worthington had monkey shit in her hair.

Elizabeth was weak from laughter after Cutter dropped her off at home. She checked on the aspics in the refrigerator, while her laughter fizzled, like air going out of a tire. She began a batch of lemon poppy-seed rolls. She started to mop the kitchen, but the yellow rubber gloves reminded her of the ones Cutter had worn and the whole sabotage operation, and she was overtaken by a fit of giggles.

She took off her apron and her dirt-smudged clothes and showered. She felt so good she got out her old makeup case, rummaged through the assortment of tubes and bottles. Good Lord, when had she last looked through this mess? Half-empty lipsticks and dusty brushes, vials of oily cream. She slathered scented lotion on her arms and legs, dabbed lavender perfume on her neck, her wrists and ankles, between her legs. She combed out her damp hair, teased a few spikes with her fingers. In the bedroom, she took out a fuchsia silk gown from the bottom bureau drawer. She unfolded it, shook out the tissue paper, plucked out the straight pins. This from her mother, two Christmases ago. She slipped the gown over her head and it fell, sleek and cool as water, down her body.

She called her mother-in-law.

"Elizabeth? What's wrong? Has something happened to my son?"

"Daniel is fine. We're both wonderful. I just thought I'd call and chat."

"But you never call." *Nevah cawl.* Davida's hard Jersey vowels, her smoke-cured rasp. Elizabeth could see her sitting there at her tiny red Formica table, the cigarette smoke snaking up from the Atlantic City ashtray, the cut-glass decanter of Chianti half empty, a *Star* tabloid or marked-up *TV Guide* crossword in front of her.

"You know, Elizabeth, I was just saying to myself the other day how my son's wife never calls me. Twelve years I know this girl, and she never calls. And now you call. Go figure." It was a kind of compliment, Davida's own coarse compliment.

"Well, I'm glad I did call, then."

"Yeah. I'll say a Hail Mary."

"Would you like to come down for a visit next weekend?"

"Am I going to be a grandmother?" Davida's voice grew loud

with excitement. "That's it, isn't it? Finally I'm going to be a grandmother. No wonder you called. You got good news, you want me to come down so you can tell me in person. Where's my son? I want to talk to—"

"Davida, no. No, it's not that. I promise. It's just—we'd love to have you visit, that's all. How about next week?"

There was silence on the line. "Daniel just called me Tuesday. He didn't say nothing about a visit."

"We can send you the airline ticket."

"I never fly, you know that."

"Greyhound then? Or the train?"

"I don't want to be no trouble."

"Of course not."

A dramatic sigh. "Well, maybe Aunt Sharon can bring me? How about Aunt Sharon coming, too?"

Yes, Elizabeth murmured. That was a fine idea.

"Elizabeth, are you still there? For heaven's sake. Speak up, I can hardly hear you."

"I said, that sounds wonderful."

"Well, I'm happy now. My daughter-in-law calls me and invites me to visit. What can I bring, Elizabeth? I can cook some, you know, and let you and Daniel relax a little. I don't mind."

"Bring a box of cannoli. You can't get a good cannoli down here."

"Sure." Davida's voice softened. "Sure, I'll do that." Davida would be finishing up a bowl of minestrone or a buttered scattering of bowties for dinner. She'd be on her fourth or fifth glass of wine. But to be fair, she'd cut back in recent years. Yes, she had. "I got to call Aunt Sharon. Is Daniel there?"

"No, he's not. Not now."

"Tell him to call me, will you, Elizabeth? What time is he coming home?"

"I'm not sure. It's hard to tell exactly when he'll be home these days."

"Oh yeah? Is he working too hard?"

"Yes," she said. "Yes, you might say that."

"Well, maybe he should think about relaxing a little. Tell him his mother's coming. When I get there, all I want is a little company, you know? All I ask is for a little conversation. He's got all his life to work. I guess he can do that much for me."

Elizabeth sat in the den with a glass of wine. She called Daniel's office, but there was no answer. After a while, she found herself at her desk, reading over her notes. *Nature, Darwinian, cruel . . . God for her is at times theistic, at times nonexistent . . . nature an extension of God . . . pantheism . . . Thus the garden imagery is indicative of . . .*

She wasn't going to kill it anymore, the poetry. When she wrote about it like that, analyzed it, took it apart, organized and explained it, she killed it. She didn't need to mutilate those beautiful lines and dry them on racks and chew the rubbery result like beef jerky to explain them.

She foraged through a box of Christmas candles, finally found an old lighter. She flicked it until her thumb was raw and ridged, but there was no spark. So there would be no dramatic flame. She gave up on the lighter. Maybe her notes and dissertation draft wouldn't be reduced to ashes after all. One hundred and fifty pages, five years of her life, and she hated it.

But she knew what to do about it.

Like thinning out seedlings. She could thin out her life, pluck out the weaknesses, the failures, and make room for the strong parts. Not flitting around delicately in white linen, heck no. Even Emily Dickinson the great American poet dug around in soil, hoed and raked, plunged her hands in the dirt like a surgeon goes in after a heart, delicately but strong, too, hands that meant business. There was dirt under those nails, those same hands that wrote about the soul selecting her own society, about Death the gentleman caller. Emily's hands were spreading cow shit, too.

She started shredding her dissertation and her notes. She was suddenly wild with energy. She tore long strips, then twisted them into paper roses, big cabbage roses. She thought it was appropriate; all those crisp leaves and curled blooms, the words peppering the petals like some kind of blight. You want garden imagery, you got it: a whole pile of manure, 150 pages of compost, transformed into a bed of roses.

Daniel arrived shortly before dusk. He got out of the car and stood looking at their yard, at the red soil. He peered down and poked a clod of clay with his foot. Ah yes, about the lawn, the failed social contract in the neighborhood. She'd almost forgotten. She would need to buy more flower seeds; she would plant them again tomorrow. By this summer—glorious!

She would go to the market tomorrow. Buy twice as many seeds. She would fill her car trunk with them.

He came in, rushed at first, flinging off his jacket, then slowed down, thinking it through. A bad sign. She stood in the kitchen, her hands covered with flour. She would tell him the food was coming along splendidly; the freezer was full of pastry crust now. She was working on the perishables.

"You're late. No doubt it's those awful office hours for young struggling Victorian lit scholars?"

"What happened to the yard out there?" Quiet and measured. He was angry. Well, yes, he would be angry at first.

"I'm planting wildflowers."

"What?"

"I'm planting flowers. It will be a while before they—"

"Elizabeth, the reception is tomorrow."

"I know."

"My colleagues, and maybe yours one day, will be here in our now lawnless home."

"Daniel, I know. I'm prepared. Come look." She opened the

refrigerator, waved her hands and did her best *Price Is Right* You've Won a New Refrigerator! imitation. He watched her warily. It had been a while since she had made an attempt at humor. He looked into the refrigerator, at the aspic, the dips, the heaps of freshly cut fruit. "I know it doesn't look like much now."

"Thirty people," he said.

"But no students, right." It wasn't a question. She watched him, the way he stopped every move on his face before it happened: how his eyebrows wanted to go up, his mouth press into a line. "I mean, I'm only prepared for a certain number. No more."

She moved to the kitchen island, her fingers cupping the ball of dough there, smooth, without a dent, a bald, featureless head. He stood ramrod straight, not even leaning on the door. Studying her.

"What's that you're wearing?"

"This old thing?" She floured the counter, the rolling pin. "Silk. I'm wearing silk."

"Why?"

"I like it. It feels good. *Carpe diem.*"

She began kneading the bread, *with the heels of your hands,* her cookbook said, and she smiled to herself; it was something she didn't know she had, heels on her hands.

He moved to the bedroom, and she could hear the dresser drawers banging. Careful, angry bangs.

She wiped off her hands and followed him, lay down on the unmade bed. He stood with his back to her, unbuttoned his shirt, peeled off his undershirt.

"Your mother's coming for a visit next week."

"My mother?"

"Yes, I talked to her this afternoon."

"My mother is coming for a visit?"

"She doesn't sound well, Daniel. Actually, I extended the invitation. She's going to have your aunt Sharon drive her."

"Next weekend? I have—you know I have to go to Durham next weekend. Elizabeth, I can't get out of that." Bewilderment deflected the full brunt of his anger. How rare, how out of the ordinary for Elizabeth to suggest a visit from Davida. Perhaps, deep down, he was a little pleased. Davida had always been a difficult mother-in-law.

"You did tell her you'd check with me, didn't you? Never mind, I'll call her and try to straighten things out."

"She won't like you changing the dates on her. She's excited about coming."

He took off his khakis. He reached in the closet for a hanger. The pants lay limply over his arm, as if they were swooning. He took off his underwear, tossed them in the clothes hamper. She sighed.

"What's wrong?"

"Nothing. Nothing. I was just thinking. Isn't it funny about male genitalia? Male sex organs are so external. So . . . demonstrative."

"Elizabeth, what in heaven's name are you talking about?" He half turned—she could have sworn bashfully—and slipped on red running shorts.

"Demonstrative. Not of love necessarily, or attachment, or even emotional intimacy. I wonder if there is always a reflexive emotional reaction, besides the biological response."

He looked at her askance, squint-eyed, like a boxer peering over his gloves. He said, "Will we need more red wine for tomorrow?"

"What if all the organs were like that? In the human species, I mean. You could look at someone and surmise so much about his life. You could observe the spleen at work, the seat of melancholia. They say malevolence is stored in the liver, so you could perceive quite clearly who meant you harm. And the heart." She gazed at the ceiling, hands behind her head, as if she were studying clouds. "Well, the *heart*. What would a *sweet* heart look like? Or a broken one? What would a cheating heart look like?"

He left the bedroom. The bathroom door squeaked in its awful, disturbing, middle-of-the-night way. "Have you gotten a lot of work done today?" he said loudly from behind the closed door, over his chortling stream of piss.

"I've been very productive." She went back into the kitchen, decided to open another bottle of wine. Red, this time. "I had a breakthrough in my research."

There was the flush of the commode, the washing of hands, the dreadful squeal of the door. After a minute, he stood there in the kitchen doorway. "Really?" he said. He laid his hand on her cheek. "That's great news."

"Glass of wine?" she asked.

"Sounds good." And then he peered at the goblet she handed him, Cutter's goblet, just as she knew he would. He said, "This is new. Isn't it?"

She nodded, handed him his wine. The goblet's curved glass reflected both of them, their faces tilted together—Daniel's uneasy glance, her own faraway gaze.

"Actually, it's very old."

"Yes, and it looks like it's seen better days."

He traced his finger over a small chip in the stem.

"Careful. I just glued it."

"Where did you get a glass like this, anyway?" He sipped his wine. He cleared his throat.

She shrugged and returned to her ball of dough, the kneading and flouring.

In the living room, he nudged a sleeping kitten with his foot. He'd asked the night before where she'd gotten them, the kittens. "I found them," she'd said. "I took a walk and found them." He didn't probe, thought it was a good sign that she'd been out, she knew, didn't want to jinx things by asking for details. And he didn't ask about her hair either, though his eyes had registered the surprise at her slick new trim.

Now, he bent down to pick up a paper rose the kittens had batted around. Playing paper hockey with her paper roses. He unfolded it slowly, his eyes scanning it like a machine.

"What the hell is this?"

"My dissertation." He had begged her to finish it for so long, and by God, it was finished now, wasn't it? *I'm weeding, I'm thinning out, I'm winnowing.* She flicked ice water on the dough. It was rolling nicely, not shredding or splitting.

He was squatting now, on a mad search, going through the wads of paper, panicked. "Please say it's not your only copy. You saved your research notes, right? I know you did everything on that damned Underwood, but you made copies, right?" His face was flushed, his hair sticking out in little horns, and he was moving about on his hands and knees like a playful father roughhousing. He walked back into the kitchen, where she stood kneading dough, her hands slowly pumping like a dying heart, and he took her by the shoulders and shook her once, hard. Like snapping a sheet before you fold it. He stared down at her fiercely as if he were talking to a child, yelling simple directions: do not cross the street, do not talk to strangers. Her teeth rattled.

"Why?"

She felt a buzzing, faraway feeling, part of her floating away. This was someone else's life, not her own. This man was not her husband. She stepped away from him, shrugged out of his grip, the kitchen stool behind her teetering, landing on the floor, banging like a shot. The kittens scattered.

"You were so close to being finished." A whisper. He turned away from her.

"No. No, I wasn't close."

"But to destroy all that work." He moved to the living room again, ambled through the tattered scraps of paper. "Goddamn it, Elizabeth." She went to him then, put her arms around him. She stroked his hair, left floury smudges and fingerprints on his shoulders. For so long she had been fighting hard to do the most ordinary, normal things—shopping, researching and writing, teaching, cooking—all that was expected of her. And now she was better— she was back to the land of the living, she just knew it—and she wanted a sanctuary, not a prison, and she wanted no more struggling over a doctoral dissertation, and no more sleeping all day. She wanted her husband back.

She buried her face in his neck and they stood there, the ragged shawl of their love, laced with her failures, wrapped around them.

"I know about her, Daniel," she said. "And I want it to stop."

Eleven

WHEN YOU HAVE A monkey lob its shit at you right in front of a prospective buyer, you are going to get a little peeved. At first I was too shocked to laugh. I just watched as she leaned over shaking her head, her fingers splayed, her hands beating at her stiff, teased hair, turds rattling around in there, trapped. By the time Mrs. Worthington screeched off in her Mercedes, Elizabeth and I were doubled over, watery-eyed.

But Mrs. Worthington would be back with a vengeance. She was mad—and she was going to get Ginnie and Barry mad, too. I had to move fast. I had to talk to Curt about some help, about a plan. He would want to help, once I explained to him what was at stake. He understood about holding on to the pieces of Sans Souci that were yours, about battling your own kin for the chance to hunker down and stay put.

My mind never strayed from Curt for very long. But I could still hear Gran's story of the Harris women's curse as if it were yesterday, as if she were standing there at the ironing board starching our Sunday dresses, going on about how the Harris women had a talent for choosing scoundrels, rogues of the worst sort. *When it comes to picking out men, we have about as much taste as a store-bought tomato. And don't forget it, girls. Don't forget it.*

My thoughts of Curt, of the two of us, were taking root in a hurry. The idea took over until suddenly, overnight, an unwieldy vine snaked through my mind with an *He's crazy about me* stem and an *He's going to be there for me* stalk. Only weeds grew that fast. Only nuisances in the garden.

When I arrived at the newsroom the next day, my blouse clinging to my shower-damp back, my hair still wet, my mother's pearl earrings dangling, my sister's Joy perfume drifting out from my wrists and neck, Curt wasn't in his office. As far as I could tell, he wasn't in the building. The way people were yawning and talking and joking, it felt as if he weren't coming back at all. I hung out in the morgue, poring over microfilm, before I stumbled upon the battered file cabinet in the corner labeled "Harris family." I came back to my desk and wrote something up.

One hundred years ago today, Henry Haynes Harris, founder of the Sans Souci Manufacturing Company, died of natural causes. Mr. Harris not only built the Sans Souci mill, but also helped create the surrounding mill village, described then as a "flourishing manufacturing town" with a population of 1,250. A major promoter of the post–Civil War textile movement in the Upstate Palmetto area, Mr. Harris was born in 1830 on his family's farm on Harris Bridge Road. In 1868, after his marriage to Jane Mays, the daughter of textile mill owner William Mays, Harris became a partner in the Maysville Mill. When that mill was sold, Mr. Harris organized the Sans Souci Manufacturing Company after securing one hundred thousand dollars in subscriptions for the stock of his proposed company. At the time of his death, Sans Souci was one of the leading mills in the region—operating 47,000 spindles and 1,300 looms.

Curt would like that I was writing about one of my forebears. I would just slip it in the conversation. Or put a note on his desk. *Here's the first '100 years ago' piece. It's about my great-great grandfather.*

At three o'clock, I walked over to Charlie. I could always count on Charlie to be sitting at his desk. He wasn't nicknamed "the Torpid Mass" for nothing.

"Listen, have you seen Cur—Mr. Sams today? I really have to talk to him."

"What's wrong?" Charlie squinted at me over his bifocals, moving nothing but his eyes.

"Oh, nothing. Just a question about a new assignment." I held up a bulging file.

Charlie hesitated, sucked his teeth.

"Don't know." We both looked over at Curt's office, the door open, the window darkened. "Why don't you just leave a message on his desk?"

His desk. Had Charlie heard about Curt and me? About our liaison in the office, on the desk? I blushed, looked at Charlie for any trace of irony.

I exhaled slowly. Was I imagining things?

"His home number is posted over there with the other numbers, you know. His mama's number, anyway. Call him if you need to. Probably drag him in from the golf course." He chuckled, a hard, wet hiccup. "All those rich boys play golf. Especially M.B."

When I finally did call, I got the answering machine, his mother's bland, smooth message.

"Curt—" I blurted, then remembered his mother might hear these messages, might be listening even now. I cleared my throat. "This message is for Curt Sams," I announced. "I'm sorry to bother you, Curt, I really am, but I need to talk to you privately." It seemed so long ago since we'd been together—days, seasons, not hours. "It's business," I added, then, "Ummm, oh yeah . . . this is Cutter . . . Johanson."

I ended up doing something I had promised myself I never would.

Even after witnessing two miserable, desperate women in the space of a week prowling and pining for a man, the same man, skulking around each other's home, I took up that obsessive, enticing, demeaning, irresistible practice of man spying myself.

Of course, my man didn't have a wife or a mistress. He had a mother.

The sunset glowed when I entered the gates of Green Mountain Estates. Sprinklers—on tripods like cameras or rising up from the ground with the stealth of periscopes—sprayed the wide lawns. I did not see Curt's Buick at 67 Wilderness Lane. The cars were sealed away in their garages like secrets. No one was out watering lawns, or talking, and there were no occupied front porches or verandas. The decks and gazebos and arbors—the people—were sequestered in backyards. The hulking stucco and stone and brick-faced houses jutted out protectively and a little fierce, like overprotective nannies glaring, their charges shoved behind them.

Gerard Avenue must have seemed as off-putting and stuffy as Green Mountain Estates at one time, as if we kept ourselves apart from the town of Sans Souci, with our side gardens and wraparound porches and protruding balconies. But at least we sat on those porches and waved.

Beyond a cluster of pitched roofs, the silver glint of golf clubs in the dusk winked at me. He was out there, on the green, I felt it. And what could I possibly say to explain my presence if I did encounter him? I hadn't thought that far. Besides, that wasn't the point. Man spying brought you a bittersweet longing, a buzzing charge, a thrum of heat in your belly. It did not usually bring out the man.

At home, I could hardly believe my good fortune. Ginnie wasn't there. The dread of a showdown with her, all that emotional wincing, left me exhausted. I washed out my uniform in the kitchen sink. I ran it through the old hand-cranked wringer. I collapsed on the sofa with a glass of iced tea and a mayonnaise and sugar sandwich. I fiddled around with the tinfoil-wrapped rabbit ears on the television, but the reception just got worse. I fell asleep. When the doorbell woke me, I was certain it was in the wee hours of the night, but my watch said it was only ten-thirty. I peered through the curtains. I swung open the door. I blinked at Curt blearily, the cool spring air clearing my mind, raising goose bumps on my arms.

"I got your message. Sounded serious. Did I wake you up?" The angry flush of a sunburn on his forehead left him white-browed, vulnerable.

"No. I just—well, tomorrow's an early Pancake Palace shift, so I try to go to bed early. But I was reading," I lied.

"I was entertaining some folks all day." He kicked at what was left of the worn welcome mat, curled up at the corners like a scab. He was wearing golf shoes. With tassels. "My mother's friends. Played golf, hung out at the club all day. I didn't get to the paper until tonight around seven." He looked at me with hooded red eyes. He'd been drinking all day out there on the golf course. "I thought maybe I could get them to up their ad space, these folks. I talked to them about it while I was out there wasting time on the green. But no go. They just—well, they treat me like a joke, like it's a hobby, my job, the paper, everything. A little fun before my real life starts."

I shivered. The spring nights were chilly. And cruel, the way they jerked you back from plunging headlong into summer, made you wait for nights as balmy and windless as the days. I could see his breath.

"Come in. It's cold."

He stepped inside, looked around the living room, studied things. He was not being bashful about it—his gaze landing on the dusty crystal chandelier above us, the sagging Queen Anne sofa, the jumble of newspapers in an old cotton basket. I turned on a lamp, harsh, too bright, a spotlight on the frayed and faded room.

"It's nothing about work," I said. "What I have to talk to you about, I mean. I know I said it was business, but . . . it's about this." I waved my hand in a little half circle, again watched his gaze sweep across the room, up the stairs, across the dank stillness of it all.

"God. This place is like a museum set or something."

"That's what I wanted to discuss. This house. Keeping my home."

"All that's missing is a velvet rope and sign-in book for visitors."

"I don't want to sell it."

"I don't blame you."

"But the others do. And I'm running out of ideas—"

He cut me short. "You don't need ideas. You need a good lawyer."

"Well, I think it's too late for—"

"It's not too late to stall. That's what you need. A specialist in wills and estates to throw a wrench in things. Slow things down, give you some time to figure out how to handle this. They'll probably ask for a partition action, when the court forces the sell. They'll have the house appraised, and they can insist the house be sold and profits divided three ways. But that's a last resort."

"My sister and brother want their cuts. They don't want to wait for me to raise the money."

"Tell you what. Our family lawyer is B. F. Haynes. I'll get you in to see him tomorrow."

"That sounds wonderful, but lawyers take money. Especially that one. And all I have is—"

"I'll work out the retainer deal with him. Explain the situation. The important thing is to stall this thing. That's what lawyers are good at, stalling. But what you have to do is, you have to get this thing to Haynes so he can put the skids on it. Throw up some obstacles. Slog it down with details. Right now, there's nothing to stop this place from being sold any day."

I swallowed. "I know."

"So I'll set it up for you with Haynes."

I nodded. I wanted my house, free and clear. I was sick of parsimony. For once, I imagined a different kind of place in life, from which I could look around and enjoy the view. I was tired of always settling for the cheapest brand of peanut butter.

"Don't worry anymore. Try to get some sleep." We stood there.

I clasped his hand. I was relieved to see the golden hair that ran from his knuckle to elbow was almost imperceptible. I was glad he wasn't hairy and dark, with a carpet on his chest and arms, like heroes I'd seen in the movies. I could see the faint, yellow bristle of his beard across his ruddy cheeks, and the slate gray of his eyes. My palm itched with a pleasant tingle. I took a step closer, entered into an embrace that began friendly and changed quickly. I felt the sharp nick of his teeth on my neck.

"Wait . . . Stop."

"Is someone else here? Your sister?"

"No, no. She's not here. But it's not that. It's not right. Here, I mean." He pulled away from me. I looked down at the floor, at my own bare feet, the remainders of last month's fire engine–red nail polish in worn splotches.

"Cutter, how old are you?"

"You know . . . I'm twenty-five."

"Twenty-five and got the run of a place like this."

"Well, yeah, but—"

"Where's your room?"

"It's at the top of the stairs."

He put his hands in his pockets, the bulky gold watch jutting out on his wrist. He turned to go.

"Don't go," I whispered. "Stay." I felt his mouth now, the bristle of his cheeks, smelled the sharp meanness of liquor. "With me."

We walked up the stairs and into my room. I turned on the lamp by my bed. He blinked at the dragonflies and toadstools and elves there on the wallpaper from my childhood, faded and buckled. His red-rimmed eyes were hooded when he looked at me, his mouth in its usual firm line. He took off his belt and pants, then his shirt. I thought how rangy he was, how triangular. His broad forehead tapered to a small, strong chin, and the pale, wide shoulders, with a sprinkling of freckles, narrowed to a slender, hard waist. He stood by my lumpy, slightly sagging bed, then fell back on it slowly, his feet still on the floor.

"This is nice."

"You forgot to take off your shoes and socks," I said, smiling. I still stood by the lamp, looking down at him.

"Oh God, this is good."

"I'll be right back," I said.

I tiptoed down the hall to my mother's old bedroom. I took off my jeans and shirt, my underwear, and kicked them under the bed. I pulled out a pale pink shift from the bottom bureau drawer, slipped it over my head. The satin cascaded over my breasts and my hips, down to the floor.

Back in my room, Curt's breath rose in a jagged snore. I sat on the edge of the bed listening to the rhythm of his breathing, his own fits and starts. His mouth had lost its resolute line, and hung open in a rubbery O. On his high, shiny forehead there were two tiny craters. Chicken pox scars, I saw when I examined them more closely. A nest of golden nose hairs, clipped and coiled, was tucked out of sight in each nostril. His pale pink eyelids, pearly and quivering, looked lashless in the rosy gloom. I took off his shoes and socks, picked up his feet, and moved his legs onto the bed, covered him with a nubby, frayed quilt I found in the closet. I considered stretching out beside him. But he kept shuddering, like a baby, moaning and turning, and it did not seem polite to witness such a restless sleep.

I went to Gran's bed across the hall, slipped off my shoes, nestled under the covers. I closed my eyes, but the rustling, scraping sounds of the rosebushes against the bedroom window kept me from sleep. The plump green buds waved in the wind like angry fists. This thicket of roses would bloom soon. Like most of our yard's ornamental flora, the roses had been put in the earth to mark some milestone of our family: a wedding or birth, perhaps; more likely a death. Last September, on the morning when my grandmother's fever spirited her off, when we'd found her here, exactly where I was, curled in her bed as if in sleep, the climbing rose was at its peak, the bloom-heavy vines shrouding the windows like tentacles.

Now they battered and thumped through the moonlit night, the vines. They stopped me from dreaming.

At dawn, I went across the hall and watched Curt rouse himself.

He squinted at his watch, then looked at me. There were angry, red sleep lines on his face. "Christ, it's five o'clock. I've got to go." He was wearing boxers. His pants and shirt were in a crumpled heap on the floor, despite my having neatly folded them. How had he managed that?

"Commmeere," he mumbled. I sat on the bed beside him. His hands moved up and down my silky gown. "This is nice," he said. I stretched out alongside him, and felt his breath at the back of my neck. This must be like married love, I thought. As casual, as common as brushing your teeth.

I sat up. "I'll make coffee, if you like."

His straw-colored hair was flattened on one side, sticking out in tufts on the other, and there was still that sharp, boozy smell seeping from his pores. He shook his head and yawned. "Stay in bed. It's chilly. I'll see myself out, lock the door behind me."

"But I have to get up anyway. I need to get ready for my morning shift at the Pancake Palace."

"Listen, I'm sorry." He did not meet my eyes.

"Sorry?"

"Sorry . . . about falling asleep. Last night."

I shrugged. "You shouldn't drink so much."

He disappeared into the bathroom. I could hear him in there, splashing and gargling. When he navigated his way down to the kitchen, I handed him coffee, watched him stand there and sip from the gold-rimmed china cup, festooned with orange and pink poppies, his finger looped through the handle, holding the saucer underneath properly. It was a ridiculous sight, like a prank, like a man wearing petticoats or heels. Is that how Barry felt? Tiptoeing through our brittle, maidenly world? Is that why my brother took refuge in the barracks of men?

I took the china cup from Curt and poured the coffee in a cracked Palmetto University mug I found in the back of the cabinet.

"There," I said, handing it to him. "That's better."

"Do you have any aspirin? God, please say yes."

"Well, let me see." I plundered through the medicine drawer in the pantry. There was Midol for PMS and three different kinds of cough syrup. There were scads of Gran's prescription bottles—for arthritis, blood pressure, nerves.

"I have these headache powders."

"Oh, fuck. Forget it. It's too late anyway. I just need some shut-eye."

He kissed me on the forehead, a hard, sour pressing down.

"See you later, then," I said.

"Maybe I'll feel human by lunchtime."

I walked over to the window, stood shivering and watched the taillights of his car disappear. The heat didn't come on. I should check the furnace. I'd been trying to hold off ordering more oil until the fall, but I hadn't expected a cold spring. I'd have to put more oil on credit. I crawled back into my bed for a few more minutes. Curt had left warmth there, proof that I hadn't imagined my night visitor after all.

I was stuck at the Pancake Palace till noon, consolidating ketchup, scrubbing the coffeepots with salt, wiping down the mirrors in the bathrooms. The worst closing duties. Punishment for calling in sick the day before. I didn't even try to argue, Jolene was in no mood to talk. She cut me off abruptly when I asked her about trading sections.

"One more stunt like that, miss, calling in sick. Make sure your guts are tore up good, before you call in. Make sure you're one step away from calling the emergency. I had to take me a damn nerve pill yesterday just to get through the morning. You never heard such carrying on from people when we got backed up, all of us in the weeds. And you at home with a hangover. I swear. You'll find yourself out of a job next time."

"It wasn't a hangover," I hissed.

I took the coffeepots off the burners and made the rounds through the dining room. Mr. Heller and Darla sat in a booth by the window with Misty and her fiancé.

"Oh, honey, if you fill this cup again, I'm going to need rubber sheets tonight." Darla was giggly. She held a half-open compact mirror, like a prop, casting a sideways glance at Rick, Misty's fiancé. She'd taken to him, offered to cut his hair for free, trim him up a little around the ears, if Misty would just bring him by her hair shop before they returned to Atlanta. "He said I looked like Tammy Wynette," Darla whispered to me earlier when she'd cornered me in the back by the ladies' room. "Can you believe that?" Her face had still been flushed from the compliment. "His aunt works in Nashville. She's a secretary at the records company. She knows Tammy Wynette. She knew Elvis. He certainly is handsome."

"Elvis?"

"No. For goodness's sake, Cutter, pay attention. Rick. Rick is handsome. Looks just like Jimmy Stewart in his young days, don't you think? Misty caught herself a good one." We both looked across the room at Misty and Rick, scrunched together in the red leather booth across from Mr. Heller. Rick was long-limbed and pink-skinned, with a wide, shy smile. He had a long neck and an Adam's apple that bobbed nervously above his button-down shirt. He had an arm slung around Misty's tensed-up shoulders as she leaned forward to say something to her father. She and Mr. Heller and Darla, too, had the same slanted features—thin, tapered noses, square, determined chins. A family semblance captured by angles. No doubt Misty's children would be embossed with the Heller square chin. There were just some family features you knew would get passed on. Curt and I both had a tendency to sunburn and freckle. If we ever had children, they would, too.

"'Course, she wants a big house in Atlanta, fancy job, kids, the works. She wants everything."

"Yeah, well, Misty was always ambitious."

"But mark my words. In a marriage, when bills start stacking up in the mailbox, sex goes right out the window."

"Oh."

"Anyway, Buddy's been talking to Rick about them setting up housekeeping here in Sans Souci."

"Misty will never go for that."

"Well, her fellow likes it here. Says it's quaint."

Now, Darla snapped shut her compact and covered her coffee cup with a hand. Mr. Heller held up his mug and winked at me. "Fill 'er up."

Misty leaned across the table and put her hand on his sleeve. "Daddy, didn't the doctor tell you to cut back on coffee?"

"Are you sure you want to get hitched?" Mr. Heller glared at Rick. "This woman is mighty bossy."

I moved on to my eight-top by the window. After a minute, Jolene caught up with me at the coffee station.

"Telephone call for you. It's your brother. You can take it back in Mr. D's office if you want."

"I don't want to talk to my brother," I said. "Can you tell him I left or something?"

"He's already called about five times this morning. Can't you take a minute to see what he wants?"

"I know what he wants. That's why I'm not going to take his call."

"Oh, all right. I'll say I can't find you. But I don't like it one bit, lying to a marine."

"Thanks. I owe you one."

"Hey, look over there," she whispered. "The weenie peddler is making the rounds." She clasped her hands together in a quick, gleeful clap.

Parker James stood talking to Buddy Heller by the cash register, handed him a business card. "You get much of a morning crowd at that filling station?" I heard him ask Mr. Heller as he clapped him on the back. "I bet your customers just love hot dogs."

"Now that takes guts," Jolene told me. "I am just so proud of my little brother."

Alfred was waiting for me on the front porch at home, a nervous flurry of chickens pacing at his feet. Today was one of his days to work at the paper, and I'd almost forgotten.

"Alfred, I just need to change clothes and I'll be right out, okay?"

"Okay." He was smiling, watching a chicken chase a grasshopper.

Inside, I saw the note on the kitchen table, Ginnie's slanted spiked handwriting like a scream: *If this guy lowballs we'll have to take it!!! Thousands of dollars gone because of YOUR FOOL STUNT!*

Curt was at lunch. A very important lunch, the office manager told me, and he was not to be disturbed. But I knew. Curt was meeting with Haynes, the lawyer. Curt was arranging things for me. Still, I worried it was too late. There was a new stack of furious messages from Barry on my desk. Were negotiations and dickering and contract terms being tossed around by Mrs. Worthington even now? I had to talk to Ginnie, call off Mad Dog Worthington.

But Ginnie wasn't to be found.

When I got to Palmetto University, double-parked in a handicapped space, sprinted up the stairs to the English Department, Ginnie wasn't in her little cubicle. I stared at the dingy, burlapped partition she shared with three students, a Highlighter parked in the middle of *Leaves of Grass*. I walked up and down the hall, casually craning my neck into offices, but I knew she was not around, sensed it, in a certain sister way.

Well, what would I say when I found her? *You've been pawning*

Gran's china, our family's heirlooms. I won't go along with this, unless you give me more time. Unless you give me a chance to stay.

I passed an office and saw Daniel Byers behind a desk. He was scribbling. I stood in the doorway until he looked up. He rose awkwardly, hit a leg on his desk, winced slightly.

"Cutter."

"I'm sorry to interrupt you. I'm looking for Ginnie."

"She's running some errands. Copying some materials for me. What's wrong?"

It was a dim, tiny office, the shelves spilling over with books, a bicycle jammed behind his desk. I shrugged.

"It's a crazy day around here," he added. "A conference our department is having starts tonight. I'm heading off to the airport myself to pick up someone shortly." He had the generic handsomeness of men in shampoo advertisements. I made a point to avoid them myself, too-handsome men. The quarterback-movie-star-politician good looks always paired with scandals and infidelities and faded, distraught wives. His eyes were more deep-set than I remembered, shadowed, distressed caves in the steep smoothness of his face.

"I'll just wait at her desk, thanks."

He shambled over in three crooked steps from around his desk and closed the door behind me.

"You seem—upset."

He cared what I thought. He knew I knew things about Ginnie. About him. The Persian rug I was standing on, for example, had given Ginnie a bad rug burn. For days she'd screeched when she stepped in the shower, laughed when I saw the pink scratches down the middle of her back, on her spine, ballooning out on her tailbone. "For love," she told me. "But it was worth it."

"You two are arguing again?"

"Well, you know Ginnie."

She's rash, hasty, careless, my sister. Shortsighted, selfish. The slimy facts writhed and knotted, unacknowledged, between us. Pregnant. And he did not know. He did not even know! *After the conference,* Ginnie said. That's when she'd tell him. He would know soon. I bit my lip, reminded myself: my sister loves this man.

A framed photograph sat at the corner of his desk, smug, half hidden beside *Barnaby Rudge.* Elizabeth and Daniel, on a boat, flushed with sunburns, a white sail flapping crookedly behind their heads. Their smiles were like little hooks, drawing me closer. I picked up the picture, studied it. Daniel at her shoulders, grinning a kiss on her cheek. She was holding one hand up, protesting to the photographer, but she was laughing hard, her dark hair spread like a fan around them both. Why had Ginnie allowed it to stay in the office? Daniel must have insisted.

He took a deep breath. "I know this situation is"—his words measured and heavy, like footsteps plodding up a steep stairway— "awkward for you."

I looked him in the eye. "When was this picture taken?"

He did not answer.

"She looks so happy there," I said. "She looks . . . different somehow. Carefree."

The fluorescent lights flickered and buzzed busily above us.

"You've seen . . . my wife?"

"I've met her."

"You know Elizabeth?"

I nodded.

"You know Elizabeth."

I swallowed. "Yes."

"How?"

"She came to . . . my house. She was upset, but I invited her in and gave her a beer and we talked awhile—"

"She would never do that. She would never go to a stranger's house. She doesn't drink beer."

"Well, she did."

"You told her."

"I didn't tell anything," I said. "She already knew. Somebody called her and told."

"The anonymous phone call."

"Yeah, that's what she told me, too."

"I just . . . don't believe it. Elizabeth showing up on your doorstep of her own volition and striking up a friendship with you? I can't see it."

"Ask her if you don't believe me."

"Do you have any idea how fragile my wife is?"

I looked at the hard vertical line between his eyes. "Well, I know she was a little reluctant to, you know, go out—"

"Do you realize how close to—how near to breaking down Elizabeth is . . ." The way he talked about her, tenderly, saying her name quiet like that, balancing it, as if he had set her on a shelf, propped her up there, wanted her to stay put. Elizabeth. Maybe Daniel Byers loved his wife. But he didn't know her.

"Look, Elizabeth isn't like us. She can't handle the world out there. She sees things differently."

"You sound like she'd melt in the rain."

"You haven't seen what I have. Her life is not safe."

I thought of Elizabeth laughing, both of us doubled over on the porch when Crusty pelted Mrs. Worthington. That was just yesterday. She was in good spirits. She even seemed plucky when she left. Upbeat.

"My wife is a gifted scholar. She's won prizes. When it comes to her work, she has stunning perceptions. But . . . I can see now where this—where I—have derailed her." He stood and turned to the window, clanged the venetian blinds to the side and peered down on a tarred flat roof and the parking lot. "She confronted me last night. I should have known, she was acting so strangely." His voice lowered, he muttered to himself, "She's self-destructive and aggressive. She's not herself."

Had our adventure yesterday pumped Elizabeth up? Had she left feeling brave enough to finally confront Daniel last night? I swallowed, tasted metallic bitterness. What had I done? I was just making everything worse. How did I ever get swept up in this horrible sticky triangle?

He closed his eyes and ran a hand over his face. "I just—I have to get us—I have to get Elizabeth through tonight. That party she insists on."

"I never told Ginnie about your wife coming over that day. I don't know why I didn't." I looked down. "Well, yes I do. I know why. Because I like her, Elizabeth. I like her. But I love my sister. And I just want all this mess to clear up on its own."

A sudden whistling, a yell; someone rambled past in the hallway, a wet, slick raincoat rustling. We looked at each other, afraid the door would fly open, preparing for an interruption. I flinched, thinking of Ginnie's angry face. After a minute, when silence returned, I cleared my throat. I wondered if I should get it all over with, tell him the big secret, the real one.

"Now I know all the variables," he said slowly. "That changes things. But it doesn't decide things. It makes things harder."

But he didn't know. *All the variables? You gotta be joking—because you're in deep, you don't even know the big one, there's one variable that I can pretty much guarantee will mess up any tidy little equation you come up with.* My lips parted stickily, the words came close to coming out, so close.

"Will you tell my sister to call me at the paper when she shows up? I know she's mad at me, but I just need to talk to her. Tell her it's urgent."

"Yes," he said, still staring vacantly in front of him. "I'll tell her. I don't know what's keeping her. She's late."

"Yes," I said. "She is."

I took care of all the funeral write-ups with unaccustomed courtesy and efficiency, keeping one eye on Curt's empty office. At five,

I began to pace. Two days away from his office, not even a walk through the newsroom. That was strange. And what about my appointment with the lawyer? And what about—us?

I walked past the lifestyle editor, who was preparing the weekend's wedding section. All those snapshots of brides spread out on her desk like an abandoned game of solitaire, a flat array of silliness. Filmy white netting, and fake pastel flowers; all those forced smiles and stiff eyes. Still, my own private image flickered: Curt in a tuxedo waiting for me at the bottom of the staircase at my house, watching me glide down, my long white silk whispering.

At five-thirty, instead of going home, I went into Curt's office. Just barged in and sat down at his desk and started figuring on a legal pad. What time would my appointment with Haynes the lawyer be? Would Curt go with me? I'd have to come up with a good excuse to tell Jolene if the appointment was in the morning and I couldn't make my Pancake Palace shift. I wrote down $1,014.09 and circled it. That was every penny I'd managed to save. No bank would approve a mortgage with my salary. I just needed some help now to tide me over, until I had some real savings.

I closed my eyes, the thoughts in my mind like smoke, floating and drifting. I sat back and folded my arms behind my head, just as I'd seen Curt do. I thought of him sleeping in my bed.

"Excuse me?"

My eyes flew open. I sat up awkwardly. My pen rolled to the edge of the desk and pinged to the floor. Curt's mother stood there. I had seen her come into the newsroom so often, I would have known her shadow. The hair, in a wavy too-young bob, the silk scarf, the heavy jewelry, the slanted, important way she held her head.

"I'm looking for my son."

I stared blankly. I needed to impress her, my future mother-in-law. And right now I needed to say something incredibly witty, a droll remark that would engender peals of laughter and admiration.

"Uh, he—I was waiting—I mean—but I think—" I sputtered.

She turned to speak to someone standing outside the office, who whispered, "Maybe he's in the back."

I moved closer to the mirrored one-way window, got myself a side view. A woman stood there. She was tall and slender, her long, dark hair falling in a glossy mahogany sheet past her shoulders. She had that uncomplicated look: good skin and straight hair. Ten seconds and I could size her up. She went once a month to the ritziest salon for a half-inch hair trim, had the manicurist put on plain gloss on trimmed nails, owned Keds tennis shoes in every color. And a horse. She was the type to own horses.

Then she squealed. I jumped. That little shriek surprised everyone else, too. The staff stared from desks, from the copier, from the drink machine. Even Alfred, who was dusting someone's penholder, looked up. Curt appeared across the newsroom. He said, "Bunny?" She bounded over to him and leapt, jumped into his arms like a ballet dancer.

She was clamped onto him, and yes, I told myself, out of courtesy or embarrassment, he seemed to be holding on to her.

"Bunny?" Something in my chest closed like a clam. Bunny? I must have whispered it. Mrs. Sams, smiling, still standing in the door, turned to me and said, "Bunny. Yes, that's correct. Well, Belinda, actually. It's a family name, as I understand it."

My knees went weak. I sat back down in Curt's leather chair.

"Curt probably doesn't tell you people at work, but he is practically engaged," she said, laughing but not really.

"I racked my brain trying to think of how I would do this, get him to take some time off—he is persnickety about his work, you know. Why, he's here half the night sometimes. So I arranged for a much-needed respite." I followed her gaze at the two of them. Curt's hand was laced through Bunny's hair. Mrs. Sams waved to them.

"Don't waste your time," I said. My voice tight, cracked. I tried to swallow. "It's a one-way window."

Mrs. Sams droned on. How Bunny was majoring in prelaw at Vanderbilt and it was just harrowing, planning this surprise visit, lining up the flight and such, without Curt knowing. How Bunny's father was a partner in the largest law firm in Kentucky, how she and Curt had dated for *"oh—just years, you know."*

I opened Curt's desk drawer in search of a tissue, found a balled-up napkin in the corner. I held it to each eye, pressed hard, until I saw colors. The napkin smelled of fixative and barbecue sauce and it reminded me of Curt. I wondered what I would do when Mrs. Sams stopped talking long enough to ask what was wrong.

"I thought, I'll just fly Bunny up from Vanderbilt. Surprise him with his sweetheart. You can't top that, now, surely."

Curt and Bunny were talking now. They would walk into his office soon. I made my way around the desk, brushed by a beaming Mrs. Sams, and shot through the door. Then I collided with them.

Curt stiffened and pulled back from Bunny.

"Cutter? Oh—w-were you waiting for me?" The twitter of a stammer gave me hope.

Bunny smiled, looked away kindly, her hand still resting on his shoulder. My vision narrowed. I saw little squares of things. I stared at her, my mind clicking like a camera, and I knew I would be mulling over those snapshots later. The thin plain gold chain around her neck curving over the smooth knolls of two delicate collarbones. A white linen blouse with a scoop neck, crisp, but with a few important wrinkles, no polyester blend in this one. Teeth, white as teacups.

Then Curt peered out from his cheerful mask, his eyes hard as buttons. He said, "Is there a problem?"

"Yes," I managed, nodding my head in assent with myself.

He looked over my head to the sports desk. He held up three fingers. "Give me three minutes, Rooster," he called. "Meeting in my office." His eyes flicked back to me meanly. "You think you could hold the obit questions? I'm swamped. And I've got to get out of here early."

Dismissed. Just like that. Dismissed!

In the bathroom, I locked myself in one of the stalls, unwound an entirely good roll of toilet paper and held it on my face like a compress over a wound. I looked up at the ceiling, the white squares like soda crackers. I pictured the sky hovering above the building and, higher still, lush, thick clouds.

The bathroom door squeaked open. A mop bucket clanged. I could see the tips of big white Nike tennis shoes.

It was Alfred, bearing bleach and ammonia to clean up my world. As usual, he'd watched everything, had picked up on what everyone else had seemed to miss.

I came out of the stall. He brushed my shoulder with a hand large and soft as a ball glove, peering at me closely.

"Cutter?"

I looked into his face: sad, scrunched up, tilted like the Magnavox dog's.

"Did you get a hurt?" he whispered.

"Don't worry about me." I blotted my eyes again, the tissue shredded and damp. "It's just a misunderstanding."

I began washing my face at the sink. After a minute, I patted it dry with paper towels. Alfred watched, the faintest wrinkle between his brows.

Oh God, I was a wreck. How could I go back through the news-room looking like this? My eyes were puffy and my eyebrows angry red slashes and . . . I looked like Ginnie. I peered at myself closely in the mirror. Yes, I looked like Ginnie that day she'd been crying, when she and Daniel had spent the morning in our house. When she'd tried to make lunch for him and then burned herself and he'd told her something about how they'd have to slow things down until he could get Elizabeth some help. She sat blubbering at the dining room table after he'd left, and I couldn't understand how Ginnie could feel so dejected, so spurned. Heartbroken.

I wouldn't be coming back. I should clean out my desk right this instant. Written notice? Two weeks in advance? Ha! Let Curt

Sams fill the dead beat with someone half as good. Let him try to communicate with the Queen of the Dead. I sniffed.

"Alfred, we're going to have to go now. As soon as I get my stuff together, okay?"

If anyone looked at me funny out there, or asked if I'd been crying, I'd just say it was the McMillan obit. That would work. The McMillan obit was particularly wrenching, I'd explain, because everyone knew Goober McMillan, the maintenance man at Sans Souci High for thirty years. He'd cleaned up generations of our after-weekend puke and our Tater Tot fights and scrubbed off the spray-painted *cocksuckers* that appeared every year on the entranceway of the school. And he never complained. Well, just a little. He complained some, like when he called us spoiled-asshole-kids-ain't-worth-a-damns, but how could you blame the man for that? Most of the time, when he wasn't laid up on a drunk and the beer wasn't seeping from his pores, he was always there when you needed him, in his soiled gray jumpsuit, tugging the aluminum ladder and box of lightbulbs. In the last few years, he'd put on weight. He'd gotten fat, so huge. Climbing ladders? Forget it. Each foot was like a little dog. And so Goober McMillan retired and within weeks was dead, found dead just this morning, Mrs. Kincaid told me, in his one-bedroom efficiency, down by the depot, not a friend in the world but three very hungry cats. One more day, she said, and those cats would've eaten his face. At that point, I'd shake my head and tell Charlie or Marti or Rooster or whoever was still listening that I was just too distraught and I needed to be alone and then I'd clean out my desk, pack up my coffee cup and African violet and favorite pens in a cardboard box. And I'd go tell Alfred to come along and—

"Alfred?"

But he was already gone. Why, he'd just turned and left silently without a peep. Without telling me—

"Oh no. Oh my God."

I whirled around and ran out of the bathroom, down the short hall, and into the newsroom.

I was too late to stop what was about to happen.

But not too late to watch.

Alfred was holding Curt by the shoulder, Curt's mother was screaming, Bunny was yelping. And everyone—Marti from her desk, Charlie standing by his, Rooster putting the phone receiver down to stare—all of them watched as Alfred shoved Curt. I could tell he didn't have the heart to put a lot into it, but even his soft-hearted push was strong. It knocked Curt down and sent him reeling into a desk chair.

I waited for the thud, the crunch that you hear in fight scenes in the movies. But there was nothing—hardly a sound at all. Just the thump as Curt fell back on the floor, hit the chair and flipped it over, its wheels spinning as he crouched beside it like a toddler off a tricycle, dazed and red-faced.

Somewhere a telephone rang, but no one answered.

Alfred stood over Curt. He pointed down at him. "You a mean man! You hurt Cutter's heart."

The whispers began, whined through the air like mosquitoes. I walked over to Alfred and took him by the arm and guided him toward the stairs, praying that no one would try to stop us. He shuffled along leisurely after me; his arm hung slack and loose in my hand. "Cutter, I left my drink in the snack room."

"Forget it," I hissed. "We'll get you another drink. Let's go."

Bunny helped Curt up. He brushed himself off. His face was still fever red. He did not look up. His shocked look was wearing off, the humiliation setting in.

Mrs. Sams came toward us. "Hurry, Alfred," I whispered under my breath and pushed him toward the stairs. But we were not fast enough.

"Mother. Mother!" Curt yelled. She didn't stop, didn't even slow down, and his calling just made things worse—everybody started staring again, this time at Mrs. Sams. She gripped my elbow. For a minute I was transported back to Miss Huffstedler's School of Dance, back in tap class, where the dance teachers regularly gripped my elbow and demanded that I *step ball change*. But it wasn't me Mrs. Sams wanted. "Somebody call the police!" she screamed. She pushed me aside and got right up in Alfred's face.

"You crazy nigger," she rasped.

"Mother!" Curt was standing beside her then, his face crimson, his nose bleeding. "Shut up, Mother! Why don't you shut up. You don't know anything about this."

She stared at him, her son, and her jaw dropped. I clomped down the stairs, pulled Alfred behind me. In the lobby, a stippled and green world beckoned from beyond wavy glass bricks, like a strange sea. We burst through the double doors and into the parking lot.

"Now listen, Alfred," I said when we got in the car. He was staring at the floorboard. "That was a mean lady, so don't pay any attention to her. And don't try to tell Father Bob about any of this. Do you understand? Let me do the talking. Alfred? Are you listening?"

"Am I fired?"

"Well, Alfred, I'll be honest. It doesn't look too good when you go around hitting the boss."

"But he hurt you. He broke your heart."

"Well, it doesn't matter. You know better than that—pushing people down."

"I will never do that again. I promise. I just wanted to fix your heart. Cutter, I just wanted to help you."

"Shit," I said. Then started the car. "At least the car's working."

Alfred had to be calmed down before I dropped him off at Father Bob's. I could just picture both of them bawling. It was more than I could handle. How I was going to explain this to Father Bob, that Alfred—a man who refused to kill the fleas on kittens—might be charged with assault and battery?

"Alfred, stop crying. You're going to have to stop crying now. It will bother Father Bob—so stop it. Okay? It makes me cry, too. Look—I've got an idea. You can come over to my house and I'll fix you some hot chocolate and then we can clean the stove."

He sniffled.

"Okay, let's just—let me think." I drove up and down our street, through the neighborhood, back to the Sans Souci main drag, finally pulled into the empty bank parking lot beside Mr. Heller's filling station.

I handed money to Alfred. "Here, go in to Mr. Heller's and buy us some Coca-Colas and a bottle of bubbles."

"You coming?"

"No, I'll wait here for you."

"How come?"

"I don't feel like talking to anybody."

"But won't you be lonely?"

"Nope, I've got plenty to think about."

The bank's new vinyl sign flapped in the breeze. I guess the bank had a new name again, I couldn't keep up. It was a splendid place, ornate, the entranceway paved with tiles, the doors wide and curved and important, like a church. It still said *Sans Souci Bank and Trust* on top, but that was from decades ago, back when they carved a bank's name in stone. Now, every six months or so, the bank was bought out and got a new name and a new sign. The only thing that stayed the same was Miss Bee, the head teller, who had worked there for forty-some years. Every week, I'd deposit my paycheck in the drive-through and Miss Bee would slide out the little drawer and it would clap open and shut like a puppet's mouth. She'd send back my deposit receipt tucked under a flat red sucker.

Maybe the bank was hiring tellers? I would ask Miss Bee tomorrow.

After a few minutes, Alfred came back to the car. He took out the bottle of bubbles.

"Why we driving round and round and round?"

"We'll just keep driving until you feel better. Until we run out of bubbles."

That was another good thing about convertibles—your own built-in bubble machine. Alfred dipped the pink wand in the bottle and held it up high.

"Go fast."

"We're already speeding."

Bubbles ripped furiously from the little wand, then floated lazily behind us. Alfred laughed, a booming, joyful explosion. I was the one with the hitched breath now, weeping.

"Go faster. Faster!" We turned onto the Palmetto Highway. The bubbles were almost gone now and Alfred was scraping the bottle with the wand, the way you might rattle a knife in an empty jar of mayonnaise.

I turned into Olde English Acres.

"Are we going home now?"

"Yes," I said. "In a minute. I'm about to turn around. It's just that I'm worried about something."

We drove past the Byers' house. There were cars parked on either side of the street. So there would be a party after all.

Alfred clapped. "Father Bob is here! He's here!"

"What do you mean? Where?"

He pointed to Father Bob's green Dodge Dart parked on a pansy bed, the driver's-side door still open.

I pulled up behind it.

"Why is it parked all crooked like that?" Alfred asked. "Is it wrecked?"

Was Father Bob looking for us? Why would he come to Elizabeth's house?

"Oh no," I whispered. "No."

Alfred looked at me. "What is it?"

"It's not Father Bob. Ginnie's here."

She had borrowed Father Bob's car. It would be easy to claim some emergency. She'd done it before. "Oh, this is bad. Bad." I groaned.

"Did she crash?"

"Yes, she crashed," I said. "A party."

Twelve

SHE NEEDED A PAIR of silver candlesticks—a candelabrum would be even better—so Elizabeth dug through Cutter's boxes. She unwrapped a silver saltshaker in brittle, balled-up newspaper from May 12, 1959. There was a dead granddaddy longlegs in the second box, along with ten teacups, the rims as thin as paper. She unpacked it all—the rose-entwined cups and saucers, the crystal goblets as striated as first frost, the heavy silverware with curved handles as solid as guns. No setting complete—just bits and pieces from mismatched settings. She didn't have the heart to put it all back.

She washed everything by hand, holding each item gingerly, not playing favorites. Spending as much time on the milk of magnesia–cobalt blue bottles as the English fine bone china and crystal glasses. When she finished drying the last piece of Blue Willow china—a large, gently sloping platter—she studied it a moment. Above the blue birds and rivers and bridges, her own serious, pert face peered hard, as if she could glimpse a tinier, perfect reflection of herself in one of those painted ponds.

She felt a strange ache, recognized hunger. The aroma of pastry wafted over to her. She hadn't felt hungry like this in a long time. She grabbed an oven mitt, slipped it on, and took out a tray of baked cheese that bubbled and sizzled like applause. She opened the refrigerator and looked at the almond-topped quiches cooling. The kittens looked up sleepily from their corner of the kitchen. They blinked at her, their small heads trembling.

She made herself a cup of tea, walked to the spare bedroom.

This would be the baby's room.

They would spend the weekend cleaning it out. That is what they'd decided. The musty twin bed, the beat-up Samsonite suitcases, all those boxes of silverfish-invaded paperbacks, the neglected exercise bike and her trays of seedlings and grow lights crammed in the corner—all this refuse from a life of waiting—would be gone by Monday. She would paint the walls a nice pastel. Powder blue, maybe. Or yellow.

Elizabeth rubbed her eyes. She was exhausted and her body still ached, unaccustomed to morning love. Last night, neither of them had slept much. At first, Daniel had tried to explain. She could still hear the whispered *I'm sorry*'s. Her ear had been moist with them, the *I'm sorry*'s. How did it start? How long had it gone on? Did he love Ginnie? The questions rose up inside her, swelled like a wound. *I love you, Elizabeth. That is what matters.* And the lid clapped down on her dangerous questions . . . and her own secret: Cutter—her friendship with Cutter.

Let's give it until the summer and we'll see a fertility specialist if we need to. By morning he had plans for them . . . how wonderful to hear them again.

She walked a slow circle around the room. A crib appeared, a sailboat mobile dangled, and Daniel was standing there peering in, smiling. He leaned over the crib, a small fist clamped on his finger. Elizabeth took a step toward them, her husband and child, but as she drew closer, they dispersed like tiny airborne droplets.

The kitchen timer blared, and she took out another tray of baked pastry. The tender asparagus grew furiously green and limp, then bent gracefully as Elizabeth lifted it from pot to tray.

She put out all of Cutter's china and crystal and silver, got out her best linen tablecloths, lighted a dozen candles. Outside, she cut branches of forsythia and camellia blossoms, plucked handfuls of pansies, and placed them in glass pitchers and vases throughout the house. Even in the bathroom, where a purple pansy harrumphed from one of Cutter's blue medicine bottles. Walking through the house, she surveyed her work. The rumblings of happiness inside her rose and hummed like a well-oiled machine.

When Daniel came home, she was in the kitchen. She came into the living room with her hands still damp, shaking them, flinging water, then stopped when she saw him, his pinched, too-thin mouth, the slump of his shoulders. Something that had hung between them black and hooded and secretive, dangling precariously and heavy, now dropped, settled in a heap on the floor. Good or bad, she didn't know, but something else had happened, something out there.

Behind him a small hunched figure hung back.

"This is Mary," he said, and he turned and took a brown bag and a large plastic covered platter from her. He set them on the table. Unloaded beer, wine, pretzels; uncovered the platter and revealed folded cold slices of meat, carrots, and celery sticks, a radish rose. A receipt lay flattened on the tray, dampness leaking purple numbers, the red *Thank you for shopping Lo-Bi* mocking.

The woman was pretending to study their stacks of art books in the corner. She wore a polyester uniform, white nurse shoes. She had a large, pale pocked face, and black-rooted, wispy yellow hair.

"Mary cleans the English Department, and I asked her . . . she has consented to help us out a little here. At my request. Just light cleaning or cooking or whatever you need before the guests arrive."

"Daniel, I don't need any help."

He walked into the kitchen with the woman behind him, and she headed for the sink, began washing pots and pans. Elizabeth following along, numbly unwrapping carrot sticks on the counter. Finally she stopped, looked at him.

"Daniel," she said, muttered it meanly under her breath, like profanity. "Daniel. Look around you. Everything is ready. I'm ready, Daniel. I mean—pretzels and cold cuts? In our house? You know I've been cooking and freezing and preparing for this thing—"

He stopped loading beer in the refrigerator and stood in his damaged, slanted way and stared down at her. She could imagine how her own face looked then, the angry flushed heart of her face. She looked into the pink-rimmed khaki green of his eyes.

"I'm sorry," he whispered. "I'm not . . ." His sentence trailed off and for a minute she thought he was on the edge of telling her something. But no, he was grabbing those feelings and pulling them in.

Mary, through tactfulness or an attack of shyness, was hugging herself and staring at a space between her feet.

"Daniel?" Elizabeth whispered it so lightly, so quietly, she wasn't even sure she'd really said his name. He gestured to the bedroom with a nod of his head, and she followed him there.

He's told her, that's what it is. He's broken it off.

"I have to go to the airport," he said. "I have to pick up Dr. Herzlov in an hour."

She wants him back.

Elizabeth nodded.

"The plates, the silver out there . . . that stuff isn't ours."

"No."

"Whose then?"

She shrugged. "I borrowed some things."

"From?"

"Patsy," she lied.

He looked at his watch. "I'll take Mary home when I get back."

"You can take Mary home now on your way to the airport. Everything is ready."

"It wouldn't hurt to have her here to help, an extra set of hands."

Elizabeth managed a shaky smile.

"Anyway, I'll be back within the hour. You can relax a little, take your time and get dressed." He kissed her right above her right eyebrow, a hard, dry stamp.

"Your husband? He's a good man." Mary put her hands in the front pockets of her blue polyester uniform. "He gives me books and jokes with me. He makes me feel good."

"I don't really need your help. I hope you're not disappointed. My husband didn't realize I'd have everything done. I think I surprised him. You keep the money, of course, for your trouble."

"If that's what you want." She dropped her eyes. "But at least let me put up this stuff."

Elizabeth grew tense as Mary finished loading the beer in the refrigerator, tipping the bottles at odd angles as she tried to wedge them in among all those platters of food. Then she turned her nose up at the aspic with vegetable curls. "That looks like a jellyfish."

"Mary, if we don't leave now we won't have time to take you home."

"Oh, don't worry about that. I'll take the bus. It stops right up there on the main road."

"Have you got an umbrella with you?"

"No."

Elizabeth darted to the hall closet, came back with an umbrella, bright red with a faux bamboo handle. "Here, it's yours."

"Oh, I couldn't keep this. It's a beautiful umbrella. I'll be sure to—"

"Don't worry. Keep it. Someone left it here. I don't know who it belongs to. We used to have people over, and they'd always leave things."

"Oh, well, if you're sure—"

"And can you carry a tray of cold cuts and a bag of pretzels?"

"I could manage."

"They're yours." Elizabeth put everything back in the bags, then handed them over to Mary.

"All this?"

Elizabeth nodded.

"Well, I wish I could be more help."

"You've done enough. Really." Elizabeth went to the bathroom and turned on the water in the bath.

"Yeah, I know how it is about running your own kitchen," Mary called to her. "You don't want people around to mess up stuff."

"Exactly." Elizabeth walked back through the kitchen, showed Mary out, locked the door behind her.

Outside, the rain began again, heavier this time. Elizabeth watched Mary balance her packages under the red umbrella.

She turned off the bathwater and pulled the plug. She ran water for a shower. She didn't need to stay still and think, she needed to forget things. His look of guilt, unalloyed, pure. Guilt. Bringing a maid. Bringing cold cuts. *He promised to tell her today.* She stood in the shower with her head down, the water steaming, hot as she could stand it. Hotter. She closed her eyes, gave herself up to the water.

"Are you all right?" His urgent whisper.

She let him in. She'd been standing in front of the bathroom sink, putting on lipstick.

"I've brought Dr. Herzlov. A few others have started to arrive."

She nodded. "I'm ready."

She was wearing a snug, fringed red dress she'd found in the back of her closet, still in the dry cleaner's plastic. And she'd unearthed pearl earrings. An anniversary present from a decade ago.

"You look beautiful."

"You don't think it's too much? I mean the red . . . and too dressy?"

"It's perfect."

She blotted the fine sheen of sweat on his forehead with a tissue. She smiled. "Go get everyone a drink. I'll bring out the food."

He nodded. "Where's Mary?"

"She went home right after you left."

"Did she say why?"

"I didn't need her."

He sighed, took her hands and clasped them in his own. "Daniel, did you tell her? Did you break it off?"

For a minute she thought he wouldn't answer. "It's . . . taken care of."

"You did, then?"

"Let's not discuss it now."

"Later tonight."

She turned from him, squinted at herself in the mirror, swiped carefully with a wet finger over her eyebrows. Added another layer of brash red lipstick.

"I want you to come with me," he said from behind her. "I want you—by my side."

Two dozen people spilled into the hall, the dining room, the living room. Everywhere people talked and nodded, hovering over plates heaped with food. They lined up at the table for food, huddled in corners, trailed through like ants. Daniel held her hand firmly and guided her. He introduced her to the man he'd picked up at the airport—Dr. Herzlov. He was a short, barrel-chested man with small, half-moon glasses and a bristly gray beard. "Elizabeth!" he said, as if he'd known her for years. But she'd never met him, had she? He flung open his arms. She let herself be enfolded into damp tweed. "I've heard so much about you, I feel as if I know you. The Dickinson scholar." She peered over his shoulder. Daniel was glowing.

Two other men standing beside Daniel—a blunt-featured chinless man, a professor of linguistics, and a bearded art professor—said nothing. Seemed in fact to be glaring at each other between bites and sips. Daniel pushed a glass of wine into her hand, put an arm around her, and she found herself talking to Bill Folger, the English Department head, who asked her how her research on Emily Dickinson, her dissertation, was going.

She keeps me busy, Elizabeth said. She stared at Bill Folger's hand, which held a glass of Burgundy in Cutter's finely etched crystal glass. His large silver ring, an oval-shaped turquoise stone, seemed to stare back at her.

She was gracious to do this, he said. Have a houseful to start this conference. The front door swung open and closed, open and closed. The room grew smaller as the crowd swelled. If you'll excuse me, she mumbled, I have to check on things. In the kitchen.

Her kitchen. She closed the swinging door behind her and stood beside the refrigerator, her cheek pressed to it, her arms around it like a dance partner. Her face on the cool metal. She listened to the murmurs and stiff laughs coming from the living room, ice cubes clinking, the din of it all beyond the door.

She needed to put in another batch of pastry, slice more cheese while she could think clearly, before the perfumed clusters of helpers invaded, chugging Zinfandel, devouring pâté. She wanted to hit the fast-forward button, for it to be morning with Daniel, their new life beginning.

She opened the refrigerator and squatted there looking in. The linguistics professor shuffled in and stood above her holding a greasy cocktail napkin and a beer. He grinned down at her. From the living room, from the outside, as she suddenly thought of it, came soft sounds of Chopin from the stereo.

"Ah—so there you are. Daniel says you made all the food. Quite an accomplishment. Everything is delicious."

"Thank you." She didn't move, hardly looked up, just answered from the floor.

"You will hear that a lot this evening. So help me out here. You don't have to reveal your recipes, but at least tell me the—"

"Honey-baked ham on sweet potato–pecan biscuits with maple mustard, blue cheese—stuffed grapes, banana–coconut custard tarts, hot asparagus canapés, crab quiche."

"May I join you?" He squatted eye-level with her, his knees popping like snapping fingers. He scooted beside her. "Not good with crowds? Neither am I."

"I'm sorry," she said, "have we met before tonight? You said you were—?"

"Lloyd Gressing. Linguistics."

She started to rise, but he grabbed her arm, held it firmly. She froze, looked in his drunk eyes.

"What is it?" she whispered. His hand pulled her back down.

His face glistened with perspiration, brown wet eyes bulging slightly. Thin mustache. Tight smile. *Toad man. Frog face.*

"Oh, come off it. When it comes to the dynamics of couple-dom, I pride myself on my perception. Just look at my Larry out there. Oh, he's fit to be tied. Just because I let it slip the two of us had a great weekend at the beach. Said it was romantic. You should have seen him glare. Like they don't know we're an item." He chuckled. "Like the whole department doesn't know everything about everybody. Larry knows I won't stay in the closet. I stayed there twenty-one years, and that was long enough for me." He stood and offered a hand, pulled her to her feet, then helped himself to a beer in the refrigerator.

"My advice is don't worry about . . . the gossip. We all have something to hide, and if we don't—well, that's a dull person who doesn't have anything to hide." So he knew about Ginnie, then. They all did. He looked at her with pity. Pity!

"Now prepare yourself. I hear the kitchen brigade coming this way. I advise one of these"—he held up his beer—"to get you through."

They invaded, barging in her kitchen. Two women gnawing celery sticks and giggling as they came through the swinging door. One of them grabbed her sleeve.

"Wonderful food."

"How did you do all this yourself?"

"Can we help in any way?"

"I'll put out more crackers."

"Beautiful dishes, and the silver!"

She moved to the stove, loaded pastry puffs on a platter, and headed out the kitchen door—back first—and before she turned around and headed to the dining room table, in that split second, she dropped the platter, and it cracked, and she found herself thinking somewhere in the back of her mind she was glad it was her cheap Noritake instead of Cutter's china. The pastries were scattered all over the floor. She stood there, apron on, blinking, her oven-mittened hands like paws.

But no one seemed to care that she had dropped and broken a platter. Some people were quietly backing into the dining room and were stepping on her puffed pastry making soft, squishy sounds like stepping on little pillows. They were backing up, all faces looking at Daniel. His back was to her, then as he half turned, she glimpsed his profile, and something else, too.

Someone else.

Ginnie. She had come. And now she was talking to Daniel in the corner, as if they were alone, as if no one could see. And she was crying. And she looked just enough like Cutter to confound Elizabeth.

Judy Folger, the department head's wife, turned to Elizabeth.

"Oh, I am so sorry. There's no excuse for this kind of—let's go to the kitchen."

Elizabeth felt weak, her knees—where were they? Her legs

almost buckled—but no. Making herself stand was what she needed to get the hell out of there. Judy Folger was tugging at her, expertly guiding her away, and already the throng was parting for them. She followed Judy through the swinging door, into the kitchen, then shook her off, flung her away, and headed to the bedroom.

She managed to find the emergency stash of pills from her closet and swallowed three pills dry, the bitter, powdery taste lingering. She crawled under her bed, beneath that creaky high post bed, the dust ruffle draping on her back, then falling back into place behind her. She muffled a sneeze. She closed her eyes, tried not to think about the dirt, about what was in the dust down there with her. Fly eyes and roach parts, dust mites and skin flakes. Under everyone's bed there were horrible microscopic creatures, things you breathed in—

She thought of biology lab, looking through a high-powered microscope to watch an aphid eating a plant. And seeing how the aphid itself was being eaten inside out by a parasitic wasp. A tiny ravenous parasite calmly eating the aphid, its tiny goggly eyes staring out of the aphid's transparent body. The meanness even in that tiny world.

Oh God, it would be so good to escape. Anything would be better than this—or nothing. Sleeping pills and Zinfandel were going to be her passport out of this. Elizabeth sneezed again. Brushed off her elbows, wiped the dust from her face with the back of her hand.

The door opened.

She went rigid, not daring to breath, listening to the whispering.

"Right now—I've got a house full of people. I can't talk right now, you know that. Goddamn it. What possessed you to do this?"

"What did she tell you?"

Elizabeth closed her eyes.

"She came in to find you, to talk to you about something. She didn't tell me what it concerned. I assumed it was something about the house."

"Alice Clacker said you were in there for half an hour. And then to just leave and not even wait for me after you were in there talking to my own sister. Just leave a note saying you'd call me"—a sob now, a squeezing out of words—"next week."

"Ginnie, we discussed this party. You knew—"

"It's not like I was expecting a detailed letter with sources in MLA format. But a sticky note—with an 'I'll call you'?"

"Ginnie—she knows. Elizabeth knows about us. She's in danger of falling apart. Right now she needs me. I can't turn my back on . . . I can't live like this. You know that. You can't either."

Another little sob.

"Don't look like that." A muffled sound. "You knew it was coming to this. Don't cry. Don't. Look at me."

"Stop pretending that you don't know! That kills me worse than anything. I was going to tell you. But when I got back, when I found out Cutter had talked to you—I knew she told you. And you—just take off. And leave that stupid, mean note!"

"Cutter said you didn't know."

"What do you mean, didn't know?"

"That they've talked. That they are friends. My wife and Cutter. Apparently their friendship developed when Elizabeth had her suspicions and came over and ended up talking with Cutter. It just shows what lengths Elizabeth has been forced to—"

"What? What are you talking about—my sister and—"

Sitting on the bed now. The bed screeching over her, her bed! Their bed! With Ginnie on it! An ankle, a sandal, a tiny silver anklet. A small pink toe, a tender little bean of perfection.

"You're telling me they've been friends? My own sister and—"

"Ginnie. What did you think she told me?"

"What I planned to tell you next weekend."

And then she knew. Elizabeth knew, even before he did, her own husband. Seconds before he did. An eternity of synapses crackling and snapping. A mind scream: *Oh my God Oh my God Oh my God*.

"Tell me what?" His voice unwavering, controlled.

"I'm pregnant."

"Ginnie. Ginnie, are you sure?"

"Yes, I'm sure. I've been to the doctor. I'm six weeks already."

More silence.

"You're so . . . cold, Daniel. Aren't you even a little happy?"

"I'm . . . I'm shocked. This isn't . . . I don't know what to say. . ."

She could hardly hear him now. Her husband's words were fading out, breaking up on her. She was listening to some permanent heavy thing grinding and colliding, changing the course of her life. Like the plate tectonics of continental drift, and she was floating off now, severed. Her own continent. The Land of Elizabeth. An arid, dry deserted isle.

Someone tapped at the door. There were voices and cleared throats. She watched their feet—his in loafers with the familiar thicker left wedge, hers in sandals.

Later, after a very long while, Elizabeth heard her name, heard Daniel calling to her. But she did not move. She did not call out. She did not feel, except for the pain in her hands, balled up in fists, the little half-moon scratches in her palms. Little crescents of blood there, she knew, she did not have to look. She closed her eyes, and the poetry gnawed at her like a parasite, obliviously and dumbly chomping inside her brain. Her own parasitic wasp.

> *The Soul stares after it, secure—*
> *To know the worst, leaves no dread more—*

Thirteen

ALFRED WASN'T GETTING OUT of the car. He only shook his head when I asked him to come in, and I was relieved, glad that he wouldn't have to see any more skirmishes. Four guests came out the front door, headed to their cars. The faculty get-together was breaking up early. A bad sign.

I walked over and closed the door of Father Bob's Dart, stood there for a minute, listened to the engine ticking. I made my way toward Elizabeth's house, around the jumble of cars in the driveway. The front door yawned open. I headed up the driveway, cut through the yard. My shoe was sucked off my foot. I hadn't been the first victim—the Byers' muddy yard was riddled with shoe-shaped holes. More people came out, walking silently past. I scraped off my mud-caked shoes on the welcome mat as best I could and walked in.

The small living room was candlelit. In the middle were two small tables swallowed with plain white tablecloths. On top I saw Gran's china—the blue delft pitcher full of forsythia, a stack of china plates, and two crystal stem glasses. The battered, faded quilt I had tossed in boxes to cushion the china was draped gracefully across the sofa. I wondered if Ginnie had noticed them.

Several people clustered together in the living room. My sister was not among them. Neither was Daniel. Or Elizabeth. I could tell they were uncomfortable. They stood together by the book-shelves, grimly shaking their heads a little, wondering if they should stay, or go, or do *something*. But a second group on the couch was smug and excited, waiting out the ending of something ugly. They stopped whispering when they saw me and stared and I knew it was because they recognized the resemblance—that problem of looking like Ginnie just enough to get me in trouble.

I walked past them to the kitchen. A man was there, standing by the sink, a wild-eyed man, reeling.

"Oh my God, it's her! It's her!" He pointed at me, then grasped the counter to steady himself, his finger waving unsteadily at me. He looked at me harder, then slumped and dropped his hand. "Oh, it's not."

"What happened?" I asked. He looked as if he were ready to talk. Getting information from the drunk in the kitchen was always a good place to start.

"First, Larry blew his top. I hate it when he does that to me. He starts with the slow burn, and then he gets icy and ignores me. Just because I said the thing about the romantic weekend in front of them—"

"I mean with the Byers. What happened? Where are they?"

"I told him from the start. I told him I will not lie. I told him, I said, 'Larry—'" He grabbed the kitchen stool and stood on it, his shirt halfway unbuttoned, his chest heaving, arm outstretched. "I said to him, 'I will not lie about us.'"

"Look," I said. "I'm looking for my sister. Or maybe you've seen Mrs. Byers?" I added weakly.

He hid his mouth with his hand. "Byers ran out the door, through the neighborhood, calling after her like he lost a dog. 'Elizabeth! Elizabeth!' Or no, no! This is better. Heathcliff on the moors calling for—"

"Then she took off? She's outside?"

He shook his head. "That I don't know."

I walked across the kitchen to the hall, turned a corner, came face-to-face with my sister.

"Ginnie," I managed, "were you standing here the whole time I was looking for you?"

"You liar." She took a step toward me. She shook her head slowly and I could hear the faint jingle of one of her dangly earrings, a soft, out-of-place happy sound. "You betrayed me, Cutter," my sister said calmly, with no anger at all.

"Don't talk to me about . . ." My voice seemed to slink off, ashamed. I swallowed. "About lying or betraying," I finished quietly.

"You're my sister." Angry now, the way I expected. "My sister. And I find Gran's china, our china, in this house? And I hear you visited Daniel today at his office. Telling him what? What, Cutter?"

"It wasn't a visit. I went there to see you. But you weren't there. I went to talk to you about the house, but I didn't tell him. About . . . you."

"Oh no. No. You just tell him about the friendship you've struck up. Behind my back, you're talking to her. You're friends with Wife?"

"She came to the house. She knew about you and what was I supposed to say? I felt sorry for her. I never wanted to get messed up in this—" A sudden wave of anger hit me. Like Gran's pressure cooker, the *zzzz, zzz* as the steam filled the kitchen, turning a pot of hard, knotted apples into applesauce in thirty minutes flat. "All I want is to live in my house and not have to worry about you and Barry and that Realtor slinking around trying to take it. You know how much that means to me—and the china and the pearl earrings and the silver. You were pawning it, all of it! Behind my back you were—"

"For God's sake, Cutter. You know I don't have any health insurance to cover this. You know I don't even have enough money for next semester's tuition or—"

"You could have asked me," I said loudly, and the silence in the living room roared like a crowd, like white noise. They were listening. The guests were listening. I could hear their vague shuffling in there, their small stirrings, like wary cattle. "We could have worked out something."

"I just took my share. I don't have to ask your permission."

"I don't recall us deciding which part was your share."

"Oh, stop it, Cutter. I'm not going to stand here and argue with you about a pile of cracked plates and dusty glasses. I'm just not." She brushed past me.

"Wait! Where are they? What happened?"

"You figure it out. You're the one with the sources. Ask her."

"Ginnie, wait. We have a home, that's what I've been fighting for, our home. You know I'd never leave you stranded. No matter what you've got—"

"I've got two to think about now, that's what I've got. Don't you realize that?"

She turned and walked back down the hall and through the kitchen, and I heard the screen door slam. Back in the living room, there were only five guests left—the drunk from the kitchen and the smug group, all of them standing by the wall, lined up with startled faces, as if they were about to be executed. They were all in their socks or stocking feet, their shoes piled in a jumble in the corner, watching cautiously as Alfred swept the floor.

"Alfred?"

"You know this man? Thank God!" A thin woman in a long black dress grabbed my elbow and the others gathered around us.

"Who *is* he?"

"Is he hired to clean up? We didn't know."

I waved them away. "He's had a hard day and so have I," I said. I walked over to where Alfred was on his knees and put my hand on his back, his shirt warm and damp.

"Let's go, Alfred."

"He couldn't find the vacuum," added the woman. "He picked up the sofa cushions and swept everything on the floor. He said no shoes were allowed. We assumed the Byers had arranged for him to come in." The rest of the group murmured among themselves, still eyeing Alfred, who looked up, stopped his sweeping—he'd made a pile of crumbs and balled-up napkins in the middle of the floor— and stood up. He walked to me, bringing the broom, now just a bundle of straw nubs.

"Let's go," I whispered.

The house was dark except for a line of light under Ginnie's room. I knocked softly. I stood there a long time. When I finally shuffled off down the hall to my room, I heard her yell.

"Friends with her. With Wife!"

"Ginnie, let me in so I can explain."

"I don't want your explanations. And I don't plan to ever talk to you again." The words rang shrill, cracked with her scream. There was a thud as she threw something at the door. "I don't even want to be here under the same roof with you."

After a while, after I had brushed my teeth and collapsed on my bed, not even bothering to take my clothes off, I heard her clomp down the stairs, our old leather suitcase obediently thudding behind her. I wondered how she was going to leave, but I heard the whisper of a car pull up outside, and I knew she'd called someone.

I lay in bed and stared up at the ceiling, my mind mulling over the sharp edges of the day. I fought drowsiness. But the night betrayed me, brought sleep.

I dreamed of Beulah, the garden angel. The house was flooding, and I was scooping up buckets of water, tossing them out the windows. But everything began to float, everything rising and bobbing, even the china, the sofa, Gran's old black purses and netted hats, and then Gran herself. My grandmother, pale and stiff, the orchid pink dress we buried her in fanning out around her, her eyes open, unblinking, like pale green glass. But I had no time to grab her, to gather up anything. I had to empty the buckets. Then I heard a grinding, a lurching. A sad groan, a lifting. The house was floating, the house was a ship! I climbed to the top, to the attic window. I stepped out onto the roof, only now it was the deck of a ship. And I could see my mother standing there at the far end, posed like the photograph on the mantel downstairs. And beside her, my father in his uniform. I watched Gran walk over to them and wring out her dress, shaking her head: "Mercy, how am I ever going to clean this up, my Sunday best, ruined." I yelled over to them, "So, that's where y'all are! All the time, you were right up here." But they didn't hear me and that made me feel lonely again. I looked down at the waves, at the rising sea below, and that's when I saw the garden angel, a figurehead now on the prow of the ship, her half smile, her filmy frock floating up in the breeze like a wave.

I woke up in a sweat. I opened all my bedroom windows and then lay still, letting the dream run through my head for hours. I was dazed and woozy when daylight finally leaked from my window shades and birdsong swelled and the roosters started crowing. After a while, there was the sound of a car door slam, footsteps on the porch.

I sat up in bed. Could it be Mrs. Worthington? Was she showing the house now? It was almost a relief, having no hope of being saved.

Someone knocked.

I went upstairs to the attic bathroom and looked out. The knocking grew louder.

The roof and porch obscured my line of vision no matter how I angled myself on the windowsill or pressed my face to the glass.

"Aw, hell." I walked down the stairs. When I opened the door, Daniel Byers stood there, ashen-faced. He was so different from the first time I'd talked with him, his jokes, his insistence on friendly conversation.

"Have you seen Elizabeth?"

"What do you mean?"

"Do you know—has she talked to you? Do you have any idea where she might go?"

I thought over the places we'd been—the farmers' market, Painters ice cream shop, Father Bob's. No place she would spend the night. "Come in," I said with a sigh.

"Maybe I should go to the police," Daniel said. He followed me to the kitchen, his uneven gait tapping out a strange rhythm as he crossed the wide wooden hallway. He squinted when I turned on the overhead light.

"She's not able to function away from home, you know."

"Yes, so you told me yesterday. I have coffee—it's instant—or tea."

"Coffee. She's been gone for hours. I can't imagine where—"

"Are you sure she's not at home now, while you're standing here talking to me?"

"No. I've checked. I fell asleep there awhile waiting and—is Ginnie here?"

"I don't know why you think I can keep up with your women any better than you can. No, Ginnie is not here. She's furious at me. She left."

He cleared his throat. "Where do you think she'd go?"

"Which one?"

He closed his eyes for a minute. "My wife."

Just days ago Elizabeth had been in the kitchen with me, shaken and pale, looking for him. And what had she said then? Something about gardening and working on her research about Emily Dickinson, how the poet wasn't kind to her. I thought about the day we'd spent together, how she'd bought all those seeds and flowers.

"If I had to guess, I'd tell you to look at the farmers' market."

"Where?"

"In downtown Sans Souci. Just take a left off Main and—"

"Why would she be there?"

"She likes it there."

"Okay, I'll look there, but I'm calling the police by noon. Although I hoped it wouldn't come to that. I'll check the hospitals first."

He gripped the table, and I noticed he hadn't touched his coffee. "Uh, I don't think I have any milk, but there's sugar."

"No." He looked startled. "No, this is fine." He picked it up, drained it like a shot. I got up, poured him more.

"Look," I said, "what all happened last night? At the party?"

"Ginnie didn't tell you?"

"I told you, she's not speaking to me. After she found out I knew Elizabeth, she was so furious—"

"Yes, and finding out that you talked to me yesterday at my office, too. That seemed to . . . She thought you told me."

There! A flinch, a quicksilver wince. It was just sinking in, the baby part.

He wrapped his hands around his cup. "Did you know?"

"You mean, about her being—"

"Yes."

"Yeah, I knew. Did she announce it there at your house in front of everyone?"

"No. No, she didn't, she wouldn't do that. She was angry, though. But I finally—I got her to move to the bedroom where there was some privacy, so I could calm her down. I couldn't reason with her. Then she told me. And I was in a state of shock myself, I think. Then I couldn't find Elizabeth."

"So she doesn't know?" I asked. "Elizabeth doesn't know that Ginnie's pregnant?"

"I . . . hope not. This kind of information travels like an epidemic. It has a life of its own."

"Well, I know and you know and Ginnie's doctor knows, but I doubt anyone else knows. Not yet."

"Yesterday, she vomited in the library."

"Are you kidding me?"

"While we were in the office and you were waiting for her. She called me from the library after it happened, and I told her to go home. I thought she had the stomach flu or food poisoning. It never occurred to me . . . you have to believe me."

"And she agreed to go home?"

"Well, no. Not initially. She wanted to talk to me, she said. But the librarian escorted her to the infirmary to be looked over, and by the time she got to my office, I'd left."

"My poor sister. Jesus."

"But I was relieved she hadn't shown up while I was there. I knew if I was alone with Ginnie—" He swallowed. "It was getting harder and harder to leave her. Every afternoon it got harder."

"What are you going to do?"

He peered down into the blackness of his coffee. That's when I knew there was no decision. He could not, would not leave Elizabeth. Wife.

Outside, Father Bob was scattering pine straw. A clattering of chickens followed behind him, and the three-legged dog. I hadn't spoken with Father Bob about Alfred yet. I would have to talk to Curt first, find out if he was pressing charges before I explained everything to Father Bob.

When I collapsed on the sofa, a cloud of dust exploded, made me sneeze. When the house was sold, I could go to college myself, maybe. Pay my tuition and get an apartment, go to school full-time and not have to worry about working for a couple of months.

I could go to Europe. Hang out in Paris, learn to speak French.

Or work across the street at Father Bob's as some kind of assistant. But I knew I couldn't look at my house every day, knowing it wasn't mine anymore.

Soon it would all be gone, and I would have nothing. I didn't have a family to come home to. I couldn't move back in with parents and take over the guest room, or settle in a garage apartment while neighbors joked about refeathering empty nests. I would have nothing, I would be homeless. I would opt out like the people I'd seen out by the Lighthouse Mission. All my possessions—a few pieces of Gran's china, an old purse, some books, and a change of clothes—in one grocery cart I could wheel around town.

I opened the refrigerator, blinked at the emptiness, and closed it. I looked at the clock in the kitchen. By now, my Saturday shift at the Pancake Palace was drawing to a close, and I hadn't shown up. Had not even called. It hardly seemed worth the effort. How could I explain that I was too busy searching for runaway wives and pregnant sisters, fighting assault-and-battery charges? Two jobs down in twenty-four hours. I closed my eyes.

I would draw myself a hot bath in the attic bathroom, I would sit in there and soak until the noon sun filtered through the bubbled-glass windows. I would run water so hot, the thick steam would caress my face, fog the mirrors, leave the tile floor slick and the windows sweating. I couldn't fix broken marriages, or a love-crazed sister, or save people from themselves. No matter how hard you tried, you couldn't make people do right. So maybe I should just try to keep myself from falling apart.

I climbed the stairs, grabbed a stack of towels from the linen closet. I turned on the water, let it splatter and splay through my fingers. I got in and leaned back. The water lapped at my neck, tickled the lobes of my ears, and just when the hot water started to run tepid—just then—the phone rang.

I ignored it. But it rang and rang and rang. I finally jumped out and walked into the hall and picked it up, bare naked and dripping.

"Miss Johanson?"

"This is Cutter." I hated myself then, for hoping that the phone call was Curt.

"Priscilla Worthington, here. An offer has been made on your house. Isn't that marvelous? And I need to discuss some contract—"

"Just a minute," I said. I walked back into the bathroom and turned off the bathtub water. I felt pink and plucked, bloodless from my soaking. I put on cutoffs and a T-shirt. I walked back down the hall, one of the floorboards screeching its usual high-pitched *uh-oh*. I picked up the phone.

"Mrs. Worthington? You may continue." We were all business now, Mrs. Worthington and I. The scent of a successful sale had blunted her scorn. Dollars made her forget monkey shit. The sale was revenge enough.

"Yes. Well, we need to discuss the particulars with the three of you—your brother and sister and you—together. The contract particulars, you understand. I can send the details to your brother, of course—"

"The apartment man? Is it the apartment man?"

"What, dear?"

"Nothing," I said and hung up. When the phone rang again, I unplugged it.

"Gran," I said out loud. "Gran, do me a favor. Y'all come on now and haunt the hell out of this place."

From somewhere I heard the crack of a beam, the house settling, shifting, and I imagined the clumpy hot pudding of magna shifting miles below us, beneath this little piece of the earth. My house sailing on, like in my dream.

I returned to my bath, where the water waited, placid, clear, the familiar rust stain around the drain shaped like a reindeer head. I undressed, stepped in and reclined, held my breath, and submerged.

The doorbell rang. The goddamn doorbell rang.

I ignored it. Well, of course I ignored it. There was nothing else I wanted to know right now. Trying to forget the last twenty-four hours was enough. But the vibrations penetrated the bathwater. I held my breath and let the water cover my ears. It was the police, maybe. Curt pressing charges. Or just Father Bob looking hurt, wanting explanations about why Alfred didn't have a job anymore. I got out again, put on my T-shirt and shorts, walked downstairs, and as I threw open the front door, I told myself be ready for anything. And I thought I was.

Fourteen

SHE WOKE UP COLD, stiff, on her back, groped for covers. Realized then there were none, realized she was on the floor, her fists clenched, her jaw set, staring up at the bottom of the mattress, a spring peeking through. She remembered then crawling down there to escape the crowd. She remembered everything. Fertilization, gestation, a fetus—a baby. Ginnie's baby. Mitosis or meiosis—which was it? The cell division that made a baby. That was going on right now, at this very instant, that complicated, fragile process. Baby making. His baby. She remembered that most of all.

Elizabeth crawled out and stood up, swayed a little, blinked. The bed was still made up. It was—she glanced at the digital clock beside her—5:10 A.M. and the bed was still made up.

Daniel. Where was he?

The room was dark, but she did not bother to turn on the light. She took off her dress, wadded it up and threw it in the closet, found a pair of crumpled jeans in the laundry basket and slipped them on. Pulled out a shirt from the bottom drawer of her bureau.

She walked through the living room, picked up a serving plate dotted with crumbs, a hardened rind of cheese, took it to the kitchen. He was not there. On the kitchen cabinet, a pile of stained and crumpled linen napkins had been gathered, corralled in the corner by three neat stacks of coffee cups. A few wineglasses had been washed, were upside down on a paper towel, but many more were crowded in the sink, the residue of Merlot glistening at the bottom of each like a jewel. The floor was a mess, but all the chairs had been pushed in neatly under the table. Maybe Daniel had begun cleaning up? No. One of them, one of the guests, someone like Judy Folger must have made an attempt, begun gathering glasses and washing them in a sink full of suds, then left when it was simply too awkward to stay. When Daniel asked her to leave, maybe.

What had he told them?

She pushed aside the curtains and looked outside. It was still dark, a few moths flirting with the streetlights. His car was gone. She opened the front door and stepped out onto the porch. The bare trellis leaning against the wall would soon be laced with her moon vine, the buds popping open at dusk, just as the morning glories closed. She would miss seeing them this year, her fragrant vines.

She would go out, now. Out with the bats, the owls, the night crawlers, the moths. Out into the nocturnal world. That was where she needed to be—out there with the secrets of night. No reason to stay here waiting—for what?

The air outside was damp and cool, and it felt good to gulp it in. Walking to the end of her driveway, the first tug, the grip of fear began, but she ignored it.

On the street now, she walked barefooted, the damp grass clippings sticking to her feet. She liked the idea of walking past all the dark houses, everyone asleep, tiptoeing past like she knew something they didn't. It felt daring and sneaky—the way a robber must feel as he planned his break-ins. With one hand she held her jeans up, realized then they were Daniel's, they were so baggy. Why, they swallowed her whole!

Up ahead she could make out the street sign of Saxon Way. She was already at the end of the block.

There was a tug-of-war inside her—between her fear of leaving, of going any farther, and the simple need to put one foot in front of the other. Not stopping to think, not stopping at all. Her mind was open now, a breezeway, just the poetry, damp and cool, coming through in gusts, sighing.

> *The first Day's Night had come—*
> *And Grateful, that a thing*
> *So terrible—had been endured—*
> *I told my soul to sing—*

Walking uphill, her calves burned. Sometimes pain reminded you that you were alive. Sometimes it was the only thing you had. She was up to the highway now, leaving the neighborhood behind. Turn around! Or find yourself crumpled on the highway somewhere, helpless, no one to rescue you, your husband gone, your friend gone, too. But Cutter was never really a friend, was she? She'd known about the pregnancy all along. Elizabeth began walking south, toward town. Toward Sans Souci.

There were no cars on the highway. She walked beside the road, her bare feet aching, soft from a winter of wearing shoes. She stepped over a Budweiser can, a diaper, a McDonald's Happy Meal box—all the trash people flung out, ridding themselves of it, pretending it was easy to unclutter your life. All that litter scattered beside the road. You never really noticed how bad it was from the car.

Or how good it was. You never noticed the good things, too. The crickets were busy with their tinny throbbing, but the dawn was peeling back the curtain of night, showing Elizabeth the bundles of daffodils playing out, the daylilies gathering and greening themselves for June blooming, the fields of kudzu beginning to climb. My God, the kudzu. Where had it come from? She stopped to look at an empty lot where someone had started to build a gas station last summer, then abandoned it. She remembered looking out the car window on one of her rare winter outings, seeing the cinder blocks and cement stacked and toppled like a ruin, the field wounded, ditches and holes bleeding with red Carolina clay. Now all that ugliness was gone, the kudzu and honeysuckle covering the blocks and stumps, snaking up telephone poles and trees, covering it all with a thick green mantle. Soon this would be a blanketed field, the gentle lumps and slopes there as sweet as the knobbed elbows and knees of sleeping children.

She could see the traffic light up ahead now, the first traffic light before you entered the town limits.

How long had they lived here in Olde English Acres? Years. And she could count the times she had ventured into town on one hand. And two of those times were with Cutter, who had insisted that Elizabeth get in the car with her and have a little excursion, "get out of this ridiculous place, this unique brick ranch capital of the world. I mean, have you ever seen a unique brick ranch?" Cutter was like a kindergarten teacher that way, chirpy but firm, luring Elizabeth out, plopping her in the car and zooming off before Elizabeth had time to think about it.

And betraying her, don't forget that. Lying. Well, maybe not lying, not exactly lying. Omitting.

Suddenly a pinpoint of light appeared, a single headlight approached. A motorcycle came speeding toward her. She could see the round, heavy helmet on the driver, that insect head turning slightly as the motorcycle zoomed past. She still clutched the gaping waist of Daniel's jeans with one hand. Her small breasts bobbed underneath a thin, faded nightshirt, some kind of garish smiling cartoon there. And barefooted. Thinking about that made her feet cold. How strange she must look. How vulnerable.

And what would she do if the motorcycle turned around? What would she do? She imagined how they would find her—perhaps dead in this ditch. Daniel would be called to identify the body— *We have a female down here at the morgue. White, five-six, short dark hair, fair skin.* How free he would be then—free to marry Ginnie, to raise their child. But not free from the guilt—God, it would kill him.

She could count on Daniel for one thing—guilt. Even now, he would never ask her for a divorce. He would never leave her for Ginnie and the child. He would stay with her, a wounded husband. If Daniel were going to leave her, he would have already done it.

Still, there was the matter of the baby. A child. His child. She wondered how she would feel about holding that baby. About taking that baby in her arms.

Behind her, the buzz of the motorcycle grew faint, then disappeared. So there would be no attack, no incident at all. She padded along, her feet no longer stinging, numb now with cold.

She was up to the traffic light, turned right onto Main Street. She passed a darkened dry cleaner's, a discount shoe store, a feed and seed, a furniture showroom full of velour recliners. She crossed the street onto Gerard.

It was morning now, the last vestiges of night magic gone. The town was stirring a little, blinking off sleep. A bread truck passed, an arm flung out newspapers from an old battered station wagon. Porch lights came on, streetlights blinked off. In the kitchens, the silhouettes of families moved slowly, opening refrigerators, holding up milk cartons, shuffling in bathrobes.

She must get back now, she must turn around.

But first—first this.

She stood in front of 102 Gerard. Gazing at it, just standing and staring. This is where her feet had led her. To this cracked, uneven sidewalk. Outside this Victorian with the sloping porch, with the leaded glass–paned door.

Elizabeth smiled in spite of herself. Poor Cutter, all she wanted was to save this house. And her boyfriend was supposed to come through and help finance her crazy plan. Or something. So what happened?

She would never know. She would never see Cutter again.

Elizabeth turned and made her way back toward Main Street. Her mouth was dry, she was thirsty. It was the pills. The pills always made her thirsty. She went into a Kwik Mart that was open and a sleepy, pimply boy looked up from his *Car Racing!* magazine.

"I'd like some water," she said simply. She had no money with her. She put her hands in her pockets. No. Nothing. Not a cent.

He leaned over the counter. Looked down. "Ma'am, you ain't got no shoes." She looked down then, too, her feet raw, tingling a little, dirty. She wiggled her toes like a child.

"No, I don't."

"We require shoes." Practiced, memorized, the way he said it. This boy was on the management track. She shrugged. He sighed. "Back there, you see them flip-flops? Get you a pair, a freebie, on the house. I'll get you that water."

She found a pair of fluorescent pink flip-flops, took her cup of water, and thanked him. He shrugged and went back to reading *Car Racing!*

Outside, she ventured on down Main again, the rhythmic flapping of her shoes pleasantly reminiscent of vacations at the beach. She stopped when she came to a full parking lot, the neon Pancake Palace sign blinking and buzzing above. She walked inside, let herself be escorted rather brusquely to a table.

"Mornin'."

Elizabeth looked up as the waitress set down a glass of ice water and a plastic menu. She took out creamers from a little pocket in her apron, flipped open a little notepad. It was Jolene. But apparently she didn't recognize Elizabeth. And why should she? Not even a purse or earrings, not a smidgen of lipstick, for God's sake. Flip-flops. But looking around, Elizabeth saw a table of hunters in camouflage and orange vests, a booth of women smoking cigarettes over coffee, a fat man sopping up gravy with a biscuit. There were all kinds here, she was not sticking out at all.

"Hey, don't I know you from somewhere?"

"I'm Cutter's friend. I . . . helped out that day when things got so busy?"

"Well, good Lord. Now I remember."

"Look, I—I don't want anything." The waitress narrowed her eyes at Elizabeth, cocked her head to the side.

"I was wondering if you could tell Cutter to come here, to my table. Is she working today? I'd like a brief word with her."

"Uh huh."

Elizabeth did not respond; the waitress did not give her time. She put the little notepad back in her pocket, crossed her arms. "She no longer works at this establishment. I'll put it that way. As of today. The bossman is not putting up with that foolishness. No, ma'am. Not coming in for two shifts, not even calling. Heard she lost her other job when she raised some kind of ruckus, that's what my cousin who works down at the pressroom of the paper said, so I don't know what has got in that girl's head. 'Course, you can't help but feel for her, driving around in that worthless bucket of bolts that don't start half the time, and the child don't have family. Not much, anyway." The waitress shook her head and her plastic globed starfish earrings spun and bobbed. "Now she ain't gonna have *no* income 'cause they're not gonna hire her back here, that's for sure." She darted over to the waitress station, came back with a cup of coffee, which she set in front of Elizabeth.

"Oh, wait. I don't have any money with me."

"My treat, hon. Looks like you need it."

"Well—thank you." Elizabeth poured in cream and stirred. But the waitress was already gone, moving to the table of hunters, holding the coffeepot high.

Elizabeth walked outside, shielded her eyes from the sun. She had to get back home. It seemed such a long way, and the soles of her feet throbbed with pain. Still, one foot in front of the other is how she got here, and it was how she would get back.

Her Sweet turn to leave the Homestead
Came the Darker Way—

The words descended on her like a fine mist, and she did not fight them, just listened this time, turned her face up, closed her eyes. After a while, she faced north, began her trek back.

Her feet still ached, so swollen she'd had to ice them before she squeezed them into her navy heels. But she had. Squeezed into her blue suit and white linen blouse, too, which she hadn't worn since she'd interviewed for her last job, the adjunct teaching position at Palmetto University.

Halfway up the sidewalk to Cutter's porch, she turned to watch Father Bob and some of the men planting a tree by their mailbox, a little willow. When she got to the front door, she remembered that day she stood right here on this porch, light-headed and weepy, her breath coming out in little gasps, until Cutter coaxed her inside.

She rang the doorbell.

After the thudding of footsteps, and the creaking of stairs, the door opened and there was Cutter, ponytailed and freckled.

"Does your husband know you're okay?"

Elizabeth moved past her and stood inside. Cutter closed the door.

"Because he's probably already called the police by now. That's what he was talking about doing this morning." Cutter not caring now how it sounded, not hiding the fact that Daniel must have been here with Ginnie this morning. Well, good. Elizabeth was through with all that tiptoeing around, too.

"When I dressed this morning, he wasn't home."

"He was here. He looked like he'd had a rough night." They moved to the living room, Elizabeth sitting on the couch, Cutter settling stiffly in a wing-back chair, taking in Elizabeth's suit with a quick, shy glance. "He said he waited up for you, then went out looking—"

"That's not my concern now."

"Oh." Cutter a little taken aback, avoiding Elizabeth's eyes.

"Are you here alone?"

"Ginnie's not here, if that's what you're wondering. She's pretty much moved out, I'd say. Not that she was here much anyway."

Cutter pushed her hands through her bangs and peered at Elizabeth timidly.

"This morning, Daniel asked about the places you and I went. He wanted to know so he could go there and look for you. He thought I'd know where you were."

Elizabeth sighed. "What else did he say?"

"Well, he was in a panic because you weren't home and he couldn't find you. He said he was going to call the police and check the hospitals. He was frantic. I think he was thinking the worst. That you might . . . do something drastic or something."

Elizabeth stood and walked over to the window, gazed at the reflection of her face. There were circles under her eyes, her festive, red-lipsticked mouth pinched in a line. But she looked braver than she felt, and that was something, wasn't it? She thought of Daniel calling for her, searching their empty house. Remembered how he'd lean in the door frame of the kitchen in their old apartment, smiling at her while she sprinkled oregano in sauce, sliding in the shower with her mornings before their classes, his wet face pressed in her hair. Where did it go, love like that? The history between them, the core of the thing, worn down, smoothed over with the dribble of day-to-day living.

She looked down at the window sash, at a dead spider, a few beetles, a fly, its body shiny metallic green, legs curled. Outside in the azalea, there was movement; a little wren lit on a branch, its mouth full of straw, its black bead eyes flickering at her. A nest in there, somewhere, she was sure.

"I heard you lost your job." She moved back to the couch, sat down. "Both jobs. Is that true?"

"How did you know that?"

"Then it's true?"

"Oh, my losses. Well—" Cutter began counting on her fingers. "I've lost my sister. I really have. She'll never forgive me. And my boyfriend. I *thought* he was my boyfriend. I guess I can't lose him if 'we' never were. And my jobs. Both of them. And worst of all, my house. I've lost my—" Her voice caught. She pulled a misshapen velvet cushion from behind her, pressed it to her face, muffled her words. "My house."

"Cutter, don't. Don't cry."

Elizabeth perched on the edge of the couch, looked down at her elegant, high-heeled, sore feet, stifled a wince. "I know something about losses, too, you know. And I could just do nothing about it. I have a lot to gain by doing nothing. His baby . . . I could make ours. I could do that. He would . . . Daniel would get me—get us through it."

"You know."

Elizabeth nodded.

"Was it horrible last night? Ginnie coming in all hysterical and . . . in front of those people. Is it common knowledge now? Did someone blab it to you?"

"I heard it from a reliable source. I'll put it that way."

"I, uh—I couldn't tell you." Cutter paused, seemed to fumble for the right words, a nonoffensive term: In a family way? With child? Knocked up? "I mean I would have. Eventually. Maybe."

"I walked here early this morning, Cutter, and I thought of you. I stood right beside the front porch in the dark, on the sidewalk, and I thought of Father Bob and Alfred and even Crusty. And I saw the gate of the dead garden and your little attic window up there. When I finally left, when I turned around and walked back to my house, I remembered what you told me once about a home. About your home. How it can root you. And I realized then why you were fighting so hard to stay. I don't think I've ever felt rooted. Trapped, yes. But not rooted."

"I was here. You could've come in and talked to me then, you know."

"This was something I had to do on my own. I walked around town, wandering up and down streets, through neighborhoods, down by the mill. I even went by the Pancake Palace. I guess you're not lost if you don't know where you're going, right? After a while, it came to me. I realized what I had to do. That I've followed one path long enough. His path. And I could continue. Part of me just wants to keep on, because I'm used to loving Daniel. But then I made a decision. And it feels right."

Cutter met Elizabeth's eyes. "You're leaving him?"

After a minute, Elizabeth said, "This morning I saw Mrs. Worthington and put a binder on this house."

Revenge. That was how Cutter saw it, her eyebrows red slashes, her eyes already swollen, hard with shock as she emerged from behind the cushion.

"Wha-at?" hiccupped by a sob. Cutter was sitting up now, rigid, her fists gripping the arms of her chair.

"I decided we should buy this house. You and I."

"How will I . . . I don't understand."

"How? Well, I don't know exactly. I just . . . I decided to put earnest money down before someone else buys it. I thought we could find a way to come up with the rest."

Cutter blinked at Elizabeth, wiped her wet face in the crook of her elbow.

"Maybe I could work. Perhaps at the Pancake Palace with Jolene," Elizabeth said. "Just until we get on our feet." She was talking too fast, the words tripping over each other. She made herself pause, take a breath.

"You were the one Mrs. Worthington called about," Cutter said quietly.

"But isn't it a good idea?"

Elizabeth closed her eyes for a minute. "I have some money I inherited from my father. And I'll also be getting money from the sale of my house, after the divorce."

"Divorce?"

"Don't forget we'll need a new roof. But maybe we can do the painting ourselves. At least the inside."

"Elizabeth, you haven't even seen the whole house yet. Or the upstairs."

"It doesn't matter." Elizabeth cleared her throat. "Cutter—please say you'll do this." For a minute she felt like the old Elizabeth, shrinking. "Please. Think about it. You don't really have a choice, do you?"

The tinny sounds of car doors startled them.

Cutter moved to the front door. She looked through the window, the slanted sun gleaming through the wavy glass.

"It's them."

Daniel would see her car across the street. He would know she was here. Elizabeth peered through the window in time to see Ginnie getting out of his car, laying a hand on his arm. It jarred her—the casual grip of his arm, her husband's arm. She sat down, her knees weak.

Cutter called out to her, "When were you planning on telling him all this?"

"I wasn't. Not now, anyway."

After a minute, the door swung open, hit the wall. "Elizabeth!" Daniel called out. Cutter winced.

"I'm in here, Daniel." The sound of her own voice was hushed and even, but not quite normal. A little thin, a little tight. She heard his footsteps—that stride like no one else's, the flawed gait, more pronounced this morning because he was tired. It got worse when he was tired, that hitch, that fragile, skimmed step. He stood in front of her, disheveled and drained, but relieved, too. She could see the relief move across his features, smoothing his forehead.

"Elizabeth? Thank God. Are you all right?"

Behind them, a flurry of movement, the soft thuds of footsteps on the stairs. Ginnie. Elizabeth wondered if Daniel might launch into an explanation of why Ginnie was there with him, excuses about why he had brought her here. She hoped not. She did not want to know.

"I was just talking to Cutter, and what I have to say is very important, so you may want to stay and listen."

"I think we should go."

"I am fine, Daniel, believe me." Looking up at him from where she sat, her eyes moving, but nothing else.

"We should talk about this at—"

"We are talking, Daniel. Right now. I want to talk about it now, and I feel fine." He would never believe her, what she was choosing, what she was not choosing.

"Elizabeth—" He took in her suit, the soft folds of her blouse. She crossed her legs, the glint of her hose shining in the noon sun.

"I'm buying this house. With Cutter."

He turned to look at Cutter. "I know it seems crazy and sudden," Cutter stammered, red-faced. "But—"

"Let's not drag Cutter into this."

"You don't know anything about it, Daniel. We're friends."

He sat across from her, and when she finally met his eyes, she was surprised. She was expecting more relief, maybe even sadness, but all she saw was worry. For a minute she saw him on his bicycle, lugging it in the front door. Remembered his hand threaded through her hair that time in the hospital, when he'd crawled in the bed beside her, the day they lost the baby.

Not being a couple would hurt. Just that morning, Mrs. Worthington's innocent question had stung: *Would you like to talk it over with your husband?*

"You've been under a tremendous amount of stress." She allowed her hand to be taken, held. She would try very hard not to be bitter. For some reason she thought of her mother's friend

Meredith, whose husband left her at forty. She had spent her days sunning herself by the pool, complaining about her ex-husband, *the baldheaded slug.* She took self-defense classes and shop classes to meet someone, anyone. No, Elizabeth would not be bitter. She might be alone. But she was already lonely. She had been lonely for a long time. And you couldn't use someone like a bandage to staunch the bleeding of loneliness.

"You've been traumatized. And it's my—"

"You don't think I can do it, do you? You don't think I can make it alone."

"Elizabeth." His voice cracked.

"You're not bound to me. You have others to think about now." Plural. *Others.* He looked at Cutter. Elizabeth watched their wordless exchange on his face. Yes, she knew.

"I'll, uh, be out on the porch," Cutter said.

Elizabeth slipped her hand out from Daniel's. She would not be bitter, but she could be angry. "I don't want your opinion, I don't want your pity, I don't want your guilt. I don't want you. And I am okay. I am fine, Daniel." *I. Am. Fine.*

"Let's go home," he whispered. "Let's go somewhere—anywhere you want—and talk."

She stood up. She could not stay here with Ginnie in the room above them. She could not stay in this room with him. "Come and get your things tonight. I've got a real estate agent coming tomorrow to look at the house. To set up a contract."

"Wait. Elizabeth, for God's sake, this is too sudden—"

"No." She interrupted him. "No, it's not sudden, not really. It's been very slow, infinitesimally slow."

He thought it was her anger fueling her now, but it was not. She was fighting weakness, fighting the urge to go over to him and wrap her arms around him and cry and leave his shirt collar soaking. She turned around, counted her steps until she reached the front door. Fourteen.

Cutter was waiting for her on the porch. She walked with Elizabeth to her car.

"Hey, Elizabeth. Ummm, are you gonna be okay tonight?"

The truth was she didn't know. She didn't know if she could get through the day, much less the night. Didn't know if she would be able to get out of bed in the morning. Elizabeth looked up at the roof then, her gaze flying, careening over the pitch, the gable, the windows. A small flutter at the drapes and she knew it was Ginnie looking down. Or a ghost.

"I think we should plan to meet first thing tomorrow," Elizabeth said. "Over breakfast. To go over the details. We'll have to set up a meeting with Mrs. Worthington."

"Okay." Cutter's face happy now, back to being cheerful, her freckles splayed like tiny flecks of paint. Her dimple a quick wink of fun. "It's just starting to hit me. Not losing the house, I mean."

Cutter did a little hop there on the sidewalk, the excitement running through her, billowing her spirits like a sail. She waved when Elizabeth started the car, mouthed *call me*. Elizabeth nodded. Cutter bounced up the steps, right past Daniel, who was standing there on the porch, still looking toward Elizabeth, like a captain scouring the sea for land. Elizabeth watched him grow smaller in her rearview mirror as she drove away. Part of her was holding it at bay, the grief of losing him; she was sandbagging the dam, preparing for the loss of that life. But she could not worry about that now. She could only do this thing, move toward this small crack of light under the door. Because now she was ready for it, the slant of light, and this time she would open the door.

Epilogue

THE SPUTTERING NAIL GUN, the screaming circular saw, the hammering and drilling and yelling—it's strange even now not to hear them. Instead, I wake to this early-morning calm: the hissing of warm air from the floor vents, the occasional groans of the house settling, like sighs of contentment. And from the eaves, the scampering of squirrels—their desperate scurrying, their scrabbling little claws.

Quiet enough now to hear the small stirrings of dawn from the open window. And just enough light to see the garden angel propped at the center of the courtyard, peering sedately at the herbs and perennials. She was too good not to share, to leave back there hidden in the dead garden. And so one afternoon, Alfred, Elizabeth, and I hauled her up in the wheelbarrow.

Beyond the courtyard, the caretaker's cottage is shrouded in darkness, but the gauze curtain billows like a flag. Elizabeth keeps the window open, night and day, through cold and heat. She likes to see the moon. She swears the hard, narrow bed is almost too soft.

As for me, I like living up here, in the attic, where I can see the lay of the land. I can just make out a few of the guests' cars beyond the camellias—the RV with the handicapped license plate, the Jaguar sporting New Mexico tags—and on the horizon, the crimson outline of Sans Souci glowing like spent coals. From here, I can watch it all. I no longer meander in the dark, the walls have moved. As I descend the narrow back staircase, I turn on the lights: the wall sconces, the hurricane lamp on the landing, the dim overheads in the hall and the parlor. For months, there was always a sawhorse or two to collide with, the crinkle of plastic sheeting underfoot. But now these spacious rooms are clad in swags and portieres and valances—window treatments that sound like royal titles. I can't help lingering for a while in the brash yellow of the dining room. It cheers me. I pull out the faded tulips from the vases, refill the saltshakers. I make myself useful.

Elizabeth and I—we have been like one person, one, single unit of industry—not leaving the house for months, not even for a day. We refinished the floors ourselves, then painted the interior. Spent our days spackling, sanding, painting. Father Bob brought us dinner every night, and a weekly supply of groceries. And then, finally, there was the contractor we brought on, not the cheapest, but the most optimistic. The one who chewed his lip and looked up at the cracked plaster ceiling and sighed and said, "Well, girls, I seen worse."

Behind baseboards, under bureaus and wardrobes, from the dark recesses of closets, we found all manner of treasures—photographs, a bill for three bolts of gingham, a water-stained postcard with a cryptic brown-inked message: *Dearest Myrtle Ann, the train ride was exhausting. Our journey liked to kill me!* From a crushed hatbox, I pulled a single braid of russet hair, thick as a rope, coiled like an intestine.

What the house gave to us, we kept. The buttonhooks, the cotton gin advertisement, the letters, the filthy lady's glove, gnarled and frozen in a claw, all of it we framed under glass, in shadow boxes, displayed in the parlor by the guest book. We even managed to save the silvery gilt of wallpaper and the peacock frieze we found like a gift under the brown and orange daisy paper in the hallway. Lost objects in a house are like memories tucked in the gray folds of our brains. They will resurface. Eventually, they will come back.

Our contractor fashioned a serviceable kitchen from the basement, culled three more bathrooms from closets and hallways, added a powder room under the stairs. Apparently, that is what we lacked for modern comfort—a plethora of private baths.

When they brought in a backhoe and discovered tree roots snaking around the pipes, gripping like talons the underground ducts and channels beneath us, it did not surprise me. "I never seen nothing like it," the plumber told us that morning. "But these kinds of things are hidden . . . like cancer. You open up the ground and there it is. The roots are choking the sewer line clear out the street past the stop sign. Could be bad. Could be real bad." It was just so used to holding on for dear life, my house. And I understood a little something about that.

Had I filled all the sugar bowls last night? I check off chores in my head: launder linen tablecloths, order new candles, fold napkins, polish silverware. I head downstairs to the basement kitchen, and Elizabeth is already there with an armful of rosemary, a clutch of sage and chives, a branch of camellias slanting importantly across her chest like a rifle.

We stick it all in the sink and she shivers, brushes off damp leafy remnants and soil from her blouse. I hand her a clean apron.

"What's on the menu?"

She hovers over a battered cookbook, bookmarks a page with a sprig of rosemary. "Omelet baskets—"

"The ones that kinda curl when you bake—"

"Yes. And pancakes. I was thinking of—"

"Apple pecan?"

She nods, begins to measure out a mountain of brown sugar, her hands callused and capable, moving over the mound as if it were soil. It reminds me of those days last summer when we turned our attention to the garden. When the house was filled with machines and loud men and we lived in paint-spattered clothes, when money worries and hassles over delayed supplies hounded us, those days when we spent all of our waking hours outside, our hands plunged into the earth, always in the dirt, always. Elizabeth began in the side yard, rescued the stubble of forgotten perennials, the vegetables gone to seed. I unearthed the marble steps that wound down to the cemetery, scraped away the dank slime of leaf blanket, then got down on my hands and knees like a desperate pilgrim and scrubbed and polished each stair. Now, in the moonlight, you can see the indentions from a century of footsteps descending, visiting the dead garden.

"Did Mr. Williams say he was coming today?"

"Yep," I say. "I think so. But you know contractors. Could be anytime this week."

"Remind him about the weather stripping around the dining room window?"

"I'll add it to the punch list."

"Did you see these?" She holds out a cupped palm, three scarlet orbs there like eggs in a nest.

"Tomatoes?"

"From the greenhouse."

"So it's working? I mean, the greenhouse garden is—"

"Not perfect, but bearing fruit."

When she is not here, in the kitchen, Elizabeth is in Father Bob's greenhouse cultivating our winter garden. You can see Elizabeth's circular route from the attic window: from greenhouse, to kitchen, to farmers' market, to porch swing, and then back to the caretaker's cottage, her own rabbit hole, where she burrows at night.

The basement kitchen sits just below sidewalk level. The windows show a strip of soil, a fringe of grass, and later in the day, a parade of feet, a swinging umbrella or two. But first, in the early light, there is always a pair of purple Converse sneakers, then a soft knock on the door. Alfred. He presents Elizabeth the morning paper in its plastic sleeve, and she hands him a biscuit or toast or waffle. She spreads the newspaper on the counter, begins reading headlines aloud while I pretend not to listen. I don't read the *Citizen* much anymore. Later, Alfred and I put on aprons and take the coffee urn and the food upstairs to the dining room.

In the article about our opening day, there was a picture of me with the mayor of Sans Souci sitting on the front porch in a wicker sofa. Underneath, a caption: *The Crazy Salad Bed & Breakfast was transformed from a familiar landmark that had seen better days into an historical establishment with a vintage home's unique charms. Pictured, at left, is co-owner Cutter Johanson, whose great-great-grandfather Henry Haynes Harris, founder of the Sans Souci Manufacturing Company, built the house.*

Such generous coverage by the *Citizen* was no accident.

He had come on our opening day, Curt had, and it couldn't have been easy for him. He sat by himself. I was running back and forth from the dining room to the kitchen, refilling water and tea glasses. He looked up, nodded, said thank you. That was all. He said thank you in that stiff, courteous way of his, and I was too surprised to say anything, too busy to pause.

A few days later, I gathered up my courage. I called him to thank him for the publicity.

He said, "It's news, Cutter. It's what the *Citizen* is supposed to do. Cover the stories that really matter. No need to thank me. I'm just happy for you."

"How are things?" I asked. "At the paper?"

He sighed. "I can't get anyone to write obits worth a damn."

"It's a dead-end job."

It was good to hear him laugh.

Later, I heard the *Citizen* lost more of its staff. A lot of them were going to the *Palmetto News*. When I saw the daily edition of the *Citizen* was getting so thin you could practically see through it, I called Curt again.

"We'd like to place an advertisement," I said. "A weekly ad. In color, with a photo. For the Crazy Salad. You can have Madge or one of the other ad people drop by to talk to us, if you like."

He said he'd come by himself and discuss the details. It was on the tip of my tongue to say, *Hey, what's this? You're selling ads now?* But I stopped myself. Maybe there were no more ad people. And maybe, just maybe, he wanted to come by.

Opening day had been good. One of those special days in your life—like a graduation or a wedding or a birth—a day that measures things, that announces you've done something in a big step, not just a little inching toward this or that. A kind of ceremonial coming together of the people you know and like and love, too; people who are proud of you. My first-grade teacher was there, so were Gran's Sunday school ladies, Miss Bee from the bank, Mr. Heller, and Mrs. Lucianne Kincaid. All those folks who knew Gran, all the town people I grew up with, people who wanted to come and cheer us on, even Jolene. Jolene showed up with her "you done good, girl" pat. "I knew you had waitin' tables in your blood," she said, sucking on a cigarette that I did not have the heart to tell her was not allowed in the kitchen.

Now Jolene helps us, she cleans the rooms, gives us a hand with serving meals. The breakfast-weenie business didn't work out after all.

With dusk, with the death of a day, comes reflection, elegiac musings. Guests need a gracious hostess, and so I sit in the dining room and preside. It's my duty to slice peach blueberry pie or dip blackberry cobbler onto the family china and pass it around. The windows grow black with night, reflect the meager gas flame in the fireplace, the portraits on the wall, the faces of the guests: the snowbirds fleeing Canada for Miami, the anniversary couples, the retirees traversing the highways, the newlyweds, the German family, the two handsome men who clutch hands even now under the table. One will ask when the house was built, another wonders aloud about my grandfather's portrait. What happened to this family? Where are they now? That's how it begins.

Along with cream and sugar, I pass around an album with a spine as wide as my hand, a red, cracked leather cover. There are pictures in there, letters and newspaper clips. I tell them about my great-great-grandfather, then move to my grandfather's madness, my parents' courtship, my father's death. *Lost when his plane exploded over Ninh Thuan, five miles north of Phan Rang in North Vietnam*—how metallic and hard those names sounded to my mother and grandmother when they wept and puzzled over the letter together in the kitchen. I recount Gran's dying in the bedroom below. I read them letters that tell of my own parents' demise, my grandparents' implosion of hatred. I weave in romance and tragedy, our downfall and endurance. The heartbreaking details of the Harris Women's Curse I leave for last.

I draw out little maps for the guests on cocktail napkins—Sans Souci mill and the baseball fields where the textile leagues played, the railroad depot where FDR came through, on past the icehouse, the mill village, down Gerard Avenue, right back up to our front porch. When they ask for a guided tour to the dead garden, I am happy to oblige. We move down the cascade of stone steps in the dusk with flashlights, like a knot of mad villagers. They squat in front of the stones and make rubbings.

I have fashioned my own Harris women time line from photographs that I paste in a new vinyl album. There is Beulah, then Gran, my mother, Ginnie and me, and Callie. Callie—short for Catherine Caroline, the newest Harris woman, named after my mother and me. The shiny, brash squares of her—a toddler now—jump out between the dull, black-and-white baby pictures of the rest of us.

When Ginnie's letters come in the mail, postmarked from Oregon, stiff with photographs, I clutch the envelope to my chest, leave Alfred and Elizabeth in the kitchen, and head to the attic bedroom. It isn't a harsh kind of sneaking, just a discreet avoidance. Like changing clothes in gym class and not looking around, busying yourself with your own quick, embarrassed movements. The pictures are always of Callie, but sometimes there is a glimpse of Ginnie's chin, the wiry forearm of Daniel. I keep the Harris women time line under my bed.

The guests forget things. We collect their leavings. What Jolene finds under beds fills three boxes. Orphaned socks and earrings, highway maps, a dream catcher keychain, romance novels, a Niagara Falls coaster set. On and on. As if our house is a portal through which the world passes. Some of the guests press their business cards on me before they depart, with a promise to come back next year. They say I am developing a following. Like a debutante. And there are those who take me to the side, who corner me in the hall, or seek me out in the garden. They clear their throats or clutch my elbow; they want to have a word.

"What a story."

"My dear, how you tell it!"

"It just breaks my heart."

"You should write it down."

I will, I promise them. Someday, I will.